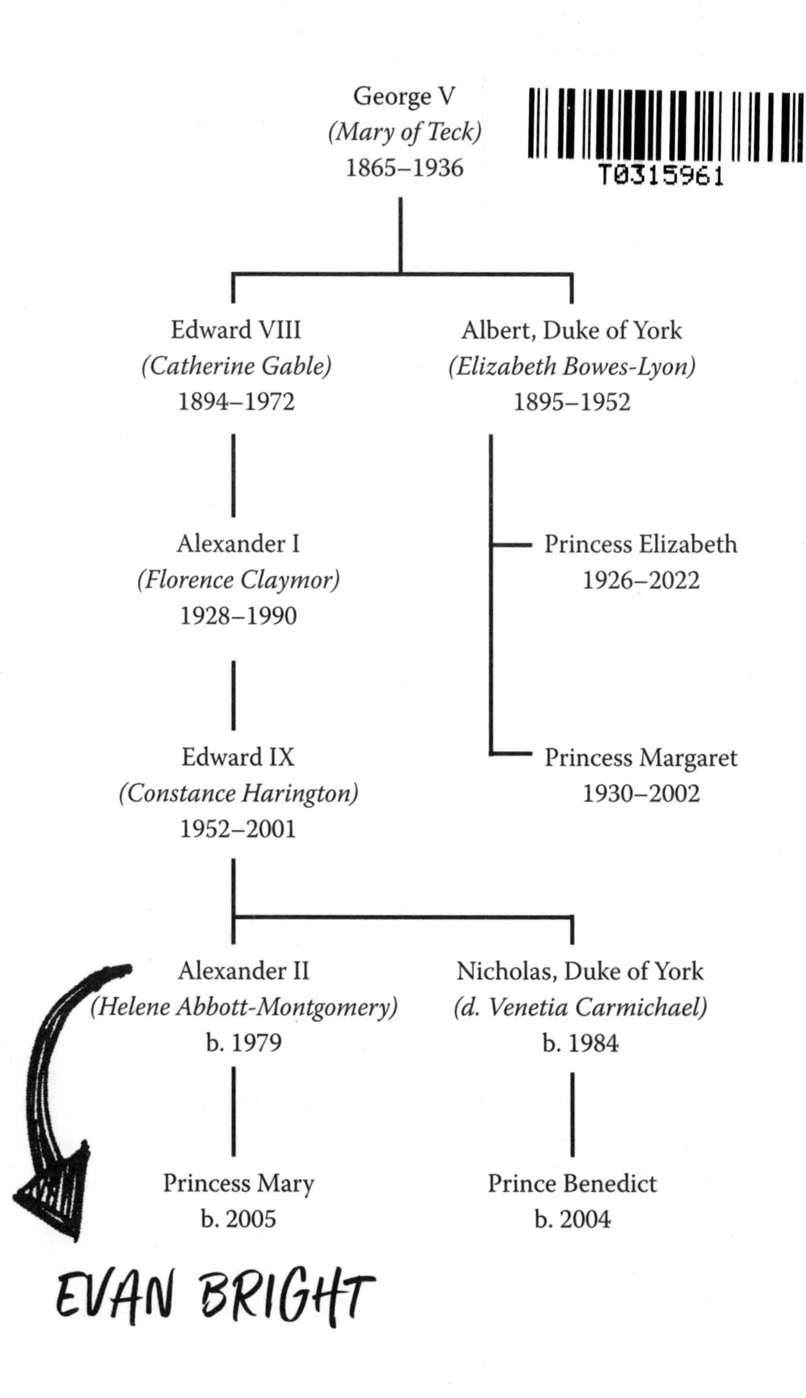
George V
(Mary of Teck)
1865–1936
T0315961
Edward VIII
(Catherine Gable)
1894–1972
Albert, Duke of York
(Elizabeth Bowes-Lyon)
1895–1952
Alexander I
(Florence Claymor)
1928–1990
Princess Elizabeth
1926–2022
Edward IX
(Constance Harington)
1952–2001
Princess Margaret
1930–2002
Alexander II
(Helene Abbott-Montgomery)
b. 1979
Nicholas, Duke of York
(d. Venetia Carmichael)
b. 1984
Princess Mary
b. 2005
Prince Benedict
b. 2004
EVAN BRIGHT

To Malcolm

First published in the UK in 2024 by Usborne Publishing Limited, Usborne House,
83-85 Saffron Hill, London EC1N 8RT, England, usborne.com

Published by arrangement with Rights People, London

Usborne Verlag, Usborne Publishing Limited, Prüfeninger Str. 20, 93049 Regensburg,
Deutschland, VK Nr. 17560

A CIP catalogue record for this book is available from the British Library.

ISBN 9781803701745 7848/1 JFM MJJASOND/24

Printed and bound using 100% renewable energy at CPI Group (UK) Ltd, Croydon, CR0 4YY.

AIMÉE CARTER

Content note

ROYAL SCANDAL is a work of fiction but deals with many real issues including mental illness, violence and references to sexual assault

Chapter One

We at the *Regal Record* hope you've been good this year, because it seems like Saint Nicholas has come early for us all. Despite rumours of a cancellation thanks to an untimely blizzard across the pond, the United Kingdom's notoriously naughty royal family will indeed be hosting a state banquet tonight for the president of the United States, Hope Park, and it promises to be chock-full of chaos.

Under ordinary circumstances, this state visit would be noteworthy considering President Park is both the first woman and first Korean American to hold the highest office in the US. But, just like every other significant event as of late, this historic achievement has already been overshadowed by the most recent addition to the House of Windsor's royal family tree.

That's right – Evangeline Bright, the King's illegitimate American daughter, will be in attendance tonight, and given her past exploits, it's safe to assume she'll do something gratingly inept to steal the thunder – and the headlines – from those who've actually earned their place at the royal table.

In the five and a half months since Evangeline's tasteless and explosive BBC One interview detailing her own sordid behaviour that led directly to Jasper Cunningham's death – of which she was cleared of criminal charges, thanks to a reported backroom deal between Scotland Yard and the

King's personal lawyers – the palace has seen fit to shove her down the throats of the British people at seemingly every turn. Hospital openings, charity appearances, even walkabouts typically reserved for legitimate members of the royal family – Evangeline has merrily joined in on all, resulting in a long list of missteps and blunders. Yet despite the efforts of the palace to make her palatable, it's becoming painfully clear that no amount of media and etiquette training can turn this American frog into a princess.

How much longer can the royal family's already-tattered reputation withstand the Bright blight? While we wait to see the fallout of tonight's state banquet and Evangeline's inevitable indiscretions, we at the *Regal Record* can only apologize yet again for revealing her identity this summer and unleashing this Pandora's box of mayhem and vexation on not only the entire country, but the world. One must own up to one's mistakes, and we deeply regret our part in this royal fiasco.

Let us hope that no one else ends up dead tonight.

– *The Regal Record*, 18 December 2023

"I'm well aware that being on time isn't a priority for you," says Tibby, clutching her phone like she's about to chuck it at my tiara. "But could you at least *pretend* to care that I'm about to lose my bloody job?"

I'm leaning against the wall in the long gallery of Windsor Castle, trying to keep my head upright as I fiddle with a strap on my stiletto. My gown isn't making it any easier, and as I set my foot down, the heel snags and comes dangerously close to ripping the shimmering burgundy fabric.

"It's my shoe," I mutter, untangling my hem. "One of the straps is loose."

Tibby arches an eyebrow as I test my weight again. Somehow, despite what has been an obscenely long day full of trivial appointments and last-minute fittings, Lady Tabitha Finch-Parker-Covington-Boyle's black pixie cut is still perfectly styled, and her tailored grey dress doesn't have a single piece of lint on it. Unfortunately for both of us, this superpower has yet to rub off on me in the six months she's been my personal secretary/babysitter, and no one is more aggrieved by my failure to develop a completely new personality than Tibby.

"I don't care if the heel's broken off and you're walking on your tiptoes," she says. "We *cannot* be late, Evan."

"We're not late." As I resume my march down the corridor, now with a noticeably uneven gait, I glance through the nearest window and into the dark courtyard beyond. A line of luxury vehicles snakes along the opposite wing of Windsor Castle, and royal footmen hoist umbrellas as tonight's guests exit their cars and step into the December downpour. "Okay, we're a little late, but—"

"There is no such thing as a 'little' late," says Tibby. "If His Majesty discovers you're missing, it'll be my neck on the block, not yours."

"He'll be too busy with the president to notice. Besides, they don't need me for the pictures, and I'm not escorting anyone inside."

"An unforgivable oversight," says Tibby irritably, as if this, too, is somehow my fault. "You're His Majesty's daughter, *and* you're American. You should be in the procession, preferably on the arm of a member of the president's family. Your absence will only start another wave of rumours in the press."

"I start rumours by breathing," I say. "Besides, it'd be an insult to pair me with anyone important."

Tibby sniffs. "Illegitimate or not, you're still of royal blood."

"Which is the only reason I'm part of this dog-and-pony show in the first place," I say. "That and the fact that the universe has a terrible sense of humour."

By the time we turn the corner and pass the royal family's private apartments, my scalp is throbbing. I reach up to adjust the Queen Florence tiara that's secured to my braided updo, but before my fingers can even graze the glittering headpiece, Tibby swats my hand away.

"Don't you dare," she says with more vehemence than usual. "Can you imagine the headlines if your tiara falls off in front of the Royal Rota? The metaphor alone—"

"The pins are digging in," I protest. "I think my scalp might actually be bleeding."

"Ignore it. The banquet won't last more than three or four hours."

"Three or four—" I gape at her. "Haven't you people ever heard of the Geneva Conventions?"

"You're royalty, darling," she says in the dismissive tone she always uses when I complain. "The Geneva Conventions don't apply."

I start to object, but before I can utter more than a single syllable, Tibby turns on her heel to face me, and I stumble to a halt.

"I understand you're uncomfortable, Evan," she says, her

voice low and hurried. "I understand you'd rather not sit around for hours listening to a bunch of politicians make each other feel important. But this is the price you pay for being royal. This is the price you pay for living in a castle with a staff of hundreds to cater to your whims. You have every resource you could ever need, every opportunity you could ever dream of, and you are one of the most famous people in the world. You are privileged in a way damn few others are, and if you tell me one more time how uncomfortable your designer shoes and couture gown and priceless tiara are, I *will* throttle you."

For a long moment, we stare at each other in silence. She's right, of course – every word of it – and I hate that six months ago, I would have throttled myself for acting like this, too.

"Sorry," I mumble, my cheeks growing warm. "I think I'm spending too much time around Maisie."

"Her Royal Highness's faults are no excuse for yours," says Tibby tartly, but at last she steps aside, and we continue down the hall towards the state apartments. "The people are watching you, Evan, and they deserve more than another ungrateful brat. Especially when you offer them hope that maybe their lives can become a fairy tale, too."

I snort. "Being accused of murder and having all my secrets exposed to the entire world counts as a fairy tale now?"

"Haven't you read the Brothers Grimm?" says Tibby. "Murder is practically a plot requirement. If we want any chance of making it in time, we'll have to go this way."

She ushers me into the royal family's private chapel – sacrilegious, I'm sure, though clearly the only sin Tibby's worried about is tardiness. She's moving so quickly now that I'm forced to do a strange skip to keep up, but when we finally reach the threshold of St George's Hall, I stop in my tracks – and so does she.

While normally the vast hall is empty, save for the ever-present paintings, marble busts and suits of armour that line the walls, a table that easily seats two hundred now stretches from one end to the other, covered in massive festive bouquets and more plates and utensils than I've ever seen. And because my life, while newly charmed, can never be fair, nearly all of tonight's guests are already inside as a fleet of footmen show them to their seats.

Tibby swears. "Keep your head up, but move quickly," she whispers, and this time I don't complain as we hurry to the nearest exit. Before we make it more than twenty feet, however, a woman at the end of the table gasps.

"Evangeline?" she says, her voice mercifully low. A few of her companions turn to look at me too, and I smile and press my finger to my lips. Her shock quickly turns to conspiratorial amusement, and even though I'm not a princess – or even an official member of the royal family – she dips in a low curtsy.

A rising murmur follows Tibby and me now, and I do my best to walk properly in my uncooperative shoe, keenly aware of all the eyes on us. It's only sheer luck that I don't trip and fall on my face, and when we finally reach the nearest exit, Tibby all but yanks me through the doorway –

And straight into the middle of an explosion of camera flashes.

"Ah, Evangeline," says a deep voice as the door closes behind us. "I'm pleased you were able to make it."

His Majesty King Alexander II, monarch of the United Kingdom and Commonwealth, stands fifteen feet away in the opulent Grand Reception Room, his blue eyes fixed directly on me. While his slightly balding head is bare, his tuxedo is heavy with sashes and medals he never actually earned, and even though he's not especially tall or commanding, everything in the room seems to revolve around him like he's the only source of gravity. Beside him stands a square-jawed woman I instantly recognize as President Park. They're posing for a cluster of photographers and members of the Royal Rota – the group of journalists whose only job is to cover the royal family – and both are still smiling widely even though every single camera is now pointed towards me.

Perfect.

Sorry, I mouth as a deep blush spreads across my face. I should curtsy, or at the very least dip my head in a show of respect. But as Tibby is so quick to lament, I'm not exactly a stickler for the rules, and as long as I have dual citizenship, I refuse to bow to anyone – even my endlessly patient father.

He doesn't seem to mind, and when he shoots me a wink before turning back to President Park, I know I'm forgiven for my unexpected entrance. By him, at least. Tibby is another story, and as she squeezes my arm in a supposed show of support, I'm sure it's only to measure how much acid she'll need to dissolve my body after she murders me for this.

As the photographers reluctantly return their attention to the main attraction, I slip into an empty corner and try to make myself as small as possible. Somehow, in the greatest show of self-restraint I've managed since arriving in England, I resist the urge to make sure my tiara hasn't slipped out of place. Given the number of pins currently digging into my scalp, it's undoubtedly right where I left it, but Tibby's earlier quip about headlines and a falling crown haunts me like a premonition I can't shake.

"And now our families," announces Alexander, and he gestures towards the other side of the room, where a small crowd is gathered. I spot two bobbing tiaras among the sea of suits and dresses, and finally Queen Helene appears with Princess Mary in tow.

Admittedly it doesn't take much to make me feel like an impostor most of the time, but one look at them and I shrink even further into the metaphorical shadows. They're both stunning – the kind of gorgeous that only money can buy, with flawless porcelain skin, shiny hair and blindingly white smiles. My statuesque stepmother is in a flowing ivory gown with her blonde hair wrapped around the base of her glittering headpiece, and it's obvious why she's been declared the most beautiful woman in the world by multiple magazines. Everyone in the room is watching her – everyone except my father.

Maisie, my equally elegant half-sister, wears a sapphire dress covered in crystals, but nothing outshines the intricate tiara perched above her strawberry-blonde waves. There's something slightly off about her expression, though – something cold and a little stiff, but not so much that she's dragging down the mood. It could be anything, from the indignity of being in a colour she doesn't love, to an actual problem she has to ignore for a few hours in order to transform into Her Royal Highness Princess Mary, heir to the throne and the future Queen of the United Kingdom, and I make a mental note to ask if she's okay.

As they make their way across the room, they're accompanied by a clean-shaven man I recognize as President Park's husband

and a teenage boy I can't place as easily. But there's no question who he is, not when he has the president's square jaw and her husband's lithe build.

When his mother was elected three years ago, Thaddeus Park was quiet, awkward and best known for his love of *Star Wars*. Now, at eighteen, he has most *definitely* grown into that jaw. And those cheekbones. And those shoulders. I give myself five seconds to stare before I tear my eyes away, reminding myself that I have my own quiet and adorably awkward boyfriend, who, less than thirty minutes ago, sent Tibby a text wishing me luck tonight, followed by a single x – which, apparently, he only ever uses with me.

Tibby lets out a low whistle as she also admires the view, and I elbow her in the side. "He's my age," I hiss. "Cougar."

"How old do you think I am?" says Tibby, aghast, and I shrug.

"Old enough to be my babysitter."

"I am not your *babysitter*," she says with familiar exasperation. "I am your private sec—"

"Miss Bright."

An older man with a short salt-and-pepper beard steps out of the crowd, and though he stands stiffly and with an air of formality, there's a twinkle of amusement in his eye.

"Mr Jenkins," I say, biting back a grin. Even though I've known Jenkins longer than I've known almost anyone, I've never seen him in a tux before, and he also has an impressive set of medals – including the star worn by Knight Commanders of the Royal Victorian Order. I'll never catch up to what people like Tibby and my half-sister have known practically from birth, but I feel some small sense of victory for recognizing this much.

"I'm sorry we're late. It's not Tibby's fault—"

"Never mind that," he says with his usual gentle understanding. "His Majesty has requested that you join him and the Park family for these photographs."

I blink. Sure enough, when I glance over Jenkins's shoulder, my father is chuckling at something Mr Park said, but his gaze quickly meets mine, and he tilts his head towards the others.

"Really?" I say in a low voice, but I already have my answer. "You're sure it won't ruin the photo shoot? Or insult the first family?"

"Quite sure," says Jenkins, and he offers me his arm. "If you please."

Tibby prods me in the small of my back, and I loop my elbow around Jenkins's and do my best not to limp. Maybe kicking off my broken shoe wouldn't be the worst idea in the world, even if it means I'll lose at least four inches. But before I can weigh the pros and cons, Jenkins is handing me off to Alexander, and it's too late to do anything about it now.

"You look lovely," murmurs my father, kissing me on the cheek. "Why don't you and Maisie stand with Thaddeus?"

While I expect him and the president to be front and centre, they both step aside and position the three of us in the middle, with Thaddeus Park towering over me and my half-sister. And as he peers down at me, I swear he smirks.

"Nice to meet you," he says in an American accent that matches mine. I'm so used to hearing the seemingly endless varieties in the UK by now, however, that it sounds strangely alien to my ears. "I was hoping you'd be here."

"You were?" I say, taken aback. "Why?"

He chuckles, and while it's the kind of laugh that probably puts most people at ease, I bristle. "Isn't it obvious?"

"Not really," I say, and before he can explain – or formulate a witty comeback, which seems more his style – the official palace photographer clears his throat. The seven of us all face forward, and I smile, hoping like hell that my sudden spike of anxiety doesn't show on my face.

"A little closer, if you would, Your Majesties," says the photographer, and while this is clearly directed at my father and Helene, who could fit half a continent between them, Thaddeus shifts towards me too.

It's a small movement – barely more than an inch or two – but instinctively I edge away, and that minor adjustment is too much for my shoe to bear. The strap snaps, and with a sharp jolt of pain in my ankle, I'm suddenly falling, dangerously close to taking the president down with me.

But then, like this is all some choreographed dance we've practised together, Thaddeus catches me effortlessly, his arms strong and secure around me. I gasp, and as I slowly absorb what's happening, I realize I'm staring directly into his dark eyes.

Click.

A camera goes off, and then another, and another, until all I hear are the echoes of shutters and phones as seemingly every single photographer and member of the Royal Rota take our picture. With a self-satisfied grin, Thaddeus helps me back to my feet, his hand lingering on my bare arm for much longer than it should. And if there was any question of which photo the press will use for tomorrow's headlines, there isn't any more.

Terrific.

@TheDailySunUK: Has Evangeline broken things off with Christopher Abbott-Montgomery, Earl of Clarence and nephew to Queen Helene? Our preview of tonight's state banquet, featuring the royal family, America's President Park, and the swoon-worthy moment between Evangeline and Thaddeus Park.
9:53 PM · 18 December 2023

@dutchessdame172: @TheDailySunUK lucky bitch.
9:57 PM · 18 December 2023

– Twitter exchange between the *Daily Sun* and user @dutchessdame172, 18 December 2023

Kit laughs so loudly that I have to pull Tibby's phone away from my ear.

"Only you, Evan," he manages, and I can picture him shaking his head, his dark wavy hair nearly skimming his jaw now despite the number of times Helene has begged him to cut it. "Turning one of those stuffy banquets into a cheating scandal. I'm impressed."

"It's not funny," I say, shifting on the cushioned window seat in one of Windsor Castle's massive libraries. The room is almost completely devoid of light, and the floor-to-ceiling bookshelves loom eerily around me, but I can take a little spookiness as long as it comes with privacy. "Everyone's saying we've broken up—"

"Have we?" he says, still chuckling. "Did you meet the love of your life tonight, and you've rung to tell me you're kicking me to the kerb?"

His voice is slightly muffled now, and I make a face. "Of course not. You're googling the photos, aren't you?"

"Naturally," he says, and a beat later, he bursts into another fit of laughter. "He escorted you *and* Maisie into the banquet? Whose idea was that?"

"His," I groan. "Alexander thought it was chivalrous. Stop – I told you it was bad."

"On the contrary, this is the highlight of my week," says Kit, and I can hear him grinning. "The snap of him catching you is actually rather stunning. If I were the one you were gazing at so lovingly, I'd frame it."

My tiara bumps against the wall, and I wince, finally giving in and digging around for the offending bobby pins. "You're terrible to me."

"Indeed. I suppose I'll just have to make it up to you at Christmas, won't I?"

I straighten, pins forgotten. "You're coming to Sandringham? But I thought—"

"My parents decided to holiday in the Maldives," says Kit. "They offered to fly me out, too, but I can think of few methods of torture more painful than spending another two weeks alone with them. And away from you."

This makes me melt a little, but considering Kit has barely seen his parents in years, it also comes with a helping of guilt. "Isn't your mother excited to spend the holidays with you?"

"Maybe. But she and my father have plenty to work through on their own, and I'd only be a hindrance. Besides, we've done nothing but partake in awkward conversations and lingering silences since the end of term, and I think we're all rather weary of tiptoeing around each other at this point," he admits. "I'll visit her again in February for her birthday."

"Okay," I say, not sure whether to be disappointed for his mother or relieved I'll get to spend Christmas with him after all. "Maisie keeps talking about how much she hates Sandringham, but it sounds kind of magical, having a tree and family and actually celebrating."

"It is," says Kit, and I can tell from the sudden softness in his voice that we're both thinking the same thing. Ever since my grandmother died when I was eleven, I've spent Christmas at various boarding schools, surrounded by a smattering of teachers without families and classmates whose parents couldn't be bothered to bring them along on whatever glamorous vacation they'd planned. Twice I was the only person left behind, save for the headmistress, and all I remember about those weeks are loneliness and desperately wanting to see my mom.

This year will be different, I promise myself. This year, even though my mother will be in Virginia and I'll be an ocean away in a secluded English manor, I'll have Alexander, Maisie and Kit there to cushion the blow. And I *will* have a good time.

"When are you supposed to arrive?" I say. "Maisie and I are taking a car there on Saturday—"

"Room for one more?"

I jump, nearly dropping Tibby's phone as a low voice floats towards me in the darkness. Standing in the doorway, silhouetted by light from the drawing room beyond, is Thaddeus Park, holding a plate and two flutes of what I think is champagne.

"What are you doing here?" I blurt, not caring how rude I must sound. "Didn't security stop you in the vestibule?"

"You mean that room with all the weapons and display cases?" He starts towards me, slow enough not to spill his contraband. "They did, but I seem to have found my way here anyway. This place is a maze, isn't it? Worse than the White House."

"You get used to it," I say, before I hear Kit's voice – distant and tinny now that I'm holding the phone by my knees. I hastily return it to my ear. "Sorry, what did you say?"

"Is that him?" says Kit. "Are you about to hang up on me for a clandestine rendezvous with your new lover?"

I make a face. "What *century* are you from?" I mutter, desperately hoping Thaddeus didn't hear that.

Kit chuckles. "Ring me later, or whenever Tibby's willing to part with her mobile again. Don't worry about the photographs, all right? It'll blow over."

I'm not so sure, but I say my goodbyes and stretch out my legs, refusing to make any room for Thaddeus on the window seat. He perches on a nearby chair instead, balancing the plate of cookies on a small accent table between us.

"Sorry," he says, but judging by his grin, he's really not. "Was that your boyfriend?"

"So you *do* know he exists," I say drily, and despite my annoyance, I take one of the cookies from the stack. I don't touch the flute beside it, though, and Thaddeus doesn't seem bothered as he sips from his own. "Shouldn't you be enjoying the party?"

"You mean the self-congratulatory political networking event masquerading as a fancy ball? I'm good," he says, popping a cookie into his mouth and chewing thoughtfully. "It's not easy, is it? Having to be two people at once."

I frown mid-bite. "What are you talking about?"

He gives me a knowing look. "When my mom was a senator from Pennsylvania, I could be myself. But as soon as she ran for president, there was suddenly all of this pressure to be...*not* me. To be presentable at all times. To stop talking about the things that made me interesting. Everything I used to like about myself became too specific, too embarrassing, too controversial—"

"That last Star Wars trilogy really did divide the fandom, didn't it?" I say, and he chuckles.

"Joking aside, I've noticed it with you, too," he says. "From a distance, I mean. Not in a stalker way, but...it's hard not to follow your story, with how often you're in the headlines. And when you joined the royal family, you seemed like this...this beautiful, wild, wilfully independent human, and no one could tell you who you were or what to do. And even when everyone accused you of murdering that dickweasel who assaulted you, and the papers broke the news about your mom's mental illness and what she did to you—"

"We're not talking about that," I say coldly, and he immediately holds up his hands in a mea culpa.

"Right – of course," he says hastily. "I just mean...you seemed indifferent to the noise. You were still *you*. But as soon as you stepped into the public eye and gave that interview, you became...polished. Predictable. You've done what's expected of you, the same way I have. And I don't know about you, but I miss the person I used to be."

This is alarmingly vulnerable, considering we just met, and a knot forms in the pit of my stomach. I don't *feel* any different. I still like the same music. I still read the same books. I still watch way too much Netflix in what little free time I have now, and I've even started to learn how to play the guitar – badly, admittedly, but it's still just for me. No one else.

I know exactly what Thaddeus is talking about, though, and I feel a stab of something unexpectedly powerful – wistfulness, maybe, or some kind of nostalgia I didn't know was there. Because I *am* two people now. Just as Maisie has to be Princess Mary, the graceful and beloved heir to the throne, I have to be Evangeline, the illegitimate daughter of the King, who's just grateful to be included. Even though Evan is the person I really am, the person I've always been, I can't be her any more – at least not where a stranger could see me. And despite his jarring candour and overfamiliarity, Thaddeus Park is still very much a stranger. "I don't think I've really changed," I say at last, keeping my voice mild as I avoid his stare and feign interest in my bracelet instead. There are only two charms on it – a music note that was a gift from a classmate, and a tiny tiara that Kit gave me for my birthday – and I roll the latter between my fingers. "I'm still me."

"And I'm still me, underneath the politics and the workouts and the curated wardrobe," says Thaddeus. "But we can't let the public know that, can we, Your Royal Highness?"

No, we can't. I let the tiara charm drop, more shaken than I want to admit that someone I met five minutes ago understands part of my life better than I do. "I'm not a princess," I say, grasping onto this instead of letting myself linger on the rest. "Didn't your handler tell you that?"

"But you're the King's daughter," he says, as if this somehow supersedes a thousand years of history and royal protocol.

"Illegitimate," I point out. "I'm a mutt in a family of purebreds, and I definitely don't have a title."

Thaddeus blinks. "Well, that's rude."

I let out a breathy laugh, because no one has actually said that before, even though it's probably true. I don't care about the title, not really – but I can't pretend not to care about the respect and legitimacy that would come with it. And that is *not* a conversation I want to have with anyone, let alone Thaddeus Park.

"You know," he says slowly, "princess or not, you and I could send the internet into a feeding frenzy, if we wanted to."

I raise an eyebrow. "I think we already have."

He shrugs. "That picture's too formal to be a showstopper. But if I post a selfie of us together, maybe of you kissing me on the cheek..."

He leans in closer, and even though it's probably an innocent move, my skin crawls as I jerk away, and every muscle in my body tenses, ready to bolt. My panic must show on my face, because Thaddeus straightens instantly, his eyes wide and his mouth gaping.

"Shit, I – that was creepy, I'm sorry," he says, and to his credit, he sounds genuinely contrite. "I just meant, you know...a cute picture. We could make finger hearts or funny faces. Something like that. Nothing suggestive or – I know you have a boyfriend, I didn't mean it like that—"

"I think Evangeline has had enough photographs of her taken tonight," says a voice from the doorway, and relief rushes through me as I look up to see Tibby standing there, hands on her hips and her expression deadly.

"Right," says Thaddeus sheepishly, and I'm on my feet before he can even shift his weight. "I really am sorry."

"It's okay," I say, even though it isn't. But that's not completely his fault. Jasper Cunningham is the real reason for my racing pulse, and why I'll never again feel safe with a boy I don't fully trust. "We're not allowed to take selfies in the royal residences anyway. It's a security thing."

"Oh." His face falls, and I'm halfway to Tibby by the time he stands. "It was truly an honour to meet you, Evangeline. If you're ever in the US and want to see the White House library…"

"I'll look you up," I say, even though I have absolutely no intention of doing so. As I reach Tibby, however, something tugs at me – some long-ingrained irrational need to make sure he, a stranger I'll probably never see again, doesn't feel bad about how this went. Or maybe the small connection we made is stronger than I think it is. And so, despite having every reason to march out of here without so much as a goodbye, I glance over my shoulder and add, "Maybe we can take that selfie there."

His grin returns, and Tibby loops her arm in mine as we disappear into the maze that is Windsor Castle.

Chapter Three

@thaddeusapark Living it up like royalty at Windsor Castle tonight. Huge thanks to Their Majesties King Alexander and Queen Helene, Her Royal Highness Princess Mary, and my very special new expat friend...

– Instagram user @thaddeusapark, below a selfie of Thaddeus Park in a tuxedo, the background dark and indistinct, and his left thumb and pointer finger pressed together to make a finger heart, 18 December 2023

"Thaddeus is using you, you know," says Tibby as we cross an empty state room with red fabric walls. Though it isn't dusty, it looks like it hasn't been used in years, and our footsteps sound hollow against the thin carpet.

"I sort of worked that out for myself," I say as she pulls on the frame of a giant ornate mirror, which swings open to reveal another lavish state room – this one with green walls, gilded furniture and massive portraits hanging in gold frames. "Thanks for jumping in back there. I wasn't sure what he was going to do."

"He wouldn't have tried anything," she says, even though she can't possibly be certain. "He's the son of the American president, and surely someone's taught him manners. But you have ten times the number of followers he does, and he clearly wanted a candid photo to boost his own profile. May I have my mobile back now?"

I hand it over, even though I'm still hopeful Kit might call again. "Is it always going to be like this? Is everyone I meet going to want something from me?"

"Yes," says Tibby, and the word sinks to the pit of my stomach like a brick. "You might get lucky and meet the rare individual who's interested in you as a person, or who believes you can't offer them anything they don't already have, but most people are always going to want something from you. You simply have to be careful who you trust."

I sigh inwardly. A year ago, no one knew who I was, and only a handful of my classmates even bothered to talk to me on a semi-regular basis. Now millions of people follow an Instagram account I don't even personally use, and based on the endless sea of comments I saw the one and only time I explored Tibby's handiwork, a disconcerting number seem to think this means they know exactly who I am. And the thought of so many strangers having a fully formed opinion of me still makes me break out in a cold sweat.

We step into an area I recognize now – the antechamber to the Windsor throne room. I can hear the faint murmur of voices filtering in from the Waterloo Chamber beyond, and I stop beside a bust of one of the Georges. "Do I have to go back to the party? I have a headache, and I lost my shoes hours ago."

"Your shoes are on their way to the royal cobbler, where they'll either be fixed or burned to ash. I haven't decided yet. But you've done your time tonight," adds Tibby, angling away from the crowded ballroom and instead leading me towards the secret passageway into the throne room. "As long as you sit still long enough for a picture while the jeweller removes your tiara, we can return to your apartment now."

The throne room isn't completely empty, but I only have to smile and say a few words before we escape into the Grand Reception Room and the more restricted areas of Windsor Castle beyond. It's a relief to be away from all those curious stares, and I drop my aching shoulders as we head back towards the private apartments.

"Are you coming to Sandringham for Christmas?" I say, hiking up the hem of my gown so it doesn't drag on the floor. My bare feet are freezing, but I'm too worn-out to care.

"Sandringham?" says Tibby. "Why on earth would I spend Christmas there?"

"Queen Victoria's your ancestor, isn't she? Doesn't that make you family?"

"If anything more distant than first cousins was still considered *family*, half of England's aristocratic marriages wouldn't exist," she says. "I'm spending Christmas at our country home in Kent, and for the New Year, I'll be in the Seychelles."

"Oh." I don't expect her to work during the holidays, of course, but the thought of Tibby not being there to cram my schedule full of lessons and fittings and appearances for three whole weeks is both daunting and exhilarating. "I'll miss you."

She gives me a strange look, though there's a softness to it that's almost foreign on her sharp features. "I'll be back before you know it. And in the meantime, you'll get to learn how to hunt and ski, and you'll have plenty of empty hours to spend with Maisie."

"Absolutely none of those things sounds appealing," I say as we approach my apartment. "Kit's coming, though."

"Is he? Should I make sure certain necessities are added to your luggage?"

It takes me a beat to realize what she means, and my cheeks instantly grow hot. "*No*," I say firmly. "We're not – *no*."

"Better safe than sorry," she hums, pushing open the door. And while my face still burns, the fact that Tibby isn't treating me like I'm about to break – especially when everyone else in my life, Kit included, avoids the topic completely – almost makes up for the humiliating breach of privacy. *Almost*.

The royal jeweller appears in record time to take possession of the Queen Florence tiara, but Tibby makes him wait a solid ten minutes while she figures out the perfect angle for Instagram. Even though the tiara is technically mine – Queen Florence, my great-grandmother, willed it to me when I was a baby – it's kept in a vault somewhere, or maybe the Tower of London, where the Crown Jewels are guarded. Either way, I won't see it again until the next state banquet, or whatever future event requires me to wear a tiara, and despite my tender scalp, I'm sorry to see it go.

Tibby sticks around only long enough to make sure my dress is hung up properly, and as soon as she leaves, I wrap myself in a fuzzy blanket, flop onto the antique sofa and open my laptop. Rather than scour British news sites – and possibly, by now, CNN and various popular celebrity blogs – for commentary about my supposed flirtation with Thaddeus, I open VidChat and click my mother's icon.

Two rings echo throughout my sitting room, which is surprisingly cosy tonight as a fire crackles beneath the elaborate mantelpiece, and suddenly my mother's smiling face appears onscreen. Her auburn curls are loose, a sure sign she's not in her studio for once, and I notice a large abstract landscape behind her – the one that hangs in her dining room.

"Evie! How did it go?" she says, and while sometimes she's distracted and agitated, especially when her doctors are adjusting her medication, tonight she's clear-eyed and fully focused on me. "I saw the photos online – you looked stunning."

I grimace. "It was fine, I guess. If you've seen the pictures, then you already know what happened."

"You mean when the president's son grabbed you?" she says. "What happened there?"

I explain everything, from my broken shoe to how late Tibby and I were, to my encounter with Thaddeus in the library, and by the time I'm through, my mother sighs.

"Missteps happen, Evie," she says. "Especially when you're in the public eye so often. You're all right, though? Your ankle is okay, and he didn't...?"

I shake my head. "He didn't touch me, except to stop me from falling on my face. My ankle's a little sore, but it'll be fine. I just..." *It's not easy, is it? Having to be two people at once.* "I'm not good at being perfect all the time."

"No one is, sweetheart," she says. "And you haven't had much of a chance to practise, either. You'll get better at the details as you go."

I'm not sure I want to, though. But while my mother broke up with Alexander, the love of her life, to avoid becoming queen, she seems to derive no end of pride and pleasure from watching me take my place as his daughter, no matter how bad I am at it.

"You haven't seen anyone lurking near the house, have you?" I say after a beat, eager to change the subject. "Alexander said the palace is still getting daily questions about you from that reporter."

"The one who's writing a biography of me?" she says. "No, security hasn't seen anything suspicious, and neither have I. But a friend said she received a strange phone call asking about the family, so it's likely only a matter of time before he figures out where I am."

I scowl. "If anything happens—"

"I'll be sure to let your father know immediately," she says. "Though honestly, Evie, sometimes I wonder if it wouldn't be in my best interest to work with...what's his name?"

"Ryan," I say bitterly. "Ryan Crewes."

"Ryan Crewes," she echoes. "If he's going to write my story, I might as well have some say in it."

While she has a point, the events of my childhood don't exactly paint her in a positive light. I have no memory of it, but my mother was arrested for trying to drown me in a bathtub when I was four, in the midst of a psychotic break due to undiagnosed paranoid schizophrenia. In her own unwell mind, she was trying to protect me from my stepmother, Helene – who, as far as I know, hadn't actually threatened me. But my mother's mental illness lied to her constantly. It still does, on her bad days, even with medication and treatment. While I know the public will draw their own conclusions with or without the real story, I don't want to see her words twisted into something monstrous in order to sell more books. And I wouldn't put anything past Ryan Crewes or the other so-called royal biographers who've been circling us for months.

"Maybe you can work with someone you've handpicked," I suggest. In a few years, once the sensational headlines that ran for weeks over the summer have faded in public memory. "But for now—"

The sharp rap of knuckles on wood ricochets through my sitting room, and I jump, twisting around to glare at the offending door. My mother leans towards the camera, her frown deepening.

"Do you need to get that?" she says, and I shake my head.

"Whoever it is will go awa—"

The urgent knocks quickly turn into demanding thuds, and I hear a muffled voice through the wood.

"Evan, you better bloody be in there. I need to talk to you."

I groan inwardly.

"Mom, it's Maisie," I say. Out of all the people in Windsor tonight, she's one of the few I can't ignore. "Could I—"

"Of course, sweetheart. I need to start dinner anyway," she says. "Call me back when you can."

After closing my laptop, I mutter a few deeply unkind things about my half-sister as I throw off my blanket and climb to my feet. The fire crackles cheerfully, its warmth fighting the castle chill, and I yank open the door that leads into the hallway. "Whatever this is about, it better be—"

"The head of palace security cornered Daddy after dinner," says my sister as she sweeps into the room, the hem of her sapphire gown billowing behind her. "One of the protection officers stationed on the reserve in Kenya called. Benedict is missing."

It takes me a beat to fully absorb what she's saying, and I stare at her, stunned. "Wait – *what?*"

Maisie rolls her eyes. "Benedict," she says slowly, "our traitorous swine of a cousin, is gone. Absent. In the wind. Vanished—"

"I know what 'missing' means," I say in a strangled voice. "How did he slip past his protection officers? Wasn't the whole point of Alexander sending him to the reserve to keep an eye on him?" And to keep him away from Maisie and me. But five months and thousands of miles aren't enough to erase my memory of the look on Ben's face when he realized he was caught, and a shiver runs through me.

I'm going to destroy you.

His Royal Highness Prince Benedict of York was the first member of the family to treat me with any decency after I arrived in London, but he was also the one who leaked a video of me pushing Jasper Cunningham off a balcony after the sleazy asshole tried to rape me. The footage was edited, of course – Jasper and Ben had drugged my drink, and I couldn't even walk straight, let alone shove an athletic nineteen-year-old hard enough for him to fall to his death. But Ben made the entire world believe it was me, and even after untangling the truth, I still have no idea why.

"Uncle Nicholas is trying to track him down," says Maisie as she begins to pace with the energy of a restless raccoon. "But Benedict has plenty of friends, and he could be anywhere by now."

"We live in the twenty-first century. Someone *has* to know

where he is," I argue, fighting the urge to pace, too.

"I've already scoured the gossip sites and social media," says Maisie. "There's no sign of him."

My hands start to sting, and with vague bewilderment, I realize my nails have dug into my palms, causing eight dark red crescent marks in my pale skin. The colour is nearly identical to the ink Ben used for the note he sent me shortly after he was shipped off to the reserve, and even though I haven't looked at it in months, I remember every word.

No matter where I am in the world, I still know your secrets.

Enjoy this while it lasts.

"What are the odds he'll disappear for good and leave us alone?" I say, rubbing my hands together to soothe them.

"Exceptionally low, unless we're lucky and he's been eaten by a lion," says Maisie. "Benedict's never been one to take blows to his pride lightly, and I guarantee you he won't go quietly."

From anyone else, I'd take this dramatic proclamation with a grain of salt. But Maisie knows Ben better than anyone, and while she's prone to theatrics – something about being a princess, probably – I saw enough of Ben's dark side over the summer to believe her.

"Do you think he'll tell everyone what really happened?" I say, almost too afraid to suggest it. No use giving the universe any ideas, after all.

For a split second, I see a flicker of very real fear in Maisie's eyes. While there's nothing Ben can do to me that he hasn't already tried, he could still destroy Maisie's life with bone-chilling ease – because while I might not have been the one who pushed Jasper to his death, she was. And even though it was an accident, even though she was acting in self-defence, if the truth gets out – if Ben goes public with what really happened that night, and everything we did to cover it up – there's no telling what the fallout might be. But I do know, without a sliver of doubt, that it would be catastrophic – not just to me and Maisie, but to the entire royal family and the monarchy itself.

"He won't," she says at last, as if her stubbornness alone can make it so. "He has no way of proving it, not after we deleted the video."

"But he's third in line to the throne," I point out, though we're both keenly aware of that nasty little fact. "He has credibility on his side, and even if the palace denies it, some people will still believe him."

"Let them," she says coldly. "There are some who believe I died at birth and was replaced with another baby, you know, but their conspiracy theories are just that."

This is news to me – weird news, but still news – and I blink. "But this is true, Maisie. And if he somehow managed to copy the video—"

A ding echoes from inside her clutch, and without waiting for me to finish, she pulls out her phone. Her pinched expression grows even more haggard at the sight of whatever's on her screen, and she turns towards the door. "I can't stay. I only wanted to warn you."

"Thanks," I say drily. "I'm sure the thought of Ben peeking through my window will lull me to sleep tonight."

Maisie gives me a withering look, though it's tempered by the way she tugs anxiously on one of her strawberry-blond waves. "Don't be daft. You have curtains."

"That's not—" I begin, but there's no point. I study her. "Are you okay?"

"What do you think?" she says waspishly, dropping her hand. "Not only has Benedict slipped his lead, but he's also got a massive vendetta against both of us, and we have no idea what he's going to try next. How could I possibly be—"

"I'm not talking about Ben," I say, glancing at her phone. "Have you heard from Gia since she got back from Spain?"

Instantly what little warmth lingers between us turns to ice. "I need to go," says Maisie. "If Benedict shows up at your window tonight, do let him know that I don't care if we share blood – I *will* turn the Tower back into a working prison if he puts even a toe out of line."

"Also a comforting thought," I mutter, but if Maisie hears me, she doesn't react. Instead, she yanks open the door and disappears into the hallway, leaving me on my own with the weight of every terrible thing Ben could do to us hanging over me, and the knowledge that whatever it is, he will relish the carnage.

Chapter Four

"Henrietta, in your twenty years covering the royal family, have you ever seen a state banquet quite like this?"

"It was certainly one for the books, though I must emphasize that the press isn't invited to the banquet itself, or the ball afterward. We're only invited for photographs and the occasional short interview before the festivities begin. The rest is a closely guarded secret."

"Even with the excitement of President Park visiting the UK for the first time, I don't imagine anything that happened behind closed doors could possibly outshine Evangeline's faux pas during the family photograph yesterday."

"She does have a knack for drawing attention, doesn't she? In her defence, it seems like this was due to a wardrobe malfunction rather than any desire to steal the spotlight, as she removed her heels immediately after the photographs were taken."

"You've been spending quite a bit of time on the subject of Evangeline as of late, haven't you?"

"I have, yes. She's lived a fascinating life so far, especially for someone who's only eighteen, and it's been a pleasure to learn more about her in my research for my new book, *Royal Rebel* – which will be released on Thursday, just in time for a last-minute Christmas gift for all the royal watchers in your life."

"Well, I'll certainly be putting it on my list. What would you say most surprised you over the course of your research?"

"A number of things, really. Evangeline may be famous worldwide now, a mere six months after joining the royal family, but very little is known about her life beforehand. As you've said, she does have a knack for drawing attention in rather scandalous ways, but I'd say the thing that surprised me most was her empathy."

"Her empathy?"

"She has a reputation for misbehaving, of course, after getting expelled from nine boarding schools in seven years. But the acts that led to these expulsions never seemed to be rooted in malice or destructive tendencies."

"Even the infamous arson mishap that resulted in her fleeing to England?"

"Especially that. According to her former maths instructor, he believes Evangeline set the fire to destroy the only evidence of her roommate's poor marks – which reportedly risked her future Ivy League education."

"Her roommate's? Not her own?"

"No, not her own. That's really the heart of the many examples of what makes Evangeline such a fascinating addition to the royal family – and, I believe, an asset to this country going forward. She's truly remarkable, and despite the occasional blunder, I feel very strongly that once she's had the chance to prove herself, we'll all agree that she's as much a royal jewel as Princess Mary."

– ITV News's interview with royal expert
Henrietta Smythe, 19 December 2023

The drive from Windsor Castle to Sandringham Estate, the privately owned country home of the royal family near the east coast of England, is almost three miserable hours long.

Maisie and I spend nearly every minute in silence, as I read a fantasy novel while she scrolls through her phone, hastily replying to every soft ding that echoes in the back of the Range Rover. I desperately want to ask if she's heard any news about Ben, but one look at the thundercloud that is her face, and I'm sure it isn't worth the risk. I might have made some less-than-stellar choices in my life, but even I know better than to test her right now.

I console myself with the fact that over the past five days, no sightings of Ben have been reported on social media, and no new rumours have surfaced about his supposed whereabouts. And while that doesn't mean he isn't still out there, it does, at least, imply that he's staying hidden. For now. And so, with the thought of an actual Christmas to look forward to, I focus on my book and do my best not to let Ben ruin this, too.

We're driving beside a low stone wall that looks older than the

United States when, for the first time in hours, Maisie looks up from her screen. Rather than say anything, however, she makes a strange sound that's halfway between a growl and a whistling tea kettle, and she shoves her phone into her purse with such force that I'm surprised she doesn't throw it out the window instead.

"Everything okay?" I say mildly.

"Marvellous," she mutters, turning away from me to stare out at the bare trees. I consider leaving her be, since it's worked out well so far. But then, with as much stealth as possible when I'm sitting less than two feet away, her hand snakes up to brush her cheek, and I realize she's crying.

With a grimace, I close my book and slip it into the bag at my feet. "You don't have to tell me what's going on," I say. "But I'm here if you ever want to talk, all right?"

A muscle twitches in her jaw. "I'm fine," she says tightly, and I can hear the thickness in her voice now. "Have you checked Instagram recently?"

This is the last thing I expect her to say, and I frown. "Tibby handles that. I don't even have the password to my account."

"Of course you bloody don't," she mutters. "Thaddeus Park messaged me the other day."

"He did?" I say, suddenly dreading where this conversation is going. "I didn't know you two were friends."

"We're not." She finally looks at me, and although it's only for a split second, it's impossible not to notice how red her eyes are. "He asked for your number, and he wouldn't believe me when I said you haven't got a mobile."

I scowl. "Probably because he saw me using Tibby's. Did he say why he wanted it?"

"No, but it's not exactly hard to guess, is it?"

No, it's not. I lean my head back against the leather seat and sigh. I've never had a phone before – they weren't allowed at most of my boarding schools, and since my mother doesn't like using them, I've never seen the point – but this only reinforces my desire not to get one. "What else did he say?"

"The usual flattery and sycophancy," she says. "Though he's really not too terrible, all things consid— What on *earth* is going on?"

She's leaning forward now, craning her neck in a direction I can't see. Frowning, I shift closer to her, the kind of close that would normally have her up in arms, but instead she barely seems to notice. And as the car slows, I see why.

Up ahead, clustered around large and extravagant wrought-iron gates, is a crowd of about a dozen people holding signs made of poster board. And even though the temperature is well above freezing, they're clad in winter coats and hats, and every single one has a scarf wrapped around the lower half of their face, leaving only their eyes visible.

Our car slows, and the crowd turns towards us, thrusting their signs in the air. They look home-made, with different handwriting and colours, but they all hold the same sentiment.

ABOLISH THE MONARCHY

NO MORE FREELOADING

REVOLT AGAINST THE ROYALS

Unnerved, I shrink away from Maisie and back into my seat. "Is this normal?" I say, trying to pretend like the hint of fear in my voice has always been there.

"No," says Maisie quietly, and in the front passenger seat, our protection officer speaks quietly on his phone, his head swivelling as he takes in the crowd.

"Additional security is on their way," he says, glancing over his shoulder and through the clear partition at Maisie and me. But it's cold comfort as the protesters surround us, their mostly hidden faces inches from ours and separated only by glass.

None of them are shouting or hurling insults our way, though. They simply stare at us through the windows, and as the seconds tick by, I feel Maisie's hand wrap around mine.

"Don't look at them," she whispers. And even though everything in me wants – *needs* – to keep my eyes on the protesters, I tear my gaze away and focus on the back of our driver's head. He, too, is tense, and I notice that both men have unbuckled their seat belts.

Finally, after what feels like an hour but is probably no more than a minute or two, the gates open, and several security officers join the fray, all holding batons. They hastily usher the crowd away from the car, and at last we continue forward. Before we make it to the safety of what must be Sandringham Estate, however, I glance out the window one more time, only to meet the menacing stare of a man in a teal scarf.

He doesn't speak – he doesn't even move – but that single look is enough, and a shiver runs down my spine. I hastily avert my eyes again, my fingers tightening around Maisie's. And even when we cross onto the private road and the gates swing shut, putting an ever-growing buffer between our Range Rover and the protesters, neither of us lets go.

Chapter Five

Maisie:

Gia, we need to talk.

Gia:

I think you've said enough.

Maisie:

You're taking this all entirely the wrong way, you know.

Gia:

Am I? How good to know that yet again, you're in the right, and I'm simply misunderstanding Her Royal Highness's intentions.

Maisie:

We've just arrived at Sandringham. Will you please answer your bloody mobile when I call?

Gia:

I'm with my family.

Maisie:

Please. There were protesters waiting for us, and security wasn't prepared. It was terrifying.

Gia:

Are you all right?

Maisie:

No. I'm shaking.

Gia:

Are you hurt? Did they attack you?

Maisie:

No, but I really need to hear your voice right now.

Gia:

I told you, I'm with my family, and I need some time. We'll speak after Christmas.

Maisie:

But that's days away.

Gia:

I need time to think. If you care for me at all, please respect that.

Maisie:

That's not fair and you know it.

Gia?

Gia, please.

Are you still coming to Klosters?

Gia:

Only if you stop with this nonsense.

Maisie:

I'm sorry.

Gia:

I don't believe you.

Maisie:

What do you want me to say? You know the position I'm in.

Gia:

Of course I do. But you can't always be the priority, Maisie. Sometimes I get to be, too.

Maisie:

You're always my priority.

Gia:

Am I? Because I'm really not so sure.

– Text message exchange between Her Royal Highness the Princess Mary and Lady Georgiana Greyville, 23 December 2023

My heart is still pounding by the time the car pulls up to the sprawling four-storey mansion at the heart of Sandringham Estate. Under most circumstances, I'd be cracking a dry joke about Maisie's standard of living, or at the very least gawking at the warm brick-and-stone facade. But for now, it takes all I have to hide the tremble in my hands as I climb out of the Range Rover, grateful that my legs are still working.

"*This* is Sandringham House?" I say, trying to feign some semblance of normality even as my thoughts keep flashing back to the man in the teal scarf.

"Of course," says Maisie, whose phone is dinging again, and she barely looks up as she exits the vehicle. "What did you expect, a hovel?"

"A house," I say as I head for the double front doors, which stand open beneath an intricate stone awning. "I expected a house. Not – whatever this is."

"We're the royal family. We do not live in *houses*. Though I do hope Tibby packed your thermal underwear," adds Maisie, her eyes still glued to her phone as she breezes past me and into the entrance hall. "You can see your breath in the bedrooms at night."

Every detail of the foyer is exquisite, from the rich dark wood panelling to the polished marble floor and the festive garlands decorating the winding staircase, and despite the adrenaline still coursing through my system, I pause to drink it all in. It really is stunning, and I have absolutely no idea what Maisie's been complaining about for the past week.

In the middle of the hall, a stout man waits for us beside a strange brass contraption, and he bows as we approach. "Good afternoon, Your Royal Highness, Miss Bright. Welcome to Sandringham House."

"Thank you, Paul," says Maisie with surprising warmth. "I don't suppose you'll take a bribe this year, will you? I have…"

She digs through her purse and pulls out half a dozen candy bars. "A Dairy Milk, a Flake, a Double Decker, a Mars bar, a peppermint Aero…"

"Your Royal Highness is too kind," says Paul with a hint of a smile. "But I fear that my honour remains unimpeachable."

"I was afraid of that," says Maisie with a sigh, and without explanation, she toes off her shoes, shoves her coat into my arms, and sits down on the odd apparatus. As I watch, baffled, Paul fiddles with a metal slide that almost looks like –

"Is that a scale?" I blurt, and as soon as I say it, I'm sure I'm right. Maisie rolls her eyes, but Paul glances at me with patient amusement.

"Indeed," he says as he nudges a few of the markers over. "The tradition of the weigh-in dates back over a century, to Edward VII, who believed that weight gain meant his guests had enjoyed themselves. Thank you, Your Royal Highness," he adds, and Maisie hops off. "Miss Bright, if you would."

I blink, horrified. "Wait – I'm supposed to do it, too?"

"If I have to, then you certainly do," says Maisie as she steps back into her shoes.

While Paul records her weight in a heavy leather-bound book, a maid appears at my side, and she takes Maisie's coat from my arms and waits for mine. I hesitate, but this isn't the only odd royal tradition I've come up against since joining the family, and I doubt it'll be the last.

Maisie disappears, her heels clicking on the marble floor as Paul carefully measures my weight. I consider asking what it is, but after months of having the media scrutinize everything about me, including my dress size and the circumference of my arms, I decide I don't want to know. As soon as he gives me the all clear, I jump down and shove my feet back in my Doc Martens, twisting around to figure out where Maisie went.

"Did you see—" I begin, but before I can finish my question, the front doors fly open, revealing an older woman with long silver hair, a fur coat and a small brown-and-white spaniel trotting at her heels. I've only met her once, but I could pick her out of a crowd of thousands.

Queen Constance, Alexander's mother – and my grandmother.

For what feels like the longest moment of an already infinite day, she and I stand fifteen feet apart, staring at each other like opponents about to fight to the death. Or at least that's how she's staring at *me*. I'm mostly just trying to stop myself from biting the inside of my cheek so hard that I draw blood.

I haven't seen her – and have barely heard a word about her – since she retreated to Balmoral, the royal family's Scottish castle, the day after I arrived in England. For the first time in fifty years, she missed Trooping the Colour and other summer traditions so she could protest my invitation into the family. Never mind that I'm her flesh and blood, or that I'm as much her grandchild as Maisie is. Constance hates me so completely that I'm positive she would rather live the rest of her life as a commoner than say a single decent word to me.

Sure enough, as soon as the maid takes her coat, Constance walks past me as if I'm not even there, pausing only for the absolute minimum amount of time it takes Paul to weigh her. "Is Her Royal Highness here?" she says in a clipped voice.

"Yes, Your Majesty," says Paul as he once again adjusts the markers on the old-fashioned scale. "Her Majesty the Queen and His Royal Highness the Duke of York have also arrived. I believe they're enjoying the luncheon buffet in the dining room."

I keep my expression carefully neutral. Helene and Nicholas's affair isn't exactly a well-kept secret among the family, and no doubt the staff has known even longer, but I have no idea if Constance is aware that her daughter-in-law is sleeping with the wrong son – and has been for several years now, according to Alexander. "Very well," says Constance, her voice impassive. With a sniff, she stands, not sparing me so much as a glance before disappearing through one of the large archways and into the corridor beyond. The dog lingers, staring up at me with liquid brown eyes, and I'm about to reach down and pet it when Constance's sharp voice cuts through the silence. "Zaffre, *come*."

Reluctantly the dog trots off, and I watch it go, doing my best not to take Constance's continued rejection personally. But even after all these months, it's still a losing battle.

"I'm sure Her Majesty is very busy," says Paul kindly, and I tear my gaze away from the archway and force a small smile.

"Probably has a massive pile of Christmas presents to wrap," I agree, even though I'm sure Constance has never wrapped a gift in her life. "Where should I…?"

"The dining room is to the left, if you're hungry," says Paul. "We're only awaiting His Majesty now."

"Right," I say, my anxiety mounting. But then I realize the implication of what Paul's said, and hope sizzles through me like electricity. "Wait, does that mean Kit's here already? Lord Clarence, I mean—"

"I vastly prefer the first," says a low voice behind me, and I spin around so quickly that I nearly trip over my own feet.

There, standing at the bottom of the winding staircase, his smile warm and his dark wavy hair somehow even longer than it was during our last VidChat, is Kit.

I don't know which of us moves first, but two seconds later, his arms are around me, and my cheek is pressed to his shoulder as I hug him in return. He buries his face in my hair, his ribcage expanding beneath his soft sweater as he inhales, but there's something about the way he holds me that doesn't feel exactly right – something slightly desperate, maybe, with a hint of relief and fear. The protesters at the gate – he must've passed them, too. I squeeze him a little tighter, hoping it's enough to reassure him that everything is fine. And as the seconds pass, the desperation fades, replaced by his usual calm and dependable demeanour. "Missed you," I mumble, and when I tilt my head up, he's there, his nose a fraction of an inch from mine.

"I missed you, too," he says softly, for my ears only. And even though we're not alone, he brushes his lips against mine, and the nervous tension in my body melts away. "Are you hungry?"

"Starving," I admit, though I don't mention it's because I was too nervous to eat breakfast. I kiss him again before reluctantly letting him go. "But I think Constance already claimed the dining room."

Kit takes my hand, his fingers lacing through mine. "The dining room is big enough for both of you," he assures me. "If Her Majesty wants to avoid you, then she ought to be the one going out of her way, not you."

As we pass out of the entrance hall, I offer Paul a smile and a wave. To my surprise, he bows his head in return, and while it's a small gesture – and definitely something no one else in the family would notice – my cheeks grow warm with both gratitude and embarrassment.

On our meandering way to the dining room, Kit gives me the grand tour of the main floor, and we pause in each new space as I take it all in. Sandringham House isn't as ostentatious as Windsor Castle or Buckingham Palace, but it doesn't skimp on the finery, either. Or the fireplaces, or the crown moulding, or the heraldry that seems to be everywhere, especially in a room Kit calls the saloon.

"Alexander usually invites the cousins here for Christmas," says Kit, his voice lower than usual as we explore a sizable white drawing room with a painting of a sky on the ceiling. "This year, however, it'll just be the immediate family."

"That'll be a barrel of laughs," I mutter. I've never met any of the other members of the royal family – the list of names that extends seemingly endlessly in the line of succession after Ben

– but it would've been nice to have a few decoys to throw in front of Constance if she gets snippy.

"It won't be so bad," Kit assures me. "There are plenty of places to disappear if Constance or Aunt Helene step out of line."

"It's not just them I'm worried about," I say darkly, and he smirks.

"Ah, yes. Maisie's been in a mood lately, hasn't she?"

"Tell me about it," I say, relieved I'm not the only person who's noticed. "The drive up here was miserable. I think she's fighting with Gia."

"They have their spats," he says with a shrug. "Though they tend to make up fairly quickly."

"I think this one's worse than usual," I admit. "Has Rosie said anything?"

"Rosie?" he says, and I give him a pointed look.

"Don't pretend she doesn't text you practically every day. I know she likes you."

Kit looks sheepish, even though her crush is entirely one-sided. "It's not every day," he insists. "But it is whenever she can think of a good excuse. No, she hasn't said anything – and she would, if she knew something was going on."

We head down a long hallway now, and I catch a whiff of beef and gravy and fresh-baked bread. My stomach gurgles, but even hunger can't make my feet move any faster towards the inevitable cold war in the dining room. Kit doesn't seem especially eager to arrive, either, and I peer up at him, searching his grim expression for an explanation I know won't be there.

"Are you okay?" I say, and he blinks, as if I've snapped him out of a trance.

"Better than okay," he promises, ducking his head to kiss

me again. "I haven't been this happy in months."

He doesn't look happy, though, not with the way his brow is slightly furrowed and his eyes look like they're in shadow. I hug his arm, but before I can press, Constance's sharp voice filters through a set of open double doors just down the corridor.

"...stop this foolishness at *once*." Somehow she sounds even more deadly than she looked in the entrance hall, and I fight the urge to drag Kit back the way we came. "I've no idea what you two expect will come of this. Certainly nothing good."

"I don't see how it's any of your business, Mother." Nicholas's voice isn't nearly as loud, but it's steady and unwavering, and it's clear this isn't the first time my uncle's had to deal with her demands.

"I'm the head of this family," she snaps. "That makes it entirely my business."

Kit and I stop at the doorway in time to see Helene's eyebrows rise so high they nearly touch her hairline. Though she and Nicholas are the only people seated at the long mahogany table, which is laden with crystal glasses, fine china and festive decorations, the pair of them are practically perched on each other's laps. Constance stands stiffly near one of the windows, and I'm suddenly positive that she walked in on a scene she wasn't prepared for. Because she didn't know about their affair.

"On the contrary," says Helene, her voice as cool as the icy-blue walls, "Alexander is the head of this family now. And he's perfectly content with the situation."

Constance scoffs. "Alexander is the reason public opinion of the monarchy has plummeted, with the consequences of his actions still ricocheting through the headlines. He's already made us a laughing stock, and this" – she gestures towards Helene and Nicholas – "*this* will only further ensure our demise—"

"Demise, Mother?" says someone new over my shoulder. "Isn't that a trifle dramatic?"

I recognize my father's voice instantly, but when I twist around, I freeze, my heart in my throat. Lingering behind me in a cosy red sweater is Alexander, looking more relaxed than I've seen him in months. But he's not alone.

Standing to his right in the hallway, her auburn curls loose and her cheeks still pink from the December chill, is my mother.

The past cannot be cured.

– Queen Elizabeth (b. 1533, r. 1558–1603)

My mom is here.

In England.

At Sandringham. For Christmas.

These are the only coherent words my mind can form as I launch myself towards her, and she catches me in a tight hug. She feels stronger than the last time I saw her back in June, and I inhale her scent, my thoughts reeling.

My mom is here. In England. At Sandringham. For Christmas.

And so are Constance and Helene.

A knot of fear forms in the pit of my stomach, and I pull away enough to look at her. "What are you doing here?" I manage, my voice already ragged. "I thought you were staying in Virginia."

"We wanted to surprise you, Evie," she says, but she must sense my apprehension, because she peers at me uncertainly. "It's a good surprise, right?"

"The best," I say, and it is. I haven't spent Christmas with her since I was ten years old. But I can feel the white-hot stares watching us from the dining room, and all I can think about is how everyone at Sandringham knows the darkest details of the worst day of her life. And I'm absolutely sure some of them won't hesitate to use them against her.

"Ah, the epitome of propriety has arrived at last," says Helene from her seat at the table. "And I see he's brought a guest."

My mother releases me and turns her attention to the dining room, though her hand settles on my back, as if she isn't entirely ready to let go. While Helene looks impossibly smug as she leans even closer to Nicholas, Constance stands frozen beside the velvet curtains, seemingly rendered speechless by Alexander's audacity. That, at least, is one thing we have in common.

"Hello, Helene," says my mother as she steps into the room with my father at her side, both of them either oblivious to Constance or pointedly ignoring her. "It's good to see you."

"Likewise," says Helene, her honeyed voice oozing with insincerity. "You look well, Laura."

She fixes her blue eyes on my mother, and a shiver runs down my spine. My mom shouldn't be here. She shouldn't have to face Helene, who's the reason everyone in the world knows about her mental illness and the psychotic break that permanently altered our lives when I was four. My mother shouldn't have to be polite to a woman who's never shown her an ounce of compassion or empathy, and who sure as shit won't start now.

But my mom is a better human being than I'll ever be, and she smiles with warmth Helene doesn't deserve. "I *am* well, thank you," she says. "It's good to be back in England. Nicholas

– you've grown up, haven't you?"

"It happens from time to time," says my uncle, and though he sounds genuinely friendly, he at least has the decency to look abashed. Good. While Helene was the one to tell the press about my mother's arrest and mental illness, all the details came straight from Nicholas – including the part about the bathtub.

But either my mom doesn't know or she doesn't hold grudges like Alexander and I do, and she flashes him a wide smile. "Alex told me you two are living together now," she says. "I'm thrilled for you."

Nicholas smiles self-consciously, and his arm tightens around Helene. "Thank you," he says. "All on the quiet, of course, but we're very hap—"

"You've brought *her* here? For Christmas?"

All at once, Constance seems to reanimate from her spot beside the window, and she fixes her livid stare on my father. Feeling like I've swallowed a lump of searing-cold metal, I tuck myself underneath my mom's arm, as if I can somehow shield her from whatever metaphorical daggers my grandmother is about to throw.

"Hello, Mother," says Alexander. "How lovely to finally see you again. No doubt you remember Laura."

Remember? I glance at my mom, who looks completely unfazed. In my mind, she and my royal relatives exist in two different worlds, completely separate from each other except for the bridge that is me and Alexander. But now that I'm standing here, face to face with the familiarity and contempt between the members of my unorthodox family, it's suddenly clear that the Venn diagram I've been picturing is much, much closer to a circle.

"Were you not content ruining my last Christmas with my late husband?" says Constance, every inch of her dripping with disdain as she glares at my mother. "Did you come to ruin this one, too?"

"If memory serves," says Alexander smoothly, "the tantrum you threw about hosting Laura – who, if you'll recall, was my fiancée at the time – was the reason Father was in a foul mood. *He* was pleased to welcome her into the family."

"Until you informed him that you intended on abdicating in order to marry your American harlot," snaps Constance. "That certainly put a dampener on the festivities, didn't it?"

"Only for you and Father," says Alexander, and he turns towards the long buffet set up against the wall. "Laura, you must be starving after your flight."

He picks up two plates, but Constance clearly isn't done with this conversation, and she steps closer to the table, her fingers curling around the back of an intricately carved chair.

"Will you and your *guest* be sharing a room again, then?" she says, her voice tight with barely contained spite. "Never mind that you're a married man."

"Helene and I are legally separated, Mother, as you damn well know," says Alexander with a hint of weariness now. "Must you make this difficult? Laura hasn't had the opportunity to celebrate Christmas with Evan in a very long time, and—"

"Which reminds me," interrupts Constance, as if an idea's just occurred to her. "Perhaps you'd prefer to use one of the other rooms this year, given the...amenities in your en suite."

Almost everyone in the room freezes at that – even Helene, whose wine glass is halfway to her lips. Only Kit and I glance at each other, both silently asking for an explanation. But I've never been here before, and Kit, no doubt, has never had a reason to explore my father's bathroom.

Oh.

Oh.

Rage washes over me, burning away my confusion until only cold clarity remains. I don't know exactly what Constance is talking about, but I recognize the shape of her verbal swipe – the insinuation that my mom can't be trusted anywhere near a bathtub without risking another *incident*. And just as Kit's hand touches my elbow, I slide away from him and towards the table, planting myself directly across from Constance.

"Do you remember the first time we met?" I say easily, even though my blood's boiling. "The day after I arrived at Windsor, before the investiture ceremony. I'm pretty sure I was wearing pyjamas."

Constance simply stares at me, her expression turning to stone.

"You don't?" I say, keeping my voice casual. "Because I do. I remember every word you said to me. It's not every day my own grandma calls me a mangy stray at a dog show."

Behind me, I hear my mom inhale sharply, and Alexander sputters. "Mother?" he says, like Constance would ever confirm it to his face, but I keep going.

"You also said I was a mistake." I glance at Helene, who was the real wordsmith there. "One that should've been corrected in the womb. You're sure you don't remember?"

Silence. Kit's beside me again, solid and warm and no longer trying to stop me, and I feel my mother's hand on my shoulder, but I don't know her touch well enough to figure out what she's trying to say.

"Does anyone know the name of the reporter who wrote that unofficial biography of me?" I ask. "Henrietta something?"

"Henrietta Smythe," says Alexander, sounding only slightly strained. "She was a member of the Royal Rota for two decades."

"Right. Henrietta Smythe." I'm still holding Constance's clear blue gaze, and neither of us blinks. "Isn't there a chapter in the book about the day I arrived in England, and the twenty-four hours before my identity became public?"

To my surprise, it's Kit who replies. "There is," he says. "Though it's almost entirely fictionalized."

I tilt my head. "I know the book's already published, but do you think Henrietta Smythe might be interested in what really happened? For future editions, I mean."

"The royal family doesn't speak directly to our unofficial biographers," says Alexander, his voice stronger now. "It offers too much legitimacy to their occasionally extraordinary claims. But I'm certain we could arrange for a proxy to contact her, if you're serious. We've certainly done such things in the past."

Constance's flinty expression doesn't budge, but I can see the wrath in her eyes – the acknowledgement of my very real threat. And I know she knows I'm deadly serious.

"I'll think about it," I say at last. "Decide after the holidays."

"Of course," says Alexander. "We'll discuss it in the new year. Mother, have you eaten? Dinner won't be served until eight o'clock, and—"

Constance whirls around, and without another word, she marches out of the dining room in a cloud of cashmere and contempt, her adorable spaniel trotting once again at her heels.

No one says anything for several long seconds, until the silence grows so heavy and awkward that it becomes unbearable. Both my father and Nicholas appear vaguely amused, while Helene finally takes that sip of her wine. But my mother looks… lost, maybe. Guarded, like Constance's blow landed, and she knows she has to protect herself from any further attacks. The rage returns, bubbling up inside me like lava, but just as I'm about to blurt out something to break the tension, Kit takes a single step towards my mother.

"Ms Bright," he says warmly, as if the entire encounter with Constance never happened – as if the only strange part about this is the fact that he and my mother have never been introduced. "It's a pleasure to finally meet you."

"You must be Kit," she says, her wariness slowly fading. "You're even more handsome in person."

"And I can see where Evan gets her looks," says Kit, his cheeks pink. But as they slip into a comfortable exchange of pleasantries, Alexander takes my elbow, guiding me towards the buffet.

"Where is your sister?" he says as he starts to fill a plate, and I shrug.

"She ran off as soon as we got here."

"Right," he says with a hint of disappointment. "I suppose we'll do introductions later, then. Did you two pass by the, er… incident at the gate?"

"You mean the weirdly quiet protesters looking for any excuse to pull out a guillotine?" I say. "Yeah, we saw them. Why is my mom here?"

I lower my voice so it carries only between the two of us, and

I can tell from the way Alexander's expression grows pinched that he understands exactly why I'm asking.

"Because she wants to be here," he says softly while he helps himself to the potatoes. "Because we would both like to spend Christmas together, as a family."

"They're going to eat her alive," I whisper. "That thing with Constance and the bathtub—"

"It will not happen again," says Alexander, moving on to the roasted chicken. "I promise. You've nothing to worry about, Evie – just relax and try to enjoy yourself, all right? You deserve it."

What I deserve is to know my mother is safe, both mentally and physically, but before I can spit that out between gritted teeth, Alexander heads back to her and hands her the plate. "Your favourites, if I recall. Let's sit, shall we?"

I remain beside the buffet as I watch them choose seats much too close to Helene and Nicholas, my jaw clenched so tightly that it aches. Kit joins me, wrapping his arm around my shoulders, and I lean into him.

"Would you like to go to the shops later?" he murmurs. "I need to buy your mum a gift."

This is obviously an attempt to distract me, but even though the idea of leaving my mother here makes me feel vaguely nauseated, he has a point. I have no idea if she received the present I sent to Virginia, and I can't stand the thought of her not having anything to open under the tree on Christmas. "Depends on whether Constance is on her way back to Balmoral yet," I mutter.

"Unlikely," he admits. "But your mum will be all right for a little while, Ev. Alexander has everything under control, and regardless of their verbal barbs, Constance and my aunt aren't ones to get their hands dirty."

"Maybe not," I say darkly. "But I am."

Kit presses a quick kiss to my temple, and despite my stewing, despite the omnipresent tension in the room and his grim mood, I swear I see him smirk.

Chapter Seven

"MAD MISTRESS" SPOTTED AT SANDRINGHAM FOR CHRISTMAS

Laura Bright, mother of the King's illegitimate daughter, Evangeline, has joined the royal family for Christmas in Norfolk.

A woman identified as the infamous American mistress was photographed early this afternoon in a Range Rover driven by the King as they entered the grounds of Sandringham Estate. Though Buckingham Palace has refused to comment, an anonymous source close to the royals confirms that Bright, 43, made the trip from the United States specifically to spend the holiday with her daughter.

This is believed to be Bright's first visit to England since news of her affair with the King broke last summer. Traditionally, only members of the royal family are issued invitations to Sandringham, though exceptions have been made for both betrothed and former partners, including Venetia, Duchess of York, who divorced the Duke of York in 2006 but continues to join the royals for Christmas each year.

There has been no word as to whether either Bright will make an appearance on the walk to St Mary Magdalene Church, which the royal family famously attends for a service on Christmas morning.

– *The Daily Sun*, 23 December 2023

Later that afternoon, when we've miraculously made it through lunch without any bloodshed, my mother goes upstairs to take a nap, and Kit and I head into the village near Sandringham.

The protesters are gone now, either of their own volition or because security chased them away, but I'm still a ball of anxious energy as our driver navigates the narrow lanes that lead into town. All I can think about is the poison Constance could whisper in my mother's ear over the next week, and while I know my mom isn't fragile, if Constance finds the right combination of words, it could cause the kind of wound that'll never fully heal – which I'm sure is exactly her intention.

"It'll be all right," says Kit as the Range Rover winds through a village full of houses and businesses all built from the same red brick. "Your mother can hold her own, and Alexander will intervene if Constance tries anything else."

I want to believe him, but he's never seen my mom when her illness is winning, when her mind is playing tricks on her and she can't tell what's real. "I wish Constance would crawl back to her Scottish castle and let the rest of us enjoy the holiday," I mutter. "It'd be the greatest Christmas gift I've ever gotten."

Kit squeezes my fingers. "We'll just have to find a way to make the best of it."

Our eyes meet, and there's a hint of something in his gaze – something dark that adds gravity to his words, an unexpected solemness that feels too heavy for the circumstances. I shift in my seat to face him. "Are you sure you're okay?"

"Positive," he says, but that darkness flickers again, even as he manages a faint smile. "It was a difficult term, that's all."

I'm not surprised. Kit's one of the most intelligent people I've ever met, but Oxford isn't exactly a walk in the park for anyone. "We'll take it easy this week," I promise. "Though I bet the Maldives is looking pretty good right now, compared to all this drama."

"On the contrary," he says, bringing our joined hands to his lips and kissing my knuckles. "There's nowhere else in the world I'd rather be. Or anyone else I'd rather be with."

As I rest my head on his shoulder, our driver parks in front of a shop on a quiet corner, which is only distinguishable from the rest of the town thanks to a faded pink sign that reads *Noble Norfolk Novelties*. While I can't tell what the shop sells, Kit seems to perk up when we climb out of the car.

"I think you'll like this place," he says as he pushes open the door, and a bell tinkles above us.

This place, as it turns out, is a strange hybrid of a bookstore, a gift shop, and an old-fashioned ice cream parlour. It's warm inside and smells like Christmas, and as I pause at the entrance, taking it all in, a woman with rosy cheeks bustles out from one of the aisles.

"Welcome," she says cheerfully. "How may I help you?"

"We're looking for a last-minute gift," says Kit as I examine a collection of jewellery beside the antique cash register. Some pieces are made of polished stones, while others show off flowers captured in resin or hand-painted earrings in the shape of tiny crowns.

"Anything in particular?" says the woman, but she must catch me eyeing the jewellery, because she adds, "All handmade by my daughter. Only fifteen and already so talented. Do you see anything you like, love?"

"It's all beautiful," I say, and as I glance up at her, recognition dawns on her round face. I smile politely, bracing myself for whatever's about to come, but other than her brief surprise, the only change to her expression is a faint hint of pity.

I touch a ring made of tiny pink stones fashioned into a miniature rose, and something subtle shifts inside me. She doesn't see me – she doesn't see a customer coming into her shop to buy a gift for an unexpected relative. She sees Evangeline, the King's illegitimate daughter, who has excellent posture and is always polite, who would never wear ripped leggings in public, and who everyone knows was sexually assaulted and accused of murder. Maybe in a decade or two, I'll have done enough for one of the worst moments of my life not to be the first thing everyone thinks of when I'm mentioned, but for now, I might as well have a neon sign above my head that screams *victim*.

"Is the ice cream parlour open?" says Kit as I pretend to focus on a pair of resin earrings.

"It is," says the woman, her voice an octave higher than before. "You *must* try our seasonal selections – they're like Christmas for your taste buds."

Mercifully the woman follows Kit to the other side of the shop, where the ice cream freezer is displayed beneath a chalkboard sign listing all the flavours, and I take the opportunity to duck into the crammed aisles. I'm not alone – a dark-haired personal protection officer trails after me with all the discretion of a lumbering grizzly bear – but I have a moment to realign myself and to become Evan again. On my first full day in England, during those precious few hours when I was still anonymous, Tibby warned me that if my identity was leaked, my life would never be the same. That I'd be stalked and hounded everywhere I went, and no matter what I accomplished, it would always be overshadowed by the accident of my birth.

She was mostly right, and despite her warning, I wasn't prepared for the level of scrutiny I've faced since. I'm still not, and even in this new place, far from Windsor and the crowds of London, I'm painfully aware that the world won't hesitate to turn on me if I even think about stepping out of line.

As I reach the back of the store, I turn the corner and stop suddenly. Two feet in front of me, on a rickety display that looks like it's balancing on willpower alone, are a dozen copies of Henrietta Smythe's new biography – complete with a black-and-white picture of my face on the cover. My cheeks grow hot as I glance around, and only once I'm sure this part of the shop is empty, I gingerly pick up the top copy and read the back.

The true story of Evangeline Bright, the secret American princess who's destined to take the royal world by storm.

"It's not a bad photo of you," says Kit softly behind me, and I jump. "Though I'm afraid that's the only good thing I can say about the book."

I wrinkle my nose and set it back down. "I can't believe you read it. Were you really that bored at your parents' place?"

He shrugs. "Maisie always asks me to read the unofficial biographies – she likes to know what they say, if only to prove them wrong. I assume that's a trait you two share. Chocolate candy cane with eggnog and evergreen swirl," he adds, offering me one of the cones in his hand.

I take it curiously and allow myself a cautious lick. To my surprise, the shopkeeper isn't wrong. It does taste like Christmas.

"Weird," I mumble.

"The ice cream, or my reading habits?" says Kit as we leave the display behind and head down an aisle full of souvenirs and knick-knacks.

"Both." I touch the spine of a purple leather-bound sketchbook, though when I start to slide it off the shelf, I realize it has a cartoon cat on the cover. "Do you think anyone's going to read it? The biography, I mean."

"I fear it's already a bestseller," he says, unearthing a wooden box that holds a miniature painting set, complete with five colours, two brushes and several small canvases. "Don't worry – it's mostly fiction."

"That's exactly what I'm afraid of." I nod towards the box in his hand. "My mom would love that."

"Really?" says Kit. "I thought she'd have a dozen like it."

I shrug. "She always says there's no such thing as too much paint."

Kit holds on to the paint set as we move down the aisle, and we both pause the conversation to lick our cones. "It's really not as bad as it could be," he says, and it takes me a beat to realize he's talking about the biography, not the ice cream. "If anything, it's surprisingly kind towards you. She interviewed some of your schoolmates and a few people who claim to be family friends, but there's nothing terribly personal—"

"Kitters?"

We both look up at the same time. At the end of the aisle stands a girl not much older than me, with flaming-red hair and a smattering of freckles so adorable that I'm instantly jealous. Beside her is a brown-haired boy – man – roughly the same age, and though his expression looks like it's set in a permanent scowl, there's something inexplicably open about him.

"Aoife? Dylan?" says Kit, his voice tight with wariness I don't understand. "What are you doing here?"

"Good to see you, too, mate," says the boy – man – Dylan. He smiles, but even though I think he means it, it comes off as pained. "My gran lives here. Aoife's visiting for Christmas."

The red-headed girl nudges him affectionately, and I notice their clasped hands. "You must be Evangeline," she says to me. "I've heard so much about you."

"Wish I could say the same," I say, glancing at Kit. His lips are pursed, and he looks vaguely like a deer in headlights.

"Evangeline," he says in that polite, formal tone he only uses around other people. "This is Dylan and Aoife. Dylan and I were at Eton together, and now we're on the same course at Oxford, while Aoife's studying computer science."

This immediately piques my interest, considering I'll be studying the same in the autumn, but Aoife laughs before I can bring it up. "You make it sound like we all nod to each other as we pass in the hall," she says. "We're friends. Good friends, I'd say. Wouldn't you?" She looks at Dylan, who grunts in agreement.

"Had to carry his arse home from the pub a few times," he says, and Kit turns pink. He's mentioned going out with friends during our VidChat calls, but for the life of me, I can't remember him ever mentioning names. Or that he was close with anyone at Oxford.

"Complete exaggeration," Kit assures me with a forced smile.

"If anything, I was the one keeping Dylan upright."

Aoife snorts. "Oh, no – *I'm* the one who had to tuck you both into bed," she teases before catching my eye. "Don't worry, it's all in good fun. Unlike Dylan and me, Kit's not a dosser."

I have absolutely no idea what that means, and I'm afraid to ask. Dylan must see my confusion, because he finally cracks a smile.

"She means he's a good lad," he says. "On the straight and narrow, as it were."

"*He's* actually at uni to study, rather than to poison his liver," she jokes. "And he talks about you all the bleedin' time. I don't know what kind of magic you've worked on him, but he's completely besotted."

Kit's blushing so hard now that he's practically scarlet. "Same magic you've worked on Dylan to get him to utter more than two words at a time," he says, but as he speaks, his phone chirps. He checks his screen, and his brow furrows. "I'm afraid we need to go."

"Bugger, really?" says Aoife, her shoulders slumping. "I was hoping you'd have time to grab a coffee. I've wanted to meet you for ages, Evangeline."

"We'll have to arrange something soon," mumbles Kit as he hastily types out a reply to whatever message he's received. I fight the urge to glance at his screen, sure he'll tell me eventually as long as this isn't a ruse to escape. "Evangeline, did you want to get something?"

I nod and take the box from under his arm. "You say goodbye, and I'll pay."

Kit doesn't argue, and considering he never lets me pay for

a thing, that's how I know this isn't some kind of ploy to shake off his friends. I excuse myself and head for the register, where the shopkeeper is beaming at my return, and as I pull the rose ring from the velvet case, I hear footsteps behind me.

"I'm sorry if I came off a bit strong back there," says Aoife, pausing in front of the jewellery display. "Oh, these are grand."

"Her daughter made them," I say, and the shopkeeper winks. "And you have nothing to apologize for. It's nice to meet some of Kit's friends. I don't really have many of my own here."

Aoife's easy grin returns as the shopkeeper rings me up. "Well, you can consider me one, then, if you'd like," she says, and there's a question there that I can't turn down – not politely, anyway. And definitely not as Evangeline.

"I would," I say, even though I'm not so sure. "You'll have to tell me more stories about Oxford."

She laughs again, any tension in her gone now. "I've got plenty of those, haven't I? Your Kit's a good lad. Brings out the best in us, or at least he tries, bless him."

He brings out the best in me, too, but I don't say that out loud. Kit and I've made more than our fair share of headlines since he took my hand at Wimbledon, and even though he and Aoife are friends, that's the kind of thing I want to – need to – keep private.

Once I pay for the gifts, Aoife and I head out onto the sidewalk together, still trailed by my personal protection officer. Kit and Dylan are waiting for us beside the Range Rover, and while they're chatting with the ease of two people who've known each other for years, Kit's posture is rigid, and his foot is tapping on the pavement to a fast and erratic beat.

"Evan," he says, too anxious to hide the impatience in his voice – or remember to call me Evangeline in front of his friends. "I'm afraid we really must go."

"No worries, mate," says Dylan, but Aoife's round eyes go a bit watery, and to my surprise, she catches me in a hug.

"Kit has my number," she says into my hair. "Stay in touch, yeah?"

"I will," I say, already feeling guilty for the lie. But I don't know how else to make a graceful exit, and it would take too long to explain that I don't have a phone. "It was really nice meeting you."

When she finally lets me go, she squeezes my free hand before latching onto Dylan's arm once more. Kit and I both pitch what's left of our ice cream, and I slide into the car, not sure whether I'm more relieved that's over or nervous about what comes next.

"They seem friendly," I say as soon as Kit joins me and closes the door. My protection officer climbs into the front seat beside the driver, and the car begins to move, leaving Dylan and Aoife behind. "Why did you never mention them?"

"Didn't I?" says Kit, even though I'm sure we both know he didn't. "I'll introduce you properly when you join us next year."

I eye him, not entirely sure how to take this gentle dismissal. But before I can press, he glances at his phone again, and while I know it's rude, I shift closer to him. "Who texted you?"

"Maisie," he says grimly, and he tilts his phone to show me. "It's a 9-9-9 text."

"A what?" I say, squinting at the screen. Sure enough, Maisie's texted a simple 999, and despite Kit's three follow-up messages, she hasn't responded. "What does that mean?"

"It means there's an emergency," says Kit. "Like your American 9-1-1."

My heart stutters, and suddenly I feel like there's a block of ice in my stomach. "My mom," I say tightly. "If Constance did something—"

"You know how Maisie is," says Kit. "It could be anything. A lost shoe, a bit of friendly gossip she's blown out of proportion—"

"But she'd be answering you, then, right?" I say, silently willing the car to go faster. "If she hasn't said anything yet..."

I trail off, and Kit takes my hand, his thumb stroking my skin. But while we don't speak for the rest of the drive, my imagination more than makes up for our silence, and by the time we finally arrive at Sandringham House, I've already come up with a dozen different scenarios, each more devastating than the last.

A footman opens the door for us, and as Kit and I hurry inside, I notice Paul packing the antique scale into a cushioned crate. He bows his head in greeting, but before he speaks, a torrent of words rushes out of me.

"Is everything okay? Maisie sent Kit a text, and she said something's wrong, but we don't know what—"

"Do you know where Princess Mary is, Paul?" says Kit, far more calmly, as he slides my coat from my shoulders.

"Her Royal Highness is in the white drawing room with Their Majesties and their guests," he says. "Should I let her know you've returned?"

I'm already striding across the entrance hall as Kit responds, "That won't be necessary," and his footsteps quickly catch up with mine. "Evan, whatever's going on, it can't be a true emergency if the staff hasn't been informed."

"You don't understand how bad things can get for my mom," I say, keeping my voice low as we round the corner. "If Constance or Helene went after her—"

"*Where* have you been?"

I skid to a stop, nearly ploughing directly into my half-sister as she paces the width of the corridor. Her face is flushed, her eyes are wild with panic, and she sidesteps me without a single dirty look – which is how I'm suddenly sure this isn't a false alarm.

"What's going on?" I say, ignoring her question. "Is my mom okay? What—"

"Your mother?" says Maisie, taken aback. "How on earth would I know? Is she here, too? Has the entire planet been invited and no one's bothered to tell me?"

Kit takes my hand again. "Evan's mother is here as Uncle Alexander's guest. What's happened? Why weren't you answering your mobile?"

"Mummy took it," says my half-sister, tugging on a lock of her hair. "She's upset I missed lunch, or she was, but now—"

"*Maisie*," I snap, and for once, she actually shuts up. "Why are we here? What's—"

A loud and vivacious laugh reverberates from the nearby drawing room, cutting me off. It's not my mother's, and it definitely doesn't sound like anything that could ever come out of Helene's or Constance's mouth. But while I don't recognize it, Kit stiffens.

"Is that…?" He trails off, and Maisie nods. "And did she bring…?"

"Of course she bloody did."

Kit grits his teeth so hard that a muscle in his jaw jumps. "And Alexander's fine with it?"

"What do you think?" says Maisie witheringly, and Kit's scowl deepens. "But she has no idea, and Nicholas isn't saying a bloody word—"

"Are you two going to speak in code all night, or do I eventually get to find out what's going on?" I hiss, and both Maisie and Kit focus on me with very real fear in their eyes.

"Our aunt is here," says Maisie at last. "*Former* aunt. But she never seems to have received that particular message, because she shows up every bloody year, and—"

"*Who?*" I press. "Who are you talking about?"

More raucous laughter echoes from the drawing room, and as Maisie and Kit exchange yet another uncertain glance, I huff. Releasing Kit's hand, I creep towards the doorway until I can peek inside.

"... and so I tell the sheik that of course it doesn't matter, it's only a Kokoschka, but he ought to be prepared to lose the Renoir auction, because my astrologer's assured me that Jupiter will be moving into my second house the day before – the *day* before! – and there's simply no way I can lose."

A blond woman lounges on a velvet sofa with her back to me, wine glass in hand as she gestures wildly. Nicholas perches beside her, though he leans into the armrest, putting as much space between them as possible. Constance sits unsmilingly in a chair nearby, and to my surprise, Alexander and Helene stand together by the fireplace, his expression stony and hers deeply troubled. It's the first time I've seen them go near each other voluntarily in months.

I'm about to pull back and ask who the blond is when she turns enough for me to see her profile, and even though I've never met her, I recognize her instantly. She's beautiful, in an overdone way that makes it clear she's fighting her real age. And while I never paid much attention to her growing up, it was impossible to miss the onslaught of skin-care ads, tell-alls, and talk show appearances that she still manages to book to this day.

Venetia, Duchess of York.

As everything Kit and Maisie said clicks like pieces of a puzzle I never should've solved, I notice that Alexander and Helene aren't watching Venetia. They're looking behind her, to the corner of the room I can't easily see.

Dread fills the pit of my stomach, and I inch forward to reveal the handsome blond boy leaning against the piano, perfectly at home in a room so full of tension that it seems to seep out of the walls. And as my blood turns to ice and my ears fill with static, his gaze shifts, and he looks directly at me.

Ben.

Chapter Eight

Has Prince Benedict of York finally returned to the UK?

Though Benedict has made a name for himself as a fixture in the London nightlife scene over the past year, he's been conspicuously missing in action since July. After weeks of questions from his loyal fans, Buckingham Palace finally released a statement in August announcing that the nineteen-year-old had decided to spend the rest of his summer – and the following autumn, putting off his acceptance to the University of St Andrews for another term – at an undisclosed wildlife sanctuary in Kenya. Though the prince has always been known for his love of animals, the trip was reportedly unannounced due to security concerns after the intense media scrutiny focused on the royal family over the summer.

But the third in line to the throne was spotted at Heathrow this morning with his mother, Venetia, Duchess of York, as the pair left the airport's private Windsor Suite. Are the prince and his mother expected at the reportedly ultra-low-key royal family gathering at Sandringham this year? The ex-wife of the Duke of York has never missed a Christmas, even in the midst of their contentious divorce, and it's no surprise that His Royal Highness has decided to make the arduous journey back for the holidays, given his close relationship with Princess Mary. After months apart, we've no doubt that their reunion will be full of good cheer.

– *The Regal Record*, 23 December 2023

I spin around and press my back to the wall, my heart racing as a picture frame digs into my side.

Ben is here.

Ben knows *I'm* here.

And if he doesn't know about my mom yet, he will soon enough.

Maisie grabs my wrist and yanks me farther into the corridor, clear of the inhospitable drawing room and Ben's unnerving stare. "Did you see him?" she whispers.

I nod and do my best to swallow the panic rising in me like bile. "Why is he here? *How* is he here? I thought—"

"Ah, there you all are. I was beginning to wonder."

The three of us turn towards the drawing room together, and my insides churn for real this time, threatening to expel the ice cream I can still taste.

Ben stands in the doorway, his hands in the pockets of his navy blazer. He smiles like nothing ever happened, like we're one big, happy family reuniting for the holidays, and as his blue eyes settle on me, a shiver runs down my spine.

"Benedict," says Kit with more self-control than I've ever possessed in my life. "I was under the impression you weren't coming to Sandringham this year."

Ben shrugs. "Mummy insisted I join her. You know how she is," he adds with what I used to think was charming geniality. "Once she has her mind set on something, there's no talking her out of it."

"I'm sure you could've come up with an excuse," says Maisie, sugary venom dripping from every word. "Like maybe the fact that none of us wants you here. His Majesty hasn't forgotten what you did, and rest assured, neither have we."

Hurt flickers across his face, so real I almost feel sorry for him. But he's Ben. He's the one who tried to ruin my life – who could still ruin Maisie's with a single slip of the tongue – and even after all these months, I still have no idea why.

"I did some terrible things over the summer," he says. "Awful things I'll never be able to erase. And I know I don't deserve a second chance, but if you'd all be willing to indulge me for a moment…especially you, Evan."

He gestures towards the drawing room, where the adults are gathered. I shrink back, a sour taste in my mouth, but before I can refuse, Maisie cuts in.

"We don't need your fake apologies, Benedict. We need you to *leave*."

"And I will," he says. "Right after Christmas. Please – this won't take long, and it'll save me from trying to explain the details of this whole mess to Mummy."

Inexplicably, this seems to be the thing that thaws Maisie's stubbornness, and she and Kit exchange a look I don't understand. "Fine," she snaps. "But in five minutes, we're all leaving."

"*What?*" I say, stunned she's given in so easily. Before I can properly protest, however, Maisie loops her arm in mine and yanks me forward, and it's all I can do to keep my balance as she drags me after Ben and into the white drawing room.

As soon as we step over the threshold – or, in my case, stumble and nearly face-plant on the rug – the hum of conversation falls silent, and all eyes are on us. I'm not surprised that Alexander's expression is a mixture of fury and concern, or that Constance's and Helene's are impossible to read. But the worry written on Nicholas's face is disconcerting, and Venetia…

Venetia, Duchess of York, Ben's mother and Nicholas's ex-wife, is looking at me like we're standing outside a chocolate factory, and I'm her golden ticket in.

"Evangeline!" she cries, rising to her feet and crossing the room in her towering heels. "At last. It's *such* a pleasure, my darling."

I stand stock-still as she presses her lips to my cheeks in a double kiss, and when she looks me up and down, it takes everything I have not to wipe off the magenta lipstick stains she's undoubtedly left behind.

"Mummy," says Ben imploringly. "I have something I'd like to say to everyone."

"Oh, yes, button. Of course," says Venetia, and she winks at me like she knows exactly what's coming before bustling back to her seat.

Ben clears his throat, gazing solemnly around the room at each of us. "I appreciate your time, and I won't waste it," he begins. "It's no secret that over the summer, I was…less than my best self."

Maisie scoffs. "That's putting it mildly," she mutters, and while Ben must hear her, he doesn't look our way.

"I won't make excuses," continues Ben. "There are none, anyway, that could possibly justify my actions, particularly my treatment of Evangeline."

Though he says my name, he still doesn't give me more than a passing glance, and I'm not sure whether to be relieved or creeped out. Kit wraps his arm around my shoulders, as if he alone can stand between Ben and whatever words he's about to wield, and I let myself lean into him.

"As a member of this family – the royal family – it's easy to forget how isolated we are from the rest of the world," says Ben. "Not just physically, but emotionally, too. It's always been hard for me to let strangers in, and I'll admit, I struggled to accept Evan. The entire situation was...jarring, and with Jasper's death and the fallout that happened...well." He gives a perfect imitation of a self-loathing scowl. "It made me question everything important in my life, and I became a person I wasn't proud of.

"But my time in Kenya gave me the opportunity to open up," he adds. "To relax, to forget about the pressures of being royal, and to re-examine my priorities. Those months allowed me to reflect on what I was doing with my life and how I was conducting myself in the name of this family, and all I felt was shame. While I know nothing will ever make up for my abysmal behaviour, these few days together are my chance to show you I've changed, and I'm asking you – *begging* you – to let me."

It's a moving speech, or at least I think it might be if anyone else were giving it. But all I feel is the cold, hard lump of anger and bewilderment settling in the pit of my stomach, and I glance around at the others, searching for – I don't know. Support, maybe. Comradery in thinking that Ben is full of shit.

Instead, Venetia is dabbing her eyes, as if Ben has just announced his nomination for sainthood. Nicholas looks reluctantly resigned, and while Constance's expression has barely changed, the corners of her mouth are angled the slightest bit upward, which is more of a smile than I've ever seen from her before. Even Helene is studying Ben like she's contemplating his request.

Only my father and Maisie look as disdainful as I feel. But rather than tell Ben to piss off, Alexander straightens to his full height, every bit a king now as he was with President Park.

"Your behaviour wasn't only unacceptable, Benedict," he says with quiet hostility that's impossible to miss. "It was a threat to this family and to the monarchy itself."

"I know," says Ben, and I swear I see him gulp. "You have every right to throw me out in the cold and slam the door, Uncle Alexander, and I don't think anyone in this room would blame you."

Venetia sniffs, and it's clear she, at least, will fight to the death to protect her monster of a son. Alexander's gaze flickers towards her, but he refocuses on Ben almost immediately and considers him for an uncomfortably long moment.

"You may be my nephew," says Alexander, "but Evangeline is my daughter. And from this moment on, you will treat her with the respect to which she's fully entitled."

"Understood," says Ben, and this time, when he looks at me, it's more than just a glance. "I'm truly sorry, Evan, for everything. I should've welcomed you into the family with open arms, and instead…" He trails off, as if he's too ashamed of the details to recount them, and I narrow my eyes.

"Instead you tried to destroy my life," I say bitingly. "You told *everyone* about—"

"Trust, once broken, is impossible to mend completely," says Alexander suddenly, loud enough to drown me out. "By virtue of blood, Benedict, you'll always be family. But if you want to be part of this monarchy, too, then you need to prove you're willing to uphold the values of the crown. You need to earn your role and your titles and every privilege that comes with them, and there will be no more second chances. Is that understood?"

Ben nods, seemingly abashed, but I gape at my father, too stunned for words. After everything Ben did, after every lie, every threat, every betrayal, Alexander is letting him waltz right back into our lives like it was all nothing.

"No," I blurt with such force that I take an involuntary step forward. "You know what he did, Alexander. You all *know*—"

"Why don't we speak outside, Evan?" says my father calmly, like I'm the one who's being unreasonable. Like he hasn't just offered a lifeline to the person who leaked the video of Jasper trying to rape me, and who might still have evidence that Maisie was the one who really killed him.

"Is this some kind of joke?" I say incredulously as Alexander strides towards me. "Or is this just good old-fashioned nepotism, and we're expected to excuse any and all toxic behaviour, so long as you were born into the right family?"

I look around the room, but while Maisie is glaring at Ben, she doesn't speak up. And as Alexander joins me and sets his hand on my elbow, I peer at Kit, expecting at least some level of support. But he won't even meet my eye.

This, more than anything – more than Constance's cold stare, more than Maisie's silence, even more than Alexander's gentle attempt to guide me towards the door – is what finally makes me move. With my jaw tight and my heart racing, I jerk away from my father and storm back into the hallway. I'm not sure where

I'm going, but it doesn't matter, as long as it's as far from Ben and the rest of my callous family as possible.

I make it twenty feet before I hear hurried footsteps behind me, and yet again, Alexander's hand is on my arm. "Evie—"

"Don't *touch* me," I snarl, whirling around to face him so quickly that he nearly runs straight into me. He hastily raises his hands and takes a step back, like I'm some wild animal threatening to rip out a chunk of his flesh.

"Evangeline," he says in a measured tone that only incenses me further. "Why don't we discuss this privately—"

"Do you not remember what he did to me? To Maisie?" I say. "Are you seriously going to forgive him just because he spent ten minutes coming up with some speech about how much he's changed? Because he hasn't, you know. You don't do the kinds of things he did and then suddenly find your moral compass because you've petted a few elephants."

"I know," says Alexander quietly. "And I would very much appreciate the opportunity to speak to you behind closed doors." This is such a strange request that the fire fuelling my rage sputters, and I still. Both Kit and Maisie linger in the corridor behind him, only a few feet from the drawing room where everyone else is still gathered, and both of them look…grim. Angry, I think. Maybe even scared.

At last, even though I have no desire to hear whatever justification Alexander's come up with, I nod stiffly. He leads me a safe distance down the hallway and into the empty dining room, and with my hands balled into fists, I take up a position near the windows, my arms crossed and my posture rigid.

Alexander waits until both Maisie and Kit have joined us, and he closes the door with a soft *click*. "This has nothing to do with how we may or may not feel about Ben," he says at last, his voice low and serious. "This is about making sure Venetia never discovers the details."

I blink, not sure I'm hearing him right. "Venetia? *That's* who you're all worried about?"

"She has the biggest mouth in the history of this family," says Maisie bitterly. "Whenever the money's getting low, she writes a new book, milking her farce of a marriage to Uncle Nicholas for all it's worth. If she finds out what really happened over the summer, then the entire world will know before the week's out."

I frown. "But she must have some idea of what went down. Ben just apologized in front of her."

"And you'll note how he took care not to mention any specifics," says Alexander. "I suspect he's told Venetia that he was unkind towards you – a bit of a bully, perhaps, or a little too aloof. But nothing that can't be forgiven in time."

"So she doesn't know Ben leaked the video of me and Jasper?" I say. "Or that he drugged my drink, or threatened Maisie, or—"

"The rule of thumb to follow with Venetia," says Alexander, "is if the press doesn't know, then neither does she."

We stand in silence for a long moment as I process this, and slowly my temper ebbs. Not completely – I'll never *not* be angry about what Ben's put me through, or what he could still do to my sister, or what passes for acceptable in this supposed family. But at least it isn't directed at the three of them any more.

I let my arms drop in a show of tentative peace, if not surrender. "If she's such a blabbermouth, then why not just kick both of them out now?"

"Because," says Alexander wearily, "we can't send either of them away without informing Venetia of all that's happened. And if Ben is whispering his version of events in her ear, and she runs to the press…"

He trails off, and I look between him and Maisie. "Then we'll deny it and tell the world about every despicable thing he's done," I say, baffled that this hasn't already occurred to them. "Wasn't that the whole reason I gave that interview? So Maisie has plausible deniability if Ben ever goes public or the recording ever resurfaces?"

Alexander grimaces. "Yes," he allows. "But…"

"But what?" I press, though no one says anything. "Maisie, back me up here."

She takes a deep breath, and even from across the room, I notice her hands are trembling. "Daddy's right," she says as Kit squeezes her elbow. "Venetia's widely seen as a credible source of insider information about our family. She embellishes from time to time, but she's never outright lied about our lives, and the public knows it."

I gape at her – at both of them. "You want Ben to stay?"

"Of course not," she snaps. Her eyes are red now, and despite the ferocity in her voice, she looks like she's about to cry. "I want him gone just as badly as you do. But Ben knows too much, and this *will* go poorly if we force them to leave."

"And you don't think it will if he sticks around?" I say, my own anger bubbling to the surface again as I turn back to Alexander. "You're really okay with us all sleeping under the same roof?"

"No," he admits. "I've already instructed security to monitor

Benedict at all times. But we'll have a better chance of controlling the narrative if he's here, where we can keep an eye on him. And, to be frank, I think more danger lies in what could – and likely would – happen if we banish him now. Not to mention the scandal it would cause."

I open and shut my mouth, momentarily speechless. "Is that what this is really about? You're going to let Ben get away with everything he did just to avoid another scandal?"

"I cannot disown him without reason – a very public reason," says my father and there's steel in his voice now. "I don't like this, either, Evan, but we're between a rock and a hard place, and certain choices must be made. Ben's entire future is wrapped up in this family, and in my allowing him to remain an active part of it. Now that we all know what he's capable of, he'll take care to earn back our trust. And until – unless – he does something truly dangerous, we must find a way to live with him."

My heart races, and I'm so furious that I can barely speak. "If something happens to one of us – to my mom—"

"Then I will destroy him," says Alexander calmly. "You have my word."

Maisie huffs. "We could just have him killed now and save everyone the trouble," she mutters.

"Only as a last resort," says Alexander, and I don't think he's joking.

But no matter what my father says, I know – from the look in Ben's eyes to the way he says my name to his charade of regret – that he isn't here to win us over. He didn't come back to beg forgiveness or to prove he loves us after all.

Ben is here for revenge. And I refuse to let him have it.

Chapter Nine

"Henrietta, would you say that it is unprecedented for the King to so blatantly flaunt his mistress at a royal family gathering?"

"In modern times, certainly, but historically, royal mistresses were extremely common and typically had a prominent place in the royal household. Anne Boleyn is likely the most famous example, though of course she eventually became the second wife of Henry VIII."

"And lost her head for it, as we all know. What about Wallis Simpson, as a more recent example?"

"As the Prince of Wales, Edward VIII certainly made no secret of his affair with Wallis Spencer – who later became Wallis Simpson – after meeting her in San Diego in 1920. This was before he married Catherine Gable in 1927, however, so he was really the third wheel of her first marriage."

"So it's been more than a century since any king has had a mistress?"

"It's been more than a century since any king was *caught* with a mistress. There have been whispers – particularly about Alexander I – for decades, but no woman was ever named."

"Until Laura Bright."

"Until Laura Bright, yes. Though while I will admit it does look rather dodgy, with His Majesty himself escorting Ms Bright to Sandringham, one might speculate that she was joining her daughter, Evangeline, for Christmas, rather than coming as the King's plus-one."

"Is there any evidence that she and His Majesty may be resuming their affair?"

"It's anyone's guess, though to do so in such a public manner would be daring, to say the least. Especially with the Queen and Queen Mother present at Sandringham."

"I expect the royals are in for an awkward Christmas, wouldn't you say?"

"That's certainly putting it mildly."

– ITV News's interview with royal expert
Henrietta Smythe, 23 December 2023

Ben is everywhere.

I have no idea how he does it, but for the rest of the afternoon, every time I venture into one of the common areas of Sandringham, he's there – lurking in a corner, perched on an out-of-the-way armchair, or seated on the opposite side of the room, rarely part of the conversation, but always watching. And usually watching me.

The rest of the family barely bats an eye, as if they've already forgotten the reason for his apology in the first place. Even Maisie seems to reluctantly accept his presence, though she, at least, never actively acknowledges his existence. Despite her unspoken support, however, the whole situation is so unnerving that once I make sure my mom is still sleeping off her jet lag, Kit and I sneak away to spend the evening on my bedroom sofa, up to our eyeballs in cheesy Christmas movies. I'm not in the right headspace to enjoy them, not with Ben skulking nearby. But Kit gets sniffly every time the inevitable happy ending rolls around, so I don't argue when he suggests yet another. At least one of us is having a good holiday.

Sometime in the middle of our marathon, we fall asleep on the couch together, and I wake in the grey morning light to the sound of indistinct whispers. They're faint at first, as if they're coming from the other side of the wall, but after a groggy moment, I realize they're murmuring my name.

"Evangeline."

"Evangeline."

"Evangeline."

The whispers repeat a dozen times over, each voice slightly different from the last. I must still be dreaming, or maybe this place is haunted, and a prickly sensation runs down my spine as I groan into Kit's chest. "Go *away*."

"I will do no such thing," says an uppity voice, and I sit up like I really have just heard a ghost.

Maisie stands in the doorway, dressed in what I can only call British country chic – a fitted tweed jacket, tan pants and brown boots so polished that they look wet. Her hair is braided and wrapped into a stylish-but-casual updo, and I shudder at the thought of what time she must've gotten up to make it all happen.

"You do know it's barely dawn, right?" I mumble as Kit stirs beside me. We're both fully dressed – which includes fluffy robes, bulky sweaters and fuzzy socks, considering it's about two degrees above freezing in my room – but Maisie's eyebrows shoot up anyway.

"Pardon me for interrupting," she says, a note of amusement in her voice. "Did you not check your itinerary? We leave for the Christmas Eve hunt in thirty minutes."

"I don't kill innocent animals," I say, rubbing the sleep from my eyes.

"But you do eat them," she says, and I shrug, too tired to defend my hypocrisy. "It's all for tonight, you know. Edward IX had a thing about hunting game for the Christmas Eve feast himself, and it stuck. You don't have to shoot anything," she adds. "The route also offers several lovely views of the estate."

"I can see it just fine from my window." My neck is sore from lying on Kit all night, and I dig my fingers into the offending muscle. "Is everyone else going?"

Maisie sniffs. "Mummy shares your soft-hearted sentiments, and Venetia's always moaning about her manicure, but as far as I know, everyone else will be joining the hunting party."

"Including Ben?" I say, and her eyes narrow. "I expect so. He has yet to miss a year."

If I was even remotely tempted to tag along, that immediately quells it. "If it's all the same to you, I'd rather not go anywhere near him while he's holding a deadly weapon."

Maisie scoffs. "I loathe Benedict as much as you do, but he

wouldn't dare try anything. Not with so many witnesses."

"Still. Accidents happen, and I'd prefer not to give him an opening. You shouldn't, either, you know."

"He wouldn't dare risk giving Daddy a public reason to cut him off," she says, but underneath her dismissiveness, there's a note of fear that she can't hide entirely. "Benedict is nothing without this family, and he knows it. He may be a snake, and I certainly won't be taking him into my confidence anytime soon, but I'm perfectly safe around him. We both are, and I assure you, he'll be on his best behaviour."

"Maybe," I mutter, though I don't know who she's trying to convince – me or herself. "His best behaviour isn't exactly setting the bar high, you know."

With a sigh that makes it clear I'm the bane of Maisie's existence, she looks at Kit instead. "Will *you* be joining us this year?"

"'Fraid not," he says as he sits up beside me. His hair is sticking out in every direction, and he futilely tries to comb his fingers through his wild waves. "I was thinking about giving Evan a tour of the gardens and the walking trails through the woods."

"At least she'll be getting *some* fresh air," mutters Maisie. "Whether you hunt or not, you're both expected at the Christmas party this evening – we'll be decorating the tree in the white drawing room, followed by a formal dinner and opening gifts. And," she adds pointedly, "the dress code is black-tie."

She eyes the cartoon reindeer on my socks with disdain, and without another word, she turns on her heel and marches out of the room, closing the door behind her.

As soon as she's gone, I lie back down in a huff and wiggle my freezing toes. "It's starting to feel like we're the only people actually trying to avoid Ben."

Kit settles on the sofa with me. "Everyone else is used to him, and it's easier to resume old patterns than establish new ones." He nuzzles my cheek. "Good morning."

"Good morning," I say, relaxing as he wraps his arms around me. "You stayed over."

"I didn't mean to," he says apologetically. "How do you feel?"

This, I know, is him asking more than just how I slept. I turn towards him and, mindful that neither of us brushed our teeth last night, I give him a closed-mouth peck. "I have a crick in my neck," I admit. "Can we please aim for passing out in the bed tonight instead?"

Kit hesitates. "Are you sure? I don't have to stay if you'd rather—"

"I want you to," I say firmly. "You're warm, and if it were any colder in here, it'd be snowing."

He chuckles and holds me a bit tighter. "Very well. I'll be your personal Sandringham space heater, but only because you insist."

Once we untangle ourselves and Kit heads to his own room to get ready, I turn the shower on as hot as it'll go and stand under the scalding water long enough to boil a lobster. By the time I dry off and dress in my warmest sweater, I have some feeling in my fingers again, and I braid my damp hair and head out into the hallway, determined to find something hot for breakfast. Before I can take more than a couple of steps, however, a door across the corridor opens, and Ben appears.

Instantly our eyes meet. He's wearing contacts instead of his typical brown frames, making his stare even more penetrating than usual, and slowly I register the fact that his hunting outfit matches Maisie's.

"Evangeline," he says, and while his tone is as genial as ever, it still turns my blood to ice. "Are you not joining us today?"

"I'm not in the mood to kill things," I say coldly, and he chuckles.

"Pity. I rather think you'd be good at it." He smiles, but there's no real warmth behind it – only a mimicry. "If you'll excuse me."

He starts to walk away, but with a surge of bravery – or, more likely, sheer recklessness and a generous lack of self-preservation – I follow, my footsteps matching his.

"I got your flowers," I say, and he slows. "I'd say thank you, but."

"Flowers?" he says innocently. There's a smirk tugging at the corner of his mouth, though, and I know he knows exactly what I'm talking about – the bouquet of blood-red gerbera daisies that accompanied the threatening note he sent to my first public appearance. "I'm afraid they must've been from someone else."

"Must've been," I agree in a tone that makes it clear I'm not the least bit fooled. "Why did you do it?"

"Send flowers?" says Ben. "I thought we just established—"

"Not that. All of it. Jasper, the video – everything that happened this summer. Why?"

Ben stills completely now, almost unnaturally so. "You've asked me that before."

"You didn't answer then, either," I say. "But I think I deserve to know. What is it that made you hate me so damn much that you tried to ruin my life?"

He tilts his head. “I didn’t try to ruin your life, Evan. You did that on your own the moment you decided to join this family.”

Before I can argue, a creak sounds behind me, and I glance over my shoulder. A member of the security team stands fifteen feet away, his grey suit a stark contrast to the rich velvets and dark woods that decorate the hallway. When I look back at Ben, his shoulders are squared and his posture is stiff as he takes in the sight of the officer.

“The family’s expecting me,” he says, his gaze once again meeting mine. We stand there for several eternal seconds until at last, with a mocking dip of his head that anyone else might assume is a bow, he turns and continues on his way down the corridor.

I watch him go, his footsteps muffled by the hunter-green carpet, and only once he’s turned out of sight do I unclench and exhale. My legs feel like they’re made of putty, and I lean against the wall, resting the back of my head on the edge of a gilded frame as I focus on my breathing.

Shit.

Chapter Ten

Aoife:

it was grand seeing you yesterday, kitters. have you and evangeline got a spare hour today? or maybe after christmas?

Kit:

We have a tight schedule today, I'm afraid, and we'll be leaving for Klosters on Boxing Day.

Aoife:

damn
I like her. she seems delightfully normal, or whatever passes for normal in that bloody family of yours.

Kit:

It's a rather low bar, admittedly.

Aoife:

some other time, then, yeah?

Kit:

Some other time.

Aoife:

you really never mentioned me or dylan?

Kit:

You know why. She has enough to worry about.

Aoife:

that's nothing, love. just a bit of fun. no reason to tie yourself into a twist over it.

Kit:

I fear our definitions of fun are very different.

Aoife:

speaking of, she said she hasn't got many friends here, and I offered up my five-star services, but you two left before we could exchange numbers. any chance you could pass mine on?

Kit:

She hasn't got a mobile, I'm afraid.

Aoife:

Oh.

Kit:

Really. I have to ring her private secretary if I want to talk to her.

Aoife:

I suppose that's a no, then.
it's only because of dylan, you know. I don't really mean any of it. not the way he does sometimes.

Kit:

I know, Aoife. I'd just rather she be kept out of it.

Aoife:

I won't say a word to her, I swear. if my secret's safe with you, then your secret's safe with me.

– Text message exchange between
Christopher Abbott-Montgomery, Earl of Clarence,
and Aoife Marsh, 24 December 2023

"Evan?"

I'm still leaning against the gilded frame outside my bedroom, my heart racing from the encounter with Ben, when my name filters down the hallway.

My eyes fly open. The security guard is gone now, and in his place stands Kit. He's in a grey sweater with fitted jeans, and his hair is tied back in a half ponytail that he pulls off with astounding ease. But even as I take in the sight of him – which is usually more than enough to make me go all warm and fuzzy inside – I can't shake the coldness that's settled over me in Ben's wake.

"I'm fine," I say, seeing the worried crease in his brow as he makes his way towards me. "Just ran into Ben."

"Did he say anything?" says Kit, taking my arm, and I shake my head.

"Nothing menacing enough to hold up in a court of law," I mutter. "I love your hair like that."

"You do?" he says, mercifully letting the topic of Ben drop as he self-consciously touches his ends. "It's not quite long enough for a full ponytail, I'm afraid. And Aunt Helene will hate it."

Sure enough, as we enter the dining room a few minutes later, Helene's fork falls to her plate in a clatter.

"Kit, I am *begging* you – allow my assistant just a few minutes with that unruly mop of yours before church tomorrow. You can't be photographed like this."

"I think he looks exceptionally handsome," says Venetia, who sits across from Helene with her green eyes now fixed on Kit. "It's rather roguish, isn't it? If I were ten years younger..."

"You'd still be a decade too old," says Helene, now delicately spearing a strawberry.

Someone clears their throat behind me, and Kit and I both turn. My mother stands with a mug of coffee in one hand and a tote bag of painting supplies slung over her shoulder, and she smiles. "Longer hair suits you, Kit," she says, though unlike Ben's mother, there's nothing creepy about the way she says this. "Thank you, Ms Bright," says Kit politely, but there's a hint of amusement in his voice, too. "May I take your bag?"

Surprisingly, my mother hands it over, and while Kit sets it down in an unoccupied corner of the room, she drops a kiss on my forehead. "Good morning, Evie."

"Hi, Mom," I say quietly, and as I hug her, I have the sudden urge to lead her as far away from the dining room as we can get. "What are you—"

"Evangeline!" cuts in Venetia cheerfully, seemingly oblivious to our private conversation. "Now that you and your mum are both here, I've been meaning to ask – what time were you born, love?"

I blink. "What? Why?" We've barely said a word to each other, and this isn't exactly the kind of question you ask without a motive.

Helene must sense it, too, because she gives Venetia a look that could melt steel, but the duchess merely waves her off. "Oh, not like *that*, darling. I simply want to do her natal chart. It'll be similar to Maisie's, of course, considering they were born on the same day, but there must be all sorts of stories in the differences. Maisie's a Leo rising," she adds cheerfully. "You're so alike, the pair of you – I bet your ascendant is a fire sign, too."

"I don't know what that means," I say. "And I don't know when I was born. I was a little busy at the time."

Venetia laughs as if I've told the funniest joke in the world. "You certainly don't get your sense of humour from His Majesty, do you? Laura, surely you know her birth time."

I peer at my mother, whose expression has gone strangely fixed. She's still smiling, but it seems glued on now, and like it's taking a considerable amount of effort to keep it there.

"I'm afraid I have no idea, either," she says. "It was a difficult birth, and the doctors gave me the good stuff. I didn't know what day it was, let alone what time."

"You've never looked at her birth certificate?" says Venetia dubiously. And for a split second, I swear Helene and my mother exchange an unreadable look.

"Evan's early life was somewhat…turbulent for me," says my mom. "Alexander has all the official documentation now. You'll have to ask him about any specifics."

Venetia opens her mouth, then swiftly closes it, her overdone lips puckered like she's swallowed a lemon. And when Helene and my mother glance at each other again, I'm sure I'm not imagining things.

Despite this awkward interaction, Venetia shows no signs of being subdued throughout breakfast. Helene and my mother make sure most of the chatter is mercifully directed towards Kit, who seems happy to talk in bland generalities about his term at Oxford, but whenever the conversation drifts towards me, Venetia's questions go from polite to probing in seconds. Again and again, Kit intercepts, turning the conversation back on himself with masterful skill, until Venetia finally seems to grow bored and excuses herself, citing an urgent need to make a phone call. As soon as she's gone, the four of us seem to exhale at once, and I shift to face my mom in the chair beside me. "Are you going somewhere to paint? Maybe Kit and I could come along and keep you company."

"I thought I'd stay here for a little while," she says, sipping the last of her coffee. "Helene and I have plenty to catch up on, and I'm not sure we'll have another chance before the boys return."

"What?" I say, so startled that for a moment, I forget we're all being polite. "But—"

"It has been a long time," agrees Helene. "And we do have quite a lot to discuss."

I look back and forth between them, baffled. Never in my life have I pictured the pair of them sitting at the same table, having a civil – let alone friendly – conversation, and the thought of all the cruel things Helene could say to my mother fills my ears with incessant buzzing and the pit of my stomach with dread. Helene was the trigger for my mother's psychotic break, and even though it's been fourteen years, those scars must still exist somewhere inside her. And I have no idea how delicate they might be. "Evan," says Kit, his fingers lacing through mine underneath the table. "Why don't we go on that walk?"

"Walk?" I say, barely comprehending the word. "But—"

"That's a great idea," says my mother. "Do me a favour and look for a spot that captures your attention. I'd like to work on a new piece while we're here, and it should be something special." I don't know how to say no to that, or how to say yes to Kit, but he stands and guides me to my feet.

"We'll be back before lunch," he promises, but before he can lead me to the exit, I slip my hand out of his grip and fling my arms tightly around my mom.

"Are you sure?" I whisper, and she hugs me gently in return.

"Positive," she murmurs. "Helene and I both have what we want now, and that makes all the difference."

I'm not convinced, but my mother releases me, and Kit's there again, apparently every bit as sure as she is that this isn't a massive mistake. I glance over my shoulder as we leave the dining room, but rather than focusing on my mother, I meet Helene's eye instead. She nods once, slowly, and this is as much of a promise as I'm going to get.

The garden, as it turns out, isn't just a stretch of flowers, but a dozen paths that lead through meticulous hedges and shrubs, past stunning fountains and statues, and into the woods that are spread out across the estate. Kit's arm is wrapped around the waist of my black wool peacoat as we meander between tall trees, the branches bare in the winter morning light, but for once, his presence isn't enough to calm the hurricane of anxiety inside me. "I hate that we don't know what they're talking about," I say, resisting the urge to look back at Sandringham House, or at least what little we can see of it from here. "If Helene says something that sets my mom off..."

"She won't," says Kit. "What would be the point? It would only upset you and Alexander, and she wouldn't gain anything. Besides, Aunt Helene may be many things, but she isn't malicious or sadistic."

"No, just spiteful and heartless," I mutter. "She told the entire world about my mom's illness."

"Because she thought it would protect Maisie. I'm not defending her," he adds gently as I start to protest. "I'm completely on your side. But I've known Aunt Helene my entire life, and if I thought for a moment that she might do something to shatter your mother's peace, I would've never walked out of that room. If anything, they're almost certainly talking about Alexander."

"What about him?" I say, silently desperate that he's right.

"Logistics, I'd expect, especially if he and your mother choose to carry on while he's still legally married to Helene."

I make a face. "I can't believe they're sharing a bedroom. Do you think – no, never mind, don't answer that."

He laughs and kisses my temple. "Are you all right with it? With them being together again, if they are. If they choose to be."

Something heavy settles over me, and I take a deep breath, considering the question. Unlike some kids with unmarried parents, I never fantasized about mine getting back together in a sweeping romance that fixed every problem in my life. If anything, the very thought makes me uneasy for reasons I'm not sure I can explain.

"I don't think I have any right to try to stop them," I admit at last. "But I don't like it. Not the idea of them – I think anyone who's ever seen them together knows how much they love each other, and they have a right to be happy. But I'm not sure that's possible. Alexander can love my mom more than anything in the world, but he's still King, and being with him will shine a spotlight on her that'll never go away. The press has already villainized her, and no amount of truth or damage control will change the fact that everyone – *everyone* knows about the darkest moments of her life."

"And because of that, they can't be together?"

I shake my head. "The media will never let it go, and the

public will never forget what happened. No matter what comes next, she'll always be the – the *crazy mistress* who tried to drown her daughter in a bathtub. At least if she's out of the limelight, she'll have a chance to move on with her life. She'll have a chance to be *more*."

Kit is quiet as we head deeper into the trees. Overhead, a bird breaks into song, and I crane my neck to find it, but it's hidden in the endless bare branches.

"What if," he says slowly, "your mum doesn't want to be more?"

I frown. "Who wants to be defined by the worst thing that's ever happened to them?"

Kit purses his lips. "For years, she's been separated from the people she loves. She couldn't be with Alexander because – well, obvious reasons, and she was scared to be around you in case she hurt you again. But now that everything's out in the open, she's here – in England, with you and Alexander. There's nothing more the press can do to her. They have all her secrets, and you...you're healthy. Thriving, even. She's still careful with you – gentle, I mean," he adds when I shoot him a confused look. "I can't pretend to know what it must be like, surviving all she's gone through, but I would imagine she'll always be gentle with you. And the important thing is that she has you now, and you have her. And you both have Alexander. What would the point of all those terrible things be if she walked away? What could possibly be worth more than the love between the three of you?"

For a long moment, I say nothing, and I let myself picture it instead. My mom and Alexander, both of them happy – really, truly happy, despite the endless storm of bullshit the media would throw at them. "He'll never divorce Helene," I say. "And he'll never marry my mom, either – it'd make her queen, and he wouldn't do that to her. It would also be the biggest scandal in the history of the monarchy, besides maybe Henry VIII and his wives."

"No monarch has divorced since, I'll grant you," says Kit. "But that's hardly the equivalent of beheading two queens and creating a new religion."

"Maybe not, but Helene's the most idolized woman in the world," I say. "There's no way Alexander can leave her without becoming public enemy number one."

"It would be…tricky," he agrees. "But perhaps—"

Crack.

A loud noise echoes through the woods, and I glance up, sure that a tree branch has broken. But before I can even comprehend what's happening, Kit's arms are around me, and he dives towards the base of the nearest tree as another crack rings out, and then another.

Kit and I hit the hard ground in a heap, his body pressed against mine, and I let out a yelp of pain as my left shoulder seems to bear the brunt of our fall. But Kit covers my mouth with his hand, stifling any sound, and I stare at him, my eyes wide.

What the hell is going on?

Another crack cuts through the still morning, and the tree trunk seems to explode a foot above our heads, showering us with wood chips.

Those cracks aren't breaking branches, I realize as cold horror spreads through me.

They're gunshots.

Kit catches my eye, and he must see my sudden surge of panic, because he presses his finger to his lips, and I manage a jerky nod. Only then does he remove his hand from my mouth, and he pulls out his phone to type a quick message, his body still covering mine.

My heart is pounding so hard that my chest hurts, and the edges of my vision slowly turn black from sheer terror. But as I lie perfectly still, my muscles taut while I wait for the next shot, I notice a dark red smear on the shoulder of Kit's tan coat. Maybe it's denial, or maybe just adrenaline, but for a split second, I can't wrap my head around what I'm looking at. When it hits me, however, all the air leaves my lungs, and the world seems to lurch sideways.

"*Kit*." His name is barely a breath, though it's enough to grab his attention. He follows my gaze, his brow furrowed, but his confusion turns to wild-eyed fear as he hastily shifts his weight off me. He's still hovering, barely an inch above me as his hair falls into my eyes, and he slides his hand between us to undo the buttons of my coat.

What are you— I mouth, but he's pushing my lapel away from my chest, and then I see it. A scarlet stain blooming in the cream of my sweater, just below my shoulder.

It's not his blood. It's mine.

Chapter Eleven

Sandringham Estate has gone into lockdown this morning after multiple ambulances and law enforcement vehicles were seen speeding onto the grounds. No further information is available at this time.

– Breaking news alert from the BBC,
9:41 a.m., 24 December 2023

I don't know how long we lie there on the forest floor, Kit's body covering mine as he presses his hand to the wound in my chest, trying to staunch the blood that flows with horrific ease. Time doesn't seem to mean much any more, and even though I'm aware of the pain spreading through me, deep and unyielding and unlike anything I've ever felt before, my mind is strangely blank.

Eventually, almost like an afterthought, it occurs to me that the gunshots have stopped. Kit's brown eyes are locked on mine, and his lips are moving, but even though I can hear the low murmur of his voice, my brain can't comprehend what he's saying. Maybe I'm panicking, or maybe I'm dying, or maybe it's something in between. Either way, I don't move, and neither does he.

The protection officer who escorted us into town is the first to reach us, and he radios his colleagues as he kneels beside us, the rush of air sending an agonizing tremor through me. Within seconds – or at least it feels like seconds – more officers appear, and when I blink, the forest is suddenly alive with blue flashing lights. More people surround us now, but even as several paramedics try to usher Kit out of the way, he stays right where he is.

I blink again, and I'm suddenly in what I think is the back of an ambulance, but something is off. There's a wall of noise around me, and I catch sight of a cloud floating level with us through a small window. My thoughts are so muddled that I can't figure out what this means, but then Kit is there, his mouth moving even though I can't hear him, and I don't care about the cloud any more.

This time, when I open my eyes, the oppressive sound is gone, replaced by a soft beeping. I'm in a dimly lit room with moss-green walls, and though a pair of curtains are covering the nearby window, a faint ray of grey light sneaks through a gap in the fabric. My body is heavy and numb, but my thoughts are clearer now, and when I notice the IV sticking out of my arm, I realize that this is a hospital room.

"Kit?" I manage, trying to sit up, but whatever medication is dripping through the plastic tube stops me from moving too much.

"Evie?"

Alexander's hoarse voice floats towards me, and he and my mother are beside the bed in an instant, both of them looking like they've aged a decade. My mother's eyes are red and swollen, and Alexander looks gaunt with worry. Which is ridiculous, because I'm fine.

"Where's Kit? Is he okay?" I say, and even though my mind is scrambling to form a coherent picture from the fragments of my memories – the gunshots, the smear of blood on his coat, the whirling of what must have been helicopter blades – I sound *incredibly* drugged.

"Kit's in the hallway," says Alexander as my mother slides her hand into mine. "He's all right – grazed in the arm, but nothing a few stitches won't fix."

Grazed in the arm. By a bullet. The same kind of bullet that somehow hit me. Maybe even the same one. None of this feels real, and I shake my head, trying to…I don't know. Make it stick, maybe. Find something solid among all this haze.

"I'm so very sorry, Evie," continues Alexander, and he covers our hands with his. With a sharpness that's in stark contrast to the rest of this soft reality, I notice he isn't wearing a wedding ring, and I can't remember if he ever did. "Police and royal security are combing through the estate as we speak, but we've no idea how this happened."

"It was Ben," I mumble, and even though I haven't actually thought about who pulled the trigger, I'm absolutely sure it was him. "Where's your ring?"

"My – what?" says Alexander, taken aback.

"Your wedding ring. Don't you have one?" There's a signet ring on his pinky, but otherwise his left hand is bare. And it's only now, with the way both he and my mother are looking at me, that I realize how strange this question is, all things considered.

He clears his throat. "Er, yes, but I haven't worn it in private in years. Evan, it wasn't Benedict – he was with me and the rest of the hunting party, and we were miles from the house. There's simply no way it could've been him. But I swear to you, we *will* find whoever did this."

Alexander's voice catches, and my mother touches his arm with her free hand. He turns towards her, his face mostly hidden from me, and for the briefest of moments, she rests her forehead against his. Before it occurs to me that I probably shouldn't be staring, it's over, and Alexander steps back as my mother shifts closer to me.

"How do you feel, sweetheart?" she says, touching my cheek with her cool hand.

"I don't know. Weird." My body feels like it's made of cement, and the harder I try to get a handle on my drifting thoughts, the more they turn into smoke. With a faint and unsettling jolt, I realize that between the loss of control over my own limbs and the disjointed confusion, this feels like the night Jasper drugged me. Except this time, danger isn't hovering nearby, whispering in my ear as he tells me to relax. It's everywhere, and the part of me that trusts the world – that believes in my own survival – has cracked.

"The doctor said that will wear off soon," she says. "You lost a lot of blood, and you'll be sore for a while. But surgery went well. The – the bullet missed your heart and lung, and there's no major damage."

I nod slightly, flexing my fingers. These, at least, still work. "When can I go home?"

"If you're feeling up to it, we'll take you back in the morning," she promises, and belatedly I realize I should've been more specific. Sandringham isn't my home. Maybe Windsor is, or maybe in my stupor, I mean Virginia. But when I think about it, all I really want is her and Kit.

"You should talk to Ben," I say, my gaze sliding to Alexander again. "He'll know what happened. He was disappointed I wasn't going hunting this morning." At least I think it was this morning. But with the curtains blocking the window and my sense of time out of whack, I can't be sure. "I think I messed up his plan."

"Security told me the two of you had an…encounter," says Alexander thickly, and he hastily wipes his cheek. "I promise, Evie, I had my eye on him the entire time. He never slipped away."

"Doesn't mean anything," I mumble. "He has other people do his dirty work for him."

My parents exchange a look I don't understand. "We'll talk about it more when you're feeling better," says my mom, squeezing my hand again. "Why don't you rest?"

I know I should. My eyelids are growing heavy, and it won't be long before whatever the doctors are pumping through my system wins. But I take a deep breath, or at least as deep as I can manage right now, and I glance at the door. "Can I see Kit first?" I have the vague sense that I could ask for the world right now, and my father would move heaven and earth to give it to me. Sure enough, almost as soon as Alexander steps out into the hall, Kit appears in the doorway. His sweater and coat are gone, and he wears a white T-shirt instead, with gauze wrapped around his right bicep. But even though he's clearly washed away the worst of the carnage, I can see a few smeared drops of blood on his neck, now dried to a sickening brown.

He says nothing as he crosses the room to my bedside, and my mother slips away as Kit carefully embraces me. His wet cheek presses against mine, and his shoulders shake as he cradles me, his breath coming in soft gasps.

I've never seen him really cry before, not like this. He's always so damn calm and stoic, taking everything life throws at us in stride, as if he can absorb any hit no matter how hard. But this is his breaking point, and I clumsily rub his back with my good hand, wishing I knew how to make any of this better.

"Are you okay?" I say, and he nods.

"How do you feel?" he says hoarsely. "Do you need anything?"

"Not any more." The stubble on his jaw is scratchy against my skin, and I nuzzle his cheek. Kit's shoulders shake a little harder at that, and as I hold him, rage burns within me. Rage at the gunman for doing this to us, rage at the terror and pain Kit and my parents must have felt, but especially rage at myself, irrational as it may be, for letting this happen in the first place.

"I'm so sorry, Ev," he whispers at last, his voice thick with guilt and grief. "I should've – I should've done more. I should've protected you."

"My memory's a little fuzzy," I say, "but I'm pretty sure you stepped in front of a bullet for me." I touch the edge of the gauze. "Several bullets, possibly."

He clears his throat, and his fingertips brush against the pulse point of my neck like he's trying to reassure himself I'm really still here. "I don't know what I'd do without you."

"Live a long and happy life with Rosie," I say, and he lets out a choked laugh that sounds more like a sob.

"You have no idea how important you are to me, do you?"

he says, burying his nose in my hair and breathing in my scent – which can't be terribly attractive right now, all things considered. But he doesn't seem to care.

"Almost as important as you are to me?" I guess, and he manages another halting laugh. Finally he pulls away, just enough to gaze at me, and for a split second, I think he's going to say it. But as he brushes a stringy piece of hair from my eyes with aching tenderness, I decide he won't. Not because he wouldn't mean it, but because he doesn't have to for me to know.

"Stay with me?" I ask, and he nods.

As he settles on the very edge of my mattress, excruciatingly mindful of my injuries, I finally look past him and notice the table on the other side of my bed. It's flush against the wall and difficult to see from my vantage point, but someone has arranged several bouquets of flowers along the imitation wood.

Most feature a variety of roses and lilies and poinsettias – the kinds of flowers that are easy to find at the height of the Christmas season. But the plastic vase set closest to my bed is full of daisies. Not bright, cheerful daisies, with sunny yellow centres and crisp white petals – these daisies, like the ones Ben sent to Wimbledon, have black eyes that seem to sink into the darkness, and even in the faint grey light, I can make out the red petals, so deep and vivid that all I see when I stare at them is blood.

I reach for the small paper card among the gaping flowers, and though my fingers fumble at first, I manage to pluck it from its plastic holder. And there, in scarlet ink and Ben's spidery handwriting, are three innocent words that chill me to the bone.

Thinking of you.

HUNTING ACCIDENT AT SANDRINGHAM TRIGGERS MEDICAL EMERGENCY; EVANGELINE REPORTED VICTIM

Buckingham Palace has announced that a hunting accident is to blame for the frightening scene at Sandringham Estate on the morning of Christmas Eve, and a well-placed palace insider has confirmed that Evangeline Bright was the victim.

While no life-threatening injuries were reported, speculation about the seriousness of the incident was fuelled by the alleged evacuation of the royal family to Windsor Castle shortly after the shooting took place, leading many to fear that foul play was involved. A Twitter post from Venetia, Duchess of York, however, suggests that the move was made to be closer to the hospital where Evangeline was taken.

@duchessvofyork What a frightening day! An unexpected detour to Windsor Castle now...there's nothing more important than being with your family on Christmas. Hug your loved ones tight.

12:23 p.m. · 24 December 2023

Bright, who is not an official member of the royal family, was airlifted yesterday morning to an undisclosed hospital for emergency treatment. Though there have been no further updates on the alleged victim's condition or location, the royal standard has not been raised at Windsor Castle, Sandringham House, or any other royal residence, suggesting that His Majesty is spending Christmas in hospital with his illegitimate daughter.

The identity of the shooter has not been released.

– *The Daily Sun*, 25 December 2023

The next morning, while most families are opening presents and drinking hot cocoa, mine is escorted back to Windsor Castle by more than a half-dozen police vehicles, complete with sirens, flashing lights and a motorcycle leading the way.

Even with the gunman still on the loose, it's overkill, but I'm too exhausted to make any kind of snarky remark. I'm stretched out across the middle bench seat in a bulletproof SUV, my head in my mom's lap and a blanket covering the rest of me, while Kit and Alexander sit in the row behind us. The three of them speak in hushed voices, and even though I drift in and out of consciousness, I catch snatches of their conversation.

"...didn't match the striations of any rifle in the Sandringham armoury," says Alexander, and I can practically hear his frown.

"That's good, isn't it?" says my mother, her fingers gently combing through the tangles in my hair. "That no one on the estate was responsible, I mean."

"All it means is that they didn't use one of our hunting rifles," says Alexander grimly. "The police are doing their best, but the estate is twenty thousand acres, and much of it is open to the public. Even if they do find evidence..."

We hit a bump in the road, and though the doctors gave me a nerve block before our trip, rendering most of my upper-left side numb and useless, I still wince. But I only have myself to blame for this whole set-up, as I refused point-blank to get in an ambulance, and this was the only alternative Alexander would accept. I must dip into sleep again, because the next thing I hear is Kit's voice. "...said you banned the family from attending the service at St George's Chapel this morning?"

"I doubt she's terribly upset," says Alexander drily. "But yes, with the service at Windsor open to the general public, it was too much of a security risk. Maisie knows that the safety of the family is paramount, and I'm sure God will forgive us, considering the..."

Alexander trails off, and Kit swears quietly under his breath.

I open my mouth to ask what's wrong, but then I hear it.

Shouts – dozens of them all at once, a wall of voices that grow louder as the car creeps forward. I remember the protesters outside Sandringham, and a chill runs through my aching body, but the people with scarves covering their faces were silent. This crowd –

This crowd is calling my name.

"How do they know it was her?" says my mom, horrified.

"Who?" I say, my throat painfully dry. "What's going on?"

I try to sit up, but her hand is there, gently holding me down. "Photographers and journalists at the gate," she explains. "There must be nearly a hundred of them. Alex—"

"I don't know," he says in a strangled voice. "I told Doyle to release a statement calling it a hunting accident. Jenkins confirmed just an hour ago—"

"There's an article on the *Daily Sun*'s site," says Kit suddenly. "A 'well-placed palace insider' told them Evan was shot."

A few long seconds pass, and I assume Alexander's reading whatever post Kit has found. "Damn," mutters my father, followed by a few more colourful snarls. "That gold-digging, bloodsucking—"

"Venetia?" says Kit, and Alexander grunts in the affirmative. "We knew she'd go to the press eventually," says my mother with a sigh. "I was hoping she would at least wait until Evan was out of the hospital, though."

The vehicle is moving at a snail's pace, and on the other side of the tinted windows, I can just make out several police officers guiding us through what must be a tightly packed crowd. My name is louder now, interspersed with what sound like questions, but I can't tell what any of them are saying. And I'm not sure I want to know.

At last, we must make it through the gate, because the shouting grows quieter as the SUV speeds up again, and I can feel my mother relax. She shouldn't be here – not at Windsor, not in the middle of everything. But I also know that nothing, not even Alexander, could send her away now. And I'm terrified.

"Security has locked down this part of the castle," says Alexander unprompted. "Though if you must go outside, do be certain to stick to the immediate grounds."

"I don't think any of us needs fresh air that badly," says Kit as the car pulls to a stop. Only then does my mother help me sit up, and I see the dozen staff members waiting for us at the door – including a man with a salt-and-pepper beard who wears a frown so deep that it's practically sliding off his face.

"Jenkins?" I gasp, wondering if I'm imagining things. But as a footman opens the door, he's there, his arms around me as he eases me gently onto the drive. And even though everyone's watching, I hug him in return and bury my face in his chest, finally letting myself feel the overwhelming grip of fear – of all that happened, of all that could've happened, and how close I came to losing everything.

"You're all right, Evan," he murmurs in a voice meant only for me. This kind of behaviour would get any other member of the royal staff dismissed on the spot, but Jenkins has been the one constant in my life since my grandmother's death, and I refuse to let something as ridiculous as protocol steal that from us.

"You're here," I say, a little dizzy as I finally step back. "What about Louis? You shouldn't have to give up your Christmas."

"There's nowhere else I'd rather be," he says. "And I assure you, our nieces and nephews won't miss me, not when Louis's baking up a storm. Your Majesty," he adds, bowing his head as footsteps crunch against the gravel beside us.

"Jenkins," says Alexander. "Thank you for coming – and please, there's no need for formalities today. Has Dr Gupta arrived?"

"He and his team have already set up their equipment in Evangeline's apartment, sir," says Jenkins, as proper as he always is, and he touches my good shoulder. "Let's get you inside, darling."

Somehow, miraculously, I manage the walk from the side

entrance to my apartment, which feels like it's tripled in the two days we've been at Sandringham. The royal physician – Dr Gupta – is waiting for me in my sitting room, and it's only after he checks my vitals and the small incision just below my shoulder that I'm finally allowed to pass out in my own bed.

Maybe it's the painkillers, or maybe the trauma of all that's happened is finally sinking in, but instead of sleeping soundly, I float from dream to dream, each more surreal than the last. Kit and I are back in the woods at Sandringham, but they're darker and full of blood-red daisies. I know what's coming – I can feel the gunman's eyes on me like heat from the sun – but when I turn, Venetia is there instead, asking me for the time I was born.

The trees morph into brick, and suddenly I'm standing in front of the gift shop Kit and I visited in Norfolk. Aoife chatters happily at me while I barely listen, too distracted by a garden of flowers made of jewel-like stones. When I look up, Dylan is there with us, staring at me with such intensity that I feel like I'm burning from the inside out. And as I cast around searching for Kit, I spot him lurking on the opposite side of the street – except as my vision focuses, I realize it's not him, but the faceless man with the teal scarf.

The buildings shift into the four posters of my bed in Windsor, almost exactly as they are, except the light pouring through the curtains is stained pink. Constance stands beside me with a silver-wrapped gift in her hand, and as our eyes meet, she doesn't look away. She opens her mouth to say something, but before she can utter a word, everything goes black. And then it's Ben standing there instead, his lips twisted into a half smirk in the indigo light.

My eyes fly open, and for a few horrible seconds, I forget where I am. My room is completely dark now, with the winter sun long set, and somewhere in the distance, I think I hear the sound of someone whispering my name again. Confused, I glance at the spot where Constance-then-Ben stood. There's no one there – of course there isn't, there never was – but I can't shake the feeling that I'm not alone.

"Evan?"

I suck in a breath, and the lamp on my desk switches on. But while the part of me that's still half-asleep expects Ben or Constance to be perched on my couch, it's my mom, her hair frizzy and the purple smudges beneath her eyes prominent. She looks like she's barely slept in days, and I feel a pang of guilt.

"Sorry," I say, clearing the thickness from my throat. My mouth is disgustingly dry, and I don't remember the last time I had any water. "Go back to sleep."

"I'm all right," she promises, climbing to her feet. "How do you feel?"

"I don't know," I say, slowly easing myself up into a sitting position. The nerve block has worn off, and there's a deep, constant ache in my shoulder that turns into a sharp stab every time I move. "Sore."

She heads to my bedside table, and as I gently probe the bandage covering my wound, she opens a pill bottle and pours a glass of water from a pitcher. "Here," she says, and I pop the painkillers into my mouth before downing the water in one go. "Are you hungry?"

As if on cue, my stomach growls. "I think that's a yes," I say, and she manages a breathy laugh.

"I'd say so, too." She offers me her hand. "Let's get you something to eat."

Once I've brushed my teeth, my mom helps me change into clean clothes – an oversized sweatshirt and ratty pyjama bottoms that Tibby has been threatening to burn for months now – and eases my arm into a sling. I'm still unsteady on my feet, but the world isn't spinning any more, and I feel more alert than I have since this all happened.

When she opens the door to my sitting room, however, I suddenly wonder if I'm still dreaming. Thousands of tiny colourful lights are strung up around the room, with longer strands criss-crossing overhead, giving everything a soft, ethereal glow. Garlands decorate the walls, and there are enough poinsettias crammed into corners that I could start my own flower shop. A wreath hangs on the inside of my door, and best of all, there's a large Christmas tree in front of the window, covered in the same colourful string lights with a glittering star on top.

"What—" I begin, baffled, but then I hear a knock on the door. It creaks open before either my mother or I can say anything, and Maisie pokes her head inside.

"Evan?" Her voice is hushed, like someone else is still sleeping in the other room. As soon as our eyes meet, however, the softness in her posture vanishes, and she strides into my apartment like she owns it. She's wearing an emerald-green ball gown and cherry-red lipstick, and when she reaches the spot where I'm rooted to the ground, she wraps her thin arms around me like I'm made of spun sugar, and one wrong move will make me collapse.

"Maisie?" I say, confused. "What's going on? Did you do this?"

She nods into my shoulder, but she doesn't say anything. And a moment later, I feel something warm drip down my neck and absorb into the collar of my shirt.

My sister is crying.

Ignoring the sharp ache in my chest, I carefully slip my good arm around her waist and hug her as tightly as I dare. "Everything's okay, Mais. I'm okay."

"Some – someone tried to kill you," she says thickly, and her shoulders shake. "You and Kit and – and we don't know who or – or why."

Privately I think I know exactly who did it, even if I don't know why. But before I can say anything, movement in the hallway catches my eye, and Alexander and Kit appear in the doorway. They're both wearing tuxedos every bit as formal as Maisie's gown, but my father's bow tie hangs loose, and Kit's sleeves are pushed up to his elbows, giving them both a strangely casual appearance.

"Why don't we let Evan sit down, darling?" says Alexander as he joins us. Reluctantly Maisie lets me go, though her fingers wrap briefly around my wrist, feather-light and delicate.

"I'm just – really, really glad you're all right," she says, eyes still brimming. As Alexander eases me down onto the nearest sofa, my mother wordlessly hands her a tissue, and she takes it, dabbing her eyes. She must be wearing waterproof mascara, because her make-up doesn't budge. "I – Kit and I, we didn't want you to miss your first Christmas with the family, so we thought we'd bring Christmas to you."

"Thank you," I say as I glance around the room again, taking in the lights and decorations. "Really. This is incredible."

"It was all Maisie's idea," says Kit, bending down over the arm of the sofa and giving me a peck on the cheek. "Happy Christmas, Evan. How do you feel?"

"Better, I think," I say, and he's still hovering close enough for me to steal a quick, but real, kiss, even though my parents are watching – and are probably the reason for his restraint. "I'm sorry for ruining Christmas."

"You didn't ruin a bloody thing," says Alexander as several footmen carry dome-covered platters into the room. "We've got a few hours left, so why don't we make the most of it?"

While he, Kit and Maisie rally around the tree, decorating the branches with glittering ornaments that look like they're made of real crystal, my mother tucks a blanket around me and brushes my tangled hair. Christmas music plays softly in the background, and even though it's probably the blood loss, there's something magical about all of this – something that fills me with warm contentment and giddiness that only seems to expand, chasing away the last of the sombre shadows. The royal family has always felt more *royal* than *family* to me, but in this moment, with the people I love most chatting and laughing together, I almost forget that my father is King, that my sister is the future queen, and that most of the country thinks my mom and I have no place here. Nothing outside my sitting room matters as we pass around plates full of food, and then presents, each more ridiculous than the last.

"Really?" says Alexander, holding up a bobblehead of himself, complete with a giant crown. When the head wobbles, a tinny voice declares, "*Gather 'round, ladies, to see the King's crown jewels!*" My mouth drops open, and from the armchair, Maisie immediately pales. "I had no idea it did that," she insists, but she's mostly drowned out by Alexander's sharp guffaw.

"Of all the bloody things...," he says, shaking the bobblehead again.

"*King Philanderer II at your service, m' lady!*"

He throws his head back, and any lingering hint of propriety dissolves into howls of laughter. My mother joins in, reaching for the toy to take a closer look, and even Kit chuckles as I manage a tired grin. Only Maisie, whose face is bright red, is unamused. "I'm going to bloody *murder* Fitz," she mutters, and I immediately feel a stab of pity for her hapless private secretary.

"On the contrary," says our father, now wiping tears from his eyes, "I think I owe him a pay rise."

We pass around the bobblehead and listen to it repeat its assortment of sordid phrases until I wince from laughter, and my mother pointedly sets the toy aside. While most of the gifts are jokes – though none of the rest are nearly as funny – her gift to me is a framed photograph I've never seen before.

It's a picture of her and Alexander, both much younger, and a baby that can only be me. We're sitting beside a Christmas tree, the lights twinkling behind us, and they're focused on me as I seemingly do my best to rip the wrapping paper from a stuffed bear. They're smiling – the kind of secret, genuine smiles not meant for the camera – and I can just make out their joined hands.

"This was your first Christmas," says my mother softly. "I know you don't remember it, but your father and I do."

I touch the frame, not knowing what to say. I wish I could remember it. I wish I could remember every moment from those first few years, when my parents were still happy and together, even if Alexander was living a double life with Helene and Maisie. I wish I could remember a time when none of us had to make room for estrangements and arrests and the scandal of just existing.

"I love it," I say, setting my head on her shoulder. "Thank you."

"You're welcome, Evie," she murmurs as she kisses my hair. "I'm just relieved we have this Christmas, too."

Maisie leans over to peer at the photo. "Oh – that's the one that was on your desk for the Christmas speech, isn't it?" she says to Alexander, who nods.

"I hoped it might go a long way to silence the conspiracy theorists," he says, and I don't need to ask which ones he's talking about. My mother's been vilified and called all kinds of names in the press, which seems fixated on the lie that she trapped and extorted him with a pregnancy he didn't want. I didn't realize it bothered Alexander so much, but as he watches my mother, it's clear that it does.

"And that," says Maisie, pointing to the record player that's currently spitting out a Bing Crosby Christmas song, "is from me and Kit. Along with the record collection beneath it."

"Really?" I say, craning my neck as much as I dare. The cabinet the record player sits on is covered in Christmas decorations, but it's definitely new, and the shelves are crammed full of vinyl records. "You and Kit did that?"

He nods. "We had to guess at some of your favourites, but I

think we found most of them. And," he teases, glancing at my sister, "only half or so are Taylor Swift albums."

Maisie lifts her chin defiantly. "She's universal. And they're signed," she adds, and I grin.

"One more reason for the entire world to hate me," I say. "I love it."

We're passing around something called Christmas pudding, which looks suspiciously like a steaming mountain of fruitcake, when another knock sounds on the door. Alexander calls for whoever it is to enter, but as soon as I see who's on the other side, I immediately wish he hadn't.

Venetia stands in the threshold, her blond hair pulled into a fancy updo that shows off the low bodice of her glittering scarlet gown. She wears a plastered-on smile that makes her Botox obvious, and a gift is tucked into her bare arms.

"I'm not interrupting, am I?" she says sweetly, curtsying to my father and Maisie. "I just wanted to see how Evangeline is feeling."

"I'm fine," I say, forcing a small smile. It quickly drops, however, when Venetia enters the room, and I spot a figure lurking in the corridor behind her.

Ben.

He, like Alexander and Kit, is also wearing a tuxedo, but his is still done up properly, and nothing about him is infused with Christmas cheer. To my dismay, he follows his mother inside my sitting room, and as his gaze slides to me, I instantly look away and suppress a shiver. Of all the brash and shameless things he's done in the past, showing his face tonight is a step too far, even for him.

"Oh, Evangeline," says Venetia, bending down to kiss my cheeks. "We're so *relieved* you're all right. I can't tell you how worried I was – my own niece, nearly killed on Christmas Eve!" Hearing her call me her niece almost makes me choke, but she shoves the gift into my hand and I busy myself with carefully undoing the sharply folded corners. I can tell it's a book at first touch, but when I finally get it open, I'm not prepared to see a younger Venetia staring up at me from the cover.

Royally Ever After: Tips and Tricks from the Duchess of York

"It's my third book," she says proudly. "I wrote it almost ten years ago, but the monarchy never changes, and it all still applies. It's about joining the royal family," she adds at what must be my blank stare. "It's meant for girls looking to marry into it, of course, but it's an excellent reference for you, too."

"Wow," I say, hoping this doesn't sound as hollow as I think it might. "This is...great. Thank you."

Venetia beams, and she takes my hands – including the one in the sling. "We're just so happy you're all right," she says again, this time with tears in her eyes. "We were so *worried*, darling."

Worried enough to cry on the shoulders of a *Daily Sun* journalist, but I don't say that. Instead, I let her kiss my cheeks again without complaint, but once she steps aside, Ben's there, and my expression drops.

Across the sitting room, Alexander tenses, and Kit shifts forward on the love seat, prepared to leap to his feet if need be. And while I'm grateful for both of them, I look straight at Ben now, refusing to offer him even a hint of goodwill.

"I'm relieved to see you up and about," he says with an amiable smile. "It seemed like it was touch and go there for a while."

"I'm not that easy to kill," I say in as neutral a voice as I can muster. There's still an edge of hatred to it, though, but Ben's smile doesn't falter.

"Lucky us," he says, and to my disgust, he leans in to brush his lips against my cheek. At his touch, I stay perfectly still, feeling like I've plunged into a tank of ice.

"You missed," I whisper in his ear.

"I never miss," he breathes, and when he straightens, there's a hint of a smirk tugging at the corner of his lips. "Here – I thought you'd like a reminder of how far you've come."

He offers me a shallow golden box tied with red ribbon, and when I refuse to take it, he sets it in my lap instead. We stare at each other for a painfully long moment, but at last Ben slips his arm into his mother's.

"We ought to get back to the party and let them enjoy the rest of their night," he says, and we finally agree on something.

"Of course," says Venetia as he leads her to the exit. "Happy Christmas, all!"

None of us says a word until Ben closes the door behind him, and only then do we all let out a collective exhale. "What did he give you?" says Maisie with an eager glint she can't hide as she kneels on the carpet beside the sofa.

"You can have it, whatever it is," I say, and my father clears his throat.

"Evan, I know you don't trust him, and I certainly don't blame you. But I truly believe he isn't responsible for this particular incident."

"It's hardly the first time someone's tried to have a go at one of us," says Maisie as she snatches up Ben's gift and starts to unwrap it. "Daddy, didn't a woman try to stab you on a walkabout once?"

"Mm, a few years after you and your sister were born," he says. "Your grandfather was shot at twice in the nineties."

"And Mummy was attacked when she was pregnant with me – broke her nose and everything," says Maisie, tossing the ribbon aside. "See? It happens."

"It won't happen again," says Alexander darkly. "I've already spoken to Victor Stephens, our head of security, and—"

"A photo album?"

We all look at Maisie now, who's staring into the box. She pulls out a red leather-bound book, and when she turns to the first page, I spot my face peering back.

It's one of the few photos the public has of me as a kid, from my third boarding school yearbook. I have uneven bangs, a zit on my chin, and I'm scowling at the camera, but Ben has blown it up so large that it takes up nearly the entire page. Confused, I reach forward to flip to another, and this time I'm looking at several pictures from a royal garden party held at Buckingham Palace this summer. But they aren't the official photos released on social media. These were taken by someone else, and I'm the focus of them all.

"Odd," says Maisie, seemingly bored of it already as she checks out one more page – which is full of more candid pictures of me at various appearances over the past month, including the one where Thaddeus Park is catching me in his arms. She eyes the photos for another beat before shutting the album with a satisfying snap, and she sets it on my lap again before turning back to her mulled wine. "The pictures aren't exactly flattering, are they? Ben may be a monster, but there's simply no excuse for immortalizing paparazzi dreck."

As she segues into a tirade about the terrible angles some of the Royal Rota have been using on her lately, I pick up the album, determined to hide it under the sofa until I can throw it in a dumpster myself. Something on the cover shimmers in the twinkling Christmas lights, however, and as I squint, I spot two lines of gold lettering embedded in the leather.

EVANGELINE FLORENCE PHILLIPA CONSTANCE BRIGHT
2005–

It's innocuous – my name and my birth year, that's all. But my heart starts to race, and as I lean forward, it takes me a moment to understand why.

The space after my birth year isn't blank. Instead, so faint that it might as well be my imagination, I can just make out the shape of four more digits that look like they've been removed.

2005–2023

Chapter Thirteen

"This past year, my family has been through a great many challenges that have tested our fortitude and courage. But it is our love for one another, and our love for our country and Commonwealth, that have allowed us to persevere in the face of trying circumstances. While the future may be – and always is – uncertain, we can count on this love, and our love for the people, to ensure that our faith and devotion to serve this great nation never waver."

– Excerpt from His Majesty's Christmas Speech,
25 December 2023

When the clock strikes midnight, Maisie has left, and both Kit and my mother are sleeping soundly on the red velvet sofas in my sitting room.

I should be resting, too, but my mind is buzzing even though my body feels like it's full of sand. The photo album Ben gave me is barely a foot beneath my mother's head now, seemingly forgotten among the other gifts scattered throughout the room, but I can feel its presence like a black hole, sucking me in whenever I so much as glance in that direction.

Alexander and I sit at the dining table now, the twinkling Christmas lights illuminating his tired face as we flip through my new record collection. I know I should say something – about the gold lettering on the cover that only I saw, about the death year that Ben didn't bother to properly remove, and about the very real possibility that his so-called gift was originally meant to be a memorial to me. But after Alexander's repeated assertions that Ben had nothing to do with the attack, I don't know how to tell him without sounding like a broken record that can't move on. Besides, I already know exactly what Ben will say – that the photo album was meant to only chronicle the first eighteen years of my life, but after the shooting, he thoughtfully removed the end date, realizing belatedly what it looked like. Or maybe he'll insist it was a simple printing error that arrived too late to correct. Either way, it'll be an uphill battle, and in the end, I still won't be able to prove a thing.

I'll tell Alexander soon, I decide. After the holidays, or if Ben refuses to crawl back underneath a rock and stay out of our lives. I can't make myself destroy the fragile contentment that's settled over my father, though, not after the few days we've all had. And so, for these last moments of my first Christmas with my family, I make myself focus on the selection of records Kit and Maisie chose for me instead. Most are predictable, from bands they know I love, but a few of them are curious choices, and I set them aside to listen to first.

"You and Kit have grown rather close lately, haven't you?"

says Alexander in a low voice as he examines the back of a Fleetwood Mac album.

"Isn't that the whole point of dating?" I say, studying one of the many Taylor Swift records Maisie included. She wasn't kidding – it really is signed specifically to me. The majority of the covers are, and it's daunting to see the evidence of just how many favours she can call in for a simple Christmas present.

"Does it feel like a long-term thing?" says Alexander, and my face grows hot as I set the album aside and select another. Ed Sheeran. Also signed.

"He jumped in front of a literal bullet for me," I point out. "I think I'm going to hold on to him for a while."

"And if none of that had happened?" says Alexander.

"Then he'd be stuck with me anyway. What about you and my mom?" I add, glancing at her sleeping form. My gaze automatically drifts to the space beneath the sofa, however, and I look back at my father. "What's the plan there?"

He clears his throat. "Your mother's the love of my life," he says. "I was a fool and walked away from her twice – once when my father died, and again when she needed me the most. I won't make that mistake a third time."

"What about Helene?" I say, picking up another album. Reignwolf. My favourite band, and definitely one of Kit's choices. "Are you planning on getting a divorce?"

A beat passes before Alexander answers. "I don't know," he admits. "That's a conversation she and I've been having for a very long time, and neither of us is eager to throw our family – your mother and Nicholas included – into that particular fire."

"So you want my mom to be your mistress again?" I say, and the words taste foul.

"Of course not. She never was my mistress," he says, and when I open my mouth to point out the obvious, he keeps going.

"She was always the real thing to me – the true centre of my life. My marriage and the rest of it…that was the part I couldn't escape."

I pull another vinyl from the stack – a Spice Girls album bearing four signatures. Apparently even Maisie's power has limits. "You're going to hurt her again."

"I'd rather throw myself off a cliff," he says without affectation. "Regardless of what happens with the status of my marriage to Helene, I have every intention…no," he corrects himself. "I *will* spend the rest of my life making your mother happy and giving her every wonderful thing she deserves. I promise you, Evan, I will never hurt her again."

He says this with more conviction than I've ever heard from him before – maybe more than I've ever heard from anyone – but I still can't help the niggling doubt worming its way inside me. "What if Helene decides she does want a divorce? What happens then?"

"What do you mean?" says Alexander.

"I mean – will you marry my mom?"

This seems to bring him up short, even though this can't be the first time he's thought about it. "Why do you ask?" he says carefully.

"Because…" I hesitate. To me, it's obvious, but apparently not to him. "Because that would make her queen. And you said so yourself – she doesn't want that."

"No, she doesn't," he agrees quietly. "And I would never force her into a role she doesn't want."

"Then you wouldn't marry her?" I say. "She'd still be your mistress?"

"Partner," he corrects. "Exactly as she is now. Exactly as she has been since the day we met."

I consider that. It's not how I see them – maybe because of the power imbalance, or maybe because of all those years I thought my mom's relationship with him was a figment of her illness. But I remember how she silently comforted him in the hospital the day before, and how she can calm both his temper and his nerves with a touch, and something about the way I think of them both shifts. He's not a king when he's with her, and she's not a mistress or a home-wrecker or any of the other disgusting things the media calls her. They're just...together.

"You don't want her to leave, do you?" I say, and he purses his lips.

"We were going to wait to speak to you about it in the new year, but...no, I don't. And neither does she."

I shake my head, more out of instinct than conscious thought. "She can't stay. I want her here as much as you do, but the press is out for her blood, and the people will never give her a chance. She won't be able to set foot outside the castle without risking her life—"

"I can keep her safe," he insists, and I give him a look. "I mean it, Evie. What happened to you won't ever happen again."

"It's not just that," I say. "It's her routine. It's everything that's familiar. You know how important that all is for her mental health. Disruptions, big changes – they can confuse her, and she's already pushing herself too hard—"

"You're important for her mental health, too."

I shake my head again. "She went seven years without seeing me in person."

"Only because she thought it was the right thing to do," he says. "Those were the hardest years of her life, and I have no desire to watch her go through that again. As difficult as it might be for a little while, she'll be happier here, once she settles in. She'll be happier here with both of us."

"But—"

"Evie." He takes my good hand. His skin is warm and dry, and there's a comforting weight to his touch that I'm still not used to. "You've spent a very long time worrying about your mum, and I understand why. But she isn't delicate, and she won't shatter, not because of something like this. She's strong – stronger than you realize, I think – and she's had to deal with more than any of us can fully comprehend. This is what she wants – very badly – and even if you can't trust my judgement, you can trust hers."

I feel like I've swallowed my tongue, and tears prickle in my eyes as I try to sort my panicked thoughts into something tangible. "If anything happens to her..."

"It won't," he says, and he squeezes my hand. "Nothing will happen to either of you again, I swear it. I've spoken to the home secretary, and starting immediately, you'll be assigned your own around-the-clock protection officers."

"Me?" I say, stunned. "Or my mom, too?"

"You," he admits. "She isn't eligible, I'm afraid, though should she choose to venture out on her own, I will ensure she has a private security team with her at all times."

My heart's beating a little too fast now, and the lights around us start to blur together. "That won't protect her from Ben."

"Benedict won't hurt her, Evie," says Alexander with a frown. "There's no denying he put you through hell last summer, and I will never forgive him for it. But he isn't responsible for the shooting. He may be arrogant and spoiled, but I've known him his entire life, and there are some things he simply isn't capable of."

Maybe Alexander means for this to be reassuring, but a hollow forms in the pit of my stomach, and I swallow, my throat dry. It won't matter if I tell him about the date on the photo album, I realize. He's already made up his mind about Ben, and nothing short of a smoking gun will change it.

"What if you're wrong?" I say. "What if he does try something? Or – what if he already has, and we just don't know it yet?"

"Then we'll cross that bridge if we come to it," he says quietly. "And in the meantime, you and your mother will be well-protected against all threats, both inside the castle and out. I promise."

He means it – it's obvious he means it with all his damn heart. But I still don't believe him.

"I want to learn how to defend myself," I blurt, and my father tilts his head like I've just suggested growing wings.

"Pardon?"

"Once I've recovered, I want someone to teach me how to fight," I say. "Not just with my hands, but with weapons, too. Something I can keep on me at all times in case security fails."

The thought of shoving a knife between Ben's ribs brings only a fraction of the comfort it should, but Alexander's nod helps considerably. "Very well. I will make the arrangements."

"Thanks," I mumble, picking up an album by a rock band called Royal Blood. Either Kit chose this because of his impeccable analysis of my musical tastes, or it's Maisie's idea of a joke. "Why am I eligible for personal protection officers when my mom isn't?"

Alexander exhales. "Well – I was going to wait until you were older, but given the circumstances…I was hoping you'd agree to become a working royal."

I blink, positive I haven't heard him right. "What?"

"It's a bit unorthodox," he allows. "Considering you're not… well, *legitimate*, technically speaking."

"I'm not a royal, either," I point out, setting the record down.

"You're my daughter. That's good enough," he says firmly. "And should you want it, I could – I would – issue a letters patent to style you Her Royal Highness The Princess Evangeline."

For a split second, the room seems to tip sideways as the weight of his words settles over me. A princess. He wants to make me an actual princess, and when I suck in a stunned breath, I damn near choke.

"That," I wheeze, "is an excellent way to start an uprising and end the British monarchy for good."

He chuckles, even though absolutely none of this is funny. "Yes, well. You're worth it."

This is almost sweet of him, minus the threat of anarchy, and I take a sip of my cooling hot cocoa to ease the sudden block of ice in my stomach. "Are you only offering because I almost died?"

"Of course not," he says. "Though I suppose the whole incident did help…clarify a few things for me. And it certainly made me see that you deserve far better than what I've offered."

I shrug. "You've given me a family. I don't need titles or jewels or – or all the rest of it. Besides, it really would cause a riot, and Maisie would literally murder me if she never got to be queen."

"I'll take that as a no, then," says Alexander, who doesn't sound the least bit surprised.

"Absolutely, unequivocally, emphatically no," I say. "I'm not really into the whole princess thing anyway."

He laughs again, a quiet rumble that only carries between us. "And being a working royal? Is that something you'd be interested in? You'd receive a generous allowance, and you're already doing the majority of the work, with the appearances you've been making with Maisie and me. Your education would take top priority, of course, and you may step back whenever you'd like. But you could do a great deal of good for many people, and the country would be lucky to have you."

That last part is bullshit, but I study him for a moment. "What does my mom think?"

"Your mother is incredibly proud of you no matter what, and she wouldn't dream of taking away your choice in the matter," he says. "But I'm certain she would feel infinitely better if you had the protection that comes with the job. We both would."

"You could just hire private security for me, too," I say, even though the thought of being followed around all the time makes my skin crawl.

"I could," he says slowly, "and I will, if you decide this isn't for you. But if you'll excuse my candour…I'm sick of the media acting like you mean less to me because your mother and I aren't married. It's absurd. You're every bit as important to me as your sister, and if you won't accept a title, then this is what I have to offer instead. An official place in this business we call a family."

I toy with a loose thread on my sling. If I'm being honest with myself, I'm sick of it, too. I'm sick of my legitimacy – or lack thereof – being brought up in every article. I'm sick of being sneered at by royalists and media commentators who've never met me. And I am really, really sick of everyone treating me and my mother like something disgusting Alexander stepped in and now can't get rid of.

"Do I get paid time off?" I say at last. "And what are the benefits like? I can't agree unless I know what kind of pension and health-care plan you're offering."

This time he laughs loud enough for my mom to stir beneath her quilt, and we immediately fall silent again until she stills. "All excellent, I assure you," he teases in a whisper. "I've no doubt we can come to a satisfying arrangement."

"Then I suppose I could consider your offer," I say. "As long as Maisie isn't my boss."

"Not for a very long time." He leans forward to press a kiss to my forehead. "I have one more gift for you."

Alexander stands and fetches the jacket of his tuxedo, which he's long since discarded. He pulls a small package from the inner pocket, and as he sits back down, he offers it to me.

"What is it?" I say suspiciously, already tucking the slim box between my knees and untying the gold ribbon with my good hand.

"A necessity," he says. "One you can't turn down this time, I'm afraid."

As I rip away the rest of the wrapping and see the logo, I groan. "Seriously?"

"You need a mobile, Evie," says Alexander. "If Kit hadn't brought his yesterday, you would have bled to death. You don't need to use it, but you do need to have it on you – charged – at all times."

"But I'll already have protection officers," I say. "Isn't this overkill?"

"No," he says simply. "It's not."

Even though I've used plenty of smartphones before, I listen closely as he shows me how it works. This one has a few features I'm pretty sure don't come standard, including a tracking app that can't be turned off, and after my father has me repeat the sequence to trigger my panic button – two short presses of the volume keys, followed by a lengthier one – he seems to breathe a little easier.

"I love you, sweetheart," he says. "Our family leads a complicated life of service to this country, but it can be good, too. If you let it."

"It already is," I promise, briefly taking his hand. "Are you going to stay?"

He nods. "Just until your mother wakes. Why don't you get some rest?"

Even though I want nothing more than to curl up with Kit, I can barely get comfortable in my own bed right now, let alone on a stiff sofa made in the Victorian era. And so I allow Alexander to help me to my bedroom door, where he hugs me again, a little longer than usual.

"Happy Christmas, Evie," he murmurs, and when he lets

me go, I smile up at him in the glow of the colourful lights.

"Merry Christmas, Dad," I whisper, and just as I turn towards my bedroom door, I swear I see his eyes glisten.

I'm so tired that I can barely brush my teeth, and I give up on braiding my hair almost as soon as the thought crosses my mind. I stumble to my bed and ease down onto the edge, warm and full and feeling more hopeful than I have in ages, despite the photo album under the sofa and the stitches below my shoulder and the ache that tells me I need to take another painkiller. But as I shift to turn off my bedside lamp, I notice something on the nightstand.

A gift wrapped in silver paper.

Instantly my dreams from earlier that day come flooding back to me, and I see Constance bathed in pink light from the window – the light of the setting sun, I realize. With my heart suddenly pounding, I gingerly tear open the present and reveal a black velvet box underneath.

Inside is a simple diamond pendant hanging from a white-gold necklace. It's beautiful, and as I touch the pendant, I can't help but wonder if it's a cubic zirconia, if only to drive home the metaphor of how I'll never be the real thing. But as much as Constance despises me, she's a queen, and I'm positive she'd never gift a fake diamond to anyone – even to me.

There's a folded piece of card stock tucked into the top of the box, and I open it. Her handwriting is cramped and almost archaically difficult to read, but her signature is clear.

Dear Evangeline,
Happy Christmas.

Sincerely,
Her Majesty Queen Constance

That's it. No explanation, no quippy insult – just a simple greeting, even less than I'd expect from a dentist or a site I ordered from three years ago trying to lure me back.

Exhausted and confused, I close the velvet box and set it aside. Maybe Alexander isn't the only one who found some clarity in the fact that I almost died, but even though I know it's uncharitable of me, I somehow doubt it.

As I finally rest my head on the pillow, however, another moment from that dream flashes through my mind. It wasn't just Constance standing over me. Ben was there, too, in the indigo of twilight.

My eyes fly open, and I look around the dark room, as if I'll find him lurking nearby, staring at me through the shadows. But he doesn't need to any more. I have the pictures to prove he's always there, even when he isn't, and I pull the blanket tighter around my aching body.

No matter where he is in the world, he'll always be watching – and waiting for the right moment to make his next move.

Chapter Fourteen

"Henrietta, it's been ten days since Buckingham Palace confirmed a member of the royal family was seriously injured in a hunting accident on Sandringham Estate, yet we've had no further official updates."

"No, and I expect we won't, I'm afraid. Though with most of the royal family now enjoying the new year at the Klosters ski resort in Switzerland, simple process of elimination has all but confirmed the rumours that it was Evangeline who was injured."

"Process of elimination?"

"She, the King and Christopher Abbott-Montgomery, Earl of Clarence, are the only three members of the royal family missing from the trip. While His Majesty has never been particularly fond of Klosters, Lord Clarence seemed to enjoy himself last year with Princess Mary and Prince Benedict, and one might expect him to be eager to ring in the new year with Evangeline, as the pair have been dating for quite a while now."

"Yet Buckingham Palace has refused to comment on any speculation regarding the incident."

"If it truly was an accident, then it's possible a devoted staff member or even a senior royal was also involved."

"Also involved? How?"

"Well, presumably someone must have pulled the trigger."

"And you believe it might have been another member of the royal family?"

"It would certainly be a twist, wouldn't it? And it would explain the palace's lack of communication regarding the matter. Royal courtiers would never allow such a thing to become public knowledge, even as a rumour."

"And if it wasn't an accident?"

"Well, that's pure conjecture, isn't it? But I will admit, there is some evidence that points to there being more to the story than we know. The police response to the incident was far stronger than one might expect from a simple hunting accident where all factors were known, and the subsequent investigation and search of the estate, as well as the royal family's hasty return to Windsor Castle, could possibly lead one to believe there may have been an active threat against the family."

"You're starting to sound rather like a conspiracy theorist, Henrietta."

[laughs] "Oh, dear me! That's hardly my intention, I assure you."

"It is all rather befuddling, though, isn't it? Particularly in light of the recent drama that has plagued the royal family."

"Yes, I rather think it is. And the fact remains – we have

no idea who shot Evangeline. Or what the circumstances were that led to such a dangerous – and potentially fatal – mistake."

– ITV News's interview with royal expert Henrietta Smythe, 3 January 2024

For the next two weeks, while most of the family takes off to the Swiss Alps to enjoy a prolonged ski trip, I'm stuck haunting the halls of Windsor.

Kit and my parents stay behind with me, and while no one says anything, I notice that my mother's wardrobe expands from a week's worth of nice sweaters and pants to paint-stained T-shirts and jeans with holes in the knees. They're not clothes she would have brought with her for a temporary holiday stay, and I'm sure Alexander's already had her things shipped over from Virginia.

Kit and I spend most of those weeks in my suite, watching Netflix, reading books and listening to my new record collection. He's attentive to a fault, and even after my shoulder heals enough for me to use my arm again, he's constantly fetching things for me and acting like I'm incapable of anything more than light conversation. The only plus to the whole situation is that, without either of us really discussing it, he spends the night – every night – in my suite. Sometimes we fall asleep on the sofa, but other times, we're both awake enough to make it to bed. And while he always falls asleep with his arms around me or his hand in mine, he's annoyingly proper and respectful about it. I wake up before him almost every morning – a switch from our usual routine, but I can't seem to sleep for longer than a few hours any more. Maybe it's the lingering pain, or maybe it's the constant buzz of adrenaline that seems to course through me, always on alert for another crack, another bullet, another near miss that doesn't this time. Either way, I spend those predawn hours on my laptop, scrolling through everything I can find about Ben. Old articles about his birth and public appearances as a child, gossip posts about his seemingly endless supply of temporary girlfriends, pictures of him spilling out of nightclubs at four in the morning, sometimes with Jasper, sometimes with Maisie, and even sometimes with Kit – anything that might clue me in as to why he's doing this, or offer a single shred of proof that he's capable of sending a gunman after me in the middle of a royal estate.

But there's nothing. He is, as far as the internet knows, an astonishingly polite and intelligent young prince with a harmless taste for partying. There's no evidence of the malicious side of him that he's kept hidden from his own family, and the only hint I find of his ruthlessness is a glint in his eyes that I'm sure no one else sees – either because they refuse to acknowledge the monster underneath, or because I'm the only one who knows it's there in the first place.

Every morning, I close my tabs the instant I hear Kit stirring, and I never tell him about my research on Ben – not because I don't trust him, but because I'm sure he'll insist that it isn't my job to figure out what happened this time. That whoever shot us won't be bragging about it on social media, and right now, the only thing I need to worry about is healing, while the police do the hard work of tracking down the shooter and figuring out why they did it.

Kit wouldn't be wrong. But when no one else is willing to admit that Ben could still be a suspect even if he didn't pull the trigger, it would feel wrong for me to listen.

For now, I feel marginally better knowing exactly where Ben is – at Klosters, with Maisie, Helene and the rest of the family. My phone remains mercifully silent for the first week of their trip, but a few days after New Year's, I wake up to sixteen text messages from Maisie, all screeching at me for not telling her about my new pocket-sized minder. She proceeds to send me pictures, videos and voice notes informing me about every minute of her day in excruciating detail, and the only reason I don't complain is because of how many times I catch sight of Ben lurking in the background. I don't like the idea of him being anywhere near my sister, but as long as he's preoccupied, there's a chance he isn't plotting my death.

"Maisie seems happy," I say to Kit as we both ignore the romcom playing on my laptop. He's on his own mobile, texting with his brows knit, and I glance at him. "Everything okay?"

"What? Oh – yes," he says quickly, switching off his screen and offering me a smile. "Just my parents. What's this about Maisie?"

"She's in a good mood, that's all," I say. "I think she and Gia made up. Rosie really hasn't said anything?"

"I haven't heard from her since the photo she sent on New Year's Eve," he says, and I snort.

"I still can't believe she managed to include that much cleavage in a single selfie. It's a shame we know she was in

Johannesburg for Christmas, otherwise I wouldn't put it past her to be the one who tried to off me."

Kit shakes his head. "She's far too good of a shot. She can fell a deer at a truly remarkable distance."

"Really?" I say, surprised. "She doesn't exactly seem like the hunting type."

"Maisie's the one who can't hit the broad side of a barn," he says. "Gia doesn't shoot, but Rosie has real talent."

"Either way, she wouldn't have risked hitting you," I say, glancing at his sleeve. The graze on his arm is well on its way to being healed, but every time I catch sight of it, dread fills the pit of my stomach as I imagine what could've happened. What almost did. And whenever Kit's eyes linger on me a little too long, I know he's thinking the same thing.

"Yes," he agrees quietly. "I think we can rule her out as a suspect."

His phone vibrates again, and he reaches for it before stopping himself, his mouth set in a thin line. As stoic as he is, he's terrible at hiding his emotions, and now it's my turn to frown.

"Are you sure everything's okay?"

"Positive," he says, and he sounds so genuine that I want to believe him. His brows are still furrowed, though, and as he pulls me into his arms so we can both settle in and watch the movie, he holds me a little tighter than usual.

Before I can decide if I want to press or not, my phone chimes, and I grumble as I grab it off the end table. "If this is another picture of Maisie's dinner…"

But it isn't. Instead, it's from an unknown American number, and with a jolt of familiarity, I notice the area code.

202. Washington, DC.

Sure enough, when I open the message, there aren't any words – only a single emoji of a tiny hand making a heart with its pointer finger and thumb.

"I'm going to *murder* Maisie," I growl, tossing my phone aside. "She gave Thaddeus my number."

"Thaddeus? Park?" says Kit, and to my surprise, he chuckles. "Perhaps she thinks you need more friends."

"She should've asked me first," I mutter.

"You're not wrong, but this is also Maisie we're talking about," he says, drawing me to him again. "The concept of asking for permission is completely foreign to her."

I grumble a bit more. "I keep seeing Ben in the background of her pictures."

"Oh?" says Kit mildly. "She did mention wanting to keep an eye on him."

"Yes, but she doesn't have to actually hang out with him all day," I say. He doesn't disagree, at least, and after a moment I decide to test the waters. "I really think he had something to do with it, Kit. I know he was with Alexander and everyone else, I know they were watching him the whole time, but the gift he gave me at Christmas…"

"Gift?" says Kit, instantly more alert. "You mean that photo album? Is there something sinister inside?"

I shake my head, though I don't actually know, because I've refused to touch it. "It's the cover. Look – I think it's still under the couch."

Sure enough, when Kit bends down to grope beneath the sofa, he straightens a moment later with the album in his hand.

His fingers brush against the gold lettering, and in the daylight, it's easier to see the slight indent of where the *2023* used to be. Without me saying a word, his eyebrows shoot up, and he leans in to get a better look.

"Is that…?" he says, and I nod.

"My death year. Obviously he was wrong, but not for lack of trying."

Kit sucks in a breath. "Ev, you have to show someone. Even if Ben had nothing to do with the shooting, this is still a very real threat."

I frown. "He'll claim it was a mistake, or that he didn't mean for it to look like a memorial album."

"Maybe, but you still need to tell your father," he insists, and I sigh.

"I will, once Maisie's back and my mom's settled into her routine here. But it won't change anything, Kit – you know it won't. Alexander will make more excuses, and everyone will think I have an irrational vendetta against Ben, especially when he has a dozen witnesses who can truthfully say he was with them when we were attacked."

"It doesn't matter what anyone thinks," says Kit, setting the album aside and wrapping his arms around me again. "What matters is your safety."

"Alexander said he won't let him anywhere near me or my mom again," I say, resting against his chest. "I think that's the best I can hope for right now. I can't prove anything, not yet, but…there's just something about the way Ben looks at me. And his *smirk* – it's like he knows something bad is coming, and he's just waiting for the other shoe to drop."

Kit nuzzles the top of my head. "When – if – it does, we'll figure out how to beat him at his own game, Ev. I promise."

"What if we can't?" I say. "Or…what if it costs us something we don't want to lose?"

Our eyes meet, and the energy between us crackles with everything we haven't said. "Then we'll make him pay," says Kit quietly. And I know he means it.

The next morning, I wake to another round of faint whispers coming from somewhere nearby. It's still early, and when I glance at Kit, he's fast asleep, clearly unbothered by the eerie sound.

I head into my sitting room on the off chance someone really is out there, but of course it's empty, and the voices disappear as soon as I cross the threshold. Too rattled to remain in my apartment, I brush my teeth and head towards the family dining room instead. Alexander is already seated at the table with a newspaper in one hand and a piece of toast in the other, and he glances up when I enter.

"Good morning," he says, managing to conceal most of his surprise. To be fair, I'm usually not an early bird. "How did you sleep?"

"Fine," I lie, plopping down into the chair beside him. Telling him about the strange whispers feels dangerous, even though I can't figure out why. "My phone kept going off – Maisie went to some party, and she sent about a hundred pictures."

"Did I not show you how to silence your mobile?" he says before taking a bite of toast.

"I know how," I say, stealing a piece of bacon from his plate.

"But I forgot, and it was on the other side of the room. Where's my mom?"

"She had a long night," he says, and at my glare, he shakes his head with faint amusement. "Painting, Evie. She had a long night painting. She hasn't been sleeping well since Christmas, and – well, we both know she needs her rest."

Yes, she does, and even though the shooting wasn't my fault, guilt slices through me anyway. A footman brings me a plate identical to my father's, and I thank him before stabbing the scrambled eggs with my fork. "How long before the press finds out she's still here, and that she didn't just fly over for Christmas?"

"A few months, if we're lucky," admits Alexander. "By then, I hope Helene will agree to announce our separation."

"And turn my mom into the bad guy all over again?" I say, and he sighs.

"I'm afraid that can't be helped at this point. But I promise you, I will do my very best to set the record—"

"Your Majesty."

Both of us turn. Jenkins stands in the doorway with a tablet in his hands, and while he's always been a master of worried looks and concerned frowns, he seems uncharacteristically apprehensive.

"Yes, Jenkins?" says my father in a voice that makes it clear he sees it, too.

"My sincerest apologies for interrupting, sir. But I've just received word that there's been an article published on the *Daily Sun*'s site, and..." He glances down at the screen. "I believe you may want to see the accompanying photographs."

I freeze, my heart pounding as Jenkins brings the tablet over to Alexander, who accepts it with the air of someone being handed a live snake.

"What is it this time?" I say, my mouth dry and my forkful of eggs forgotten. "Was someone taking pictures at the hospital? Were you and my mom photographed together? Did Maisie and Gia—" I stop and resist the urge to look guiltily at the footmen still in the room with us. Their relationship isn't a secret in the family any more, but I'm not about to out my sister to the entire damn world.

Alexander swipes the screen methodically, his expression unreadable. The passing seconds are agony as a dozen possibilities flash through my mind, each worse than the last, but eventually his hand stills, and to my shock, he starts to chuckle.

"It isn't you or your mother or Maisie," he says. "It seems Helene and my wayward brother were caught together in a hot tub in Switzerland."

I gasp and scramble to his side, ignoring the protest from my healing shoulder. Sure enough, there are more than a dozen photos taken last night that show Helene and Nicholas in a private hot tub together, and there's no mistaking their steamy kisses and intimate touches for anything short of a hot and heavy affair.

"Holy shit," I whisper, and I look at Alexander, my eyes wide. "Holy *shit*."

He laughs again, a strangely dignified sound that carries two decades of relief with it, and he hands the tablet back to Jenkins. "Well, then," he says. "This will certainly be interesting."

Chapter Fifteen

In case you've been living under a rock for the past six hours, the *Daily Sun* has obtained pictures taken last night that show Queen Helene in a very compromising position with her brother-in-law, Prince Nicholas, the Duke of York.

While we can hardly fault the *Daily Sun* for posting the risqué series of exclusive photographs – we've been known to do so from time to time as well, after all – one must wonder if it might be considered high treason to do so of one's beloved Queen.

After all, who can blame Her Majesty for finding comfort in the nearest pair of exceptionally handsome arms, considering the decades of turbulence and humiliation she's suffered in her marriage to His Majesty? Not only has Queen Helene had to endure the knowledge that her husband was involved in an extramarital affair that produced a child he refused to denounce, but eighteen years later, she's been forced to accept his illegitimate issue into her home and treat her like family – and host the King's mistress during what should have been a private Christmas gathering.

Frankly, Her Majesty deserves a bit of fun, and we at the *Regal Record* congratulate Queen Helene and His Royal Highness on their affair. We very much hope this turns out better for both of them than their marriages.

For more fascinating royal relationships that might be more than they appear, click through our gallery below.

– *The Regal Record*, 4 January 2024

For once it's not my name in the headlines, and even though I feel bad for Helene and Nicholas and the sudden white-hot scrutiny of their relationship, I can't pretend it isn't nice to get a break from all that attention.

What worries me, however, is the fact that the photographs were clearly taken by someone inside their private château. A member of the staff, maybe, but Alexander confirms that Helene and Nicholas brought their own personnel with them – all of whom have known about their affair for ages. Which means that if there is a mole, it's someone in the royal party. And while I can't pinpoint a motive, the part of my mind that's fixated on Ben tries to come up with a way that he could be responsible for leaking this, too.

I text Maisie twice that morning, but she doesn't respond. By the time noon rolls around, I'm on the verge of actually calling her when the protection officer now stationed outside my room – a no-nonsense woman in her thirties named Ingrid Straw – informs me that Her Royal Highness has returned to Windsor.

I pause just long enough to scribble a note for Kit, who's showering in his own suite, before I sprint down the long gallery. I'm at my sister's door fifteen seconds later, my shoulder aching and my lungs burning, and taking a deep breath, I knock with all the delicacy of someone defusing a bomb, not entirely sure what I'll find on the other side.

Silence. I scowl.

"Maisie, it's me," I call through the thick wood, glancing at the burly protection officer standing outside her room – a development I'm sure she's as thrilled with as I am. "I know you're in there. You can't text me non-stop and then decide to ignore me when—"

The door flies open, and a hand reaches through the crack, grabbing my good arm and yanking me through the tight space. As soon as I'm inside Maisie's apartment, which is easily twice the size of mine, the door slams shut behind me, and my sister faces me with a mixture of annoyance, fury and very real fear mingling on her features.

"I can't believe Daddy's allowing someone to *stalk* me all bloody day," she says, and it takes me a moment to realize she's talking about the protection officer.

"Between the two of us, you're the logical choice," I point out.

"Hardly. *You're* the one who was nearly killed, not me."

"But you're the one inheriting the throne. I have a shadow now, too, if it makes you feel any better."

"It does not," she says with a sniff, and she whirls back around and marches to a cream-and-gold sofa, where she's strewn the contents of her purse. "I can't find my bloody mobile. I think I left it on the plane."

"You mean this mobile?" I say, picking up the phone that's lying face up on a side table, half-hidden by an enormous vase of hot-pink roses. "Who sent the flowers?"

Maisie snatches her phone out of my hand, checking it over like she expects it to be damaged. "No one," she mutters, but there's still a card nestled among the fragrant petals, and even though I don't mean to snoop, it's impossible to miss the blocky signature.

Thaddeus

I barely – *barely* manage to suppress a choked laugh. He's definitely barking up the wrong tree. "I'm sorry about the photos," I say. "How's your mom doing?"

"How do you think she's doing?" snaps Maisie as she scoops her things back into her purse. "About as well as you were after that bloody video of you and Jasper was posted, I'd expect."

That's not a fair comparison by any stretch of the imagination, considering Helene was fully conscious and consenting – to Nicholas, at least – but I bite my tongue. "It'll blow over. She and Alexander are already separated anyway, and—"

"I don't bloody *care* about the photos," my sister explodes, throwing her purse towards the white piano positioned in front of her floor-to-ceiling windows. The leather hits the keyboard in a discordant array of notes, and the contents go flying.

Right. Not just a run-of-the-mill bad mood, but a full-blown temper tantrum. I let her seethe for a few seconds before I say quietly, "What's really going on, Maisie? And don't tell me it's nothing. You've been blowing hot and cold for weeks."

She takes several deep breaths, each one with the kind of crescendo that makes me think she's going to hurl her phone at my head. But at last, after nearly half a minute of this, she sinks onto the sofa and buries her face in her hands.

"You already know what's going on," she mumbles, and I approach her slowly, still not convinced she won't lash out.

"Gia?" I guess, and she nods miserably.

"We tried to patch things up over the New Year, but I was awful to her this morning after we found out about Mummy's pictures, and..."

I ease down beside her. "Why were you awful to her?"

"Because—" The words seem to stick in her throat, and she swallows hard. "The *Regal Record* posted a bunch of photos."

"Of Nicholas and Helene?" I say, confused. "I thought that was—"

"Of me and Gia," she says, and she glances my way only long enough for me to see how red her eyes are. "As a bonus feature to their story about Mummy and Uncle Nicholas. 'Royal relationships that may be more than they seem', or some other nonsense."

My hand twitches towards my phone, and Maisie must notice, because she sighs.

"Go ahead. It's the only way you'll understand."

With an apologetic look, I fish my phone out of my pocket and pull up the *Regal Record*. It's a simple blog with black text and a white background, free of the frills and ads of most other royal gossip sites, and that somehow makes it all the more unnerving – especially when they get things right.

It takes a few clicks to find the gallery she's talking about, and I swipe through it, studying each photo in turn. They're not all bad – most of them are paparazzi shots of Maisie and Gia leaving clubs or walking into exclusive parties together, and even with how close they're standing, their heads occasionally bent together, it could all easily be considered innocent. But two of the images stand out – both grainier than the others and clearly taken from a distance.

The first is a picture of Maisie, Gia and Rosie inside the VIP area at a club I don't recognize – which isn't surprising, considering I've only joined them on their midnight excursions a handful of times. While Rosie is tugging on one of her blond curls and making eyes at a server holding a bottle of champagne, Maisie and Gia are leaning close together, and their heads are tilted in such a way to make them look like they're kissing. For all I know, they were.

That doesn't sound like my sister, though, who always at least pretends to be careful with her secrets. From an unbiased perspective, it's obvious the angle and lighting aren't doing them any favours, and I could easily argue that nothing is really happening. But when I find the second damning photo, I take a slow breath and release it, trying to keep the shock off my face.

It's impossible to positively identify Maisie and Gia in the shadows of the dimly lit room, which is full of people drinking and dancing. But the innocuous previous photo does the detective work for the viewer, plainly showing them arm in arm in the same distinct outfits they're wearing in the second picture. Maisie's hand – identifiable from the golden bangles she's wearing and the ring on her thumb – is resting dangerously high on Gia's deep brown thigh. Gia's fingers are tangled in Maisie's strawberry-blond waves, and while their faces are obscured, it's clear that they're taking advantage of the darkness and stealing a quick kiss. Or more.

"No one's supposed to take pictures at those parties," says Maisie miserably. "That's always been the deal. Anyone caught trying has been kicked out, but..."

"But someone got away with it," I say, flipping through the photos again. "Do you remember when this happened? Is there any chance you might be able to figure out who took it?"

"It's always the same people at those bloody parties," she says, pressing her palms into her eyes. "That was from October –

Rosie's birthday. I had a little too much to drink, and I wasn't thinking—"

"It's not your fault," I say. "Whoever sent this in—"

"Of course it's my bloody fault," she bursts, her temper flaring again. "I should've known someone would be watching. I should've never trusted any of them, I should've never taken the bloody risk—"

"You're allowed to kiss your girlfriend at a party," I say firmly.

"*You* might be, but I'm the future queen," she snaps. "If I'm outed, all hell will break loose. There are already whole social media accounts dedicated to Gia and me, watching our every move, reading far more into things than they should—"

"Are they, though?" I say, and she gives me a look that could set the ocean on fire. "Listen, I'm not trying to push you into something you're not ready for, but explain it to me – what's the worst that could happen if you and Gia go public?"

Maisie laughs suddenly, humourless and borderline hysterical. "That's easy. Benedict gets the crown."

"Well – yeah, obviously, if you two don't have kids. But—"

"You've no idea how the succession works, do you?" she says, and there are tears in her eyes now. "It's what you and your American sensibilities might refer to as *archaic*. I'll be the head of the Church of England as Queen, and while a portion of the world may have moved on from certain narrow-minded prejudices, I assure you that the archbishops have not."

"So this is a religious thing, not a royal thing?" I say slowly, and she scoffs.

"They're one and the same. Succession law very clearly dictates that my heirs – who I'd have to give birth to – would only be allowed to inherit the throne if I'm married to their biological father. Adoptees aren't eligible, and forget any sort of *donation*." She laughs again, raking her nails through her hair and grabbing fistfuls of it. "And the line of succession is set now, isn't it? Mummy and Daddy obviously aren't going to have any more children, and Nicholas is second in line after me. As soon as we all die, Benedict's going to win. No matter what I do, he's going to get exactly what he wants."

"Dunno," I say. "From what you've said, you might destroy the whole monarchy before he ever gets the chance to sit on the throne."

She buries her face in her hands, and her shoulders start to shake, but I don't know if she's laughing or crying. I set my hand on her back anyway, rubbing circles against her sweater, and my eyes fall on the hot-pink roses once more.

Oh.

"Does Thaddeus know about Gia?" I say delicately, and she sniffs.

"No."

"Are you going to tell him about Gia?"

"I don't know," she whimpers, and I wrap my arm around her shoulders in an awkward hug. She doesn't push me away, though, so that's progress.

"Is that what you're fighting about?" I say, but by now, I'm pretty sure I know the answer.

Maisie nods, wiping her wet eyes and smudging her mascara. Clearly she didn't think to wear the waterproof kind today. "I don't know what else to do. A few dates with Thaddeus would get the rumours off our backs, but Gia's furious."

"Thaddeus probably will be, too, if he finds out you're using him," I say. "Usually both halves of a fauxmance know they're in one."

"A what?" She turns her head to look at me properly, and I gently wipe the black smudges from her face with my thumbs.

"A fauxmance. A fake romance," I explain. "They're common in Hollywood, I think. There's always some rumour going around that two actors are together to publicize their new movie, or that they have a relationship contract—"

"A what?" she says again, and this time I see the spark of something I don't like in her eyes.

"I'm not here to give you ideas, Mais, and I don't know what to say to make any of this better. Just that…we'll figure it out, all right? I promise. And who knows – maybe Ben will do us all a favour and die young."

She focuses on the cream rug, and I notice her nails are short and ragged. I've never seen her with anything less than a perfect manicure before, and this more than anything tells me exactly how upset she really is.

"There are several monarchs whom historians suspect also… favoured the same sex," she says softly. "They all married, though, and most of them had children. Queen Anne was pregnant at least seventeen times. *Seventeen.*" She looks at me again, her blue eyes almost pleading. "Maybe it wouldn't be so bad."

In that moment, my heart breaks for her. She has all the privilege and wealth and status anyone could ever ask for, but what's the point if it's really just a gilded cage?

"I can't tell you what to do," I say, taking her hand in mine.

"But I will say that while those kings and queens didn't have much of a choice, you do. We don't live in the eighteenth century any more, and the people love you – even the ones who are… less than open-minded. You have a right to be yourself. You have a right to be happy and to be with the person you love and to not give up such a huge part of who you are just so you don't make strangers uncomfortable. I mean – look where prioritizing the crown got our parents. They're all miserable. Or they were, at least, for longer than we've been alive."

Maisie shakes her head and, in what's possibly the most shocking thing I've ever seen her do, she wipes her nose on the sleeve of her cashmere sweater. "I really don't want to end up like them."

"Me neither," I admit. "Especially your mom. No offence."

"None taken." She sniffs again. "I don't think I've ever really seen her happy before, except when she's with Nicholas."

"And I don't think I've ever really seen you happy before, except when you're with Gia. Or ordering me around," I add as an afterthought.

Maisie sighs again, ignoring my quip. "I love her. I hate that we're fighting. I hate that this might be the end, all because of things we can't control. It isn't fair. Thaddeus is the perfect solution, and it wouldn't be for ever."

"I'm not sure that would end well for anyone, though," I say.

"I know," she mumbles. "I don't want to lose her. I've tried talking to her about it a million times, but—"

Abrupt staccato footsteps sound in the hallway, growing louder as they approach Maisie's sitting room. No one knocks, however, and we both fall silent, listening as they fade – until the muffled but unmistakable sound of Helene's shrieks echoes down the corridor.

"Mummy's home," says Maisie grimly, and with one more pass at her face with her sleeve, she grabs my good arm and yanks me to my feet, dragging me to the door.

Chapter Sixteen

I am born for the happiness or misery of a great nation, and consequently must often act contrary to my passions.

– King George III (b. 1738, r. 1760–1820)

"Maisie," I hiss as we creep towards the doorway that leads into Windsor's white drawing room. "*Maisie*. We shouldn't be doing this."

"Since when have you had a moral objection to eavesdropping?" she whispers, pulling me closer to the threshold. Though she and I are sneaking around like we're thieves in the night, our protection officers walk normally behind us, both looking vaguely bored by the whole thing as Helene's rising voice reverberates through the open door.

"…all over," she cries. "Everything I've worked for, every terrible thing you've done that I've excused or ignored or endured—"

"This is hardly the end of the world," says Alexander's measured voice, far quieter than Helene's. "Does it truly matter if everyone knows you and Nicholas are a couple? You live together, after all, and that was hardly going to stay a secret for ever—"

"No, of course not. How could it, with you parading *her* around?" snaps Helene, and it's only when I catch a glimpse of my mother's auburn hair through the doorway that I stop caring about being spotted. With Maisie still attached to my arm, I'm the one leading us inside the room now, over the threshold until the whole miserable scene is laid out before us.

My mother's seated with her back to the large bay window, facing an easel and a canvas I can't see, paintbrush poised in her hand even though it isn't moving. Nearby, Alexander sits unperturbed on one of the white-and-gold sofas beneath a massive portrait of some long-dead queen, and Helene paces frantically in front of him. Her thin frame is rigid and her silk skirt catches between her knees, and no amount of concealer can hide the dark hollows beneath her eyes – which, every time she turns towards the window, are glaring daggers at my mother.

"Oh, lovely," says Helene when she catches sight of me near the doorway. "Precisely who I was hoping to see at this very moment in my life. Shall we tell your secret family about all our private affairs, Alexander, and call it a day?"

"You're being unreasonable," he says, which even I could tell him is exactly the wrong thing to say. Sure enough, Helene sputters and whirls on him again, her face twisted into a caricature of its usual beauty.

"*I'm* being unreasonable? I didn't get a say in any of this, Alexander. I was twenty years old when I agreed to marry you – *twenty*. I didn't know what I was getting into, and *you* certainly didn't tell me you were in love with someone else."

"You knew it was an arranged marriage," says Alexander in a tired voice that makes it clear this is an argument they've had countless times before. "You knew you weren't the first woman I proposed to. And we both knew we didn't love each other—"

"So that made it all right for you to sneak around behind my back?" she snarls. "That made it all right for you to ruin my life barely a year into our marriage?"

Alexander is quiet for a moment. "Why is it," he says at last, "that whenever something goes wrong for you, you insist on laying it at my feet?"

"Because *everything* is your fault," she explodes. "You never tried to love me. Nicholas was the only one who ever paid me any attention, and—"

"When did your affair start, Helene?" says Alexander, now deadly quiet. She stops in her tracks, her face draining of colour beneath her make-up.

"That has nothing to do with—"

"We both know that's not true," says Alexander. "If you want to have this argument here and now, then we will. But I don't think you do."

Helene swallows convulsively, and for a moment I think she might actually scream. "You didn't love me, Alexander," she says, so pitifully that I feel like an intruder. Which I am, but with my mom so close to the line of fire, I can't back away now.

"Yes, I did," he says. "Just not the way you wanted me to."

"Not the way you were supposed to," she counters. "Not the way you promised to."

"I loved you the only way I could," he says. "I'm sorry it wasn't enough. I mean it – I've always been sorry. And I'm especially sorry it's come to this."

"So am I," she says, and there's such an undercurrent of bitterness beneath her words that I take half a step back, nearly running into Maisie. She shifts beside me, and we stand shoulder to shoulder in the doorway, watching our parents have the fight that's been brewing for twenty years.

"I'm sorry, too, Helene," says my mother softly. "What we did to you was inexcusable. You deserved better, and we will never be able to make it up to you."

"No," she says. "You won't. Neither of you can give me my life back, can you? And we're all stuck now. There's no wriggling out of any of this."

At last Alexander stands, his entire body heaving with a sigh. "I'll tell Doyle to draft a statement announcing our separation."

Helene's mouth drops open. "Alexander – *no*. You can't. The entire world will blame me—"

"I will make sure he is very clear on when, precisely, our separation took place," continues my father. "And that we are still deeply devoted to the country and to our family, despite this egregious intrusion into our private lives."

There are tears in Helene's eyes now, and she doesn't bother to wipe them away as they roll down her cheeks. "The details won't matter," she says. "Everyone will think it's my fault."

"I cannot erase those pictures, or go back in time and stop them from ever being printed," says Alexander. "But I will do everything I can to place the blame squarely at the feet of my affair, and to make it clear that the accusations of infidelity against you are baseless. I will also ask the courtiers to inform the press that I wholly and happily support your relationship with my brother." He glances at my mom. "In a few weeks' time, when we're ready, the four of us will make a joint appearance together, and we will all look happier than we ever have in our lives. Is that acceptable?"

"What?" I blurt before either my mother or Helene can say a thing. "You want to make a public appearance with my mom? *No*—"

"That's something for me and your father to discuss," says my mother, but I hear the apprehension in her voice, even if it doesn't show on her face.

"Mom, please – it's too dangerous," I insist. "The press will eat you alive—"

"I know," she says so quietly that I can barely hear her. "Evie, please, it's not the time—"

"Evangeline's right," says Helene suddenly, and I'm so taken aback that I fall silent. "The media will insist it's a cover-up, and they won't just go after Laura. They'll make up stories, call me horrible names, claim I'm some – some *villain* who went after your brother for revenge. They'll destroy me, Alexander. Everything I've worked for, everything I've ever wanted, everything I've had to put up with because of *you*—"

This time, she rounds on my mother, and I automatically move forward again, my pulse racing. Maisie's there beside me, though, her fingers curling around my elbow, and a hint of pain twinges below my shoulder.

"You should've left us alone," says Helene tearfully. "You should've never let him back into your life. You've ruined *everything*, all because you two had to have your way, consequences be damned. My family – my *life* is now a joke because of you, and—"

"And we will pick up the pieces as best we can," says Alexander, a few steps closer to my mother now, too. "Our marriage may have fallen apart, but we are still bound together, Helene, and I will not let you crash and burn."

"How can you possibly save me?" she says with astounding vitriol. "You can't even save yourself. Your reign is in tatters, Alexander, and history will hate you. Your people already do."

"That is entirely their prerogative," says Alexander, but I can tell this blow has landed.

Helene turns to me now, and the force of her animosity is so strong that only Maisie's grip keeps me in place. "None of this would've happened if you'd just stayed where you were," she hisses. "That was all you had to do, Evangeline. Live your life as far away from mine as possible. But you couldn't even manage that much, could you?"

"We all know I've never been very good at following directions," I say drily, even though I feel like I'm staring down a rabid bear. "But all *you* had to do was learn to lock the door."

Maisie looks at me sharply, but it's Helene whose fingers twitch like she's itching to wrap them around my throat. "I was right the first time," she says thickly. "You *were* a mistake."

"That's enough—" snaps Alexander, but I'm already speaking over him.

"Maybe I was," I say. "But so were you."

Helene's face turns a sickly purple, and she pulls her shoulders back, drawing herself up to her full height. Slowly she turns to Alexander, her expression strangely unreadable.

"You're absolutely right, Your Majesty. It is enough. And if you can't protect me any more, then I'll just have to protect myself."

She curtsies, a mocking gesture that oozes contempt and revulsion, and then storms straight towards me. Maisie finally lets me go, and I quickly step aside, knowing damn well that Helene will win this game of chicken if I play.

Sure enough, she breezes past me at speed, so close that I can smell her perfume, and only when she reaches the door does she pause. "Coming, Maisie?"

My sister, who hasn't said a word during this entire exchange, is staring at Helene like she's never seen her before. When she finally looks at me instead, I can see the apology in her eyes, but I don't try to stop her. Obviously she's always going to choose her mother.

And so, like Constance's dog trotting after its master, Maisie follows Helene out of the white drawing room and into the long corridor beyond, leaving Alexander, my mother and me on our own. Or at least as *on our own* as we'll ever be in a place with footmen, courtiers and protection officers lurking in every corner.

"That wasn't your fight, Evan," says my mom, finally setting her paintbrush down. "You shouldn't have gotten involved."

I shrug. "Helene's always going to make it my fight, too. I might as well get a few hits in while I can. Are you okay?"

I'm speaking to my mom, but I also watch Alexander. He's already sunk back onto the sofa, his hands clasped and his lips pressed together so hard that the skin around them is colourless. My mother nods, but he doesn't respond right away, instead taking a deep, shuddering breath that seems to burrow into his soul and expel something with it.

“More than all right,” he says with a hint of forced cheer.

“Now none of us has anything to hide, and that’s all we’ve wanted, isn’t it?”

I manage a nod, but I’m not convinced. And as I glance at the empty doorway once more, dread nags at me, bringing with it a sense that somehow, this is about to get a whole lot worse before anyone finds their peace.

Chapter Seventeen

@duchessvofyork My heart goes out to Her Majesty and His Royal Highness the Duke of York for this abhorrent invasion of their privacy. Happiness shouldn't have to be sacrificed in the name of crowns and thrones, and they have my deepest sympathy.
12:52 a.m. · 5 January 2024

@yorkiesfurever @duchessvofyork Does that mean it's really true? I'm so sad. I always thought you two made such a lovely couple and hoped you'd get back together.
12:55 a.m. · 5 January 2024

@dutchessdame172 @duchessvofyork did you know?? how long have they been together? and with her husband's BROTHER??? #ew #twotimingqueen #offwithherhead
12:59 a.m. · 5 January 2024

@mrshrhnickofyork @dutchessdame172 Can't you read? Those photos are revolting, and the Duchess is right. Even if they aren't photoshopped and the Queen and Duke are sneaking around behind His Majesty's back, maybe we should all be asking ourselves why.
1:05 a.m. · 5 January 2024

– Twitter exchange between Venetia, Duchess of York, and users @yorkiesfurever, @dutchessdame172, and @mrshrhnickofyork, 5 January 2024

#OffWithHerHead trends for a full week after the pictures are released.

I think it starts as a joke, but soon enough, a terrifying number of people are taking it much too seriously, and death threats – real, actual death threats against Helene and Nicholas – flood in. Each morning at breakfast, Jenkins briefs Alexander on the worst of them, and they grimly discuss the measures both the police and palace security are taking to ensure none of those threats turns into bloodshed.

In light of the scandal, Alexander cancels all royal appearances in hopes that the furor will die down, but it quickly becomes apparent that this isn't going away anytime soon. Helene and Nicholas retreat to Kensington Palace, where they remain for the week as a specialized crisis management team works overtime to quell the uproar, and Maisie joins her mother during the day to offer her support. I'm not surprised – if our positions were reversed, I wouldn't leave my mom's side. But I still check on my sister every night when she returns to Windsor Castle, if only to make sure she hasn't gone to pieces again.

By that Monday, four days after the photos are released, seemingly every royal correspondent in the UK has dived head first into the mess. Some insist it can't be true, while others write exposés about the whispers they've heard and the moments they've witnessed between the royal pair that gave them pause. Helene's die-hard fans spend countless hours online defending her, refusing to believe the pictures aren't photoshopped, but others gleefully jump to the conclusions those images offer, delighted to watch her downfall in real time. Every known photo of Helene and Nicholas is unearthed and dissected, and every glance they've ever exchanged in public suddenly becomes a conniving – or occasionally lovelorn – look between two people pulling a fast one on the entire world.

The promised press release from Buckingham Palace is simple and to the point, with no wordsmithery to manipulate the facts: Alexander and Helene have been separated since early July, and though my father deeply regrets the pain he's caused his wife of twenty years, he wishes her and Nicholas well in their new relationship. Most of the commenters and posters seem to take his statement at face value, but there's more than one corner of the internet that doesn't believe a word of it, and the rage against Helene only grows.

Amidst the chaos of the monarchy all but burning down around us, I start both physical therapy and, even though I'm nowhere near fully healed, self-defence lessons with Ingrid, my protection officer. She's careful with me, despite her gruff demeanour, and Kit is a ready and willing participant when she needs to demonstrate something she can't yet do on me.

"*Oof*," he grunts as he hits the mat that's been laid out in the green drawing room, his hair fanned out in a wild tangle. "That one hurt."

"That's the idea, Lord Clarence," says Ingrid without the faintest hint of apology, and she offers him a hand up.

"Just Kit, if you would," he says as he takes it, and she hauls him to his feet.

"I'm afraid that's against protocol, sir," she says, and he winces again.

"Considering you've been throwing me to the ground for the past twenty minutes, perhaps we can consider ourselves above protocol. Just for the time being."

Ingrid makes a non-committal sound in the back of her throat, and when she turns away, I see Kit's expression grow pained. His courtesy title, Earl of Clarence, is only his because his older brother died, and even though I never met Liam Abbott-Montgomery, I know without a doubt that Kit would give up every penny of his inheritance – titles and estates and future dukedom included – if it meant having him back.

"Call him Kit," I say suddenly. It's as close to an order as I've ever given, and he looks at me, surprised. "Or else I'll tell His Majesty that you call me Evangeline."

Ingrid raises an eyebrow, and I think I see a hint of amusement on her sombre face. It's hard to tell, though, considering I'm pretty sure she hasn't smiled since she was in diapers. "If you insist, Miss Bright."

"I do," I say, amazed that this actually worked – and admittedly a little worried that Maisie is rubbing off on me. "Thank you."

The rest of our lesson goes off without a hitch, and though Ingrid slips up once or twice, she corrects herself immediately. She does seem to throw Kit a little harder than before, though, and by the time our session is over, I notice he's favouring his right side.

As soon as we return to my sitting room, I request an ice pack from the kitchens, and we spend the rest of the afternoon on my sofa together, lamenting Ingrid's unyielding toughness and fantasizing about the day I'm strong enough to throw her. Eventually Kit's phone buzzes, and as he checks it, his head resting in my lap and the warm ice pack discarded on the side table, I reach for my own. To my mild astonishment, I have no messages from Maisie, but there's a notification about a new post on the *Regal Record*. And as I read it, I swear under my breath.

"Everything all right?" says Kit, and I shake my head.

"The *Regal Record*'s reporting that Helene and Nicholas are living together at Kensington Palace," I say. "How do they know? How could they *possibly* know?"

"Someone trusted the wrong person," says Kit simply, and I grumble.

"Maybe Ben's still feeding the *Regal Record* information."

"It's possible," he allows. "Though as far as I know, Ben hasn't been anywhere near Kensington Palace in ages."

"He's in Florence with Venetia," I say, and Kit doesn't seem surprised I know this. "Nicholas probably told him."

"Son or not, you'd think he'd know better by now," says Kit, though his gaze is focused on his own screen again, and we lapse into silence.

As I scroll through the latest posts, a thought occurs to me. "I bet we could figure out who runs the site."

"The *Regal Record*?" says Kit, his thumbs typing furiously. "You know all about that computer stuff, don't you?"

"A little, but not enough to get around any privacy protection." I pause and glance at him. His frown is deeper now, but it's directed towards his phone, not me. "What about Aoife?"

Instantly he stills, and his brown eyes meet mine. "What about her?"

"She's studying computer science, isn't she? She might have some ideas."

Kit watches me for the space of several heartbeats, and I can practically see his mind turning this over. "You...want me to ask?" he says slowly, and I shrug.

"It's probably easier if you give me her number. If that's all right," I add, because based on his scowl, it isn't. But the moment I say this, he seems to realize his face is telling its own story, and it relaxes into a neutral expression.

"Er, yeah," he allows. "I'll text it to you. Just..." He hesitates. "She hasn't been vetted. By the palace, I mean. Whatever you say to her might end up in the papers, so be careful, all right?"

Now it's my turn to frown. "I thought she was your friend. Your *good* friend, according to her."

"More of an acquaintance," he mumbles. "We wouldn't know each other if it weren't for Dylan, and I'm not particularly chummy with him, either. We just go out to the pub together sometimes."

"Oh." This is at odds with the conversation they had in the gift shop near Sandringham, and I sift through the memory, trying to decide whether I'm imagining things. I don't think I am, but I also know the royal family and those connected to it are the evergreen targets of social climbers and sycophants. And Kit, who's a tabloid staple now because of me, is no exception.

"Just...promise me you won't trust her, yeah?" says Kit. "Not completely. That's all I mean."

"Okay," I say. "I'll be careful. I promise."

I watch as he types into his mobile, and a moment later, mine dings with her number. I add it to my contacts, but instead of messaging her, I set my phone aside and study him. He stares unseeingly at the ceiling now, and though he hasn't moved from my lap, I can sense a strange distance between us that wasn't there a minute ago.

"Are you okay?" I say at last. His gaze drifts to me, coming into focus as the faint furrow reappears between his eyebrows.

"Of course. I might be a bit sore in the morning, but it's nothing I can't handle."

"That's not what I mean," I say, running my fingers through his waves. "Something's been off for a while."

"We did both get shot," he points out, and I automatically glance at the pinkening scar on his bicep, visible now that he's wearing a T-shirt.

"You know it's more than that," I say quietly. "Something's going on, and I think it started before the attack. You don't have to talk about it if you don't want to," I add. "But if you do, I'm here to listen."

A moment passes, and then another, and part of me is sure he won't say anything. But then he lets out a weighty sigh, and his hand finds mine.

"I've been thinking about Liam a lot lately," he admits as he laces our fingers together. "When I went home over the summer to see my parents, my mother told me she'd kept a box of his things hidden from my father in the attic. I was looking through them, and..." He exhales again. "I don't know. I was hoping they'd offer answers. About why he did it, about...about who he was as a person towards the end. I didn't see him much in those last few years," he adds. "With him at Oxford and me at Eton. I just wanted some insight, I suppose. Some closure."

"Did you find it?" I say, and he hesitates.

"No. Not yet. But I've been doing more research about his time at university now that I'm there, too. His professors remember him. He was part of certain social groups and clubs, and…well, it's almost like following a ghost. Everywhere I go, a part of him is there."

I rest our joined hands on his chest, directly above his heart.

It's racing, and I don't fully understand why. "I'm sorry."

"Don't be." He smiles, but it's weary. "Maybe there were never any answers to be found. But I do have to try."

"When I start in October, I'll help you," I offer. "If you're still looking, I mean."

He draws my hand to his lips and kisses it. "I'd like nothing more."

We fall asleep early that night, and it's a damn good thing, too, because there's a tap on my door well before the sun rises. Though the knock isn't loud, it sends a jolt through me, pulling me from my dreams so quickly that I'm dizzy, and I mumble a curse as Lady Tabitha Finch-Parker-Covington-Boyle strides into the room.

"Good morn—"

As light floods the room, she stops dead in her high-heeled tracks, her eyebrows climbing nearly to her hairline.

"Well, then," she says, and it takes me a beat to realize what's grabbed her attention.

"Get your mind out of the gutter, Tibby," I grumble as Kit

shifts beside me, rubbing his eyes in the unexpected light. "What are you doing here?"

"What your father pays me to do," she says, and she resumes her stroll to my armoire, where she starts to rifle through a selection of designer dresses. "Doesn't your new term start in a few days, Kit?"

"I'll be there when it does," he says, his voice thick with sleep. "Does she always wake you up like this?"

"Every morning except Sundays," I mutter.

"I feel like I understand so much more about your relationship now," he says, and he gives me a quick peck. "I'll see you at breakfast."

Both Tibby and I watch as he rolls out of bed in his flannel pyjamas, and once he's pulled on a robe and left my apartment, I turn the full force of my glare onto my smug private secretary.

"It's not a big deal," I say, and she hums in agreement.

"If anything, it's about bloody time. I expect the precautions I included in your luggage to Sandringham were put to good use, then?" she adds, and I flush.

"That's definitely none of your business."

"Everything you do is my business, Evan. It's my job to know the details, so I can help keep your private life private and prevent any sordid affairs from becoming public knowledge."

"Yeah? Then Helene probably needs you more than me right now."

"Mm. The staff at Kensington Palace *is* going through a rather brutal restructuring at the moment, but you're a far better long-term prospect. Speaking of," she adds as she pulls a burgundy coat dress from my closet, "His Majesty has decided to go ahead with your and Maisie's scheduled joint appearance today at the Royal London Children's Hospital."

"Really?" I say, still trying to digest the compliment I think is in there. "I thought everything was cancelled."

"Yes, well, it seems the monarchy is currently in desperate need of good press, and Doyle believes that you and Maisie are the best bet. She's universally adored, and you provide…well, a distraction, shall we say?"

I narrow my eyes. "Is this about the *hunting accident*?"

"If you'd like to call it that. The public will no doubt be relieved to see you whole and well. You *are* whole and well, yes?" she says with something that sounds suspiciously like concern, and she studies me more intently now.

"I probably won't be able to wear strapless or low-cut dresses any more," I say, pulling aside the collar of my shirt to show her the healing scar. "But that's Louis's problem."

As Tibby takes in the sight of the bullet wound, her throat contracts. "I see," she says quietly. "I was led to believe it was a shoulder injury, but that is…very close to…"

"Missed by a couple inches," I say, straightening my shirt. "The bullet nicked an artery, so there was a lot of blood, but it didn't hit anything else important. I keep asking if I can have it as a souvenir, but Jenkins ignores me every time I bring it up."

"I will see what I can do," says Tibby a bit shakily, and it might be the lack of sunlight, but her face has a slightly grey cast to it now. "In the meantime, it would be good for…for the people to see that you're all right."

"And you think the best way to do that is to send me to a hospital?" I say, and she sniffs.

"*I* didn't arrange it. Fitz did, ages ago, and I'll happily let him take the blame for any perceived blunder."

I finally climb out of bed and carefully start one of the morning stretches my physical therapist recommended. "This isn't going to steal headlines away from Helene, you know."

"Darling," says Tibby in a dry tone that's much more her usual style, "you and Maisie could walk into the middle of Piccadilly Circus and stab someone, and it still wouldn't steal headlines from Helene right now. But Doyle's desperate."

"Clearly," I say. "And you never know – maybe he'll get lucky, and whoever shot me will try again. That would probably make a few front pages."

As Tibby goes ashen once more, my phone buzzes on the nightstand, and I glance at the screen. This early, I shouldn't have any messages, but there's a single text from an unknown number I don't recognize. And as I open up the conversation, my finger already hovering over the delete icon, I freeze, and every single cell in my body goes cold.

Good luck in London today. I'll be watching.

Chapter Eighteen

You are a member of the British royal family. We are never tired, and we all love hospitals.

– Mary of Teck (1867–1953)

The crowd waiting for Maisie and me in front of the Royal London Children's Hospital is enormous.

It's not just the usual group of fans and photographers. A clamouring mass of tabloid journalists is there, too, held back by a single line of police, and I can hear the questions they hurl at my sister and me as we greet well-wishers behind the metal barricade on the opposite side.

"Mary! Are your parents getting divorced?"

"How do you feel about your mother shagging your uncle?"

"Evangeline! Is it true the affair started after you arrived?"

"Is your mother sleeping with the King?"

"Mary! Do you have anything to say about your father's mistress?"

"Evangeline!"

"Mary!"

"Evangeline!"

"*Mary!*"

The fans aren't much better, with their worried looks and sympathetic words of support – some for Helene, some for us. A few want to know how I'm feeling, and more than one dares to ask Maisie directly about the Switzerland photos. But her dazzling smile never falters, and I follow her lead, not wanting to be the weak link.

At last a frazzled-looking Fitz and a steely Tibby usher us through the front doors, and we're greeted by an official photographer, members of the Royal Rota and nearly two dozen hospital employees and board members. Doctors, nurses, administrative assistants, charity representatives – their names and positions all blur together, and my face starts to hurt from all the smiling. Maisie is a consummate professional, though, and she more than makes up for what I lack in grace and charm, asking questions, offering compliments and laughing at every terrible joke. The photographer mercifully spends much more time focusing on her, and I take advantage of his inattention to find my footing.

I start to relax halfway down the line, and my interest is genuine as I ask about the hospital and the role each person plays. It's one of the things I've learned from Maisie over the past six months – my job here isn't to be the centre of attention, but to make our hosts feel like the most important people in the world. My sister does it flawlessly, and while I'm still learning, it helps that I feel like I have to earn the welcome that's always given to her. Finally we reach the end of the line, where the well-dressed head of the hospital charity greets Maisie like she's known her for years. They exchange kisses on the cheeks, and Maisie turns towards me with a flourish.

"And this is my sister, Evangeline," she says warmly. "Evangeline, this is my godmother, Lady Peggy Merrit, director of the Children's Trust."

Suddenly it makes sense that Alexander felt comfortable sending us here, and I take her offered hand. "It's really nice to meet you."

"And you, Evangeline," says Peggy – or Lady Merrit, I suppose, but I'm still stubbornly adverse to titles. "We've all been so very worried about you."

I smile graciously. "I feel great, and I'm honoured to have the opportunity to learn more about the incredible things you do here," I say, which is the line Tibby's fed me in case anyone asks about the supposed hunting accident. It's not a lie, exactly, and it swiftly turns the conversation back to our visit.

"We've certainly been looking forward to it," says Peggy. "Come – we have a wonderful tour planned, and the children are so very excited to see you both."

Maisie takes the lead, as she always does, and I end up a step behind. But as we move through the lobby, I spot a collection of flower arrangements lining the front desk, and a chill runs down my spine.

Every single vase is full of blood-red daisies.

In an instant, the eerie text I received this morning makes sense, and a strange buzz hums in my ears, growing louder with each second. Of course it's Ben. Of course he's the one who's watching, who somehow knows exactly where I am and what I'm doing, even though he's hundreds of miles away.

Suddenly I'm acutely aware of the healing wound in my chest, and as my pace starts to slow, Tibby is by my side in an instant, every bit as calm and collected as she always is.

"Are you all right, Miss Bright?" she says, and I nod, even though I'm not really sure.

"The crowd was just…a lot," I say quietly as we fall a few steps behind. "And those flowers…"

"What about them?" says Tibby, glancing at the bouquets. But if she recognizes them from my appearance at Wimbledon, she says nothing.

"Ben sends them to me," I admit, my voice falling to a whisper. "And I got a weird text this morning that I think—"

"Miss Bright?"

I look up. Peggy has stopped at a pair of double doors, and both she and Maisie – and everyone else tagging along with us – are watching me, concerned.

"I'm sorry," I say with what I know isn't a convincing smile. "I was just admiring the flowers."

Peggy beams. "Oh, aren't they lovely? They arrived from the palace this morning. Just the touch of cheer we needed, wouldn't you say?"

I nod in polite agreement, ignoring the fact that Tibby is now in a hushed conversation with one of the protection officers nearby. "They're beautiful," I say, my mouth dry.

Peggy continues through the double doors, happily chatting away about the opening of the new wing we're touring, and Tibby presses something into my hand – a cold bottle of water. "Small sips," she says under her breath. "And if you feel like you're about to faint, tell me so we can go somewhere private."

"I'm fine," I whisper, but I sip the water as instructed. The moment I'm done, Tibby steals the bottle back and hides it in her handbag, as if admitting that a member of the royal family can be thirsty is a cardinal sin.

The water helps, and I fall into step beside my sister as Peggy guides us through the wing, introducing us to more members of the staff and showing us the latest technological advances funded by the trust. Even among the bustle of saving lives, the atmosphere is warm and comforting, and everyone seems delighted to see us. It's such an about-face from the crowd outside that my overwrought nervous system finally begins to unclench, and by the time we reach a playroom full of waiting children, I'm sincerely happy to be there.

The kids are lined up to meet us – or at least the older ones are, while the younger ones are too busy with their toys to bother with two strangers in heels. There's a colourful banner stretched across the windows that reads WELCOME, PRINCESSES, and it's so damn sweet that I almost feel like one.

Maisie and I read handmade cards, admire drawings and listen to countless stories from the parents who hover nearby as they tell us all the hospital has done for their children. We split up at one point – Maisie sits at a low table to make paper flowers with a group of chatty kids, while I kneel on the floor in my coat dress to play blocks with a little girl named Elsie. Her mother looks on, a bit misty-eyed, and the official photographer spends an uncomfortable amount of time focused on the three of us. Maybe everything in the lobby was for show, but these moments feel personal.

At last, after more than ten minutes, I hug Elsie and thank

her mother for her time. By now my feet are half-asleep, and I stumble slightly as I stand, using the back of a nearby chair for support. But before I can even right myself, Tibby is there, her arm looped through mine and a fake smile plastered on her face.

"Miss Bright," says Tibby smoothly, "why don't we step out into the hallway for a moment?"

This is definitely not a suggestion, and before I can protest, she starts to lead me forward. I try to dig my heels in without making it obvious, but then Ingrid is there, and between the two of them, I don't stand a chance.

"Really, I'm okay," I insist once we've stepped into the hallway. "My foot fell asleep, that's all."

They both continue to ignore me as Tibby guides me into a nearby room, where a nurse is waiting, clearly on call for exactly this scenario. Ingrid stands guard outside, and I reluctantly sink into a chair, though only because my leg is tingling with pins and needles.

"This is totally unnecessary," I protest as the nurse takes my blood pressure. "Tibby, seriously, I'm fine—"

"Your colour is off," says Tibby. "And you looked like you were seconds away from passing out in the lobby. While I expect that might do the trick of commandeering a few headlines from Her Majesty, that is *not* how your father wants it to happen."

"Her Royal Highness's pressure is low, and her skin's a bit clammy," says the nurse apologetically, like this is somehow her fault.

"I'm not a Royal Highness," I say with a sigh. "And I'm sweaty because the playroom was warm. Tibby, come on – I'm *fine*, and people are going to notice that I'm missing."

She sniffs. "If by some miracle Fitz is doing his job, Maisie ought to be handing out plastic tiaras and swords right about now, and I expect that will be enough to distract everyone for a while. *You* need to take a moment."

I grit my teeth, but no matter what I say, I know Tibby won't budge, not when she's convinced I'm one misstep away from collapsing in public. And so, when the nurse leaves us with another bottle of water and some cookies, I nibble on them grudgingly as Tibby checks her phone.

"Those flowers in the lobby," she says without preamble. "What did you mean, Ben sent them?"

"I'm sure it was him," I say, and in between bites, I explain everything – the bouquet and menacing note at Wimbledon, the flowers beside my hospital bed, and even the Christmas gift and Ben's insistence that he never misses.

"The photo album is unnerving, I'll grant you," says Tibby once I'm finished, her expression troubled. "But gerberas aren't exactly a rare flower."

"No, but they're the exact same shade, and it can't be a coincidence. He's trying to get under my skin."

"Clearly it's working." She raises an eyebrow. "And you believe he's doing this for what reason, precisely?"

"I don't know," I say, slumping in my chair. "A warning? A reminder that he's always watching? At Sandringham, he pretended everything was fine, but it isn't, Tibby. I'm the reason he was practically exiled last summer, and he wants revenge. But I don't even know why he did it all in the first place."

Tibby sighs. "Whatever his reasons were, you must remember that he's half a world away—"

"He arrived in Paris this morning," I say, before I can stop myself. Tibby gives me a strange look.

"Very well," she says slowly. "He's in Paris. Which means he isn't here, Evan. He could send an entire field of flowers, and it still wouldn't matter – they can't hurt you."

I shake my head, and my throat tightens as I resist the urge to press my palms to my tearing eyes. "He doesn't need to be here. He wasn't in the room when Jasper attacked me, either, and he was miles away when I was shot, but I'm sure he's behind that, too. Someone tried to kill me, and he just happened to show up the day before? But Alexander refuses to even acknowledge the possibility, and I can't talk to my mom about it, and Kit is supportive, but he isn't convinced, and – I just need someone to *listen* to me."

She takes a slow, steady breath and tucks her phone away. "I am listening, Evan," she says. "And I'm worried. Maybe Ben is behind it all, but it isn't your job to figure it out."

"Who else is going to do it?" I say. "No one believes me. No one's even looking for the person who tried to kill me and Kit—"

"On the contrary, your father has half the Home Office working round the clock to find the shooter," says Tibby.

"But no one's caught them yet. The shooter's wandering around free as a bird, and if they come after us again—"

"What happened at Sandringham was a fluke," says Tibby. "Someone was impossibly lucky, sneaking onto the grounds like they did, and you and Kit were undoubtedly victims of opportunity. Not intended targets. If it had been Maisie out there instead, or Helene…"

This has never once occurred to me over the last seventeen

days, and I open and shut my mouth, not sure what to say. "But…but what about the date on the photo album? I know there are other explanations, but – what if Ben *was* involved? What if it was all planned, and he tries again?"

Tibby says nothing for a long moment, and she eases down into the chair across from mine. "Where is this coming from, Evan? You were joking about the shooter this morning, and you certainly didn't seem worried then."

"I don't know. I don't *know*." I bury my face in my hands and take a shuddering breath. "Maybe it's the crowds, or – or being out in public again. I didn't think about that part. I didn't think about what it would feel like to be around hundreds of strangers when any one of them might want to kill me."

I feel Tibby's hand on my knee, but I can't make myself look at her. "You've no idea what kind of effort goes into your security, do you?" she says, but for once, there's no judgement in her voice. "You're safe, Evan – as safe as anyone in the world could possibly be. Your father wouldn't have sent you here otherwise. There are snipers on the roof as we speak, and an entire tactical team no more than fifty feet away, ready to set the world on fire to save you and your sister from every threat imaginable. Each room of this hospital has been searched, and everyone inside has been background-checked within an inch of their lives. Millions of pounds every year are spent protecting your family—"

"From other people," I say in a choked voice. "From crowds and overzealous fans who think they know us thanks to some twisted parasocial relationship. But who's supposed to protect us from each other?"

Tibby doesn't seem to have an answer to this, and she watches me with the intensity of someone trying to read between the lines – to see the three-dimensional shape that's hidden in the magic picture.

"I'll speak to Fitz," she says at last. "I think it's time for us to cut this visit short."

"What? *No*," I insist, rising to my feet and hastily wiping my cheeks. "Tibby, I'm fine. Really. And I'm obviously not going to mention any of this to the kids."

"They're not the ones I'm concerned about," she says, and I give her a withering look.

"I'm not bailing. And I know you don't want to be responsible for the rumours that'll inevitably crop up if I do," I say. "I just – I haven't been sleeping well lately, okay? I'm tired, I hate hospitals, the flowers rattled me and I promise I'll rest when we get back. But we can't leave early – these kids deserve better, and Maisie will never forgive me. You know how she is when she's holding a grudge."

Tibby eyes me for a long moment. "Fair point," she allows reluctantly. "The Maisie bit, that is. And I'd rather not give the press another nasty headline, so you get one more chance, Evan. But if I so much as see you slouch, we're going back to Windsor."

"Deal," I say, and even though my eyes are still brimming with unshed tears, I plaster on my sunniest smile. "Let's go, then, before there aren't any swords and tiaras left to hand out."

After Tibby cleans up my smudged make-up, we spend another hour touring the rest of the facility and visiting patients in their rooms. Tibby watches me like a hawk the entire time, but I refuse to let my Evangeline mask slip, not wanting to give her a single reason to follow through with her threat. And at last, once we've hugged dozens of children, shaken what feels like hundreds of hands, and smiled for countless photos, Peggy escorts Maisie and me back down to the lobby.

As we say our goodbyes, I refuse to look at the flowers lining the front desk. But I can feel them there, like stares burning a hole in the back of my head, and it's a relief when our protection officers usher Maisie and me out the door and into the waiting crowd.

That relief doesn't last long, however. The teeming mass of onlookers is bigger than it was this morning, with so many rows of people packed against the creaking barriers that a wave of claustrophobia threatens to drown me. Even though all I want to do is climb into the Range Rover, Maisie heads straight for the fans eager to catch a glimpse of her, and I follow with an iron fist wrapped around my heart, knowing exactly how it'll look if I don't.

With a smile still glued onto my aching face, I shake hands and accept bouquets – none of which are daisies, thankfully, but there are plenty of deep-red roses. The roar of the crowd grows louder as Maisie and I make our way down the barriers, and anxiety spreads through me like a weed, choking what little composure I have left until I can barely speak. I want to leave – I *need* to leave, but when I glance at my sister, she's still chatting happily with her well-wishers, seemingly oblivious to the unrest around us.

"Miss Bright?" says Tibby, who lingers nearby with an armful of bouquets. I force another smile, afraid of what will happen if I open my mouth, and though she eyes me warily, she doesn't press. Maybe because there are a dozen cameras pointed our way, and a hundred more phones documenting our every move.

Or maybe, unlikely as it is, I look more convincing than I think I do. Either way, for the first time that day, I desperately want her to take my arm and march me out of there, appearances be damned. But despite her many talents, even Tibby hasn't yet learned how to read my mind.

We're only ten feet from the SUV when I notice a flash of colour in the crowd – a vivid teal. At first I think it must be someone's hat or sweater, but as I pose half-heartedly for a selfie I know Tibby will berate me for, I see it again. And this time, when I look up, he's there – the protester who stood outside the Sandringham gate.

I recognize him instantly. His face is once again covered in a teal scarf, and he has a beanie pulled down over his ears, leaving only his deep-set eyes exposed as he stares at me with the intensity of a predator who's found his prey. Though he's several rows back from the barrier, he elbows his way closer with each passing second, ignoring the protests of those he shoves out of his way.

Despite the frigid January weather, a drop of sweat trickles down my spine. The crowd is seething now, crushed against each other, fighting for enough space to breathe. Hands reach for me, touching my coat and gloves, but my heels are rooted to the pavement, and I can't take my eyes off the man with the scarf.

When he's less than three feet away – so close now that I can make out the ring of gold around his pupils – the sun breaks free of the heavy clouds. And as he pushes aside a woman filming me with her phone, I catch the glint of something metal in his hand, and unadulterated terror strikes me like lightning.

"*Gun!*" I cry as panic erases everything in my mind except the singular need to escape. A chorus of screams pierce the air as I spin away from the crowd, my vision blurred and my breath caught in my throat, but I don't look back.

The car – I have to get to the car.

As I stumble forward on my teetering stilettos, however, an ear-splitting *crack* reverberates off the building, and I lose my footing completely. Cries of surprise and pain echo behind me, and I hit the ground hard, my injured shoulder taking the brunt of it.

Agony cuts through me, and for a split second, I think I've been shot again. I gasp, the edges of my vision going black, but when I glance down at the front of my coat dress, there's no sign of a bullet wound – only some slush from the sidewalk.

"*Evan!*"

My sister's scream rises above the commotion, and when I look up, the pathway between me and the hospital entrance has disappeared. Instead, the crowd surges past an overturned barrier, propelled by the crush of bodies behind them as they flood the empty space.

"Maisie!" I shout as I scramble to my feet, pain momentarily forgotten. I've lost sight of the man with the teal scarf, and the thought of him getting anywhere near my sister chills me to the bone. "*Maisie!*"

But before I can dive recklessly into the throng, a pair of arms wrap around me, and Ingrid drags me away from the tangle of human bodies. I fight to break free, but she's incredibly strong, and before I know what's happening, Ingrid shoves me unceremoniously into the back seat of the Range Rover.

I tumble over the soft leather, dazed and panicked and desperate to find Maisie. But by the time I right myself, ready to dash back into the melee, another protection officer bursts through the edge of the crowd – and he's holding my sister in his arms.

"Evan!" she sobs as he lifts her into the car. She's chillingly pale, and a button hangs loose from her lavender coat, but to my relief, she looks mostly unscathed. Ignoring my throbbing shoulder, I throw my good arm around her and hold her tight, and she clings to me like I'm the only thing in the world that can keep her from sinking into oblivion.

"They attacked me," she babbles, her voice too high and tight. "Evan – did you see? The crowd, they came out of nowhere, and – and they were everywhere—"

"I saw," I say, swallowing my own hot fear. Out of the corner of my eye, I notice Tibby and Fitz hastily climb into the vehicle behind ours. "Are you okay? I heard a gunshot, and—"

"Gunshot?" Her wide eyes brim with tears. "Someone had a gun?"

"In the crowd," I say shakily. "The man pushing his way up to me – he had a teal scarf—"

"He wasn't holding a gun, Miss Bright." Ingrid climbs into the passenger seat and pulls her door shut, cutting out the worst of the crowd. "It was a mobile with a metallic case."

"A – what?" I say, stunned. I glance out the window, part of me expecting to see him staring me down like he did outside Sandringham, but a line of police officers stand between us and the crowd now, blocking my view. "Are you sure?"

"Positive," she says, and despite her gruff demeanour, there's a hint of softness in her voice, too. "I had eyes on him the whole time, Miss Bright, I assure you."

"But – the gunshot—" I say as Maisie finally lets me go and digs a tissue out of her purse.

"The sound you heard was the barrier breaking from a surge in the crowd," says Ingrid. "You were never in any danger, Miss Bright."

As I stare at the back of her head, speechless and reeling, Maisie dabs her eyes. "But they attacked me," she insists. "They ran straight for me and knocked me down, and – and I understand them hating Evan, of course, but I'm their future queen. They love me. They *love* me."

Despite her barb, I take her trembling hand in mine as we pull away from the chaotic scene. And though my shoulder continues to protest every tiny move I make, I look out the window once more at the countless faces that watch us go. But I'm only searching for one.

Finally, just as we turn a corner, I see him – the man in the teal scarf. Despite the Range Rover's tinted windows, he's staring straight at us, and in that moment, I know beyond the shadow of a doubt that this won't be the last time we meet.

Chapter Nineteen

Kit:

Maisie, I've just seen the news – are you all right?

Evan isn't answering my texts.

Maisie?

Maisie, please tell me you're both safe.

Gia:

What news? What's happened?

Kit:

A barrier broke during their walkabout, and the crowd rushed them.

Gia:

What?? Are they safe? Do we know anything?

Kit:

Their PPOs got them into the car, but that's all the footage shows. There had to be hundreds of people there.

Rosie:

were they attacked??? xx

Kit:

I don't know. I'm waiting on them at Windsor now.

Gia:

Kit, tell the front gate to expect me. I'm on my way.

Rosie:

me too!! xx

– Text message exchange between Her Royal Highness the Princess Mary, Lady Georgiana Greyville, Lady Primrose Chesterfield-Bishop, and Christopher Abbott-Montgomery, Earl of Clarence, 10 January 2024

While Maisie spends our entire drive back to Windsor Castle in tears, babbling non-stop on a phone call to her mother, I don't say a word.

I replay the scene outside the hospital again and again in my mind, trying to figure out what happened, but once my heartbeat slows and the panic seeps from my body, it's obvious.

The surge was my fault. I'm the one who thought I saw a gun, after all – I'm the one who caused the crowd to panic, and I'm the reason the barrier broke. It doesn't matter that my fear was born out of trauma and the very real fact that I almost died seventeen days ago. No excuse will erase that terrifying moment for anyone, least of all myself, and I spend the rest of the ride staring unseeingly out the window, trying not to think about how many people must've been injured in the crush.

When we finally return to Windsor, Alexander is waiting for us with Jenkins at his side, and both look about as bleak as I feel. Maisie goes to our father as soon as her feet are planted on the gravel drive, and he embraces her while she sobs into his shoulder. I turn towards Jenkins, determined to give them some privacy, and he regards me gravely.

"That will never happen again," he says, and I shake my head.

"It was my fault," I say, my voice breaking. "I thought – I thought I saw someone in the crowd with a gun, and…"

As I take a shuddering breath, he opens his arms, and I go to him, pressing my cheek against his suit jacket. It wouldn't be the first of his that I've ruined, but even though I'm trembling now, my eyes are dry.

"The barrier broke, and the police were unprepared for the turnout," says Jenkins. "Neither of those things are your fault, darling, and I'm afraid you can't take the blame for this one."

Except I definitely can. "Where's my mom?" I say, hating how small I sound. But as Jenkins starts to reply, I hear hasty footsteps on the gravel.

"I'm right here, sweetheart," she says, and in an instant, she sweeps me into a comforting embrace, and Jenkins steps aside.

The smell of her shampoo floods my already-overwhelmed senses, and as my mom holds me close, I melt into her, inhaling that familiar scent. The maelstrom in my mind finally begins to calm, and I suddenly feel every bit as exhausted as I am.

"You're all right?" she says softly into my hair, and I nod.

"Just tired," I mumble.

"Nothing else for the rest of the day," she says firmly as she rubs my back. At first I relax at her touch, but when she gets a little too close to my shoulder, I wince.

"Are you injured?" says Jenkins, and the alarm in his voice must alert my mother, because she immediately lets me go. I shake my head.

"I fell, but I'm fine. I don't know why Tibby makes me wear heels," I say, trying to play it off as a joke, but I can't dredge up any humour right now. "The crowd swarmed Maisie. I don't know if they hurt her."

"Dr Gupta is already waiting," says Alexander, still holding my quaking sister. "Come – let's get you both inside."

My exam is mercifully quick, with the doctor prescribing me nothing more than rest and another round of anti-inflammatories. But Maisie's arms are red and already starting to bruise, and she seems startled when the nurse notices her left wrist is swollen.

"It doesn't hurt," she says, dazed, but when she tries to bend it, she whimpers.

"An X-ray, I think," says Dr Gupta. And as Maisie dissolves into tears once again, guilt gnaws at me until I can't stand to be here any more.

While everyone's busy tending to my sister, I slip out of the room and into the corridor, grateful for the cooler air. For a moment, I close my eyes and take a deep breath, trying to push the sounds of Maisie's sobs out of my head, but a familiar voice echoes down the hall.

"Ev?"

When I look up, Kit is hurrying towards me, and his arms are around me before I know what's happening. He's gentle with me – he's always gentle with me – but I still wince into his shirt as he accidentally jostles my shoulder.

"Are you all right?" he says thickly, and with a start, I realize he's been crying.

"I'm okay," I say. I can feel his pulse hammering through his sweater. "It was just – scary, that's all. One of the barriers broke, and I thought…"

I trail off. After everything Kit and I've been through together,

I can't bring myself to tell him about the gun I thought I saw, or to admit that this was entirely my fault, no matter what Jenkins says. Kit's already terrified, and I can only imagine the scenarios that have been running through his mind since he heard. There's nothing he can do to fix this for me, and in turn, I don't want to make it any worse for him.

And so, even though I hate keeping secrets from him, I swallow my own jagged unease and hug him tighter. I'll tell him once we've both healed, I decide. Once this overwhelming fear doesn't matter any more, and this is all just a footnote in our history that reminds us how far we've come.

To my relief, Kit doesn't push me for more, and instead he exhales into my hair, his breath warm against my skin. "You weren't answering my texts."

"Tibby has my phone, and she and Fitz were in the other car," I say apologetically. "I should've asked Maisie to let you know everything was okay. I'm sorry."

"Don't be," says Kit. "She wouldn't answer me, either. I was afraid..." His Adam's apple bobs.

"She's bruised, and her wrist might be sprained, but I think she's more shaken than anything." I brush my lips against his cheek. "We're both okay, Kit. I swear. Everything's okay."

It takes him a minute to release me, and once he does, I slip my hand into his and lead him back to my apartment. Ingrid trails us as we go, and for once, I'm grateful for her presence.

"Gia and Rosie are on their way here," says Kit as he rubs his swollen eyes. "I should let them know everything's okay."

"I need to change anyway," I say. "Do you want to track them down, and I'll meet you in Maisie's room?"

His frown makes it clear he doesn't want to go anywhere without me right now, but when we reach my door, I stand on my tiptoes and give him a lingering kiss.

"I'm fine, Kit. I promise," I say. "I'll join you in a few minutes, all right? Maybe you could order Maisie something from the kitchen. She was pretty shaken."

"Tea ought to steady her," he agrees, and he kisses me again. "Do you want anything?"

"A peanut butter and jelly – jam – sandwich," I request, even though my appetite is long gone. It gives him something productive to do, though, and I'll eat every sandwich in Windsor if it helps him feel a little less lost.

He sees me into my sitting room before heading off, and as soon as I'm alone, I head into my bedroom and sink down onto the edge of my mattress. For a moment, I stare at the cream carpet, my vision unfocused and my head swimming. But at last, without any conscious thought, I bury my face in my hands and finally let myself cry.

I don't know why the crowd scared me so damn much. I don't know why I'm suddenly afraid of everything outside the castle walls. But even though the broken barrier was an accident, even though the man in the scarf didn't have a gun and I was never in any real danger, every inch of me feels like I've escaped some horrible fate.

Was he the one who shot me and Kit? The thought is so preposterous that I almost dismiss it immediately, but it's no less possible than the idea that Ben was somehow behind it. The man was at the protest in front of Sandringham, after all, and the fact that he was here today, too…

My head is spinning as the adrenaline finally leeches from me, leaving me with limbs that are too heavy and a body that doesn't feel quite right. I take one more deep breath before forcing myself to stand, and then, like I'm going through the motions, I wash the make-up off my face, change into a cosy sweater and leggings, and head back into the corridor.

Ingrid is waiting outside my apartment, and when I open the door, she greets me with a nod. "All right, Miss Bright?"

"Just tired," I mumble, echoing the same reply I gave Jenkins, and I hesitate. "I'm sorry about today. I really thought that man had a gun."

Ingrid regards me for a long moment, her light blue eyes studying me like she's not sure what she'll find. "Years ago, a sniper almost killed me in Afghanistan," she says, and I blink. "It took me a long time before I felt comfortable out in the open again, even after I came home. Our brain exists to try to keep us alive, and it'll take yours a while to realize there isn't a bullet with your name on it lurking around every corner. In the meantime, be kind to yourself. No one blames you for a thing."

I should say something – tell her I'm sorry she went through this, too, or thank her for putting herself in harm's way again just to protect me. But when I open my mouth, no words come out, and a lump forms in my throat.

She doesn't seem to expect a response, but as we make our way down the long gallery towards Maisie's apartment, Ingrid walks a little closer to me than usual, a comforting presence now rather than an unwanted shadow. And when we reach the turn near the dining room, I pause, still a couple doors down from Maisie's.

"Could you do me a favour?" I say, my throat still tight. "Will you ask the other protection officers to keep an eye out for that man in the scarf? He was at the protest outside Sandringham, too, and...I don't know. I just have a bad feeling."

"Of course, Miss Bright," she says, and even though I know this is part of her job, I'm absurdly grateful that someone else will be on the lookout for him, too.

As we approach Maisie's suite, I hear the sound of rising voices echoing from inside, and I pause, not entirely sure what to do. But as I'm reaching out to knock, the door opens, and to my surprise, Kit appears.

"There you are," he says softly, and he slides his arm around me. "Gia and Rosie are here, and—"

"—sent you *roses*?"

Gia's incredulous voice rises from somewhere inside the sitting room, and Kit grimaces. "We should—" he begins, but Maisie cuts him off.

"I didn't bloody ask for them. I didn't even know they were coming until they were already here, and what was I supposed to do? Reject them?"

"Are you texting him?" demands Gia.

"I – yes, a little, but only as friends—"

"Does he know about me? Did you tell him you have a girlfriend?"

Silence.

"We should go," Kit says to me, looking distinctly uncomfortable. "Your sandwich should be arriving from the kitchen soon, and I can ask them to deliver it to your room instead—"

"Is that Evan?"

Gia's voice is much closer now, and Kit steps aside to reveal her standing only a few feet inside the door. She's in a purple leotard and sweatpants, with her hair pulled into a tight bun, and it's obvious she came straight from ballet practice.

"Kit and I were just leaving," I say, but Gia steps towards me, her eyes blazing.

"Did you know about this?" she says, and over her shoulder, I see an anguished Maisie standing beside Rosie, who's picking nervously at the end of a single blond curl.

"About the flowers?" I say slowly. "Or the texts?"

"About how she's trying to replace me with a cocky American *boy*," she spits out, and Maisie immediately protests.

"I'm not *replacing* you! Gia, please, be reasonable—"

"I'm being perfectly reasonable," she snaps, though her furious gaze is still fixed on me. "You're accepting flowers – *roses* – from someone who's very clearly interested in you, and you haven't bothered to tell him you've been in a relationship for the past three years."

Rosie gasps. "You've been together that long?" she says in an injured tone, but both Maisie and Gia glare at her, and she falls silent.

"I really don't want to get in the middle of whatever's going on between you," I say, taking half a step back, but Gia closes the distance between us, grabbing my wrist and lowering her face so it's only inches from mine.

"Did you," she says, "or did you *not* know that she's planning on dating that American narcissist in front of the entire world because she's ashamed of me?"

"I'm not ashamed of you!" cries Maisie, her voice thick with tears. "I'm trying to protect you. Gia, please, that's all it is, I swear—"

"You're trying to protect me by pretending I don't exist?" says Gia, finally whirling around to face her again, though her grip on me doesn't loosen. "Even in your world, Maisie, that makes no sense."

"Yes, it does," she says, wiping her eyes as Rosie loops her arm around her. But Maisie slips away, walking towards Gia instead, and Rosie sinks dejectedly onto the sofa. "If they find out about you, they'll hunt you like you're prey. They'll stalk you. They'll dredge up every slightly scandalous thing about you and your family, and they'll turn it all into headlines—"

"Do you think I don't know that?" says Gia incredulously. "Do you think I've spent the past three years keeping my head down and my nose clean because I *like* being invisible? I've turned down modelling jobs, parties, friendships, business partnerships – Maisie, I don't even have a bloody Instagram account because I know what it could mean for you. Everything I *do* is to make sure that when we go public, when you finally pull your head out of your arse and stop feeling so bloody ashamed of something that isn't the least bit shameful at all, the press will have nothing on me. *Nothing*."

Gia's in tears now, too, and the two of them stand only a few feet apart, but it might as well be a mile. Maisie's hugging herself even though her left wrist is wrapped in a bandage, and her pale face is splotchy, her lips parted in disbelief.

"It doesn't matter," she says brittlely. "They'll find something anyway, or they'll make it all up. Or – or they'll go after you because you're Black, or because your mother's Kenyan, or because you're stunningly beautiful and people will always be jealous of you—"

"I don't care," says Gia. "Don't you see? I don't care about any of that as long as I have you. I know the risks. I've seen what you and your family have to go through, I've seen how the press tortures you all, and I know what I'm getting into, Maisie. And it's worth it – every last bit of it – as long as it means getting to be by your side."

I try to ease my arm out of her grip, painfully aware that this should be a private conversation, but Gia's fingers tighten around me, and I still.

"I want you by my side more than anything," says my sister tearfully. "But I have a duty to my country and the crown—"

"Sod the bloody crown," spits Gia. "I didn't fall in love with a tiara. I fell in love with *you*. What's it all worth if you're not allowed to be happy?"

Maisie's lips are white, and she's shaking again. "You know I don't have a choice. I'm the only person who can stop Ben from inheriting the throne, and if the public turns on me—"

"There's no bloody reason you can't have both me and everything you've spent your life working towards," says Gia, and there's a hint of desperation in her voice now. "All you have to do is take a chance, Maisie. All you have to do is trust that it'll all work out, and it *will*. I'm not saying it'll be perfect, and I'm not saying that it'll be a fairy tale every step of the way, but whatever the world throws at us, we can face it together. Doesn't that sound better than a lifetime of lies and misery with Mr America and those hideous roses?"

Maisie wipes her eyes with her uninjured hand. "I want that more than anything in the world," she manages. "But the press will destroy you—"

At last Gia drops my wrist, and she moves towards Maisie, towering over her even without her heels. "Let them try," she says in a dangerous voice. "It's worth it to me – every last risk, every last consequence. I know what I want, and it's you. But you're the one who needs to decide what *you* want."

"I want a life with you," she says in a tiny voice. "You know I do. But it's not that simple – it'll never be that simple."

"Of course it won't be," says Gia. "But that doesn't mean it isn't worth fighting for."

"I – of course, but—" begins Maisie, but Gia shakes her head and takes a step back, seeming to lose her last thread of patience.

"I don't care what you are or who you're going to be," she says, her tone ripe with heartbreak and disgust. "If you keep playing these games, one day, you'll finally look up, and you'll realize you've lost me for good."

Without another word, Gia slips past me and Kit and out the door, disappearing down the corridor as Maisie breaks down into gut-wrenching sobs.

Chapter Twenty

We at the *Regal Record* can exclusively report that Princess Mary is under the care of the royal physician after a barrier broke outside Royal London Children's Hospital shortly after noon, causing a crowd surge that swarmed the heir to the throne.

The frightening incident was caught live by BBC World News, with footage showing Her Royal Highness and Evangeline Bright being ushered to safety after greeting fans outside the hospital, where they had spent the morning supporting the Children's Trust. Even though the event was thought to be cancelled, the crowd that gathered to meet the royal sisters was reported to be in the hundreds – not exactly surprising, considering the bombshell photos that were posted by the *Daily Sun* exposing the affair between Queen Helene and Prince Nicholas. One must wonder why His Majesty, in all his wisdom, sent his daughters out into the chaos like lambs to the slaughter, particularly when their security was clearly unprepared to handle the size and scope of the crowd. While Evangeline is reportedly unharmed, Her Royal Highness was swept up in the surge, causing significant bruising and a sprained wrist. Royal insiders have revealed that Mary is resting comfortably at Windsor Castle, and we wish our brave little princess a speedy recovery.

– *The Regal Record*, 10 January 2024

Maisie is inconsolable.

I try for a while, but there's nothing I can say – nothing anyone except Gia can say – that will offer her any comfort. She sobs until she has no tears left, and Rosie, Kit and I spend the rest of the day with her in her suite, alternating between listening to her rant, assuring her that she's not a terrible person, and discreetly picking up the trail of used tissues in her wake.

Rosie leaves after dinner, and Maisie ends up falling asleep with her head in my lap in the middle of some insipid vampire movie, but I don't have the heart to wake her. Instead, Kit drapes a pair of blankets over us, and even though I know I'll be sore tomorrow, I lean my head against the back of the sofa, close my eyes, and do my best to convince myself that no one will try to kill any of us in the morning.

I don't remember my dreams that night, but when I jolt awake shortly before sunrise, I have the vague sense of having just escaped something terrible. It takes me a moment to realize where I am, and I glance around the darkness as I try to calm my racing heart. Maisie has migrated from the sofa to the nest of pillows Kit's created in the middle of her sitting room, and they're lying with their feet inches from the other's face, in a way that feels so casually familiar that I'm sure this isn't the first family sleepover they – and likely Ben – have had.

Tap tap tap.

"Your Royal Highness?"

To my surprise, it isn't a member of the household staff or even Fitz who cracks open Maisie's door. Instead, as warm lamplight filters into the sitting room, I see Tibby standing in the doorway, hovering like she isn't sure whether she's allowed inside. "Still asleep," I mumble, and Tibby breathes a sharp sigh of relief.

"*There* you are. I've been looking all over for you."

I sit up and run my fingers through my hair. It's sticking up in every direction thanks to the hair spray my stylist used yesterday, and I make a face. "Maisie had a rough night. What time is it?"

"Nearly eight o'clock," she says softly. "His Majesty wishes to see you."

"Everything all right?" says Kit from his spot on the floor, and when I glance down, his eyes are open, though he hasn't moved. Maisie, mercifully, is still fast asleep.

"I couldn't say," says Tibby. "All Jenkins told me is that the King and Evan's mother have requested that she join them for breakfast."

"What about Maisie?" I say, slowly stretching my sore shoulder. It's better than it was last night, but the ache is still persistent.

"I believe it would be best to let Her Royal Highness sleep," says Tibby pointedly. And considering my sister's puffy face and the dark shadows beneath her eyes, I can't disagree.

After I leave a note for Maisie beside her phone, Kit and I extract ourselves from her sitting room, careful not to wake her. He ducks into his suite while I head into mine to shower and get dressed, and twenty minutes later, we're walking down the long gallery together, towards the private dining room.

"Any idea what this is about?" I say, and Kit shakes his head.

"Maybe just a family breakfast."

"Maybe," I echo, but considering everything that happened

yesterday, I'm not convinced. And with each step we take, my anxiety grows, until I'm absolutely sure that whatever this is, it isn't good.

Alexander and my mother are waiting for us in the private dining room, and immediately I notice that it's just us – there are no footmen lingering nearby, no kitchen staff bustling through the door with fresh dishes for the buffet, and I have to fight the urge to turn around and walk right back out.

"Good morning, Evie," says my mom, and she joins me and kisses my hair. "How do you feel?"

"Sore," I admit, gingerly flexing my shoulder. "We stayed the night with Maisie."

"How is she?" says Alexander from where he stands near the dining table. The smell of eggs and sausage and pancakes permeates the air, but my stomach only turns.

"Not great. Relationship stuff," I add as he frowns. "You should ask her."

Alexander nods grimly, but when I move to the buffet with my mom, I notice Kit is still lingering near the entrance.

"Should I…?" he says, his hands behind his back and his body angled towards the door.

"If you wouldn't mind excusing us—" my father begins, but my mother cuts him off.

"Stay," she insists, beckoning for him. "There's plenty for everyone."

"Laura," says my father, but she gives him a look.

"He should be here for this," she insists, and though Alexander purses his lips, he doesn't argue. And while Kit looks about as nervous as I feel, he doesn't protest, either.

With my fear that this isn't a normal breakfast confirmed, my throat is tight, and all I get from the buffet is a cup of black coffee that's too bitter for me to enjoy. We stick to small talk until we're all seated at the table, with Kit beside me and my parents across from us, and as I study them both, I realize they look like they're bracing themselves for a fight. Terrific.

"What's going on?" I say, my stomach doing somersaults, and though my mother picks nervously at the dried paint on her nails, her gaze doesn't leave mine.

"We have something we'd like to speak to you about, Evie. Something important."

Instantly my exhaustion evaporates, and I glare at Alexander. "We talked about this."

He turns pink. "This isn't that, darling," he reassures me. "Nothing's changed between your mother and me. We simply..."

"We'd like to take you back to Virginia," says my mom. "For the time being, until everything settles down."

Despite all the possibilities running rampant through my mind, this one didn't even occur to me. "What?" I say. "Why?"

My mother glances at Alexander, but she doesn't wait for him to explain. "After everything that happened at Sandringham, and then yesterday, with the crowd surge...it isn't safe for you here," she says. "Not until we know who was behind the shooting."

"I already know who was behind the shooting," I protest. "Ben. Why isn't anyone looking into him?"

"Evie..." My mom presses her hands together, and I think I see her fingers twitch. "Tibby told us about your suspicions, and how they've been affecting you."

I grit my teeth. Of course she did. "That's no reason—"

"And if Ben is harassing you, then that's certainly something I can address with security," says my father, as if I haven't spoken. "But your mother's right. It would be safer for you in the States for a little while."

"Safer how?" I argue. "Tibby made it clear that you're taking every precaution during our appearances, and the castle has armed guards surrounding it at all times. Unless you've significantly upped the security at my mom's house, I'll always be safer here."

My mom hesitates. "It isn't just about your physical safety, sweetheart. The incident outside the hospital—"

"That was an accident," I say. "The barrier broke, Mom. No one did it on purpose."

Alexander clears his throat. "Your protection officer mentioned that you thought you saw a man with a gun."

Beside me, Kit stiffens, and any warmth I feel towards Ingrid instantly evaporates. "I was wrong," I say. "Ingrid's positive he was only holding his phone."

"Yes, but..." My mom stares at a spot somewhere behind me, her gaze unfocused. "We're worried about you, Evie. What happened to you at Sandringham...it would rattle anyone. You need time to recover properly, and you won't have that here."

I open my mouth, but nothing comes out. They're not talking about physical recovery, I realize. They're talking about my mental health.

"I'm not going," I say flatly. "Maisie's falling apart, and she needs me."

"*You* need rest and recuperation—" begins Alexander, but I cut him off.

"Then I'll do that here," I say. "I'll even go to therapy if you insist. But I'm not leaving."

Kit takes my hand below the table, and I look at him, the edge of my anger melting away. He looks…hollow, I think. Deeply, utterly, bone-wearily wrung out, exhausted, and just – sad. It's so startling that I don't know what to say, or even what to think.

"They're right," he says, so quietly I can barely hear him. "The past seven months have been extraordinarily difficult, and you weren't given the proper time or space to come to terms with it. After what Jasper and Ben did to you, and after what happened at Sandringham…"

"I've spent almost three weeks up to my eyeballs in TV shows and movies and books and music with you," I say, my voice breaking slightly. "That's plenty of time. I'm fine, really—"

"I don't think you are," he says, sandwiching my hand between both of his now. "I'll go with you, if you'd like. You can show me where you grew up, and we'll go for walks in the park and order from your favourite restaurants, and we'll just…relax."

"But you have to go back to university," I say, and he shrugs.

"I can put it off. It won't be the end of the world. What will be the end of the world, though, is if something happens to you because of – all this." He gestures around the room, but he's not just talking about Windsor Castle. He's talking about everything. "Please, Evan. Consider it."

I swallow convulsively, my eyes growing hot with tears of frustration. "How long do you want to banish me?" I say acidly to my parents.

Alexander clasps his hands together so tightly that his knuckles are white. "We wouldn't be banishing you, sweetheart.

You'd be welcome back anytime you'd like, and—"

"At least a few months," says my mother softly. "Maybe more."

I exhale sharply. Not days or weeks, but *months*. "Why can't I start therapy here? And if things get worse, maybe then—"

There's a knock on the door, and Alexander scowls. But before he can send whoever it is away, the door to the private dining room opens, and Jenkins steps inside. He's pale and his expression is drawn, and for one horrible moment, I'm sure something devastating has happened.

I'm not alone, and Alexander's anger seems to die in his throat. "Jenkins? What's going on?" he says, his hand finding my mother's.

"I beg your pardon for interrupting, Your Majesty," says Jenkins with a bow of his head. "But I fear this couldn't wait. I've just received word from Doyle – it seems Her Majesty recorded an interview with Katharine O'Donnell late last week, and as a courtesy, the BBC has let us know it will be airing tonight."

"An interview?" says Alexander, confusion muddling the worry on his face. "What sort?"

Jenkins hesitates. "While my source was not especially forthcoming, it seems Her Majesty has taken it upon herself to...disclose private information regarding her affair," he says. "And yours."

Instantly Alexander's expression darkens. "Of bloody course she did. Do we know how bad it is?"

"I fear it doesn't look good, sir," says Jenkins. "We're trying to negotiate a delay, especially in the aftermath of the incident with Miss Bright and Her Royal Highness yesterday, but I'm afraid the head of the BBC is refusing to reschedule. Or allow us access to the interview before it airs."

Jenkins crosses the room now, and he wordlessly offers my father a tablet. Alexander accepts it with some reluctance, and I stand, my fury at my parents' so-called intervention temporarily pushed aside as I lean over to get a better view.

Jenkins has already queued up a video, and when Alexander hits Play, Helene's face fills the screen, her make-up plain, her hair down, and her blue eyes brimming with tears.

"...spent the best years of my life loving him," she says in her honeyed voice, soft and sweet and devastating. "But now that I know the real truth of it, I know it was all a lie."

Her face fades, and then, in big block letters, words appear.

HELENE – HER TRUTH, HER LOVE
AND HER GILDED CAGE

"Your Majesty, we have all watched with shock and awe over the past seven months as the private affairs of your family – of the royal family – have been exposed in a way that the country has never seen before."

"It's been devastating. Not just the emotional turmoil, but also that it's played out in such a terribly public way."

"It all started, didn't it, with the arrival of Evangeline Bright?"

"No. That marks the time when the public finally found out, but this particular storm has been brewing for longer than anyone knows."

"When would you say it all began?"

"During His Majesty's first year at Oxford, I suppose. That's when he met Laura Bright."

"They knew each other at university?"

"Oh, yes. My husband likes to call it love at first sight, and they were together quite a while – years, really. They were even engaged at one point, in the months before Alexander ascended the throne."

"Yet the public never knew?"

"It was easier in those days to keep secrets, before the invention of smartphones and social media. There were paparazzi, of course, but the intense focus on the family that exists now simply wasn't there in the nineties and early aughts."

"One might argue that that intensity exists because of you and your incomparable popularity after your marriage to His Majesty in 2003."

"Yes, so I've been told. But before Edward IX died so tragically and at such a young age, the royal gears turned rather like clockwork. The media didn't scrutinize the family's every move, and Alexander and Laura took advantage. She was even a guest at Sandringham the Christmas before Edward IX passed – as Alexander's fiancée."

"Yet the public was never told that the then-heir to the throne, the Prince of Wales, was set to be married?"

"No. I believe his intention was to quietly remove himself from the line of succession before the marriage took place."

[pause] "His Majesty wished to abdicate?"

"Laura had no desire to be queen – it's a job that comes with a great many responsibilities, after all, and they both anticipated pushback from an American assuming the role. Which I always thought was a rather silly excuse, considering Mary of Teck, who became queen in 1910, was the first royal consort to be born in England since Henry VIII's sixth wife, Catherine Parr."

"You don't believe that was the real reason His Majesty

planned to give up his birthright?"

"It played a part, no doubt, but he never wanted the crown in the first place – it was only the tragedy of his father's death that made him set aside his own desires and accept the throne. He was never happy about it, though. He made that clear when we were discussing the possibility of becoming engaged. Alexander had a particular need to make sure I was willing to take on the duties that he so strongly resented – duties that, by then, had lost him the woman he called the love of his life."

"Did you know about Laura during your engagement?"

"In a sense. I knew he'd been in a relationship when his father died, and I knew that relationship had fallen apart because of it. He was forthcoming about that much, and I've known the royal family for my entire life – our mothers were close friends, after all, and I've been privy to a great many secrets over the years. I was aware he'd been away in America with a girlfriend, even though I didn't know the details."

"Would you have married him if you'd known he was still in love with her?"

[pause] "No. Looking back on it, I was very much hoodwinked, though I had no idea until more than a year into our marriage."

"When did you find out that they had rekindled their relationship?"

"The day I discovered I was pregnant. It was a tragedy, really, the way it played out – for all of us. I was over the moon about the baby, of course – Alexander and I had been trying for an heir since our wedding, and by then, I was starting to worry that perhaps something was wrong with me. He'd grown a bit distant, and I thought it was my fault. He had a great deal of pressure on him, after all, being King at such a young age, and my inability to give him an heir...well, I was convinced I was only making things worse."

"What happened that day?"

"I was pleased and relieved – and frightened, admittedly. We were still young, but I loved him so very much. All I wanted was to make him happy." [pause] "I took the test that morning, and it was that evening that he...he asked to speak with me alone. He'd been out all day – working, I thought – but...that was when he told me he was still in love with her. With Laura. And that they'd been seeing each other again for months by that point, and she..." [pause] "She was pregnant. And he wanted to abdicate to be with her and their child. It was the most devastating moment of my life."

"And that was when you told him about Princess Mary?"

[nods] "As I said, it was a tragedy for us all. He finally had a chance at the happiness he so desperately wanted with Laura, but when I told him I was pregnant, too...well, that changed things, didn't it? He couldn't leave me then, not when it also meant leaving his heir. And I couldn't let him go. We'll both have to live with that moment for the rest of our lives, and I don't think either of us will ever fully recover."

"Did you love His Majesty when you married him?"

"Yes. I think so. As much as I could, given we didn't know each other very well."

"And did he love you?"

"He was fond of me, and I truly believe that he very much wanted to love me and had convinced himself that he would, in time. I was so certain that our love would grow, too, and it did – for me. I spent the best years of my life loving him. But now that I know the real truth of it, I know it was all a lie. Not just for me, though. Alexander also lied to himself, and we've both had to live with the consequences."

"And what were those consequences?"

"For him, a double life – a mirror life he could never truly have. A child – a daughter, Evangeline – he could only watch from a distance. They did meet a number of times when she was very young. Alexander and Laura spent some holidays together, playing family, but in the end, he always came home to me and Mary. And I could see it eating away at him, bit by bit, right before my eyes."

"And for you?"

"Well, that's rather obvious, isn't it? I had the love of the people, the love of my country, but never the love of my husband. And it's a very difficult thing, not being loved by the person who ought to love you most."

"Do you resent him?"

"No. How could I? Even to this day, I still love him – and in a way, he does love me, but it's not the kind of love I needed, then or now. It wasn't his fault, though. His father died, and everything rather snowballed from there."

"Do you believe that your lives would've been different if Edward IX had lived longer?"

"Certainly. If he had, Nicholas would've been old enough to take the throne instead. That was what Alexander was waiting for – time to prepare his brother, the spare, for the role of the heir instead. Alexander has made many mistakes, but he's always put his family first. He would've never walked away without being certain that Nicholas was ready to lead the institution – the country and Commonwealth – without him."

"During the time after Princess Mary was born, when you knew Alexander was leading a double life...did that draw you and the Duke of York closer together?"

"No. By then, he had his own wife and son, and he was far too busy with his military career to bother with me. Don't get me wrong – he was considerate, of course. He checked in on me occasionally, as did all members of the family who knew about Laura and Evangeline. But we didn't grow closer until recently."

"When Evangeline joined the family?"

"Yes. By then, my marriage was over – had been over for years. Alexander and I are still friends. We'll always be friends, and we both take our duties to our country very seriously. But we decided many years ago that when our daughter turned eighteen, we would quietly separate. And we did."

"And is that when you and the Duke of York started seeing one another?"

"Yes. The stress of having Evangeline at Windsor Castle...

well, it's no secret she struggled for several weeks after she arrived, between her identity being leaked and all that the Cunningham boy did to her. As a family, we were there for her, of course, but...it was difficult for us all, facing our new reality while the public sifted through the intimate details of our lives."

"How did your relationship with Prince Nicholas begin?"

"Innocently. Reluctantly. We both love Alexander, and neither of us wanted to hurt him. But he's known from the beginning, and he's been very supportive of us – very supportive of our happiness, as Nicholas and I've been supportive of his renewed relationship with Laura."

"The rumours are true, then?"

"Of Alexander and Laura being together again? Yes, I'd say so. She joined us at Sandringham for Christmas, and in truth, I've never seen Alexander happier. It's as if the weight of the past twenty years has gone."

"Do you resent her?"

[soft laughter] "Well...no, not really, though I've certainly had some difficult days. I think she made some poor choices, as did Alexander – choices that are ultimately inexcusable. But she's also faced a great deal of hardship in her life, and in the end, I'm truly happy to see her overcome it all. I'm truly happy for them both."

"Do you believe that one day, you and His Majesty will divorce?"

"No. As I've said, we've always taken our duties seriously, and in this family...in this institution, happiness always comes second to the crown. Sometimes third or fourth, and occasionally it isn't a consideration at all. We both know that, and we've both accepted it. And I expect – I hope, rather – that we've both found the relationships that will see us to our graves, but our friendship and partnership haven't diminished."

"What would you say to those who might feel... uncomfortable with knowing that the head of the Church of England is living such an...unconventional lifestyle?"

"I would say to them that we have both – that we have *all* made the best of what has been an unbearable and suffocating situation for the past two decades, and that I hope a loving and compassionate God would understand. And that the good people of the United Kingdom will, too. Our past mistakes, and what we do now in our private lives, will never affect our love and our devotion to this country."

"And Princess Mary? How do you believe this will affect her?"

"We've never lied to her about the situation, and I rather think she's relieved. While it may seem like we're setting a poor example for her in the present, I believe the poor example was set during those first eighteen years of her life. She's only now had the opportunity to see both her parents truly content, and that, I feel, will only make her a better queen when the time comes for her to take the throne."

"Do you have any regrets?"

[pause] "I regret it all. But time only goes one way, and no matter who we are or what lives we lead, the only thing

we can really hope for is the chance to find our happiness any way we can."

– Excerpt from Katharine O'Donnell's interview with Her Majesty Queen Helene, 11 January 2024

As the hour-long interview ends, the lights in the Windsor Castle conference room go up, and every single one of my father's advisers looks utterly shell-shocked.

None of it was new information to me, or at least nothing so significant that I'm speechless. But the fact that Helene has said it – openly, willingly, and in front of the entire world – is jawdropping. Alexander is completely still at the head of the table, while my mom, who sits to his right and my left, has tears in her eyes. Maisie's on his other side, so pale that she seems ill, and Kit's hand is on my good shoulder, gently massaging the tension from my neck.

"How did we not know about this?" says Alexander as the screen that descended from the ceiling slowly retracts with a faint whir. He's holding my mother's hand beneath the table, and Jenkins, who stands behind us, silently offers her a tissue.

Doyle, the royal press secretary, clears his throat. "It seems that part of Her Majesty's agreement with the BBC included keeping us in the dark until the day the interview aired," he admits. "Sir, if I may, we'll need to issue a statement—"

"More than a statement," says the dark-haired woman sitting beside him. Yara, whose title I still don't actually know, but she's the only person who ever challenges Doyle. "The claims Her Majesty has made could be extraordinarily damaging to the monarchy, and the sooner we refute them—"

"The problem is," says Alexander, "they're all true."

Silence. Several advisers glance between one another, clearly not knowing what to say, while Doyle sputters indignantly. But I shake my head.

"They're not, though," I say, looking at Alexander. "The timeline's wrong. Her affair with Nicholas started before—"

"A trivial detail," says Alexander quietly. "And if we go after her for it, it will come off as a personal attack when, arguably, Helene went out of her way to make it clear that no single one of us is at fault for what happened."

"Your Majesty," says Yara carefully, "if we're able to point out one inconsistency, then that would throw her entire interview into question—"

"And how do we prove that the timeline is wrong?" says Alexander. "More photographs? Personal testimony from the staff? Whispers from courtiers? I will not wage a war in the media against Her Majesty. Not when there's nothing to be gained from it, and so very much that we could lose."

"Sir, if we do nothing to contain the situation, we already stand to lose a great deal," argues Doyle. "The people expect the royal family to uphold the values of the Church, to offer consistency and stability when the country is in turmoil—"

"We certainly haven't been living up to our side of the bargain lately, have we?" says Alexander wearily. "But perhaps this is the moment we need to get back on track. Ripping off the plaster, so to speak."

"Sir," says Doyle, appalled. "You cannot possibly suggest that this could be *good* for the country."

"No," says Alexander, a hint of steel in his voice now. "I expect we're in for a rather bumpy ride. But the fact remains that Helene's spoken the truth – in far more detail than we would've liked, admittedly, but it *is* still the truth. She did not demonize me, she did not demonize Laura, and in the end, all she was trying to do was exonerate herself from the claims that the media has been making against her – and I certainly can't blame her for that."

The throng of advisers and senior staff members exchange yet another round of baffled glances, and for a long moment, no one seems to know what to say.

"What would Your Majesty prefer we do, then?" says Jenkins at last, as cool and level-headed as always. "If you do not wish to speak out against Her Majesty or condemn the interview, then it will be accepted by the public as fact. Which will come with consequences we cannot predict."

"I am aware," says Alexander. "But they are consequences we must live with regardless."

"And the consequences that will be directed towards Ms Bright and Evangeline?" says Jenkins, and only now does Alexander's resolve seem to waver.

My mother sits up a little straighter, still holding his hand. "I've known the risks from the start," she says. "I knew it would be bad if we were caught, and we were – when Evangeline's identity was revealed. What Helene's interview gives us is context. It lets the world know that Alexander and I have been together for a very long time, and that Evangeline isn't..."

"The bastard product of a one-night stand?" I supply, and amidst the soft gasps from around the room, my mother's lips thin.

"Helene has cleared the air around a lot of things that Alexander and I were never going to be able to address on our own. Things I know have been bothering you," she adds as she looks at my father.

He nods, his throat working for a moment. "Yes," he finally manages. "Helene did not have to be kind or compassionate, but she was. And in the process, she offered us an opportunity – one I would very much like to take."

"And what opportunity is that, sir?" says Yara, unable – or maybe unwilling – to hide her scepticism.

"The opportunity for us all to have what we want," he says. "Myself, Helene, Laura – even my brother. We will continue to serve the country as we always have, without feeding into this situation or making it worse. I will speak with Her Majesty, and we will find a way to put forth a united front."

My fingers curl around the cuff of my sweater. I know what *a united front* means, and I don't like it. "It doesn't exactly sound like she's willing to play nice right now," I mutter.

"Perhaps when she knows there will be no retaliation, she may be more open to having that discussion," says Alexander, but even he doesn't sound convinced.

Doyle scowls. "Sir, with all due respect, burying our heads in the sand won't stop the media – and the people, for that matter – from turning this into a circus. We'll be lucky if it doesn't start a riot—"

"We will let it play out as it will," he says. "If it gets out of hand, then we'll reassess our strategy. But as it stands, there is nothing in the interview to refute, and Laura is right. It offers the people context that she and I would never have been able to publicly divulge. Perhaps this will, in the end, be a blessing to us all."

That doesn't seem likely, and as I glance around at the averted gazes and shuffling papers, it's clear no one else agrees with Alexander, either.

"We should, at the very least, cancel your upcoming appearances," says Yara, turning to what must be Alexander's schedule. "The Modern Music Museum opening tomorrow, the veterans' lunch next week—"

"No," says Alexander softly, though his voice still carries around the table. "Business as usual, Yara. I insist."

Her mouth opens and shuts several times. "Sir, we are on the precipice of a crisis—"

"We have been in crisis for months," he points out. "This is merely another chapter. Should there be security concerns, then I will certainly reconsider the matter. But unless there are any valid objections, I will continue my public duties."

Jenkins grimaces. "Sir, I understand the desire to maintain status quo in the face of something that we are all still… processing. But without any official rebuttal, I must very strongly advise against it, at least until we have a better idea of what the fallout will be."

"And you know I value your opinion greatly, Jenkins," says my father. "But I will not hide from my people. Or my past."

"Can't we have it both ways?" I say before I even realize the thought's formed in my head. All eyes turn towards me, and I try to keep my expression neutral. "I mean – Alexander can stick to his duties, but we can also find a way to send a message to the public, too."

"What sort of message?" says Alexander, and I shrug.

"That we support you, I guess. That's what this is about, right? Who has more support? It wouldn't mean much coming from me, all things considered, but—"

"It would mean something coming from me," says Maisie. They're the first words she's spoken since the interview aired, and even though her hands are clasped together, I notice a slight tremor.

"It might mean something from me, too," says Kit quietly from behind me.

Faint amusement flickers across the deep shadows on Maisie's face. "Mummy may be your aunt, Kit, but we all know where *your* loyalties lie," she says, glancing suggestively at me.

"It's not a bad idea, Evangeline," says Jenkins as I narrow my eyes at my sister. "A display of unity, particularly from Her Royal Highness and Lord Clarence, might quell any rumours of a fracture within the family, and perhaps take the teeth out of the worst of Her Majesty's revelations."

"We could go with Alexander to the museum," I offer. "It sounds interesting anyway."

"No," says my father firmly. "You girls need your rest. It was a mistake sending you yesterday, and I won't compromise your safety."

"What happened at the hospital was an accident," I say, exasperated. "And this is important. If you won't issue a statement, then the best thing we can do for you – for the monarchy – is to show a united front."

"Evangeline is right, sir," grunts Doyle from his spot a few seats down, and I'm so surprised that I do a double take. "If she, Her Royal Highness and Lord Clarence wish to support you publicly, then I can think of no better way for them to do so. It would certainly be the most efficient and effective way to signal the royal family's stability in the face of such…public uncertainty."

But even though Maisie nods in mute agreement, she pales and pulls her hands into her lap. I frown.

"Maybe Maisie shouldn't go," I say. "Not with her wrist wrapped up like that."

"I'm fine," she insists, but nothing about the way she looks or sounds supports this particular claim.

"You were nearly trampled yesterday, and you look like death warmed over," I say. Not to mention the emotional turmoil from her fight – and potential break-up – with Gia. "You really do need to rest."

"I agree," says Alexander before my sister can continue to argue. "It wouldn't do any good to bring you along, darling, not while you're injured. And without Mary, there's little point to Evangeline and Kit joining me—"

"Of course there's still a point," I protest. "I know I'm not Maisie, but I'm still your daughter, and I can support you. And Kit—"

"—is still an Abbott-Montgomery," says Doyle brusquely. "Despite his relationship with Evangeline, the press will expect him to side with Her Majesty. To show the three of you together, perhaps a few friendly moments between you and Lord Clarence…"

Alexander clenches his jaw, clearly unhappy about how this

conversation is turning out. But he's the one who wants to carry on like nothing is happening.

"And we can all take a picture together tomorrow at breakfast, before the three of you head out," says Maisie, who sounds considerably more optimistic now that crowds aren't involved on her end. "I'll post it on Instagram with a suitably supportive caption – without mentioning Mummy's interview, of course – and everyone will see that you're wearing the same outfits from your appearance, so they'll all know it was taken that morning."

Our father shakes his head. "I'm afraid I must insist on going alone. The crowds tomorrow—"

"We'll skip the walkabout," I say. "But I *am* coming. If you don't want me there, then cancel the appearance, but those are your only options."

He scowls. "I am still your king—"

"You're also my dad," I snap. "And I'm not letting you go out there on your own tomorrow. If you do, you'll just be giving Helene and the media exactly what they want, and you know it."

Alexander and I stare at each other for a long moment – too long, probably, considering more than two dozen people are now gawking at us – and it's only when he straightens in his seat, clearly about to issue some kind of command, that I cut him off.

"I'll do it," I say quickly. "That – trip we talked about at breakfast. I'll do it, no argument, for a minimum of three months and a maximum of six. But only if you let me do this for you."

This seems to instantly take the wind out of his sails, and he glances at my mother, as if asking for her opinion. Or maybe her help.

"It's one appearance," she says quietly. "An hour or two at the most, and then Doyle will have his rebuttal, and you'll have your dignity and the public support of your family. And Evangeline…"

She trails off, but I know what she isn't saying. I'll have the break they think I so desperately need. I'll be out of this mess long enough to recover, and maybe, by the time my parents let me come home, this will all be sorted out. Or at least the rancour will have died down.

And maybe, just maybe, someone will finally believe me about Ben.

Alexander exhales. "Very well," he says at last. "One appearance as a family, and then we will carry on as we were before this abominable interview ever happened. Do we have a deal?"

"We have a deal," I say, and even though I'm the one now facing up to six months in purgatory, I still feel like I've won.

Chapter Twenty-two

Nat4leele: Alexander's been seeing that American slag for TWENTY FIVE YEARS??? How did we never find out?? DIVORCE HIS ARSE.

gemino604: wait – so QH just put up with it all that time? girl. take that royal money and RUN.

MarciOSurley: The Queen is right, this is a tragedy. I hope they all find peace, happiness, and love.

guardenia93: I can't be the only person who thinks she and Nick make a super hot couple. Like, yeah, it's sad that she and the king didn't work out, but what an upgrade. Rooting for them. #royalwedding2025

AshPecla: What kind of person shags their husband's brother? Disgusting.

GRANdeVENtie3: yawn. rich people cheating on each other and being miserable. who cares.

yeetherish: Why are we deifying these inbred adulterers?

Cancel the whole lot. They're nothing more than worthless grifters who've been living off the people for far too bloody long. Britain deserves better. DutchessDame: time to bring back the guillotine. #offwithherhead

– The comments section of "Heartbroken Queen Regrets All," The *Daily Sun*, 12 January 2024

I barely sleep that night, and when I do, it's only to wake with a start, drenched in sweat, the last fragments of my nightmares already gone.

At first I can't figure out why. I was fine on Maisie's couch, after all, hours after the barrier broke in front of the hospital. But I didn't know then that I'd be facing another crowd so soon – an angry crowd this time, with every right to hate me and Alexander for what we did to their beloved queen.

Our protection officers will be more cautious now, I tell myself, after what happened to Maisie and me. But this does nothing to soothe my anxiety – if anything, it only makes me fixate on what else they've overlooked, and what other small things with big consequences can go wrong. And how Alexander, Kit and I will be the ones paying the price.

After I jerk awake for the second time, Kit rubs my back until his hand stills and his breathing evens out. Not wanting to disturb him again, I slip away and settle onto the sofa in my sitting room instead, taking my laptop with me.

I spend the next three hours distracting myself by reading the comments about Helene's interview on various gossip sites. Some call her a liar and insist she's trying to save face, while others support her wholeheartedly and drag my mother's name through the mud – and occasionally mine, calling us leeches and her a succubus and all kinds of things that would make Constance proud.

Most of all, though, the people blame Alexander. Not everyone, of course. Some empathize with him, or pity him, or focus on the real villain in all of this – an archaic system that imprisons everyone born into it, then drapes them in gold and jewels and privilege beyond compare so no one will ever believe their pain.

But too many push their anger onto him, assigning him motivations and emotions and sinister traits that turn him into the worst of humanity, ignoring that he was in an impossible situation and allowed to make mistakes. All they want is a demon to hate, and in Alexander, they've found one in spades.

The revelations from Helene's interview dominate the news cycle, with her face plastered on the front page of every single news site I visit. But when I type out the *Regal Record*'s address – more out of habit than any desire to see what they're saying – I'm instead faced with a paparazzi shot of Maisie and Gia exiting a club in what I think is Soho.

I recognize the outfit Maisie is wearing – a cute blue dress I helped her pick out sometime in September, before it grew too cold to need a jacket. Despite the packed pavement, there are several feet between her and Gia as they walk past a cluster of photographers, and unlike the shots featured in the round-up the *Regal Record* posted last week, they both look miserable.

PRINCESS MARY AND LADY GIA SUFFER FALLING-OUT AMIDST ROYAL ADULTERY SCANDAL

While the rest of the world is focused on the sensational surprise interview with Queen Helene that aired earlier tonight on the BBC – and we' ll certainly get there, too – we at the Regal Record have received word of yet another royal break-up: Princess Mary and Lady Georgiana Greyville, who have known each other since nappies, have reportedly suffered a dramatic falling-out.

Lady Gia, as she's known to close friends and family, allegedly rushed to Windsor to check on her princess after a crowd barrier broke yesterday morning at the Royal London Children's Hospital, leaving Her Royal Highness with a sprained wrist and other minor injuries. Their reunion was short-lived, however, as Lady Gia stormed out of the heir to the throne's private apartment mere minutes later, leaving the princess utterly bereft. The catalyst behind their fight? A bouquet of roses from a very presidential American suitor.

While we wouldn't dare presume that these two besties have ever been anything more than the closest of friends, one must wonder why a sweet, but hardly personal, gift would lead to a shouting match heard throughout the halls of Windsor Castle.

To remember happier times between Her Royal Highness and Lady Gia, click the gallery below.

I read the article twice, too exhausted to be sure I'm not imagining things. But there they are, in neat black font on white background – details that no journalist or gossip blog should know about Maisie and Gia's fight. And as I scroll through the most recent entries, I realize it's more than the roses or their break-up. The *Regal Record* knew about Maisie's injuries, too. And the time stamp is less than an hour after we returned from London.

Someone in the castle – someone close to the royal family – is running directly to the *Regal Record* with insider information.

My mind races through the names and faces of everyone I saw at Windsor Castle that day, tripping over possibilities and half theories that don't make any sense, and I'm so distracted that I don't notice the whispers at first. They start out soft – so soft that they sound like a faint buzz, or maybe the rush of blood through my pounding heart. But as soon as I realize they have nothing to do with my too-fast pulse, they grow louder, and I slowly register the fact that the whispers are saying something – something I can't make out until I do. And this time, it isn't my name.

"*You die today.*"

Terror cuts through me, so sharp and tangible that it might as well be a knife. I slam my laptop shut and leap to my feet, heading straight for the only weapon I can think of – a weighty silver candlestick on my mantel. Though it isn't much, I clutch it in both hands as the whispers surround me, repeating themselves again and again like some demonic nursery rhyme.

"*You die today.*"

"*You die today.*"

"*You die today.*"

"Evan?"

I jump. Kit is standing in the doorway to my bedroom, his hair wild, his pyjamas rumpled, and his eyes half-closed with sleep, and I'm so relieved to see him that I almost burst into tears.

"Can you hear that?" I say, not entirely sure I want to know the answer.

He cocks his head, listening for a long moment, and I can't

tell if the faint whispers that echo in my mind are real, or if they're nothing more than figments of my imagination now.

"I'm sorry, Ev," he says at last. "I don't hear anything."

I close my eyes and take a deep breath, but the strange sounds have already disappeared. "I don't know what's wrong with me," I say, my voice tight and frantic and one wrong note away from snapping. "I keep hearing these whispers, ever since Sandringham. Mostly they say my name, but sometimes it's laughter or even music I've never heard before, and – and I can't tell where it's coming from, but today – just now – they said – they said—"

"Evan." Kit gently takes my shoulders and leans down so our foreheads are pressed together. "Just breathe, all right? Just for a minute."

I stare into his liquid brown eyes as we both inhale and exhale at the same time. I'm dizzy again, but at least the whispers are gone, and when he touches my cheek, I don't know what to say.

"Did you sleep at all?" he murmurs, and I shake my head. "Not really," I manage. "I was on my laptop."

He brushes his lips against mine. "You're exhausted. We have a few hours before you have to be at breakfast, so why don't we go back to bed? I'll chase Tibby off and wake you in time."

Breakfast. Maisie's Instagram picture. The museum opening. I can't do any of it like this – not when I feel like I'm about to jump out of my skin. "The whispers were saying I'm going to die today."

"You're not going to die today," he murmurs, tucking my tangled hair behind my ear. "You're not going to die for a very, very long time."

I blink hard. "What if my mom and Alexander are right?" I mumble. "What if I really am losing my mind?"

"We'll figure out what's going on when we get to Virginia, okay?" he says, but I shake my head.

"You need to go back to Oxford."

"What I need right now has nothing to do with university," he says. "But we'll talk about it later, all right? For now, let's get you tucked into bed."

He leaves a note for Tibby on the dining table, and once we're back in my bedroom, he chooses an ocean soundscape on YouTube and plays it just loud enough to drown out any other noise – real or imagined. It reminds me of the nightmares I used to have when I was a kid, the ones where no matter what I did, I always ended up drowning. But this time, as he holds me and I slip into that same dream, he's on the shore with my mother and grandma, ready to show me the way back.

By the time he wakes me, a streak of sunlight sneaks in through a crack in the curtains, and it's nearly nine o'clock. Tibby is waiting in the sitting room, and though she's done an exceptional job of keeping to herself, as soon as she knows I'm up, she's back to ordering me around like I haven't been getting myself ready in the morning for practically my entire life.

I don't know what, if anything, Kit told her, and I don't ask as I brush my teeth and get dressed. A stylist is waiting for me in my sitting room, and thirty minutes later, my hair is dried and pulled into an artful half ponytail, my make-up is done, and Kit and I walk hand in hand to the breakfast room, where Alexander, Maisie and my mother are all waiting for us.

I force a smile as Tibby takes picture after picture, some with all of us, some with just me and Maisie and our father. Even when we start to eat, I notice her sneaking a few shots when she thinks no one is looking. And although I'm calmer now, as I look around at my family gathered together, I can't shake the feeling that this is somehow a morning I'm always going to remember. Or that maybe those voices were right, and this is the last happy memory I'll ever have.

Our regular Range Rover is replaced with a Rolls-Royce bearing the royal standard, bulletproof windows and an emergency airlock that, in case of a gas attack, will keep us safe. Security has more than doubled, with Ingrid accompanied by three other protection officers specifically there to keep an eye on me and Kit, and no fewer than six to protect Alexander.

Kit holds my hand the entire way, and he and my father chat about the museum we're about to visit – a newly renovated building along the Thames that's been nearly two years in the making. They pretend that nothing's wrong, that neither of them noticed there were no newspapers waiting for us at the breakfast table this morning, or that I've barely said a word. And none of us mentions the protesters lining the sidewalks as we approach the museum, or that the crowd waiting for us behind reinforced barriers is booing.

"Ready?" says Alexander, looking straight at me.

I try to take a steadying breath, but it hitches in my throat, and suddenly I want nothing more than to say no, to tell him we have to drive away and forget this photo op, forget this opening, forget that he has duties and responsibilities. The crowd is tense. The sky is an overbearing grey. And every cell in my body is screaming at me that we shouldn't be here.

But Alexander won't leave, even if I beg. And if I don't go into that museum, Kit will stay behind with me, and my father will be alone. The photographers will have their iconic picture of him walking up the steps surrounded by bodyguards, with no family or loved ones there to offer support, and I have to do this. I *have* to do this.

"Ready," I manage, trying to smile away the anxiety coursing through me, replacing my blood with ice and panic. It will be fine. It will be fine. It will be *fine*.

But as we step out of the car – Alexander first, then me, then Kit – I nearly freeze on the spot. A wall of jeers hits us like an avalanche, and I notice a muscle tightening in Alexander's jaw as he smiles and waves to the hostile crowd. Our protection officers surround us, not letting us anywhere near the barriers, and I'm enormously grateful as Ingrid joins me on our walk to the front doors. Kit is on my other side, and I clutch his hand, afraid that if I let go, I'll never find it again.

Among the endless questions and accusations hurled at Alexander, none of which he acknowledges, the sound of my own name catches my attention. The voice is deep and clear, and out of habit – or maybe because I don't expect to be addressed today – I glance over into the sea of people watching us.

And there, right up against the barrier, is the man with the teal scarf.

He's not alone – there are three others with him, the lower half of their faces also covered by thick scarves, though I notice a single lock of red hair sticking out from beneath the smallest figure's hood. They're all staring at me, and I grip Kit's hand so tightly that he leans in until his lips are an inch from my ear.

"All right?" he says, barely audible. I shake my head.

"Ingrid," I manage. "To your right – the man with the teal scarf."

"I see him," says Ingrid quietly, and she hangs back for a moment to speak to the protection officers behind us. I feel strangely exposed without her there, and I practically glue myself to Kit's side as we finally ascend the steps.

The curator, who's willowy and blond and looks jarringly like Helene, greets us at the arched entrance with a curtsy. After introducing herself, she dives straight into a gushing speech about how grateful she is that we were able to make it, though she doesn't say a word about the interview or the antagonistic crowd. Alexander is polite and down-to-earth, without any indication that his estranged wife has just aired his dirty laundry to the entire world, and only when the doors close behind us do I release my death grip on Kit's hand.

"Sorry," I whisper as he flexes his fingers. "There's someone out there – he was at the hospital, too."

"The one you thought had a gun?" he says, and I nod grimly. But our conversation is quickly cut short as the curator introduces her team, and Kit and I both work our way down the line to greet everyone.

The lobby of the museum is an architectural wonder, with soaring arched ceilings and marble columns that seem to shimmer as we move. The curator tells us about the design of the museum – that everything was built with acoustics in mind, and that it could double as a concert hall if need be. Kit and I join Alexander, who looks thoroughly intrigued, and I almost manage to focus – until I see them.

Three vases of blood-red daisies, spaced perfectly apart on the welcome desk.

I take Kit's hand again and, without letting my own fake smile falter, I meet his questioning gaze and glance at the desk. He freezes in place for a moment, clearly seeing the flowers, too, and we fall out of step with the others.

"Is everything all right?" says the curator, and Alexander pauses.

"Evangeline?" he says, his worry obvious, but my mouth is dry, and I'm not sure what to say.

"We were just noticing the flowers," says Kit after a beat. "They're beautiful – and rather distinct, wouldn't you say?"

"Oh, yes," says the curator. "We were so pleased to receive them, Your Majesty. It was a lovely gesture from the palace."

"We're very glad," says Alexander, so smoothly that for a moment, I think he doesn't understand. But he steps towards the welcome desk, the curator at his elbow, and I notice the slight tremble in his hand as he touches the card tucked in the middle bouquet. Finally, *finally*, he might actually believe –

Boom.

A noise unlike anything I've ever heard before seems to shatter the very air around us, rocking the marble beneath my feet. And before I can process what's happening, before I can wrap my head around the way the entire lobby is disintegrating before my eyes, Kit's hand is ripped from mine as something collides with me with the force of a concrete wall, and the world goes black.

Chapter Twenty-three

An explosion has been reported at the Modern Music Museum in Central London, during an official visit from His Majesty the King, Evangeline Bright and Lord Clarence. The area surrounding the museum has been evacuated, and there is no word yet on casualties.

– Breaking news alert from the BBC,
11:17 a.m., 12 January 2024

All I hear is silence.

I don't know where I am. I don't know what time it is, or what day it is, or why I can't see. Vaguely I'm aware that I hurt – that my body is aching in ways it shouldn't, that something has happened, something I should remember. But all I can feel is a strange tingling that seems to be holding the real pain at bay.

There's something warm beside me – warm and wet, I think, but I can't be sure. My senses aren't working properly, and I'm floating in the dark, yet at the same time held down by something foreboding and impenetrable. None of it makes sense, and I want to slip back into nothingness when a high-pitched sound pierces my eardrums, and the world around me seems to shift.

Suddenly it's daylight, bright and overpowering and filled with dust as it chases away the darkness. I squeeze my eyes shut, but not before I see the white arched ceiling of the museum high above me, partially collapsed where two of the shimmering columns should be.

"I've got Evangeline here!" The deep voice mingles with the whine in my ears, and I'm vaguely aware of someone touching the pulse point on my neck. That brush is enough to ignite the rest of my dormant nerves, and suddenly the pain hits me like a tidal wave, leaving me gasping for breath.

I open my eyes again, and there's a man in a firefighter uniform peering down at me as others clear the debris around us. It's mostly plaster, I think, but there are some heavier chunks of marble, too, and only then do I slowly start to understand what happened.

"What—" I manage, but it comes out as a gurgle. Another emergency worker lifts a piece of stone that landed inches from my head, and he inhales sharply.

"Found a body," he calls, and I notice the dark red stain on the bottom of the marble. Some small part of my mind is screaming at me, but I don't understand why – until I turn my head and see the mess of blood and bone beside me, so close that I can feel what's left of its heat.

"Keep still," orders one of the men working to excavate the rest of me. "I need a collar over here!"

I'm still staring at the body, mostly buried under marble that missed me by inches. That voice in my mind grows louder, clawing away at the fog until I finally hear what it's saying.

Kit. Kit. Kit.

Kit was next to me. Kit was exactly where this body is now, and—

The world goes dark once more, and when I come to again, I'm lying on a stretcher, surrounded by medics. There's an oxygen mask over my mouth, and a woman is doing something to one of my legs. When I glance up, I see the grey sky again, but this time there's no hole to look through. We're outside.

"Kit?" I whisper, but if anyone hears me, they don't react. Someone shouts nearby, and another team of medics rolls a second stretcher past mine, though I can't see who's on it. When it's gone, however, my blurred vision focuses on the top of the steps, where several long black bags are lined up side by side, one after another.

Body bags.

"Evangeline?" A woman with black hair and a nose stud shines a light in my eyes, and I blink, not sure if I'm crying or not. "Can you hear me, Evangeline?"

I nod – or at least I try to, but something is holding my neck in place. "Kit?" I repeat, louder this time.

"We're taking you to hospital now," she says like I haven't said anything at all. "We'll get you sorted there, all right?"

Time slips away from me again, even though I think I'm still awake. I hear the sirens, can feel every bump in the road as the ambulance rushes through traffic, and when we arrive at what must be the emergency room – *A&E in England*, says a dry voice in my mind that sounds an awful lot like Tibby – I'm surrounded yet again by a medical team.

"Kit?" I say desperately as a doctor removes my oxygen mask. "Is he okay?"

"Can you tell me where it hurts?" she replies, and if I wasn't crying before, I am now. I try to sit up, but hands hold me down as I babble Kit's name again and again, and all I can see is that crushed body in the rubble.

The doctor must sedate me, because the next time I open my eyes, I'm in a room that's eerily similar to the one I woke up in on Christmas Eve. The whining in my ears is fainter now, and in its place, I hear a steady *beep-beep-beep* that must be my pulse.

"Kit?" I say before I can even think of why. But then the memory of that morning hits me, and I suck in a breath. "Kit—"

"It's about bloody time," says a clipped voice from my bedside. "The doctors said you'd be awake an hour ago, but as always, they're utterly incompetent and haven't a clue what they're doing." For a split second, I'm positive I'm dreaming. But sure enough, when I turn my head, I see my grandmother sitting straight-backed in a plastic hospital chair, her expression drawn, her eyes red and swollen, and her designer coat dress buttoned to her throat.

"Constance?" I manage. "What are you doing here?"

"You will address me as Your Majesty," says my grandmother sternly. "And I am here because I've long since done my duty to the crown, and no one cares what happens to me."

This doesn't make any sense, and I lift my head. The brace I wore on the stretcher is gone now, and even though every inch of my body aches, I can still move my fingers and toes. "Where's Kit?" I say as I struggle to sit up. "Is he—"

"Would you *please* lie still? For the love of..." Constance reaches forward, and a moment later, my bed begins to whir and guides me into a sitting position. "You're a very lucky girl, you know. You have mild concussion and a nasty gash on your leg that needed stitches, but beyond that and a few bumps and bruises, you ought to be perfectly fine. *If* you don't strain yourself over the next few days."

I shake my head. I don't feel lucky – I don't feel anything but creeping dread. "There was a body beside me," I whisper, my fingers digging into the thin mattress. "There was blood – so much blood – and before…before, Kit was there, and—"

"My understanding is that Lord Clarence is awake and being treated a few rooms down," says Constance so matter-of-factly that it knocks the wind out of me. "*He's* not the one who had the bloody ceiling fall in on him."

I look at her sharply, not sure I've heard her right. "Kit – he's alive?"

Constance sniffs. "Honestly, Evangeline, your life would be so much easier if you learned to listen."

Something hot and liquid seems to explode in my chest, and before I realize it, I'm sobbing. From relief, from shock, from delayed fear – I don't know what it is, but I'm crying harder than I ever have in my life.

Kit's alive. He's okay. It wasn't him. *It wasn't him.*

Constance stiffens, seemingly frozen in place by a show of actual emotion. But eventually I feel her tentative touch on my back, and a moment later, she snakes a thin arm around me with the kind of awkwardness usually reserved for middle schoolers at a dance.

I don't care that we've never said a nice word to each other.

I don't care that she hates my guts and is only here because she has to be. I bury my face in her shoulder as every last emotion wrings itself from my body, leaving me quaking and boneless when my sobs finally start to subside.

"Who was it, then?" I say hoarsely as I let her go. "Who—" But then another possibility occurs to me, and I study her face. Her swollen eyes. Her haggard expression. The way she suddenly looks every single one of her seventy-plus years, despite a lifetime of facials.

"Where's Alexander?" I say as cold horror sweeps through me, taking every ounce of my relief with it. "Constance, where—"

"Your Majesty," she corrects, but her voice hitches. "You will call me Your Majesty, Evangeline, or I—"

"*Where is he?*" The guttural sound that comes out of me is inhuman, and all I can think about is that broken body beside me, and how I know beyond a doubt that my father, king or not, would have done everything he could to protect me. Even if it meant taking the death that was supposed to be mine.

Constance swallows hard. "His Majesty was pulled from the rubble shortly after you were," she says slowly, like it's taking everything she has to keep her voice steady. "He sustained crush injuries to his legs and chest, and—"

"Is he alive?" I demand, sick with fear all over again. Her chin quivers now, and I reel, trying to brace myself for the reality I don't want to face.

"Yes," she whispers. "He's still alive. But he is critical, and the odds the doctors have given him..."

She closes her eyes, and twin tears escape down the sides of her nose. Before I can think better of it, I'm hugging her again, numb to the inconsequential aches and pains in my own body now. And when she slumps against me, all her carefully crafted royal veneer vanishing in a single shudder, I know that there's a very real chance I'll never see my father again.

Chapter Twenty-four

A total of eight deaths have been reported so far in the bombing of the Modern Music Museum in London during an official visit by His Majesty and members of the royal family. The identities of the victims have not yet been released, and Buckingham Palace has refused to comment on the status of the King.

– Breaking news alert from the BBC, 2:11 p.m., 12 January 2024

Constance remains with me throughout the rest of the afternoon as we wait for an update on Alexander.

All details of his condition are kept from the media – a matter of national security at this point – and the hospital is crawling with police and personal protection officers, both for our safety and to hold the rabid journalists that surround the building at bay. No one is allowed to leave their room without a damn good reason, and while neither of us is thrilled about it, especially when I'm desperate to see Kit, Constance and I settle into something that resembles an uneasy truce.

After she dabs her eyes and resumes her prickly royal demeanour, I pepper her with questions, and she tersely explains that both Maisie and Helene have been told by the prime minister and home secretary to stay where they are, in case of another attack. This is what she meant when she said that no one cares what happens to her, I realize – she's not in the line of succession, and she's considered as expendable as I am. But Alexander is also her son, and as much as she and I don't like each other, I'm glad someone from the family is here.

Our shared fear and frustration with the lack of updates does a strange thing as we wait – it makes me feel like we actually have something in common. It's far from a familial bond, but by the time the sound of an argument filters in from the corridor outside my room, I'm almost starting to warm up to her. Almost.

"What on earth…" mutters Constance as she stands and marches towards the door, but despite the high-pitched tone that still lingers in my ears, I immediately recognize one of the voices.

"That's Kit," I say urgently, climbing out of bed, but Constance flings open the door before my feet touch the ground.

"What is the meaning of this?" she demands. Kit stands a few steps away, physically blocked from the entrance by two protection officers with their holstered weapons now on full display.

"I just need to see – Evan!" says Kit, the relief in his voice palpable as he spots me over Constance's shoulder. "Are you all right? Would you bloody let me *go*?"

"Get your hands off him," says Constance sharply as I stumble across the freezing floor, my injured leg protesting as a dozen stitches tug against my skin. "Lord Clarence is family and well within his rights to be here."

The protection officers step aside, and Kit offers my grandmother a grateful bow of his head before hurrying past her and into the room. He catches me in his arms, lifting me off the ground as he holds me to him.

"Bloody hell, Ev," he mumbles into my hair, his voice choked with tears. "You have to stop doing this to me."

"Not my choice, trust me," I say, wrapping my arms around his neck. I can feel the edge of a bandage against my skin, and when I pull away enough to peer at him, I see several small cuts across his face, including one beneath his eye that required stitches. "You're okay?"

"Fine," he promises. "Climbing the bloody walls trying to find out how you are. MI5's here, and they wouldn't tell me anything—"

"No one is being told a thing," says Constance. "The press *must* be kept in the dark about the King's condition, is that understood?"

"He's alive?" says Kit, and I can tell by the catch in his voice that he wasn't expecting this. "At the museum, I thought…he was buried, and when they found him…"

His throat works hard, and I press my cheek to his. Dust still clings to his hair, turning parts of it ashy grey, and I realize he's dressed in hospital scrubs. "You saw what happened?"

"Only bits," he says. "One of the PPOs pinned me to the ground, but I could still see you. Ingrid threw herself at you, and then…then the column fell, and…"

My insides churn, and suddenly I think I'm going to be sick. "Ingrid?" I manage. "She was – she was with me?"

I see the body again, the blood and the bone and the parts I don't want to identify, and I press my lips together, as if that'll stop the contents of my stomach from coming up. But when Kit nods wordlessly, I let him go, and he sets me down just in time for me to grab the plastic bin next to my bed and be sick.

Someone calls for a nurse, and Kit crouches beside me, rubbing my back as I retch. He murmurs something, but the high pitch in my ears grows louder, drowning out his voice.

Ingrid was only there because of me – because I demanded that Alexander bring me. If I hadn't, if I'd listened to him and stayed behind, or if I'd trusted my gut and not gotten out of that car in the first place, she would still be alive. The other people in the body bags – maybe they'd still be alive, too. Alexander wouldn't have noticed the flowers, and he would've been in a different part of the lobby. And maybe, maybe –

I'm sick again, and a few seconds later, I feel the prick of a needle in my arm. I expect to black out – I expect them to sedate me like they did in A&E – but instead all that happens is that my nausea subsides as quickly as it came.

"There we go," says a nurse, offering me a tissue as I sit back up. Her voice is muffled by the ringing in my ears, but that, too, slowly eases until I can hear myself panting. Kit presses a glass of water into my hand, and I'm so dazed that I don't think twice before drinking it.

Ingrid's dead, and this time, it really is my fault.

Kit helps me back onto the bed as the nurse fetches some crackers, but I sit sideways, my legs dangling and my head in my hands. "I shouldn't have been there," I whisper. "Alexander didn't want me to go. If I'd listened to him, then Ingrid…"

"That's not fair," says Kit. "You didn't know this was going to happen, Ev."

"I think I did," I say, so softly I'm not even sure my voice carries. But he squeezes my knee, and I know he heard. "Those whispers in my sitting room…"

"That had nothing to do with this," says Kit. "Okay? You didn't know this would happen, and it isn't your fault. You had no control over any of it. Whoever did this—"

I look at him suddenly, my eyes bleary as I feel myself go pale. "The man in the teal scarf," I say. "The one in the crowd—"

"Who?" says an unfamiliar male voice in the doorway, and Kit and I both turn.

Constance has disappeared into the hallway, and in her place stands a tall man with thick black hair, dark skin and a sharp charcoal suit. There's something overwhelmingly intimidating about him – even more so than the protection officers carrying loaded guns – and I look nervously at Kit.

Kit clears his throat. "Evangeline, this is Suraj Singh. He's from MI5."

"It's nice to meet you, Miss Bright," says Singh, stepping into the room and extending his hand towards me. "Though I wish it were under different circumstances."

I eye his hand like it might bite me. "MI5. Isn't that like the CIA?"

"More like your FBI," he says with the ease of someone who expects me to be difficult. "MI5 is the British security service, while MI6 deals in foreign intelligence. It's entirely possible they'll also be assisting with the investigation, but for now, you're stuck with me."

My experience with the police hasn't exactly endeared me to any kind of government authority, but his hand still hovers between us, and reluctantly I take it. His grip is firm, but brief, and as soon as he lets my hand go, I wedge both of mine between my knees.

"Lord Clarence was kind enough to tell me all he remembers about the incident at the Modern Music Museum this morning," he says smoothly. "And I was hoping you might feel up to the same, particularly if there's someone you've noticed or—"

"Who gave you permission to be in here?"

Before today, I never would've thought I'd be relieved to see Constance, but as she steps through the doorway, her face hard as stone, I could actually hug her.

Singh clears his throat. "Your Majesty," he says, bowing his head. "Forgive me. I'm Agent Suraj Singh, and I've been sent by the home secretary—"

"I don't care who sent you," says Constance, drawing herself up to her full height. "You've no right to be in this room, or to question a member of the royal family."

My mouth goes dry, though I'm not sure what part surprises me more – Constance being protective of me, or her referring to me as a member of the royal family.

"Ma'am," says Singh patiently, "we need Miss Bright's statement—"

"And you'll have it," says Constance. "Once Evangeline is out of a hospital gown and in the safety of a royal residence."

Singh purses his lips, and suddenly, in the face of Constance's ire, he doesn't seem nearly as intimidating. "My team is in the process of tracing the terrorists now, ma'am, and time is of the essence—"

"You know who did this?" I cut in, and Singh hesitates. "We made several arrests at the scene," he admits. "And an anti-monarchist group that calls itself the Army of the British Republic has taken credit. But situations such as these can be chaotic and confusing, particularly in the initial hours and days, and the more information we have—"

"There is nothing Evangeline can tell you that other witnesses cannot," says Constance. But as Singh looks at me again, I can see he thinks otherwise.

"You said you saw a man in the crowd – one wearing a teal scarf," he says. "He seemed suspicious to you?"

I open my mouth, though I'm not entirely sure what's going to come out. Before I can make a sound, however, Constance steps between us, her arms crossed as she blocks his way.

"One more word, and I'll be having more than a few with the home secretary over your conduct in the hospital room of a traumatized eighteen-year-old girl," she says sharply. "Now go, before I have you physically thrown out in front of every single journalist camped outside."

Singh manages a tight smile. "Very well, ma'am," he says, and he pulls a card from his pocket, reaching past her to offer it to Kit. "When Miss Bright is ready to speak."

Kit takes the card, and Singh offers Constance another bow before exiting the room. As soon as he's gone, Constance shuts the door and begins to pace in her heels, clearly fuming.

"The nerve of that man," she mutters. "You must never

answer any questions without legal representation present, is that understood? No matter how innocent you are, you mustn't say a word."

"I know," I say quietly. "I promise, I know."

Her frown deepens, but at least this seems to satisfy her for now. "I've just spoken to the doctors," she says, and Kit and I immediately sit up straighter.

"About Alexander?" I say. "Is he—"

"He's out of surgery," she says in a clipped voice. "Which was more than he was expected to survive. For now, he's in a medically induced coma, though the doctors can't say much more at this stage. If he..." Her voice catches again, and she takes a steadying breath. "If he survives the night, then we'll have a better idea of what the future might hold."

If. I swallow hard as Kit's fingers slip between mine. "Does my mom know how bad it is?" I say, and Constance shoots me a withering look.

"What have I been saying about how important it is that his condition not leak to the press?"

"My mom won't tell anyone," I insist. "Helene's the one who runs to the media every chance she—"

"I'm well aware," snaps Constance. "But she is still his wife, and she still has the right to make medical decisions for him. Which unfortunately means she is the only other person currently being updated on his condition."

Constance and I stare at each other, my mind racing as I try to put my thoughts into words. "So you're saying – you're saying my mom has no idea if he's even alive?"

She purses her lips. "No."

"What about me?" I say, my heart pounding. "Does she know I'm okay?"

Constance sets her jaw, and I slide off the bed, closing the distance between us.

"Go get her," I say in a low, dangerous voice. "Wherever she is – go get her, and bring her here."

Her eyes narrow. "Watch your tone with me, Evangeline. The hospital is on lockdown—"

"I don't care," I say. "And you shouldn't, either. I get why you don't trust her, but she loves him more than her own life, and we both know he feels the same. You can't keep her in the dark. Not now, not when…" I shake my head. "He'd want her here. You know he would."

Constance glances away, the lines in her forehead multiplying. I try to think of what to say next – of what combination of threats and pleas might make her relent – but just as I open my mouth again, she sighs.

"Very well," she says, so quietly that I almost don't hear her over the ringing in my ears. "I shall send for her."

Instantly the tension in my body deflates, and my limbs feel like rubber. "Thank you," I say, but it's all I can manage right now. She nods tersely, and as Kit helps me back onto the bed, she goes to the door to speak to one of the officers in the hall.

"Fetch Ms Bright," she orders. "She's downstairs with one of your colleagues. Don't allow her to speak to anyone, and bring her directly to me."

"Yes, ma'am," says the officer, and when Constance re-enters the room, I'm gaping at her.

"My mom's been here the whole time?"

"Of course she has," she says blisteringly, but there's no real bite in her voice now. "You're her daughter. Where else would she be?"

My mother arrives less than five minutes later, and I know instantly from the hollows beneath her eyes and the grey tint to her face that she's spent the entire afternoon desperately trying to convince herself that Alexander and I aren't dead. "I'm sorry," I say as she clings to me. "I thought someone would tell you. I didn't know – I'm so sorry—"

She shakes her head. "You're all right," she manages. "That's all that matters."

"Alexander's alive, too," I say, ignoring Constance's glare. "But...he's in really bad shape, Mom. They don't know if..." My mom holds me tighter, and a dry sob escapes her. We stay like that, tangled together in the middle of the room, until my legs start to give out from the effort of supporting our combined weight. And once we've separated, me perched on the bed and my mom gripping my hand in both of hers, Constance looks between us, as if coming to some kind of decision.

"How far can you walk?" she says to me, and I glance at my leg. The cut is deep and jagged, and it's yet another scar to remind me of what's turning out to be the worst month of my life. But in the face of everything else, it's barely a blip.

"As far as I need to," I say, and she nods.

"Put on your dressing gown and follow me – both of you. Kit, stay here. I'll bring her back soon enough."

He doesn't argue, and I tie the sash of a hospital robe around my waist as my mom and I follow Constance into the corridor. The protection officers assigned to my room start to protest, but she silences them with a single look, and I tuck myself underneath my mom's arm as Constance leads us down the hall.

I don't know where we're going until we stop in front of a door guarded by two more protection officers. And as they exchange a grim look, I'm positive I know what's on the other side.

"You will let us all in," says Constance, "or you will lose your livelihoods."

There's a moment – just a moment – when I see both of them weighing her threat and wondering if she actually possesses the power to have them fired. But she's the former queen consort, mother of the current sovereign and grandmother to the heir to the throne. If anyone has the power to do anything in this country, it's her.

And so they step aside and open the door, and with her head held high, Constance leads us into Alexander's hospital room.

The first thing I notice is the beeping. It isn't just a single steady *beep-beep-beep*, but several layers of tinny noise, all indicating that he's still alive – or, at the very least, that the machines are keeping him going for now. A nurse sits in the corner beside a computer that displays his vital signs, and another pair of protection officers stand near the door, eyeing us like we might be threats. I ignore them and, mustering up all the courage I have left, finally look at my father.

He lies in an oversized hospital bed, with so many bandages wrapped around his broken body that there's no real way to tell who he is. The only sign that it's him is the part of his swollen face not hidden under gauze, and even then, he's barely recognizable. I freeze, completely unprepared for the sight of him like this, and Constance stands stiffly beside me, also unmoving. But my mother doesn't hesitate as she walks towards his bedside and takes his bare hand, gently sandwiching it between hers.

"Oh, Alex," she says softly, her eyes raking over the damage. "My Alex. Look at you."

There's something so achingly tender about the way she says his name that tears well in my eyes, but I blink hard, refusing to lose it right now. Not in front of my mom. Instead, I force myself forward and push a plastic chair beside the bed, giving her a place to sit.

"We should know more about His Majesty's condition in the morning," says the nurse in a gentle Scottish accent. "For now, the doctors have stabilized him, and we'll do all we can to help him make it through the night."

"He will," says my mother with quiet certainty. Her eyes linger on his face, and her thumb strokes the back of his hand. "I'd like to stay with him, if it's allowed."

The nurse looks at Constance, who still stands by the door, her cheeks bloodless and her eyes haunted. For all her arrogance and bad temper, right now she's nothing more than a mother faced with the possibility of losing her son, and her throat tightens before she nods.

"He would want you here," she says, and my mom offers her the tiniest of smiles before turning her gaze back to my father. And as she lays her head down beside their intertwined hands, I drag another chair over and join her.

ARRESTS MADE IN MUSEUM BOMBING; KING'S CONDITION STILL UNKNOWN

The Home Office has announced that several arrests have been made related to the bombing of the Modern Music Museum in London yesterday, which has claimed the lives of eight people. While the identities of the suspected terrorists have not yet been revealed, the Army of the British Republic, a previously unknown and self-declared anti-monarchist group, has reportedly taken credit for the bombing in a video posted anonymously to social media. Though the Home Office has yet to confirm their claim, several international leaders, including President Hope Park of the United States, have already condemned the organization for the attack.

While the King's condition remains unknown, a palace insider has revealed that Evangeline Bright, illegitimate daughter of the King, and Christopher Abbott-Montgomery, Earl of Clarence and nephew to the Queen, survived the attack. Both have been admitted to an undisclosed hospital for treatment, though the extent of their injuries remains unknown.

– The *Daily Sun*, 13 January 2024

In the early hours of the morning, long before the sun rises, Jenkins appears in the doorway of my hospital room.

Kit is asleep in the bed beside me, his body tense with nightmares that aren't hard to guess, but I'm awake, staring at the ceiling as I try not to think about what's happening down the hall. Every time I hear someone hurry past my room, my adrenaline spikes, and I'm sure this is it – that Alexander's finally let go. But neither my mother nor Constance comes to break the news to me, and each time my anxiety drags me out of bed to check with the protection officers stationed outside my door, all they do is offer a reassuring nod. Somehow, against all odds, he's hanging on.

"Jenkins?" I whisper as he slips inside the room, closing the door softly behind him. He startles slightly, clearly not expecting me to be awake, and in the dim light, I see his apologetic grimace.

"Good morning, Evan," he says softly. "How do you feel?"

"Like a building fell on me," I deadpan, and to his credit, he tries to smile. "Is Alexander still…?"

"His Majesty is a fighter," says Jenkins, and I breathe a sigh of relief. "Do you feel well enough to come home?"

"Already?" Technically Kit and I have both been discharged, but no one's argued about us staying in the room for a little while longer, considering Alexander's the only other patient on this floor.

"Her Royal Highness has asked that you be present for an emergency meeting this morning," he says. "In order to discuss the, er…plans for what will happen while His Majesty is incapacitated."

"Plans?" I say, confused. "What does that mean?"

"It means..." Jenkins clears his throat. "It means that though we all very much hope His Majesty will make a full recovery, we must decide how to carry on until he is ready to resume his duties. Her Royal Highness is the heir to the throne, of course, but until she is twenty-one, she is bound by the Regency Act of 2005, and that...complicates matters significantly."

I stare at him for a long moment. "Jenkins, I *just* learned the difference between MI5 and MI6. I have no idea what the Regency Act of 2005 is."

This finally gets a real – albeit faint – smile out of him. "It's an act that was put into place by Parliament shortly after your sister was born. It outlines what would happen – what will now happen – should something befall His Majesty before Her Royal Highness reaches the age of twenty-one."

"But he's not – he's not gone," I say. "He could wake up, right? Isn't a regency permanent?"

"The situation we're now in is...rather delicate, and we do not yet know if a true regency will be required. But it is possible."

I don't want to think about that, especially not now, in the early morning, with my ears still ringing from the bomb. "Why twenty-one?" I say. "I thought Queen Victoria was eighteen when she took the throne."

"She was," says Jenkins. "But while the Regency Act of 2005 was being drafted, your father asked to include a clause ensuring that so long as Her Royal Highness is under the age of twenty-one, she will be assisted by a council of senior royals, who are able to help make decisions and carry out the monarch's duties in his absence, whether temporary or permanent."

"So it won't all be on Maisie," I say, though I'm still confused.

"Precisely," he says. "And she wishes for you to be present during the discussion of the finer details."

I have no idea why, and spending hours listening to a dozen royal advisers arguing over political minutiae sounds like the worst way to spend any morning, let alone this one. But I nod, because the thought of what Maisie must be going through right now makes me shiver, and the idea of her facing it alone makes me ache with something I can't name. Protectiveness, maybe. Or maybe some kind of sibling connection I don't recognize. If Alexander takes a turn, or if he can't find his way back, my sister will be queen. And I don't think any of us are prepared, least of all her.

"Okay," I say. "But when it's over, I'm coming back to sit with my mom."

"I'll make sure no one stops you," says Jenkins. And after another beat, he wordlessly takes my hand, as if reassuring himself that I'm really there. "Sometimes I wish I'd never brought you to England in the first place," he admits so quietly that I barely hear him.

"But I'm glad you did," I say.

"Even after all this?"

"Especially after all this." I glance at Kit, who's still asleep. He looks calmer now, like his nightmare has passed. "I like having people in my life who are worth a few bombs and bullets."

"It's hardly our typical British welcome," he says, and I shrug.

"You're all worth it."

After I check in on my mom and Alexander, whose condition hasn't changed, Jenkins and several protection officers escort Kit and me into a parking garage beneath the hospital, and we emerge into the predawn London morning in a Range Rover with bulletproof windows and armoured plating around its frame.

Even though our location is supposed to be a secret, half the journalists on the planet are waiting for us at the exit, and Kit and I watch wordlessly through the tinted windows as they try to swarm the vehicle. The police hold them back behind the barriers, though, and our security team sees us swiftly onto the dark city streets, where we speed away from the hospital towards the relative safety of Windsor Castle.

"How bad is it?" I say to Jenkins. "The press coverage, I mean."

"It's the top story in virtually every English-speaking country around the world, and the majority that aren't," he says. "The BBC has been running wall-to-wall coverage of the bombing, though with no official word on His Majesty's condition, it's all speculation. I'd imagine our exit is already being shown on a loop."

"Are they wearing black?" says Kit, and though I don't understand the reference, Jenkins shakes his head.

"Not yet. Though there are plenty of rumours that it's only a matter of time."

Kit grimaces. "Are there plans to release an official statement?"

"As soon as Her Majesty feels it will not be misleading."

Kit must notice my confusion, because he says quietly, "Aunt Helene is – or was – waiting to see if he makes it through the night."

"Oh." I don't know how I feel about the thought of Helene

still being such an important part in all of this, not when she hung my parents out to dry less than two days ago. But her interview feels so inconsequential now that I can barely muster up any anger towards her. Just bone-deep exhaustion I'm not sure will ever go away.

We reach Windsor Castle as a hint of pink appears on the horizon, and even more journalists are waiting for us at the gates. This time, security has already cleared the road, and we speed through without so much as slowing down.

Tibby stands at the entrance nearest the private apartments, clutching her tablet as she watches us approach. I notice she's wearing low heels today, along with a grey dress that's so dark it's almost black, and somehow these are the details that make it all feel real to me – that make me realize this is going to impact the rest of our lives, and nothing will ever be the same.

She hugs me fiercely as soon as we're inside, and I let her fuss over me on our way to my apartment. She doesn't ask any questions about Alexander or the details of the bombing, and I don't know if it's out of respect or because there's a blanket ban on trying to wheedle information out of us. Either way, I'm grateful, though when she notices the bandage on my leg, I actually see her bite her tongue.

Kit and I separate long enough to wash the dust and blood away, and once I'm dressed, I head out into my sitting room, fully expecting Kit to be waiting for me alongside Tibby. But there's no sign of either of them, and instead I'm greeted by my frantically pacing sister.

"It's about bloody time." She pounces towards me with the speed and grace of a jungle cat, and I do my best not to grunt as she tackles me in a hug. I'm sorer now than I was in the immediate aftermath of the bombing, and my shoulder still aches, which doesn't exactly help. But I can tell from how tightly she holds me that she needs this, and I delicately hug her in return.

"Good call, staying home yesterday," I say in a pitiful attempt at a joke. But as soon as she pulls away and I see the tears brimming in her eyes, I immediately regret it.

"Have you seen him?" she says, her lower lip trembling. "No one will let me leave. Mummy told me it's touch and go, but beyond that, I don't know a thing, and I've been going mad trying to figure out a way to visit him—"

"I saw him right before we left," I say, trying to sound reassuring. "My mom and Constance have been with him all night. He's…"

I pause. I don't want to scare her more than she already is, but I don't want to give her false hope, either. My ears are ringing again, faintly now, and I suck in a breath.

"We'll find a way for you to see him after the meeting," I say at last. "Even if we have to sneak you out of here."

She wipes her eyes, and I can tell she understands everything I'm not saying. "I don't know if that'll be possible," she admits. "The prime minister himself told me to stay put. It's a matter of national security, apparently."

Privately I agree. I don't want to imagine the chaos if Maisie is somehow hurt in all this, too. "Then we'll VidChat my mom, all right? We'll figure it out. Now tell me about this meeting and why you decided to drag me out of bed so early."

I expect this to be a neutral topic, or at the very least easier to bear than the thought of Alexander's mangled body, but Maisie's lower lip quivers again, and I think she might actually burst into tears.

"The entire senior staff will be there," she manages, her voice not much more than a squeak. "I'm of age now, and – and they'll all be – looking to me for instruction, but—" She sniffs and dabs at her cheeks with the cuff of her midnight-blue sweater. "I don't know what to do, Evan. This wasn't supposed to happen for decades."

"It hasn't happened yet," I say, trying to sound reassuring, even though the idea still makes me reel. "Everyone coming to this meeting was hired by Alexander for a reason, and they know what they're doing. Listen to them. Listen to your mom and Nicholas, and remember they're all there to support you, not the other way arou—"

A sharp knock cuts me off, and even though this is my apartment, Maisie calls for whoever it is to enter. A beat later, Jenkins opens the door, his expression even more sombre than it was when he left me in Tibby's hands.

My heart drops to my knees. "What's wrong? Is Alexander—"

"His Majesty's condition has not changed," he says hastily. "But I fear there is a…situation in the conference room that requires Her Royal Highness's immediate attention."

I glance at Maisie, and she smooths the fear from her face and draws herself up to her full height. In the space of a single heartbeat, she goes from my terrified half-sister to heir to the throne – one who could become queen at any moment – and I bite my lip, silently wondering if this is the last time I'll see her like that. Raw and vulnerable and genuine, without the weight of the entire country and Commonwealth on her shoulders.

As the three of us head into the long gallery, we're joined by a nervous-looking Tibby and a silent but steady Kit, who gives me a questioning look. I shrug. Whatever's going on now, I suspect there are a lot of *situations* that are going to require Maisie's attention, and this kind of grave urgency is something we all need to get used to.

As we climb the staircase to the upper floors, I wince at the pain in my leg, and Kit wordlessly takes my elbow. I have no right to complain, not when Ingrid's dead and Alexander's fighting for his life, but I'm still embarrassingly slow, and by the time Kit and I catch up to the others, they're standing in front of the closed doorway to the conference room.

Fitz, Maisie's private secretary, is already waiting for her, his suit jacket wrinkled and his red hair sticking up like he hasn't brushed it in days. Tibby doesn't even try to hide her disdain, and as he briefs Maisie in a low voice, she joins Kit and me, her scowl deep and her jaw set.

"Utterly incompetent. Has he never heard of a bloody comb?" mutters Tibby before refocusing on me. "I expect you won't have to do or say much. Just listen, and remember that everyone inside that room is there to keep things running as smoothly as possible in His Majesty's absence. And if Maisie seems like she needs a break, it's completely within your rights to call for—"

"*What?*" My sister's voice cuts through Tibby's murmur, and Fitz flushes.

"I – I'm very sorry, Your Royal Highness, but there was nothing I could do—"

Maisie lets out a curse so vile that even Tibby looks taken aback, and Jenkins steps forward. "Security is on standby, Your

Royal Highness," he says. "Should you choose that particular route."

I have no idea what he's talking about, but my sister grits her teeth and pushes open the door with the force of a tornado. I glance at Kit, both alarmed and intrigued, and we follow her into the room just in time to see Maisie round on someone sitting near the empty seat at the head of the table.

"How *dare* you show your face now," she says, her voice shaking with fury. "You've no right to be here. *None*."

"I think you'll find that I have every right to be here, especially now," says a mild voice that chases away every trace of exhaustion inside me, leaving nothing but adrenaline and anger behind.

Sitting beside his father, with his blond hair pushed back casually from his face and his lips twisted into the faintest hint of a smirk, is Ben.

Chapter Twenty-six

A job well done.

That depends entirely on whether he's still breathing

No updates yet.
I'll let you know as soon as I hear.
How did you manage it, anyway?

What did I tell you about asking questions?

It's already done.
There's no harm in telling me.

I lost loyal followers to this, and I've taken enough of a risk without giving you something else to hold over me.

What happened to mutually assured destruction?

Forgive me for thinking you'd ever pay the price.
Send me an update as soon as you hear.
I need to plan our next move.

I've already moved forward with the photo.
It should hit the news cycle any moment now.
Was she one of them?

Yes. Not an easy loss.

It'll all be worth it. For both of us.

– *Text message exchange between two prepaid mobile numbers, 13 January 2024*

While there are more than two dozen people crammed around the long conference table, no one says a word as Maisie takes a menacing step towards Ben, her fists clenched like she actually knows how to use them.

"Did you hit your head?" she says nastily. "Or have you conveniently forgotten what His Majesty told you before we left for Klosters?"

Ben leans back in his chair and surveys her with the arrogance of someone who thinks he's untouchable. "I believe the word 'banished' may have been batted around once or twice," he says. "By all means, if Uncle Alexander feels the need to remind me, he's more than welcome to do so."

"That is *enough*," says Constance sharply from the seat across from him, while Maisie looks like she's about to burst into flames. The Queen Mother sits beside an expressionless Helene, who, to her credit, seems like she's only barely managed to pull herself together for this meeting, with her hair limp, the cords of her neck strained, and the circles beneath her eyes so dark they're purple.

Ben's smirk is unmistakable now as he looks at us one by one, and while it may be my imagination, I swear his searing gaze lingers on me for a beat longer than the others. "I can't be the only one who's actually *read* the Regency Act of 2005," he says. "That is why we're all here, is it not?"

I barely have time to wonder how he knows that before Maisie speaks up again. "It has nothing to do with you, Benedict—"

"I think you'll find that it does," he says. "I don't have the exact wording in front of me, so forgive me if I'm paraphrasing, but I do believe it states that should the heir to the throne be eighteen at the time of ascension or regency, then the four most senior members of the royal family shall gather to advise her, and to rule by council until she turns twenty-one. Am I wrong?"

Maisie slowly turns a shade of red I've never actually seen on a human face before. "It doesn't mean *you*."

"As I said before, dear cousin, I think you'll find that it does," says Ben, and there's a hint of victory in his voice that makes me want to wring his neck.

My sister narrows her eyes. "Then I suppose we'll just have to remove you, won't we?" she says. "It should be a simple vote. Four to one, I think—"

"You aren't Queen yet, Your Royal Highness," says Ben. "And even if Uncle Alexander dies today, I believe you'll find that you won't have the power to get rid of me for another two and a half years. The act is ironclad. Uncle Alexander's rather clever that way, isn't he? Or...wasn't he?" He drums his fingers against the mahogany table. "I'm afraid I've been remiss in asking how our beloved King is doing. Or not doing, so to speak." It's only Kit's tightening grip on my elbow that stops me from launching myself at Ben, and Maisie actually takes a step towards him. But whether it's the dozens of curious eyes on her, or the very real possibility that Ben does in fact know what he's talking about, she stops herself from getting too close and instead turns to Helene.

"Mummy," she demands, "he can't be here. He can't be part of this."

Helene exchanges a look with Nicholas, who's leaning slightly away from his son. "I'm afraid Benedict is correct," she says, her honeyed voice brittle. "Alexander was...very specific about the requirements in the event of his incapacitation, and unfortunately we're all bound to them. Any change would require an act of Parliament, which would surely take time, and it would, I fear, also require an explanation. A public explanation."

Ben pushes a lock of hair out of his eyes, practically basking in the glory of his win. "Would you like to be the one to explain to Parliament and the entire world why you don't want me here, Maisie? Or would you prefer I elaborate for you?"

For a split second, she tenses in a way that makes it seem like she really is about to knock him upside the head. But Jenkins clears his throat, and he pointedly positions himself between them, heading off the fight that Ben is so gleefully stoking.

"If I may, Your Royal Highness," he says to Maisie. She nods stiffly, still glaring at Ben with the heat of a thousand suns, and Jenkins turns towards him. "Your recollection of the Regency Act of 2005 is mostly correct, Your Royal Highness. But I fear there is one point in particular that you have misinterpreted."

Ben goes very still. "Is that so?" he says, an edge to his voice.

"Indeed," says Jenkins. "The act asks that the four *blood* relatives closest to His Majesty and the heir to the throne, including the Counsellors of State, step up to advise Her Royal Highness. It never specifies that they must be designated senior royals – or even royalty at all."

In an instant, all eyes are on me, and with sharp horror, I realize why I'm here. "Wait," I say suddenly. "*Wait*—"

"Is this a joke?" says Ben, leaning forward in his chair so quickly that he nearly leaps out of it. "Evangeline isn't any older than Maisie—"

"She meets the age requirement of eighteen," says Jenkins mildly. "And forgive me, Your Royal Highness, but you yourself are only nineteen."

Ben sputters. "But – she's *American*. That alone invalidates her eligibility—"

A peal of laughter escapes from Maisie, so unexpected that even Ben looks taken aback. "Evan has a British passport," she manages. "And I'm fairly certain that as far as close relatives go, *daughter* trumps *estranged nephew* by a bloody mile."

I'm still reeling, trying to absorb what no one has actually said out loud, but Ben stands rigidly, fixing his glare on me. "A matter of interpretation," he says, like this is somehow my fault. "And I'm certain the palace lawyers will see it my way."

Jenkins clears his throat again. "I fear it is not a matter of interpretation," he says. "I helped His Majesty draft the clause in question, and he was exceptionally clear about his intention. He worded it in such a way to specifically ensure that Her Royal Highness would have the support of the three Counsellors of State – Her Majesty the Queen, Her Majesty the

Queen Mother and His Royal Highness the Duke of York – and her only sibling, Evangeline Bright, once they both turned eighteen. There was, in fact, no discussion regarding your involvement in any potential regency. Sir."

Jenkins says this last word with just a hint of bite, though his posture is straight and his expression unmoving. And I'm absolutely sure that even if Ben enlists half the lawyers in the UK to fight him on this, Jenkins will stand his ground until the bitter end.

Someone knocks on the door jamb, and Kit and I turn to find two members of the palace security team standing directly behind us. They don't say a word, but they don't have to, and when I look at Ben again, he's turned an unhealthy shade of puce.

"I see," says Ben through his clenched jaw, and yet again, he eyes us one by one until his stare falls on me. There's a new layer to his hatred now – a malevolence so intense that it chills me to the bone. "Then I suppose that settles it. Though I wouldn't be terribly surprised if the public were…less than enthusiastic about Evangeline playing a role in this, all things considered."

He lets this hang in the air like it's an invitation, but I know better than to give him that kind of opening. And no one else, not even my viciously smug sister, takes it. After a beat, his smirk returns, and he smooths the front of his jacket.

"I'll see you all rather soon, I suspect," he says, as if he's the victor in this battle. And maybe, in his own mind, he is. "Father. Grandmother. Aunt Helene. Good luck."

He slides past Maisie without a second glance, but Jenkins, I notice, has to step aside to avoid being directly in his path. And when Ben reaches the door, he pauses as he peers down at me, and the air between us is so charged that a single spark could set it on fire.

"Rest assured, Evangeline, that this is only the beginning," he says with eerie calm. And just when I think he's about to keep going, he leans down so close that his lips brush against my ear. "It was meant to be you."

I suck in a breath, stunned. "What the hell is that supposed to mean?" I say raggedly, but as he tilts his head, the picture of innocence, I already know the answer.

I was the one who was supposed to die under a mountain of rubble. Not Alexander, not Ingrid, not the seven other victims – that bomb was meant for me.

Kit steps forward, danger radiating from him. "I believe Her Royal Highness has made it clear that you are no longer welcome here," he says with inhuman calm, and Ben chuckles.

"My condolences on your most recent failure, Lord Clarence," he says. "Perhaps you'll finally get the job done next time." And with an enormous wink at Kit, he finally passes through the doorway, waving aside the officers as he strides down the hall and out of sight.

The room is deadly silent. Rattled, I try to catch Kit's eye, but his gaze is focused on the empty doorway, and his lips are parted, almost like he's seen a ghost.

"What is he talking about?" I whisper, but Kit shakes his head and slides a protective arm around my shoulders.

"You should sit," he says, and before I can protest, he leads me around the table to the now-empty chair beside Nicholas. I hesitate, ready to insist that I'm perfectly fine standing, but once again, all eyes are on me. And so I ease down into the chair, my skin crawling when I discover the leather is still warm.

I don't want to be here. I don't want anything to do with Parliament or politics or a maybe-regency for my critically injured father, but even though no one's said it out loud, it's clear now that I'm the only thing standing between Ben and a position on this royal council. And while his whispered words and their terrible implication still slither through my mind, I can't discount the likelihood that they're designed to do exactly this – to shake me so badly that I race out of there and never come back, leaving his seat vacant once more.

And so, knowing I need to tell someone but also painfully aware that now is *not* the time, I shove my trembling hands between my knees and make myself as small as possible. Kit remains behind me, and I take all the comfort I can from his presence, though for once, it isn't enough.

"Well, then," says Maisie as she sits at the head of the table – Alexander's spot. "Shall we get on with it?"

"How is His Majesty?" says Yara immediately, her complexion bloodless. "Is his condition really so poor as to require...this?"

"The King's injuries are grave," admits Helene, her gaze fixed on the table in front of her. "And if he does survive, there is a... significant possibility they will have a permanent impact on his quality of life. And, potentially, his ability to rule."

This is new information to me, although considering I'm one of the only people in that room who's actually seen Alexander, it shouldn't be. Shock and devastation flicker across Maisie's face, and it's only thanks to what must be a supreme act of willpower that she pulls herself together before she falls to pieces.

"*When* my father recovers," she says, as if challenging not only her mother, but the entire universe to prove her wrong, "we will of course dissolve this council. But until then, we will do our solemn duty to protect and uphold His Majesty's rule."

I stay silent as Jenkins situates himself in the empty spot beside me and leads the meeting from topic to topic, starting with when to release a delicately worded statement about Alexander's condition, and then moving on to how to divide his duties between the members of the royal family – which, to my relief, doesn't seem to include me. Maisie and Helene take the lion's share, but when the topic of public appearances comes up, Nicholas stands.

"There will be no public appearances until we can be certain that all participants of the attack on His Majesty have been rounded up," he insists. "We will not put other members of the family at risk."

"MI5 has already made several arrests in the case, Your Royal Highness," says a man I recognize as the head of palace security – Victor Stephens. "We're working closely with the Home Office to ensure the royal family's safety."

Nicholas nods. "Good. And when we do start to venture out into the world again, I insist that Princess Mary be accompanied by another senior royal whenever she is in public."

Maisie stares at our uncle. "Pardon me?" she says, though there's no politeness in her voice. "With all due respect, our security is the best in the world. I don't need a minder."

"You're in an exceptionally vulnerable position," says Nicholas, "and you will need support from those of us with the experience to guide you."

"And I will have it, in private," says Maisie fiercely. "I suppose *you'd* prefer to escort me everywhere I go?"

"Yes," says Nicholas. "After what's happened to my brother, I very much would."

She gives him a contemptuous look. "You're not superhuman, Uncle Nicholas. You're not going to single-handedly stop a building from falling on me."

"Likely not," he agrees, "but my military background gives me insight into the security of public events that the other members of this family do not have."

"And you don't think our *actual* security team might have a problem with you stepping in to play bodyguard?" She shakes her head. "We need to give the people a sense of stability – a sense of continuity and safety and peace, and the last thing they need is a steady stream of images of their princess being followed around like a child who can't be trusted. I know I'm young, and I know I have a lot to learn, but I will *not* give the country a reason to doubt me, and I will *not* offer the media a single bloody excuse to claim I'm incapable of upholding my duties as the future—"

Suddenly the door flies open, and a sweaty Doyle bursts into the room, clutching a tablet. Despite the sea of people now staring at him, his wild eyes immediately find me.

"Pardon me, Your Majesties, Your Royal Highnesses," he says with a quick bow to the head of the table. "I'm afraid there's a matter that needs immediate attention."

"Is there something more important going on than the attempt on His Majesty's life?" says Jenkins calmly, and Doyle reddens.

"I—" He shakes his head, seeming to think better of it. "Jenkins, you need to see this."

Doyle manoeuvres past an irritable Maisie, and Kit presses against my chair to give him enough space to reach Jenkins. Breathing heavily, Doyle hands the tablet over, and as Jenkins examines the screen, he grows very, very still.

"What am I looking at?" he says in a quiet voice that doesn't carry any farther than a few feet.

"That one right there..." Doyle reaches over to swipe to a separate page, still panting like he's run a marathon. "Her identity was just released. And as you can see, she's—"

"*Everyone out.*"

Jenkins's commanding voice echoes off the walls, louder than I've ever heard him before, and a shocked murmur ripples through the crowd. Confused, I glance up at Kit, but his eyes are fixed on the tablet, and his fingers dig so deeply into the leather of my chair that I can't even inch back enough to stand.

"You forget yourself, Jenkins," snaps Constance, while Helene looks like she's been slapped across the face.

"My apologies, Your Majesty," says Jenkins, his words unnervingly sharp as he pulls the tablet to his chest. "But I'm afraid we need to adjourn this meeting. I will be in touch with the Privy Council to make all the necessary arrangements, and in the meantime, it is my strongest recommendation that the royal family take a few hours to rest. The days ahead are bound to be difficult, and you will need your strength."

But Maisie climbs to her feet, her annoyance with Nicholas transferring seamlessly to Jenkins. "Nothing could possibly be more important than this meeting," she says hotly as she marches over. "We still have several matters to discuss, and—"

Jenkins bows his head as she approaches. "Forgive me, Your

Royal Highness. Now that the royal council has been established, I fear this is currently a more pressing matter."

"What—" she says, but he shows her the tablet, swiping between what seems like two pages, and her perfectly plucked brows furrow. "Is that—"

"Yes, ma'am," he says.

"And that's one of the people who…?"

"Yes, ma'am."

She goes white, and her eyes lock on mine for an unbearably long moment before she straightens. "You heard Jenkins," she says. "Everyone out. Not you," she adds, her gaze flickering towards me once more. "And *certainly* not you."

This is directed towards Kit, who visibly gulps. By now, I'm practically burning with both curiosity and dread, but Jenkins and Maisie don't offer a single hint as every senior adviser except Doyle shuffles out, all looking as baffled as I feel.

"I must insist that we stay," says Constance once the room is nearly empty. Helene and Nicholas stand together at the head of the table now, but the Queen Mother hasn't budged from her seat.

"And I'm afraid I must insist that you excuse us for the time being, Grandmama," says Maisie. "I'll see you all at breakfast as soon as we're done here."

Constance opens her mouth to argue, but Nicholas sets his hand on her shoulder. "Mother, let's go," he says quietly. "Whatever this is, the sooner it's resolved, the sooner we can return to the matter at hand."

She doesn't look convinced, but after several seconds, it becomes clear that Maisie isn't going to cave, and Constance narrows her eyes. "You're every bit as insolent as your father," she says as she stands. "Do try to remember that you aren't the sovereign yet, darling."

"A fact for which I am exceptionally grateful at the moment," says Maisie hotly, glaring at Kit once more.

As soon as they've left, royal protection officers in tow, I wiggle out from between my seat and the table and finally stand. "What's going on?" I demand, facing the four of them. "Kit?"

He shakes his head, his dark eyes focused on the carpet now. "I'm sorry, Evan," he says with a desperate note in his voice. "I didn't know. I thought..." He rakes his fingers through his hair and finally looks at me, and his face is full of such naked vulnerability and fear that my insides turn to lead. "I didn't *know*."

"Out of all the things you two could've done," says Maisie, and to my shock, her voice catches like she's about to cry. "Are you both out of your bloody minds?"

"What are you talking about?" I say, alarmed. "*What is going on?*"

At last, with the reluctance of someone about to saw off their own limb, Jenkins shows me the tablet. I don't know what to expect, but the possibilities racing through my mind are too horrible to contemplate for long – and not at all like the innocuous picture on the screen.

The red-brick buildings of the town near Sandringham fill the background, and in the corner of the image, I can just make out the sign from Noble Norfolk Novelties, the ice cream-slash-gift-shop Kit and I visited. I'm standing on the sidewalk with the red-headed Aoife, who hugs me like we've known each other our whole lives. Kit lingers beside us, looking nervously over his shoulder, while Aoife's boyfriend – Dylan, I think – is facing away from the camera, his knit hat hiding any trace of his features.

Bewildered, I search the photo for some hidden image – some clue as to why they're all panicking. "Those are Kit's friends from school," I say. "We ran into them when we were picking up presents for my mom. That's right after Maisie texted Kit about Ben – we were heading back, and—"

"So you do know her?" says Maisie like this is somehow a massive betrayal.

"Aoife? No, not really. This is the only time we ever met. She hugged me before I could get away, that's all. Kit—" I say, turning to him for confirmation, but his entire body is hunched over the back of my chair now, and he looks like he's about to collapse.

"Evan," says Jenkins in a measured voice. "This woman's name is Aoife Marsh. You're *absolutely* certain this is the only time you two have met?"

"Positive," I say, my heart thumping so hard that I can hear my pulse. "Please, just tell me what's going on. You're scaring me." For a split second, no one replies. But at last, with a heavy sigh, Jenkins swipes to another tab, and the BBC home page appears. A single headline dominates the screen:

TERRORISTS BEHIND BOMBING IDENTIFIED

"The Home Office has released the names of the suspects arrested yesterday in connection to the bombing," says Jenkins. "And Aoife Marsh – the girl you're hugging in this photo – is one of them."

Chapter Twenty-seven

We at the *Regal Record* can exclusively reveal that Evangeline Bright, illegitimate daughter of the King, is allegedly a close friend of one of the suspected terrorists in the bombing of the Modern Music Museum in London.

Evangeline and Aoife Marsh, 19, pictured together below, met last year through Christopher Abbott-Montgomery, Earl of Clarence, and the two have reportedly been in constant contact ever since. Marsh was one of three suspects arrested at the scene of the bombing yesterday morning, during an official visit from the King, whose condition remains unknown. Eight others were killed in the blast, including two royal protection officers thought to be guarding His Majesty.

Both Evangeline and Lord Clarence were present during the attack, though the couple, who began dating this past summer, were released from a London hospital in the early hours of this morning. Evangeline was infamously involved in the death of Jasper Cunningham this past June, but was not charged despite alluding to her guilt in a live interview that aired weeks later.

There has so far been no word from the Home Office on the connection between Evangeline, Lord Clarence and Marsh, though we can only hope that with eight families mourning the loss of their loved ones today, no one, not even the daughter of the King, will be above the law this time.

– The *Regal Record*, 13 January 2024

Aoife, Kit's sweet and bubbly friend from university, tried to kill my father.

Aoife, whose beaming face is clearly visible over my shoulder in the image on Doyle's tablet, is responsible for the deaths of Ingrid and seven other innocent people.

Aoife, who's hugging me like we're best friends and have known each other our entire lives, is an actual terrorist.

And somehow the only picture of us together has surfaced barely twenty-four hours after the bombing.

My stomach twists so violently that I think I might be sick, and slowly, as if one wrong move will make me fall apart, I sink down onto the edge of the mahogany table, my head spinning.

I don't know what to say. There's nothing *to* say, not when the media will take this picture and wring every last drop of conjecture and bad-faith assumption out of it. Even if the palace tries to claim it's photoshopped, even if the royal press office manages to convince the BBC and CNN and every other major news outlet that Aoife and I've only met once, this single photo will inevitably make headlines around the world. And this time, it'll be my name trending with *#offwithherhead*.

"Do we know where it came from?" says Jenkins to Doyle, who grunts ambiguously.

"A gossip site called the *Regal Record* posted it fifteen minutes ago," he says, and Maisie sneers. "I already have my team trying to get them to take it down, but—"

"They won't," says Jenkins grimly, pinching the bridge of his nose. "Bloody hell. How do we get ahead of this?"

"I don't know that we do," admits Doyle. "We can release a statement making it clear that she and Evangeline have no connection, but it won't do any good, not if Lord Clarence knows her. The media will immediately frame it as a cover-up."

Maisie crosses her arms tightly over her chest, her lower lip caught between her teeth before she speaks. "Talk to us, Kit. How do you know these people? *Why* do you know these people?"

Kit's eyes are still glued to the floor, and when he speaks, it seems to take him an enormous amount of effort. "I knew Dylan at Eton," he rasps like he hasn't had water in days. "We ended up on the same course at university. I...I didn't suspect anything was off until recently, but—"

"Until recently?" I blurt, stunned. "You knew they were...?"

"No," he says firmly, and finally he looks at me. "I didn't know they were involved in this sort of thing, Evan, I swear. They—" He grimaces. "They're members of a group called Fox Rex."

"The dinner club?" says Doyle, seemingly flabbergasted. "I remember it from my Christ Church days. Wasn't it banned years ago?"

"Yes," says Kit, but his focus is still on me. "Though apparently it was resurrected as a secret society. Over the summer, I discovered that my brother was a member, and...they invited me to join at the start of term."

Secret societies aren't news to me – there were plenty of those at the boarding schools I attended, but as far as I know, none of them turned into terrorist organizations. "What does that have to do with the bombing?" I say.

"I'm getting there," he assures me, his Adam's apple bobbing. "I turned them down at first, and they started to push, particularly

Dylan and Aoife. Dylan has always been...outspoken about his politics. He's a republican," he adds, and he must see the question on my face, because he clarifies, "In the UK, it means he's an anti-monarchist. He doesn't support the royal family."

"Oh," I say. "Is that why you were nervous when we ran into them?"

"One of the reasons," he admits. "And...because it's relevant, if my aunt weren't who she is, I'd likely lean that way as well. Which I made the mistake of mentioning to Dylan while we were at Eton, before I ended up with a bloody courtesy title."

This is news, and I stare at him. "You're a...republican, too?"

He shakes his head, and I can see the pleading in his eyes. "Not in the way they are. *Never* in the way they are. The things Dylan would let slip when he was drinking..." A muscle in his jaw twitches. "He told me on Bonfire Night that among the more senior members of the club, it isn't Fox Rex. It's *Fawkes* Rex. As in Guy Fawkes."

"The fifth of November guy?" I say, and this earns a loud snort of derision from Maisie.

"Honestly, what *have* your tutors been teaching you?" she mutters. "Yes, the traitor who tried to blow up Westminster Palace in the Gunpowder Plot of 1605. He and his co-conspirators wanted to assassinate King James I. Though *they* intended to place a Catholic monarch on the throne in his stead," she adds. "Not abolish it entirely. That was far more of a Cromwellian thing."

"I don't know what that means—"

"And not one of us is surprised," she says, cutting me off. "Kit, will you *please* get to the bloody point?"

He flinches, and when he continues, he's looking at me again, as if I'm the only thing that matters about any of this. "The more Dylan let slip, the more I wondered if...perhaps it didn't have something to do with the reason why Liam..." He pauses, pain flickering in his deep brown eyes. "I was chasing ghosts, and Dylan could tell. He mentioned my brother a few times, hinted that I might find some answers, and finally I agreed to join. I didn't question *why* they wanted me so badly, but as soon as I became a member, it was clear my presence offered their more... extreme political leanings legitimacy."

"In what way?" says Jenkins. Kit exhales.

"I discovered that everyone invited was an anti-monarchist to some degree. And while I'm not – I'm *not*," he insists at Maisie's quirked eyebrow. "Even then, my courtesy title, my future dukedom, Aunt Helene...it was as if they could put me on a pedestal and claim they were surely on the right side of history, if even the nephew of the King and Queen wanted to be part of it. As soon as I realized what sort of mess I'd gotten myself into, I tried to disengage. We were nearing the end of term by then anyway, and it was easy to prioritize exams."

"Why didn't you tell me?" I say, my voice small and pathetic, but the words are out before I know they're coming.

"I'm sorry, Ev," says Kit, and his hand flexes like he wants to reach for me, but he doesn't close the distance between us. "I'm so bloody sorry. I wanted to tell you, but...I could never find the right words. And you've had enough on your plate lately, with everything that happened over the summer, and I didn't want you to worry."

Part of me isn't surprised, though that doesn't stop it all from hurting anyway. "You should have said something," I say. "I could have helped. Or – I would've at least listened."

"I know," he says, his voice barely audible now. "I'm sorry. It wasn't you – it was never you. I was…ashamed that I got taken in like that. That I didn't see them coming, and the last thing I wanted was for you to get tangled up in it as well."

"Too late now," I mutter, glaring at the tablet. "That picture… Kit, it makes it look like – like—"

"I know." His eyes are shining with tears now. "I had no idea. It must've been a set-up – it was too much of a coincidence to run into them, and now the photo…"

"Do you have reason to believe there's a connection between this Fawkes Rex club and the Army of the British Republic?" says Jenkins. "They're the ones who've taken credit for the attack, though MI5 has yet to confirm their involvement."

Kit shakes his head, but at the same time, he gestures towards the screen. "Aoife's proof, isn't she? And the other names that were released…I recognize them, too."

Doyle mutters several curses under his breath, while Maisie's posture stiffens. "You're certain?" she says.

"That I recognize the names? Yes," says Kit. "That Fawkes Rex has any direct ties to this Army of the British Republic outside of Aoife and her cohorts? No. It could feed the other way – Aoife could have been involved with the bombers before she joined the club, or the other members could've roped her into it. I thought – I thought it was all theoretical," he adds, pinching the bridge of his nose. "If I'd known for a second that there was a plan, or any chance they might've taken action…"

He trails off, and my sister watches him, her expression

unforgiving. "You need to speak to MI5 immediately," says Maisie. "The photo's already out there, and we've no hope of getting ahead of it now. But we can at least come up with a reasonable explanation that has a chance of mitigating the damage and proving your innocence. And Evan's," she adds, glancing at me. "But the fact that you two were there yesterday… it doesn't look good."

No, it doesn't, and as I stare at the picture again, I finally begin to understand just how bad this all is.

"Doyle," says Jenkins, "draft a statement for anyone who asks about the photograph. Make it clear that Evangeline's met thousands of people during her time in the UK, and find pictures of her hugging other fans to send to journalists who are friendly to us."

"I could spin it into a security issue," suggests Doyle. "Make it seem like we're deeply concerned that someone like Aoife Marsh was able to gain access to Evangeline and accost her in the street."

"Do whatever you have to do to steal the narrative," agrees Jenkins. "Lord Clarence, I'll have one of the palace lawyers join you before MI5 arrives. Follow their directions to the letter, is that understood?"

Kit nods mutely.

"Good. Your Royal Highness, as soon as everything is taken care of, I'll update you and the rest of the royal family."

"Please do," says Maisie with stiff bravado, but I can see the fear in her eyes.

"And Evan…" Jenkins takes my hand in his, and it's only then that I realize I'm trembling. "It's likely that you'll need to speak to MI5 as well, I'm afraid. Is that something you're willing to do?"

I try to nod, but it's taking everything I have not to cry. Jenkins watches me for a long moment before pulling me into a gentle hug, and I cling to him as a single sob finally escapes.

"We'll sort this out, darling," he murmurs into my ear. "I promise. None of this is your fault."

But as bad as it all is for me, that's not the reason I'm crying. Instead, I watch Kit over Jenkins's shoulder, both furious with him and terrified for him at the same time.

"I need to..." I try to say, but the words come out as a croak, and I clear my throat. "I need to talk to Kit. Alone. Please."

Doyle looks dubious at best, and even Maisie hesitates, but it's Jenkins who shakes his head. "I don't think that's a good idea, sweetheart."

I pull back. "What? Why not?"

"Because this way, the three of us can assure the Home Office that there's been no collusion between the two of you now that we know about Lord Clarence's connection to the suspects."

"Collusion?" I stumble over the word. "Jenkins, this isn't some spy movie—"

"He's right, Evan," says Kit thickly. "If this gets...sticky for me, the palace is going to focus on protecting you. And they can't do that if you're trying to protect me."

"I—" I look between them, stunned. "So what, you're going to separate us?"

Doyle dabs his forehead with a handkerchief. "For the time being, it would be...wise for Lord Clarence to keep his distance from the royal family," he says. "Not only from a legal perspective, but the optics—"

"But he didn't do anything wrong," I protest. "If you kick him out, it'll look like we think he did. *Jenkins*—"

"I'm sorry, darling, but this is all rather serious, I'm afraid," he says, still holding my hand. "We'll know more once you and Lord Clarence speak to the Home Office."

I open and shut my mouth, momentarily speechless, and finally I look at my sister. "Maisie, please," I beg. "He's your cousin."

"So is Ben." Her eyes are red as she meets mine. "I'm sorry, Evan. You told me to listen to my advisers, and...I'm listening."

I push off the edge of the table with such force that my leg nearly buckles beneath me. "This isn't fair," I say jaggedly. "You know it's not fair. You can't just throw him to the wolves because it's easier—"

"We're not throwing anyone to the wolves," says Jenkins. "You're right, Evan. He didn't do anything wrong. But we need the opportunity to prove that. He'll have our best lawyers with him, and when it's all said and done, everything will be fine."

"How can you say that when—" I begin, but a tentative brush against my shoulder startles me, and as I whirl around, Kit snatches his hand back, every bit as fearful of touching me as he was during those first few weeks we knew each other. This, more than anything, is what breaks me, and when I finally close the distance between us and throw myself into his arms, it's a relief to feel him embrace me in return.

"It's all right," he murmurs into my hair – not a whisper, not a secret Jenkins and Doyle and Maisie can hold against us. "As soon as we talk to MI5, it'll all be settled. Dylan and Aoife have been texting me about the club for months, and I have everything I need to prove I had nothing to do with any of this. And that you didn't, either."

The ringing in my ears grows louder again as I hold him, refusing to let go. All I can picture are the terrible ways this could end – the worst-case scenarios that have Aoife and Dylan claiming Kit was part of this all along, that he offered them access and information and gave them everything they needed to pull this off. I can see the headlines. I can hear the jeers and the boos. I can imagine the talking heads and media figures tearing him down, mentioning his name in the same breath as Aoife Marsh and acting like they were in this together the entire time. And I'm terrified.

At last it's Kit who gently pushes me away, until I'm clutching the fabric of his jacket and staring up at his blurry face. "I'll see you soon, Ev," he promises, resting his forehead against mine. That small gesture is enough to remind me of what my parents have been through and how everything in their lives conspired against them, and I am desperate – *desperate* to not let that happen to us.

"I love you," I say, the words easy even if I have to force them past the lump in my throat. And despite the way everything is going so incredibly wrong, he manages a tiny, genuine smile.

"I love you, too," he says, pressing his lips to my temple. And then it's Jenkins's arm around me instead, leading me to the exit. I watch Kit over my shoulder until we reach the doorway, and the last image I see of him is of his hand pressed to his mouth, and the utter despair he must've been holding at bay finally creeping over him, stealing the last of his smile.

Chapter Twenty-eight

"Henrietta, with all that's happened in the past twenty-four hours, I scarcely know where to begin."

"It's all been rather shocking, hasn't it? But with the statement that was just released from Buckingham Palace regarding the King's condition, we're finally starting to see some answers."

"His Majesty is alive – that's certainly more than some were speculating."

"Alive, yes, but given the news that the royal family is invoking certain clauses of the Regency Act of 2005, it's clear that his injuries are extensive and potentially life-threatening."

"Can you tell us more about the Regency Act, Henrietta? And how it may affect us all in the days and weeks to come?"

"The first modern-day Regency Act was passed in 1936, after Edward VIII took the throne when his son, who later became Alexander I, was only seven years old. Parliament wanted to ensure that there was a clear path forward if Edward VIII died before his heir reached the age of eighteen, and that involved creating the position of Counsellors of State – members of the royal family over the age of twenty-one who may perform most of the sovereign's duties, should he be temporarily incapacitated or abroad. Traditionally these include the monarch's consort and the first four adults in the line of succession, though as the royal family began to slim down in recent generations, the number has fluctuated. Now the heir to the throne is included, should they be over the age of eighteen, as well as the consort of the former sovereign."

"The Queen Mother, you mean?"

"Indeed. Queen Florence, His Majesty's grandmother, was also a Counsellor of State until her retirement from public duties shortly before her death."

"And who are the Counsellors of State today?"

"Officially, the Queen, the Queen Mother, the Duke of York, and Princess Mary, now that she's eighteen, are the only four Counsellors of State. Prince Benedict, of course, is still under the age of twenty-one, and Prince Edgar, the fourth in line to the throne and second son of Alexander I, does not reside in Britain, nor do his descendants. After him come the descendants of Edward VIII's daughters, Princess Victoria and Princess Phillipa, none of whom have titles or are actively involved in royal life."

"So in this time of great need, we are short a Counsellor of State."

"Indeed. But there are several curiosities regarding the Regency Act of 2005, most important of which deals with precisely the situation we've found ourselves in now –

what happens if His Majesty is incapacitated, either temporarily or permanently, before Princess Mary turns twenty-one."

"Presumably the monarchy would become a regency, yes?"

"It's possible, though a regency will only be established if His Majesty is permanently unable to perform his duties. In either case, after Princess Mary was born, the King worked with Parliament to outline a plan to ensure she would not be burdened with the full weight of the crown whilst still a teenager."

"And this is where this...royal council comes in, yes?"

"Precisely. His Majesty requested that should he be temporarily incapacitated, or should Her Royal Highness be placed in a position of regent or monarch before the age of twenty-one, she be assisted by four individuals: the Counsellors of State, and should this equal less than four, then her closest blood relatives over the age of eighteen."

"Which, until now, we all assumed was included to allow for Prince Benedict's involvement, considering he was born the year before Princess Mary."

"Yes. But it seems His Majesty has, as they say, pulled a fast one on us all. At the time the clause was drafted, he was very much aware that he had a second daughter – Evangeline Bright. And the statement from Buckingham Palace announcing the arrangement has made it clear that *she* was always the intended final member of the council, *not* Prince Benedict."

"A rather unusual choice for His Majesty to make,

considering Evangeline's existence was only revealed to the public last summer."

"'Unusual' doesn't even begin to cover it, I'm afraid. Parliament almost certainly wouldn't have accepted the wording as it stands had they known an illegitimate half-sibling would be involved, and I'd imagine that this won't help calm the inevitable chaos in the palace at the moment."

"What should we expect from this royal council, moving forward?"

"It's difficult to say, as such a council has never been established before, let alone placed in a position of authority over the monarchy. But I have no doubt that everyone involved wishes to work together towards the best interests of this country and its people, and with the experience of two queen consorts at Princess Mary's disposal, we can only hope the transition – whether temporary or permanent – is as smooth as possible, given the tragic circumstances."

"And if His Majesty, God forbid, succumbs to his injuries?"

"Should the unthinkable happen, then with the royal council's continued guidance, Princess Mary will officially ascend the throne, and the United Kingdom will have our first queen regnant since the age of Victoria."

– ITV News's interview with royal expert
Henrietta Smythe, 13 January 2024

I spend the rest of the morning in a much smaller conference room with Wiggs, the grey-haired palace lawyer who represented me during the investigation into Jasper Cunningham's death, as he takes me through every excruciating detail of my meeting with Aoife Marsh.

For the most part, he's sympathetic, but he has me repeat my story more than a dozen times, in different ways and from different angles, and I start to notice that his questions are designed to trip me up and catch me in a lie. And while I know that it's his job to make sure he has as much of the truth as I do before he squares off with MI5 for me, especially with the stakes so high, by the time Suraj Singh strides into the room with a laptop tucked under his arm, my nerves are frayed and my patience is dangerously close to zero.

"Miss Bright," he says politely, but instead of sitting down, he opens the laptop so I have a clear view of the blank screen. His suit is identical to the one he wore in the hospital the night before, and even though it looks clean and pressed, part of me wonders if he hasn't gone home.

"What's this about?" says Wiggs gruffly, eyeing the laptop. Singh taps a key, and the image of a human silhouette appears, its identifying features in shadow.

"This video was posted by the Army of the British Republic less than twenty minutes ago," says Singh as he sets the computer down on the table, and before Wiggs can ask any more questions, he hits Play.

" – rocked the entire world with our message, and we're only getting started," says a pitched voice as the silhouette shifts. "We have shown our so-called rulers that they are not and will never be our betters, and that they sit on their thrones because we the people allow it. Because we the people *tolerate* their existence, not because they have any true power, and the time has come for us to refuse to stand by and endure the shame of their lechery and depravity in the name of our great country."

A chill runs through me at the sheer loathing in those words, but even though there's nothing really happening on-screen, I can't tear my eyes away.

"For now, we must live in the shadows, loyal soldiers dedicated to a single cause. We rejoice in our suffering because we know it will lead to a future where the people will no longer have to live with the corruption, the theft, the *evil* with which our kings and queens built their empires, and we know that we alone have the will to stop them.

"But not all of us have remained hidden," continues the voice, and the silhouette seems to lean closer to the camera. "We are proud of those who have risked their lives for our cause, and prouder still of those who have risked their legacies. To have their names among ours, to know that even those who live in the nest of snakes can see the cruelty and immorality of their existence – this is what sparks us all into action, for even those who benefit from the systems that have held the people hostage are able to see that justice must be served."

The silhouette fades, and to my horror, a video clip starts to play – one of me and Aoife on the street outside the gift shop, filmed from at least thirty feet away. We're chatting like old friends, and as we move towards the Range Rover, she throws her arms around me as she says goodbye – and in my attempt not to offend her, I look like I'm hugging back. It's everything that damn photograph is, but worse, because no one, not even the palace, will be able to claim it's fake now. Or that it was a simple meet and greet gone terribly, unthinkably wrong.

"Our undying thanks to Evangeline Bright for the important role she played," says the pitched voice again, and I clutch the table so hard that I break a nail. "Without her contribution, our cause would have been lost, but now we are stronger than—"

Singh taps the keys again, and the screen goes blank. I open and shut my mouth, my head spinning as I try to think of something – *anything* – to explain why the apparent leader of the Army of the British Republic thanked me personally.

"I – I didn't have anything to do with—" I begin shakily, but Wiggs covers my hand in a silent attempt to get me to shut up. I don't, though – I physically can't stop myself, and I pull away. "I don't know these people. I only met that girl once, I swear—"

"I believe you," says Singh, and the rest of my protest dies on my tongue.

"You – what?" I say as he glances at me, then at Wiggs, who must wear a similar expression of incredulity, because despite the fact that I'm staring down the barrel of treason, there's a faint smile tugging at the corners of Singh's mouth.

He finally sits in a chair at the head of the table, next to me rather than across. "Tell me, Miss Bright," he says. "If you were running an underground organization determined to destroy the monarchy, and you were lucky enough to convince a member of the royal family to help, would you turn around and thank them publicly after failing to assassinate the King?"

This time I know better than to answer the question, and Wiggs clears his throat instead. "Miss Bright had nothing to do with the attempt on His Majesty's life, and was herself a victim who very nearly died—"

"Yes," says Singh with compassion I don't expect. "I was sorry to hear about your personal protection officer, Evangeline. I've been to the site of the bombing, and there is no question that that could have been – perhaps was meant to be – you."

I dig my nails into my palms as I remember the words Ben whispered to me only a few hours earlier. "She died to protect me," I say roughly. "I would never – *never* help these people try to kill my family and friends."

"On the outside looking in, there seems to be no sense in it, I agree," he says. "Though just because I don't see the connection right away doesn't mean there isn't one. In this particular case, however," he adds, gesturing towards the laptop, "it is far too neat. It's so perfect that it's sloppy."

I don't know what to say to that, or if I should say anything at all, and so I let Wiggs do the talking yet again. "Miss Bright only met the alleged bomber once, during a brief outing in Norfolk—"

"A fact which Lord Clarence has confirmed – multiple times, each more insistent than the last," says Singh. "I *will* need to hear your version of events, Evangeline. But for now, I'm far more curious why the Army of the British Republic would name you, specifically, as their accomplice."

"Miss Bright had nothing to do with—"

"Yet again, Mr Wiggs, I believe her." Singh eyes the pair of us. "Do you think it might be possible to work under the presumption that I am an ally, not an enemy? My goal is to find out what happened to His Majesty and the victims of the bombing, and to identify the members of this organization before they can do any more harm. It is quite curious to me that they would name Evangeline rather than the much more plausible Lord Clarence, and I'd like to hear her thoughts on why."

After a brief pause, Wiggs nods slightly towards me, and I gulp. "I don't know," I say at last. "None of it makes sense. That picture, the video – all of it had to be a set-up, but I don't know *why*."

My voice breaks on this last word, but I force myself to hold it together, and again I hear Ben's whisper.

It was meant to be you.

That wasn't the only thing he said before leaving the conference room, though. And with a sudden stark clarity, I look at Singh, my eyes wide.

"Ben," I blurt. "Prince Benedict, my cousin. He said something to me and Kit earlier—"

"Miss Bright," says Wiggs in a warning tone, but when I feel his touch again, I jerk away.

"I'd like to hear what His Royal Highness said," says Singh to Wiggs, but the words are already tumbling out of me.

"He told Kit – Christopher Abbott-Montgomery – he said something like, 'my condolences for your most recent failure. Maybe you'll finally get the job done next time.' I didn't understand what he was talking about," I add quickly, before either Singh or Wiggs can interrupt. "But I didn't know about – about the group Kit joined, or that Aoife was working for the bombers, or any of it."

Singh pulls a small notepad out of his suit jacket and flips through a few pages. "I don't recall Lord Clarence mentioning this interaction."

"Ask him," I say. "He'll tell you. Ask everyone seated by the door in the conference room – they could hear it, too."

Singh scribbles a note. "So you believe that your cousin, His Royal Highness Prince Benedict, is also trying to frame you?"

"That's quite enough," blusters Wiggs. "It's one thing to question Miss Bright about her involvement when she has been named by the organization in question, but to drag His Royal Highness into this when he is not here to defend himself—"

"He told me it was meant to be me," I say, and my voice wavers as my face grows hot. "In the conference room, before he accused Kit of being involved in the bombing – he whispered in my ear and said it was meant to be me."

Singh leans forward before Wiggs can come up with a coherent response. "And you believe His Royal Highness was referring to…?"

"Ingrid," I manage shakily. "Or maybe Alexander. I don't know. It was a threat. All he does is threaten me. Back in June, he told me he was going to destroy me, and now every time I see him, it's like he's trying to decide what to put on my gravestone. He was there at Sandringham when someone tried to kill me and Kit, but even though he was with Alexander and the rest of the hunting party, I'm sure he had something to do with it, and—"

"I'm afraid Miss Bright has had a very difficult few days," says Wiggs suddenly. "Unless you have any further questions regarding her single brief meeting with Aoife Marsh, then I must insist that you allow her time to rest."

My eyes are blurry with tears of frustration now, but I can still see Singh watching me. I want to say more – I should say more – but Wiggs is right. I have no evidence. I have no proof that Ben is behind any of this, only a bone-deep certainty that every terrible thing that's happened somehow points back to him. But he has an alibi for all of it, and while Ben may be many things, he isn't the kind of reckless that would ever let him slip. At least not where anyone else could see it.

"Yes, I think it might be prudent to continue this conversation at another time," agrees Singh, his dark eyes still on me as he closes his notebook. "For now, I would suggest you remain in the comfort of the royal residences, Evangeline. We don't have a full picture of what the Army of the British Republic's intentions are, nor what other plans may already be in motion, and it's best not to give them any opportunities."

Opportunities. "You mean chances to try again," I mumble, and he nods.

"Yes, among other things."

I stare at the grain of the polished wooden table as all the fight and stubbornness drain out of me. If I stay at Windsor, then I won't be able to sit with my mom at Alexander's bedside. But the thought of making her a target, too, is enough to nauseate me all over again, and I take a deep breath and nod.

"Everyone's going to think Kit and I were behind this, aren't they?" I say in a small voice.

"It's likely, for the time being," says Singh plainly. "Should this all be a misunderstanding, however, no doubt the public will be relieved to hear it."

That's definitely not true. I'm still being blamed for Jasper's death in plenty of corners of the internet, and no matter what happens next, I know that those same people will latch onto these accusations like leeches until there's nothing left of the truth to believe. And by the time this is over, even if the prime minister himself declares on national television that I had absolutely nothing to do with this, it'll be too late.

Everyone in the world is going to think I tried to kill my father. And I have no way to prove I didn't.

Chapter Twenty-nine

BOMBERS CLAIM EVANGELINE BRIGHT AS ALLY

– BBC News, 13 January 2024

AMERICAN PRINCESS REPORTEDLY INVOLVED IN ROYAL BOMBING

– CNN, 13 January 2024

HEAD OF ARMY OF BRITISH REPUBLIC: THANK YOU, EVANGELINE

– *The Daily Sun*, 13 January 2024

ROYAL FAMILY ON LOCKDOWN – EVANGELINE REMAINS AT WINDSOR

– BBC News, 14 January 2024

PRESIDENT PARK WISHES KING ALEXANDER SPEEDY RECOVERY, CONDEMNS TERRORISTS RESPONSIBLE FOR MUSEUM BOMBING

– CNN, 14 January 2024

EVANGELINE NAMED OFFICIAL SUSPECT IN BOMBING BY HOME OFFICE

– *The Daily Sun*, 14 January 2024

EVANGELINE REMAINS AT WINDSOR WITH PRINCESS MARY DESPITE CONNECTION TO ROYAL BOMBING

– BBC News, 15 January 2024

PALACE INSIDER REPORTS EVANGELINE FROZEN OUT OF ROYAL FAMILY

– CNN, 15 January 2024

PRIME MINISTER ISSUES STATEMENT SUPPORTING KING, CALLING FOR FULL INVESTIGATION INTO EVANGELINE'S CONNECTION TO ABR

– *The Daily Sun*, 15 January 2024

Over the next several days, I'm practically a ghost.

Singh confiscates my laptop and phone, leaving me with no way to see what the world is saying about me. Tibby, on the other hand, is glued to her screen, and while she refuses to spill any details about what's happening in the headlines and on social media, her favourite new pastime is declaring it all *utter bollocks*. And though part of me knows that remaining blissfully ignorant is undoubtedly for the best, the possibilities still eat away at me until I feel like I'm losing my mind.

My schedule isn't completely empty. Every morning, I sit in the conference room with Maisie, Helene, Constance and Nicholas, along with a revolving door of senior advisers, as they all make plans and decisions I barely understand. While Jenkins attends the first few meetings and goes to significant lengths to make sure I'm included, he's conspicuously absent from the rest. And from then on, no one will look at me, and I never speak up. My only job is to fill a seat that would otherwise be Ben's, and that, I know, is the sole reason Helene hasn't thrown me out on my arse. Though she and Constance are both cold to the point of being unapproachable, neither seems to actually believe the ABR's claims about me, probably because it would also mean believing that Kit was involved. But the truth doesn't stop either of them from treating me like the whole wretched scandal is entirely my fault.

To make it all worse, Kit officially leaves Windsor for his family's town house in London. While he isn't far, we have no way of communicating – and even if we did, I'm sure he wouldn't risk it, not when it might give Singh a reason to reconsider my supposed innocence. But either way, the solid foundation Kit has offered me for the past seven months is gone, and I constantly feel like I'm walking on shaky ground, and one small push could send me spiralling into oblivion.

On the fifth day after the bombing, I wake up to another round of whispers. They're more frequent now that I'm on my own, and I lie in bed, my eyes squeezed shut as I try to ignore them.

"*Evangeline.*"

"*Evangeline.*"

"*Evangeline.*"

At first my name is almost white noise in the quiet of the early morning. But as the seconds pass, the whispers seem to converge until they become a single voice pulsing in the air, and even when I roll over and bury my head underneath the pillow, I can still hear them. With a curse, I shove the blanket off me and sit up with dizzying force.

"Go *away*!"

The words ring through my bedroom, and silence rushes in as the whispers abruptly disappear. Startled, I look around in the darkness, but before I can figure out what just happened, my door swings open, and Tibby stands silhouetted in the lamplight from the sitting room.

"Evan?" she says. "Are you all right?"

"Fine," I mutter, though my heart is racing. I push a loose lock of hair from my face, and I can hear the faint thud of Tibby's heels as she walks towards the windows. "What are you doing here so early?"

"Fitz is a wreck, so I stopped by to help him arrange Her Royal Highness's schedule for the rest of the week," she says as she opens the curtains, even though the sun hasn't come up yet. "Naturally the job took all of ten minutes. Did you have a nightmare?"

She says this in a strange, almost sympathetic tone that doesn't sound natural on her, and I shake my head. "It doesn't matter," I say, climbing to my feet. "I need to shower."

Tibby lets me trudge off to my bathroom without further comment, but I can feel her eyes on me as I go. And once I emerge half an hour later, she speaks to me like I'm a feral animal that's one wrong word away from biting her, and I know it's going to be a very long day.

I barely manage to choke down a croissant at breakfast, and I don't say a word during the meeting that follows. Vaguely I note the dark circles under Maisie's eyes – ones that are slowly beginning to rival Helene's – but she, like everyone else, does a remarkable job of acting like my seat is empty, and the moment the meeting is adjourned, I escape into the hall and make myself scarce.

This time, however, the thought of returning to my room and enduring Tibby's sympathy is too much to bear, and so rather than turning left when I reach the bottom of the staircase, I turn right, heading for the drawing rooms instead.

Even though seemingly every adviser is on call, the household staff has been reduced in the wake of the bombing, and the long gallery is empty. As I pass the series of doors that lead into the royal family's private apartments, I pause in front of one that's identical to the rest, but as far as I know, no one except cleaning personnel has been inside in months.

Ben's suite.

My fingers wrap around the handle before I know what I'm doing, and I give it an experimental twist. The knob doesn't give, and I take a deep breath, standing perfectly still. I shouldn't be here. I should keep walking and disappear into the maze that is the state apartments and not give this door another thought. But something compulsive – something irresistible – makes me slip my lockpicks out of the narrow pocket in the waistband of my leggings, and after a quick glance up and down the corridor to make sure no one is coming, I slide them into the keyhole.

Fifteen seconds later, I'm inside, my back pressed against the closed door as I look around the room. It's different from the last time I was in here – less lived-in, somehow, even though none of the blue-and-gold furniture has changed. But the floor-to-ceiling bookcases are full of generic leather-bound books and artfully arranged knick-knacks, and when I peek inside the credenzas near the dining table, where Ben stashed the rest of his seemingly endless supply of paperback novels, they're empty.

That should be the end of it – solid evidence that any sign of Ben's time here has been vacuumed and dusted away. But something pulls me towards the door that leads into his former bedroom, and when the handle turns easily, I cross the threshold, feeling as if I'm entering a tomb.

It's nearly pitch-black inside, with heavy velvet curtains covering the windows and blocking out the sun, but I don't bother fumbling around for a switch. Instead, I let the light from the sitting room spill inside as I move straight towards the large wardrobe and open the doors. It's also empty, without even so much as a single stray sock or hanger left behind, but I'm not surprised. If his books are gone, then his clothes must be, too.

I crouch down and feel around the bottom of the wardrobe, until my fingers brush against a slight gap at the edge. With dread settling in the pit of my stomach, I lift the false bottom of Ben's favourite hiding spot and hold my breath.

At first, all I see is darkness. My body is blocking the light from the sitting room, and it isn't until I shift that I notice a shadow lurking inside. The last time I was here, the contents of the drawer were mostly organized, save for the pile of adult magazines that served as a decoy to keep anyone from searching too hard. But now, the Polaroids and media and manila envelopes are gone, and in their place sits something strange and irregular. Gathering my courage, I reach inside, and my fingers brush –

A flower.

I snatch my hand back, and it takes me several long seconds before I can make myself touch it again. The petals are velvety soft, and gingerly I pull it out of the hiding place, not at all surprised when the light reveals it's a blood-red gerbera daisy. Ben must have stashed it here before Maisie kicked him out of Windsor, but the daisy doesn't look like it's been lying at the bottom of a dark wardrobe for the past five days. It's healthy and thriving, as if it were plucked straight from a vase full of water. As if Ben placed it here minutes ago, knowing I was about to come looking.

Suddenly my skin prickles like something – or someone – is watching me, and I scramble to my feet, the flower clutched in my hand. I don't bother to close the wardrobe as I hurry out of the bedroom. Ben will know I was here whether or not I cover my tracks, and I dash through the rest of his suite, my pulse racing and my vision blurring – with anger, with determination, with every answer I know I have, but can't prove. And maybe that's the point. Maybe, like a predator taunting its prey, Ben wants me to know I'm right – that his fingerprints are all over what's happened since the attack at Sandringham, and I'm the only one who knows he's playing the game.

I'm three long strides into the corridor when I run straight into something warm and solid, and it's a minor miracle I don't fall flat on my face. Instead, as I stumble, a hand reaches out to steady me, and I hear Jenkins's voice.

"Evan. *Evan.*"

I blink, and his face swims into focus. The line between his brows is deep with concern, and his blue eyes are so intensely fixed on me that it looks like he's trying to keep me upright through sheer willpower alone.

"Jenkins," I choke out, still clutching Ben's daisy. I didn't close the door to his room, I realize. And Jenkins isn't oblivious. "I – I was just—"

I trail off, the lump in my throat too big for me to finish, and to my horror, hot tears roll down my cheeks. Without a word, he pulls me to his chest, and we stand like that for a long moment, my face buried in his shoulder as he murmurs in my ear – murmurs that sound eerily like the whispers that I can still hear if I focus on the silence.

I don't know how to explain this. I *can't* explain this, not without telling him everything, but part of me – a very small, terrified part of me – wants to. Jenkins has spent half my life fixing my problems, but right now, with the monarchy on his shoulders, I refuse to add to a burden that must already be impossible to bear. And what can he do, anyway? Reassure me that Ben isn't allowed in Windsor any more? Tell me everything will be all right, even though we both know it won't be?

"I'm worried about you, darling," he says at last. "You haven't been reading the papers, have you?"

"Tibby won't let me near them," I mumble. "Or social media. Or her phone."

"Good," he says, tucking my hair behind my ear as he studies me for a long moment. "Do you have any plans for the rest of the day?"

I wipe my eyes with the back of my hand. "I think Tibby has me down for a long, aimless walk around the castle from now until lunch, and then after that, I'll be busy staring at the walls and, if I can squeeze it in, having a minor breakdown before dinner. The major one comes after," I add, trying to smile, but my face won't cooperate. "And then, of course, there's the two to four hours of lying awake at night, worrying about everything. Sleep is optional."

"Mm, quite busy, then, I see," says Jenkins, and he plucks a handkerchief from his pocket and presses it into my hand. "Do you think, just for today, you might be able to make some room in your schedule for a hospital visit? Your mother's been asking after you, and I think it'd do you both some good to spend time together."

I open my mouth, but for a moment, nothing comes out. She hasn't left Alexander's side since the bombing, and I miss her so much that just the thought of her makes me feel like I've swallowed acid. "MI5 told me to stay here."

"And since when do you do what you're told?" says Jenkins kindly. "Or is it only me you refuse to listen to?"

I shake my head. "Singh told me that if I go see her, I could make her a target."

"We'll be discreet," Jenkins assures me. "There's no safer place in England right now than your father's bedside. And, if you'll excuse my candour, given the state you're in, I think the real danger is what may happen if you stay away any longer."

I should say no. I should keep as much distance between my

parents and me as possible until every member of the ABR is behind bars. But those damn tears start again, and my chin trembles as I nod.

"Okay," I say, barely audible, and he sets a comforting hand on my shoulder to guide me back down the corridor. My fingers tighten around the daisy stem, and I know that no matter how much space I put between me and that wardrobe, it – and Ben – will taunt me until I find a way to trap him in his own snare of lies.

LORD CLARENCE PICTURED COSYING UP TO BOMBER MONTHS BEFORE ATTACK

Christopher Abbott-Montgomery, Earl of Clarence, has been having a secret affair with close friend Aoife Marsh, one of three suspects arrested at the site of the Modern Music Museum bombing that claimed the lives of eight people and has left His Majesty the King in critical condition.

Photos of the pair cuddling at a local pub last November have surfaced, months after they met through mutual friends at Oxford University, and a member of the couple's inner circle has confirmed the relationship.

"Everyone knows Christopher and Aoife have been sneaking around, spending the night together and snogging in dark corners when they think no one is watching," says the source, who wished to remain anonymous. "He's tired of the constant drama surrounding Evangeline, and when he's had too much to drink, he always goes on about how she won't let him touch her after what that Jasper bloke did to her. I guess he finally got tired of waiting. I know I would."

Clarence, 19, is currently rumoured to be a suspect in the bombing, along with his girlfriend of seven months, Evangeline Bright, illegitimate daughter of the King, who was specifically thanked by the Army of the British Republic for her participation in the terrorist attack. Both the Home Office and the Palace have declined to comment on the duo's connection to the ongoing investigation.

– The *Daily Sun*, 17 January 2024

An hour later, Jenkins and I walk down the hallway of the hospital together as every single person – staff and guard alike – eyes me like I'm about to pull a grenade from my pocket and lob it into the nearest crowd.

It's jarring, to say the least, and it leaves me both queasy and questioning why I'm here in the first place. "Does my mom know?" I say softly as we pass through yet another checkpoint of the seemingly infinite layers of security that surround my father.

"She doesn't know anything about the investigation or the claims against you and Lord Clarence," says Jenkins at a volume that matches mine. "You may tell her if you'd like, and perhaps it would be good if you did. But I didn't want to do so without your permission."

The thought of telling my mother that the world thinks I helped plan the bombing is enough to make me wish I had a vomit bin. "Not yet," I mumble, and Jenkins nods, mercifully leaving it at that.

As we approach my father's hospital room, both protection officers at the door shift their stance as they scrutinize me. I try to pretend I don't see their hands twitch towards their hidden holsters, but they're not exactly subtle about it.

"Gentlemen," says Jenkins as we stop in front of the room.

"Miss Bright is here to visit His Majesty."

The larger of the two steps towards me. "All visitors are required to be searched—"

"We've been searched three times already, as you very well know," says Jenkins. "Both the palace and Home Office have already determined that the claims against Miss Bright are baseless, and that she is not a threat. Do you know something we don't?"

The protection officers glance at each other, and one picks up a walkie-talkie to mumble something into it. A burst of static responds almost instantly, and he grimaces.

"Lovely," says Jenkins, as if this has all been settled, and with a grudging nod, the first guard opens the door for us. If the situation were any different, I'd be fascinated by this rare display of Jenkins's power. But as we enter the room, all I can do is stare at my father's prone and broken body, and my mother's hunched form on the small sofa that's situated a few feet from the edge of Alexander's bed. A new nurse sits at the computer, scribbling something down on a clipboard, and while she nods to us both in greeting, she returns to her work immediately.

"Whenever you're ready to leave, let the protection officers outside know, and someone will come to escort you," says Jenkins. "There's no rush, though, darling. Stay as long as you'd like."

I nod, but even though I want to be here, I'm not sure how much I can take. A heaviness surrounds this place, muffling any sense of the past or the future, and even though I knew exactly what to expect, it still feels like another world.

My mom looks up then, and her eyes are distant, like she's

focused on something no one else could ever possibly see. The haziness clears up after a beat, however, and she manages a smile. "There you are, Evie," she says, beckoning for me, and I notice a large open sketchbook resting on her lap. As I cross the room to join her, she clears a place for me among the pencils, brushes and various other art supplies that always seem to follow her wherever she goes, and to my surprise, I notice the paint set Kit gave her for Christmas.

"You're really using that?" I say as I ease down beside her.

"This? Of course," she says, opening it to show me the half-empty tubes of paint. "It's incredibly useful. Your Kit has excellent taste, you know."

I try to smile, but I still can't manage it. Part of me knows I should tell her about the ABR's claims and about the picture with Aoife, but even if I wanted to, I don't know how. She'll find out eventually – there's no way to hide the accusations of murder and treason from her for ever – but for now, her ignorance is a balm, and I need it more than I realized.

"Are you okay?" I say. "Do you have your medication with you? Is everyone treating you all right? Have you been eating?"

My mother pulls me closer and kisses my forehead. "I'm perfectly fine, sweetheart, don't worry. Jenkins is making sure I have everything I need."

Of course he is, and I make a mental note to thank him. "How is Alexander?" I say, glancing at the bed and the beeping machines presumably keeping him alive. She sighs.

"There hasn't been much improvement," she admits. "But he isn't getting any worse, either, and that's the important part. It can take a while for the swelling to go down, and until it does…"

She trails off, and instead of finishing, she rubs my back for a moment before focusing on her sketchbook. It's only because she isn't trying to hide it that I let myself look at the unfinished drawing, and when I do, I'm startled to see my own toddler face peering back at me.

I can't be older than two or three, and I'm laughing, all baby teeth and chubby cheeks as someone tickles me. The hands are large and nothing like my mother's, and as soon as I spot the rough sketch of a signet ring on the pinky, I realize they must be Alexander's.

"Wow," I say as my mother defines the knuckles, her pencil moving so quickly that it looks like she's revealing what's already there beneath the blank page. "Did that really happen?"

"Of course," she says, and she pauses long enough to flip back a page. There's another picture, this one of her and Alexander sitting in what I recognize as her backyard in Arlington, and she's filled in the garden with bursts of watercolour. They look young in the painting – just a few years older than I am – and it seems so real that it's almost like I'm staring into her memories.

"That's beautiful," I say softly, as if speaking too loudly will ruin it somehow.

"It's nothing," she says, but her cheeks grow pink as she turns to a third drawing. It's a detailed study of Alexander's sleeping face, whole and well, and his fingers peek through towards the bottom of the picture, laced with someone else's – my mother's, no doubt. He's young in this one, too, but as she moves to another page, there's a near-identical drawing, and this time, there are lines around his eyes, and his hairline isn't as thick as it was in his twenties.

One by one, she shows me each of the nearly two dozen drawings, all memories of their history together. By the time we reach the very first sketch, my vision is blurred, and I blink hard before taking in the details of a large building with remarkably detailed Gothic architecture. A girl – my mother – sits on the edge of a fountain in the foreground, sketch pad in hand, as a figure that can only be my father walks towards her. His face is hidden, but I'm struck by the look in her graphite eyes. Somehow, my mother's managed to convey an entire lifetime of love and joy with only a few pencil strokes, and I brush the tip of my finger against the page, far from any spot I might smudge.

"This is the day Alex and I met," she says, leaning her head against mine. "I used to think the idea of love at first sight was a fairy tale, but from the moment I laid eyes on him, I knew he was it for me."

"He told me the same thing about you," I say quietly as I gaze at those pencil figures, who have no idea what kind of heartbreak and tragedy are lying in wait for them. "Do you regret it at all? Going to Oxford, I mean. Meeting him. Maybe if you hadn't…"

"If I hadn't met him, I wouldn't have you," she says. "And even if Alexander and I hadn't worked out, even if he'd never spoken to me again after you were born, you're worth every moment of it, Evie. Good, bad, devastating – I'd do it all again a thousand times over if it meant bringing you into this world. You know that, right?"

My mom peers at me with such naked vulnerability that I nod, even though I don't know this. Even though I can't imagine that I really am worth the pain and suffering she's faced. She must see my uncertainty, because she sighs and sets the sketchbook aside.

"I hate that you only remember the worst parts," she says, clasping my hand between both of hers. "My mother – your grandmother thought it was best for me to keep my distance from you while I was still recovering. And she was right at first, especially…well, especially in the immediate aftermath. But it robbed you of seeing the good parts, too, even when they were messy and might've seemed like our darkest moments from the outside looking in."

"Like what?" I say, not entirely sure I want to know. Hearing her talk about Alexander makes me ache in a way I can't entirely face, but it's a good kind of pain, too, I think.

She hesitates. "For instance, when I was hospitalized after… well, after what I did to…what happened to you, I didn't see anyone for months. I refused, and I was…" Her throat tightens, and she glances at Alexander for a split second. "I was in a bad place. But your dad visited me every week. Every single week, he would take a red-eye from London, and he would sit in the visitors' lounge, waiting for me to come out."

"He did?" I say, but I'm not surprised. Nothing about how much they love each other surprises me any more.

"He did. And eventually I started to look forward to it, even though I refused to see him. Just knowing he was there…during a time when I hated myself more than anyone else ever could, it gave me something to live for. And I think he knew that. I think he knew how much I needed him, even though I couldn't admit it. But when I did…when I finally worked up the courage to see him, he didn't blame me for hurting you. He didn't tell me what a terrible mother I was, even though I deserved it."

"You're not—" I begin, but she squeezes my hand.

"I thought I deserved it at the time," she amends. "But your dad made sure – still makes sure – that I know *he* didn't believe it. He made sure I knew that he understood what had happened, and all he wanted was to help me heal."

She looks at him again, and even though he's lying motionless on the bed, covered in bandages and bruises and stitches that will undoubtedly leave scars, there's no fear in her eyes. Just a depth of love I can't even begin to fathom.

"Now it's my turn to make sure that he knows I'm here for him," she continues, "and that I'm not going anywhere. And I won't pretend it's not one of the most difficult things I've ever done, seeing him like this, not knowing if he'll ever wake up or be the person he was before. But in a way, it gives me the chance to love him the way he loved me then, as painful as it is. And there's nothing more worthwhile than that. So no, I don't regret any of it," she says, turning back towards me. "How could I? You're the brightest stars in my sky, and without you, life wouldn't be worth living."

I don't know what to say to that, and so I just hold her hand as she shifts closer to me.

"All I want now," she says, "is for the three of us to have the chance to make new memories. Alexander's fighting to stay – I know he is, just like he's always fought for you and me. But even if he…even if he doesn't make it, even if these memories are all we'll ever have together, I'll always be here for you, Evie. I won't ever be able to make up for the time we lost, but I also won't ever leave you again. Okay?"

"Okay," I whisper, resting my head on her shoulder. Maybe it's the weariness, or maybe it's the number of times I've cried in the past five days, but suddenly all I want is to believe that she really is a permanent part of my life, in a way she's never been before. It seems like some distant dream – like a fantasy I'll never really have – but in that moment, leaning against her and listening to the soft sound of the beeps, I desperately want to believe it.

"*Evangeline*."

My eyes fly open as the sound of my name seems to filter through the air, little more than a soft whoosh as a distant door closes. "Did you hear that?" I say, sitting up straight, and my mom frowns.

"Hear what?"

"Someone said my name," I say. "I heard it earlier, too, in—" I cut myself off, but I can already feel the concern radiating from her. For a long moment, I listen, waiting to hear it again, and I'm so focused that when she touches my hair, I jerk away.

"Do you want to talk about it?" she says with gentleness I can't stomach, because I know what she's thinking. It's the same thing I've been afraid of ever since the voices began, and my mouth goes dry.

In the weeks and months that followed, Laura Bright was diagnosed with schizophrenia, a lifelong mental illness that often has a genetic component.

They're the words from the *Daily Sun* article that revealed my mother's history and diagnosis to the world. At the time, it was a not-so-subtle swipe at me, considering the paper is owned by Robert Cunningham, who was convinced I'd killed his son. But that sentence is seared into my brain, and finally I admit to myself that I'm terrified it might be right.

Auditory hallucinations. Paranoia. Confusion. The absolute certainty that I'm seeing something that no one else will admit is there. I feel like I'm standing at the edge of a cliff, painfully aware of my mother's worried gaze, and at last I bury my face in my hands.

"I've been...hearing things," I say softly into my palms. "Mostly whispers when I wake up and go to sleep at night. Sometimes they say things, like my name, or – or threats." I bite my lip, but now that I've admitted it, the words spill out of me like a waterfall. "And the flowers Ben's been sending me...he's behind this, Mom – I *know* he is, but whenever I try to tell someone, they make me feel like I'm – I'm—"

"Paranoid?" she offers quietly. "Imagining things? Connecting dots that aren't really there?"

I nod and finally work up the courage to look at her. "Nothing feels right any more," I say thickly. "But I'm also so sure I'm not making any of it up that – I don't know what to think. I don't know what's *real*."

My mom sighs and gathers me in her arms, her auburn waves tickling my nose as I breathe in the scent of her. Even after nearly a week at Alexander's bedside, she still smells like home.

"You've been under an enormous amount of stress lately, Evie," she says. "It would take a toll on anyone. We'll find someone to help you sort through this, all right?"

I nod, though my heart feels like it's being squeezed in a vice. "But what if it's not just stress? What if...?"

While I can't force the words out, my mom understands. "Then we'll make sure you have the care you need," she says.

"It'll be okay, sweetheart, no matter what happens. I promise."

There's no fear or pity or disappointment in the way she says it. Instead, she's so calm about it, so matter-of-fact, that even though I'm all but clawing at the walls of my own mind, I let myself believe her. And for the first time since the bombing, I relax. Not entirely – not when I'm feet away from my father, whose chest rises and falls only because a machine is breathing for him – but enough that the crushing weight of anxiety inside me lessens to the point where, at least for the moment, it's bearable.

My mom nuzzles my hair. "Why don't I head back to Windsor with you tonight?" she says. "We can spend a little time together. Watch a movie, maybe, if you're up for it."

"Don't you want to stay with Alexander?" I say warily.

"I'll let Constance know so she can sit with him. He won't be alone."

And while I know I should say no – that every minute she's away from him, she'll only worry – I selfishly don't want to. Because even during all those years on my own at boarding school, even after everything Jasper did to me, even in the thick of the shooting and the bombing and every awful thing that's happened lately, I don't think I've ever needed her more than I do right now.

"Okay," I say. "But we'll be back tomorrow morning, all right? First thing."

"First thing," she agrees, and she kisses my hair again as we settle into silence, both of us lost in our thoughts as we listen to the steady beat of Alexander's heart.

Chapter Thirty-one

Is it time to admit, once and for all, that teenagers are too young to rule?

Princess Mary might have been groomed from birth to be our future monarch, but at eighteen years, six months and sixteen days old, she can barely be trusted to sign her name in the right place, and we as a United Kingdom and Commonwealth ought to be shaking in our boots at the very notion of her taking on the lifelong job of queen.

After all, what teen today isn't far more occupied with their follower counts and ever-evolving trends than with politics and diplomatic relations? The royal family has always been an exception to the plague of modernity, or so we're led to imagine. But while Princess Mary has been a shining star during her dozens of official appearances over the past six months, smiling for the cameras and shaking hands hardly qualifies her to lead on the global stage.

I know what many of you must be thinking – no doubt of the last great queen who ruled our nation, Victoria, who ascended the throne at the age of eighteen. But times were different nearly two hundred years ago, and children were far more prepared to take on the responsibilities that came with their station. Now one cannot make small talk with anyone under the age of twenty without being accused of a slip of the tongue that leads to theatrical claims of offence. And while we have watched Her Royal Highness as she has grown from fragile newborn to the sunny young woman she is today, the palace has only recently begun to present her as our future sovereign, and in a time of great turmoil, the British people deserve the stability and reassurance that comes with the known.

Though the Regency Act of 2005 makes it clear that Her Royal Highness would be assisted by a so-called royal council, with the third in line to the throne being deliberately passed over in favour of the King's illegitimate American daughter, it's time to pose the question we've all been thinking: just how seriously are we meant to take this farce of temporary rule?

Should the worst come to pass and His Majesty fail to recover from his reportedly severe injuries after the 12 January bombing, would Britain not be better off in the hands of a prince who has decades of experience as a working royal? A proper regency would require that Prince Nicholas, the Duke of York, rule in Princess Mary's stead until her twenty-first birthday, allowing her more time to grow and mature into the monarch we all wish her to be. It would allow for fewer hiccups, no doubt, and certainly less wariness and scrutiny both within and beyond our borders.

With as much turmoil as the King and his wayward family have caused over the past seven months, is it too much to hope that perhaps the royals might finally prioritize the people and the stability of this country over their own privilege and entitlement? Or could we as a country finally find relief from this never-ending roller coaster of drama?

– Op-Ed in the *Daily Sun*, 17 January 2024

The first thing my mother does when we return to Windsor Castle is head straight for the shower.

"I'll meet you in your rooms in twenty minutes, all right?" she says, her fingers running through my hair. "I just need to wash the hospital smell off."

She says this with a slight shudder, and I'm too wrung out to tell if she's trying to keep things light-hearted, or if it really does bother her. Either way, I agree, and I drop her off at Alexander's apartment before sniffing my own hair. It also smells vaguely like antiseptic, and I wrinkle my nose.

"Evan?"

I whirl around. Rosie stands outside Maisie's door, only twenty feet or so from Alexander's. Her freckled face is pale and free of make-up, and she looks so startlingly lost that for a second, I'm sure something else has happened.

"Rosie?" I say. "What are you doing here? Is Maisie—"

"She's in her sitting room," says Rosie quickly, like she knows I can't take any more bad news right now. "Your mum's still in England? I thought..."

There's something strange about the way she says this, like she's putting the pieces of a puzzle together, and I can practically see the gears turning in her mind. "Yeah, she's still here," I say, glancing at Alexander's door. There's no point in lying, after all, not if Rosie's already seen her. "She's been staying at the hospital with Alexander."

"Oh." Rosie's lips thin. "I didn't know."

Even though I'm not exactly her favourite person, not when I'm the one dating Kit, I expect her to ask something else – why my mom's hanging around, maybe, or even how Alexander's doing. But instead she tugs nervously at one of her blond curls, and I swear I see her gulp.

"Is Gia here, too?" I venture, and she shakes her head, her green eyes growing round.

"Maisie texted me earlier. She's having a really bad day, and I thought maybe I could help, but all she's really done is throw things and scream. I don't…I don't know what to do any more." Her voice breaks, and I feel a sudden stab of pity for her.

"I can try to talk to her, if you think she'll let me," I say, even though I know this is a terrible suggestion. Maisie's barely been able to look at me since the news of the photo broke, and there's a very real chance I'll only make things worse. But Rosie nods eagerly, as if this is the greatest idea she's ever heard.

"Maybe she'll listen to you." But as she says it, the faint sound of shattering glass echoes from inside Maisie's apartment, and Rosie flinches. "Or at the very least, maybe she'll stop breaking things. Some of those are priceless, you know."

Taking a deep breath, I steel myself and approach Maisie's door. I can feel Rosie's nervous gaze on me as I knock, and I'm not at all surprised when Maisie's snarl cuts through the air like a knife.

"I told you to piss off, Rosie!"

"Off to a great start," I mutter before raising my voice. "It's me. Can I come in?"

Maisie lets out a string of curses so obscene that I nearly abandon the whole idea. But before I can talk myself out of this entirely, her door flies open, and I'm face to face with my seething sister.

"*What?*" she says, and over her shoulder, I notice several picture frames and chunks of glass scattered across her cream carpet. After almost seven years in boarding schools, I'm no stranger to tantrums, but the ones I've witnessed didn't involve artefacts older than most trees.

"My mom and I just got back from the hospital," I say with all the nonchalance I can muster. "I thought you'd like an update."

Maisie's jaw is clenched, and her entire body seems to vibrate with pent-up emotion as she inhales. "Rosie," she says after a beat. "Have someone bring us a pot of tea. Make sure it's hot."

The thought of Maisie being anywhere near boiling liquid right now isn't exactly comforting, but Rosie nods and scurries off, and finally my sister stalks back into her apartment, leaving me room to step inside. I do so carefully, eyeing the floor for pieces of glass, not in the mood for another round of stitches.

"How is he?" she says waspishly, walking through the shards in her high heels with several loud crunches. I skirt the edges of the room as I head for her antique white telephone, which is set on an end table near her sofa.

"He's not getting worse," I say. "Which is about all anyone can ask for right now. My mom said the swelling takes time to go down, and when it does—"

"Daddy has to be okay," she says, cutting me off. "He has to be."

"I... No one really knows yet," I admit. "But my mom said—"

"I don't care what your bloody mother said," bursts Maisie, and I'm not sure which startles me more – her words or the fact that she's suddenly a teary mess. "I can't do this, Evan. I can't – I can't be queen, not yet. It's too bloody soon, and I'm supposed to have years – *decades* before I have to make these kinds of decisions, but suddenly everyone's looking to me like I have the answers, as if genetics alone is enough—"

"It's not all on you, not yet," I say, easing around the remains of what I think might've been a snow globe. "You have your mother and Constance and Nicholas—"

"The papers are calling for a regency," she says with such venom and heartbreak all at once that the words come out guttural. "If Daddy – if Daddy never wakes up, they want Nicholas to reign until I'm twenty-one."

I study her. "Is that a good thing, or…?"

"Of *course* it's not a good thing!" she explodes, grabbing the nearest item – a lamp – and hurling it at the floor. As it shatters, a streak of red appears on her leg, though she doesn't seem to notice. "The people don't trust me. They don't think I'm up for the job, but of course *Nicholas*, perfect bloody Nicholas, is exactly what this country needs right now. Never mind that Victoria became queen when she was eighteen, or that Mary, Queen of Scots, was six days old. *Six days!* And obviously it's disputed, but Lady Jane Grey was fifteen when Edward VI, who was *nine* when he became king, died and named her his heir, and King Henry VIII was seventeen—"

"It's alarming that you know all this off the top of your head," I say.

"It's my bloody *job* to know this," she snaps, marching past her sofa towards her bookcase, where there's a hand-painted music box sitting beside a leather-bound set of Shakespeare plays. "My entire education has been to prepare me for becoming queen. I've studied history, politics, economics, constitutional law – all to be the best monarch I can be when the time comes. It didn't matter that I like maths and science. I learned some, of course, because I can't count on my bloody fingers in front of the world, can I? But who I am and who, in another life, I might've wanted to be – none of it matters, because I'm going to be queen. It's destiny. And now these people – *these bloody people* – are trying to take it from me like I'm not singularly qualified. Like I'm some – some *teenager* who can't control herself and who'll throw a tantrum if I don't get my—"

Maisie stops abruptly as her fingers close around the music box, and without any prompting from me, she looks around at the utter destruction that is her sitting room. Picture frames torn off the walls. Trinkets and teacups and paperweights that are little more than dust now, and several antique books with freshly torn pages. Her hand falls to her side, and without warning, her face crumples as she dissolves into sobs.

Inwardly cursing the thin soles of my flats, I tiptoe as fast as I can through the wreckage until I reach her. She tries to push me away, but her attempts are half-hearted, and I capture her in a hug.

"From where I'm standing, you're doing an incredible job," I say. "Every single meeting, you take charge, and even when you don't know what the answer is, you listen, and you process, and you decide. Nicholas might have more experience, but you're a born leader, Maisie."

"I don't want to be," she whimpers, her arms snaking around me until she's the one holding me to her. "I want him back. I want more time. I shouldn't – I shouldn't have to *do* this yet."

"No, you shouldn't," I say quietly. "I'm sorry."

Maybe no one has actually said this to her, or maybe all she wants is for someone to understand, because this seems to trigger another flood of tears, and she clings to me like I'm a life raft. We stand there for a minute or two as she cries so hard that her entire body is wracked with sobs, until at last, with several wet sniffles, she lets me go.

"Sit down," I say, nodding towards a nearby love seat. "You're dripping all over the carpet."

"What?" she says, dazed, and only then does she notice the blood still trickling down her leg. With a curse, she limps over to the sofa, and I grab a cushion to keep her injury from ruining the white velvet.

As she's inspecting the cut, I pick up the corded handset of her telephone, and I'm instantly connected to an operator. "Yes, Your Royal Highness?" says a low female voice on the other end.

"This is Evangeline," I say. "I'm with Princess Mary. Everything's okay, but we need a maid and a doctor, please."

"Yes, Miss Bright," says the operator smoothly, as if this is hardly an unusual request. "I'll send for both right away."

"Thank you," I say, and I hang up the phone with a click. Almost as soon as I do, there's a knock on the door, and without waiting for a response, a protection officer steps inside.

"Your Royal Highness," he says, and I notice his hand is resting on his holster. "Is everything all right?"

As soon as he says it, he seems to notice the debris, and his gaze snaps straight to me. "Maisie had a rough afternoon," I say drily, not at all appreciating the implication of his stare.

"I'm fine," she mumbles without glancing up from her leg. "I just need a bandage, that's all. And for you to go."

The protection officer heads for us anyway, the glass under his shoes crackling with each step he takes. He pulls a small first-aid kit seemingly out of nowhere, and I watch as he snaps on a pair of latex gloves and removes several alcohol swabs, gauze and medical tape from the pack.

"Thank you," says Maisie testily as he starts to mop up the

blood for her. "That will be all."

"Ma'am—" he begins, but she cuts him off.

"I said *go*. I'm hardly going to bleed to death from a scratch."

The officer looks between us dubiously, but Maisie's glare doesn't waver, and at last he stands.

"I'll be outside if you need anything," he says, and this time, I notice that he takes the long route around the worst of the carnage before heading back out the door.

As soon as we're alone once more, Maisie lets out a muffled screech. "Do you see?" she says, tears flooding her eyes all over again. "This is my life now, and the people won't even let me have that. There are already rumours about what sort of queen I'll be, or that I'm impulsive and can't make decisions, and – have you read the *Regal Record* lately?"

"No," I say, offering her a tissue. She snatches it from me and dabs the cut with a distinct lack of gentleness. "My phone and laptop were taken by MI5, remember?"

"Probably for the best," she says with vague irritation, and though I want to know what she means, I don't push. "Yesterday, at the meeting, I asked Grandmama about how we might approach the weekly session with the prime minister today. If it ought to be all five of us, or if it should just be me and Mummy."

"I remember." Thankfully, Nicholas was the only one who voted for the entire royal council to attend.

"Well, less than three hours later, there was an article up on the *Regal Record* about it," she says with a sniff. "They went on and on about how I shouldn't be allowed to meet the prime minister without Nicholas, not when I'm not even regent yet, and since he's next in line after me, it'd only be prudent if…if…"

She wipes her eyes with the back of her wrist, and I offer her another tissue. "Can I tell you something?" I say uncertainly, and this immediately grabs her attention.

"You can tell me anything."

That's definitely not true, but I press on anyway. "I think there's a mole in the castle," I say. "One who's been leaking information to the *Regal Record*."

"Well, obviously," she mutters. "It was Ben, wasn't it? We figured that out ages ago."

"Yes, but – he hasn't been here," I point out. "He's in Belgium right now. But the *Regal Record* is still getting little scoops like that – information that no one outside of that meeting should have."

Her hand stills. "You think someone else is going to them now?"

I nod. "They knew about your injuries after the crowd surge, Maisie. And about your break-up with Gia. There are other things, too – little things they shouldn't know, but do, and it's *constant*. Someone close to you is selling secrets to the *Regal Record*."

Maisie looks up at me, the second tissue now pressed against her cut. "Who? And don't you dare hold back," she adds as I hesitate. "You wouldn't tell me this if you didn't have a theory."

"I..." I rip open an alcohol swab and hand it to her. "I don't know who. But it has to be someone close to you. Close to both of us. The break-up with Gia, for instance...who else knew about that except the five of us in the room?"

"I was upset," says Maisie defensively. "And with the way Gia stormed out of here, anyone could've guessed."

"Maybe," I say. "But they knew it was because of the roses that Thaddeus sent you. Did you tell anyone else? Your mom, maybe? Or even Alexander?"

She grows quiet for a long moment. "No," she says at last. "I didn't tell anyone. Just you, Kit, Rosie and Gia."

"Then one of us is the mole," I say. "Unless someone else found out, it's the only possibility."

"But—" Maisie stops. "It isn't me. *Obviously* it isn't me. And it can't be Gia or Rosie, either."

"Why not?" I say, and instantly I know I've waded into dangerous territory.

"Because," she says sharply, "they've been my best friends since we were in nursery together. They've never betrayed me – not once – and there's no reason in the world they might start now."

"No reason that you know of," I say, and her glare is so withering that I have to fight the urge to flinch.

"What about Kit?" she retorts. "He was there, too, *and* he's the one who's chummy with terrorists. Maybe he also tipped off the *Regal Record* and sent in that photo of you hugging the bomber. He's the only one of us who knew about it, after all, and with everything else the papers are saying—" She cuts herself off and shakes her head. "*He's* the most likely suspect."

I open my mouth to tell her in no uncertain terms that it couldn't be him – that he wouldn't do something so awful, that there's no way he would ever betray either of us – but it's the same knee-jerk reaction she had to my suggestion of Gia and Rosie. And instead, even though it takes every ounce of willpower I have, I press my lips together and consider it.

She's right. He *has* been there for all of it. He was the one to suggest the trip to the shop. He was the one to introduce me to Aoife. He also knew about Maisie's injuries, and the break-up, and the roses – everything that Gia and Rosie knew and more.

On paper, it makes sense. It more than makes sense – he really should be our prime suspect. But as I think about the things he's said, the things he's done to protect me, the changes he's been willing to make in his own life to keep me safe and unafraid...maybe I'm every bit as in denial as Maisie is, but it doesn't fit. It just doesn't.

"Did I ever tell you that I blamed him for leaking the story about my mom's illness to the press?" I say. "Back in June, the morning the news broke. He was the only one I ever told."

Maisie scowls. "What does that have to do with—"

"I was wrong. It wasn't Kit," I say. "Even though he let me believe it was, even though I almost lost him, it wasn't him. And I'm not going to put Kit through that again. Not unless we have irrefutable proof."

"And I'm not going to blame the only two friends I have because *you* can't see what's right in front of you," she snaps. "He was there for all of it."

"Yes, he was," I say. "And maybe that's the point. Maybe the real mole is trying to frame him, too, just like Ben tried to frame me last summer."

Maisie lets out a derisive snort and shakes her head. "You think this is still about Ben? The bombing, the attacks—" She shakes her head incredulously. "You're absolutely mad."

After the conversation I had with my mother that morning,

her words are a slap to the face. But I swallow the sting and press on, refusing to rise to her bait.

"Ben knew about the photo with Aoife before it was posted," I say with all the steadiness I can muster. "During that first meeting after the bombing – he said that he wouldn't be surprised if the public wasn't thrilled about me being part of the council."

"Yes, but that could've meant anything—"

"He offered Kit his condolences for his failure," I say, and this time it's my voice that rises. "Maisie, he meant the bombing. He knew Kit was in the picture, too – he knew Kit was part of that group. He knew it all. He even said—"

I stop suddenly, and Maisie pulls her leg from the pillow so she can face me properly.

"What, Evan?" she says, fury radiating from her. "What awful thing did Ben supposedly say that made you think he knew about the bombers?"

"He said..." I stare at her, positive she won't believe me. She didn't hear it, after all – no one else did. But I'm sure it was real. "He said it was supposed to be me. The people who died in the bombing – the ABR was after *me*, Maisie. Ben said—"

She laughs, a cold sound that seems to drop the temperature in the room a good twenty degrees. "You just have to make this all about you, don't you? Never mind that eight people died, and that Daddy's in hospital and might never wake up. Oh, no – this *must* all be about the great Evangeline Bright."

My mouth drops open, and for a long moment, I have no idea what to say. "Maisie, I'm not making this up—"

"And that's the worst part," she says. "That you actually believe it. Fine, there might be a mole – I'll give you that. And yes, they're feeding secrets to the *Regal Record*, which Ben also manipulated for his own personal gain. But as awful as last summer was, there is an entire universe between blackmail and the murder of eight people."

"That doesn't—"

"I've known Ben my entire life, Evan. He's my cousin. I know how he thinks, what he's capable of—"

"You didn't seem to believe he was the one behind the video, either," I say, my voice breaking again.

"No, but this is *treason*, Evan. This is – it's unthinkable." She shakes her head, her face twisted with incredulity. "He loves this family. He loves the monarchy, and he would never do anything to destroy it. I *know* he wouldn't. You, on the other hand..."

Her words hit me like a semi-truck, and as muffled voices sound in the corridor, I gawk at her, wondering if I've imagined this, too.

"What...?" I say, but it's all I can manage to squeeze out of my rapidly tightening throat.

Something that might be a hint of regret flickers across Maisie's face, but it's gone before I'm sure it's real. "You're the only newcomer, Evangeline. Everyone else in my life has been there practically from the start, and they've proven time and time again that they're loyal. But if you want to talk about who might be feeding information to the *Regal Record*, let's look at you, shall we? Because *you* knew it all, too."

I open and shut my mouth so many times that I feel like a fish trying to breathe. "Maisie, it wasn't me—"

"And it wasn't me, it wasn't Gia, and it wasn't Rosie," she snarls. "I know why you hate Ben. I hate him, too. But everything that's gone wrong in my life lately only happened after *you* showed up, and I'm beginning to think it isn't a bloody coincidence."

I try to speak – to defend myself, to swear it wasn't me – but the words don't come. And as the door opens once more, this time to a voice I recognize as Dr Gupta's, I slowly step back from the couch.

"That's what I thought," says Maisie with such searing malice that it feels like she's ripped out some vital part of me and smashed it, too. "Leave, before I call security. And if you *ever* try to accuse my friends of treason again, I will make you regret the day you ever stepped foot in my country. Is that understood?"

My mouth is as dry as a desert, and I can't speak, but I can't nod, either. Because nodding feels like an admission somehow, and even though every bone in my body feels like it's turned into concrete, I can't give her that. Not when it isn't true. Not when she has it all so impossibly wrong that I don't know which way is up any more.

Instead, as Gupta and his assistants file into the room, along with a small army of cleaners who immediately start picking up the glass, I turn around and slink towards the door. I wait for her to say something else – to get in a few last words, or maybe, impossibly, to take it all back. But she doesn't. And as I step over the threshold and into the cold corridor beyond, it feels like the delicate fabric that is our relationship has shredded into threads, and nothing will ever be able to weave it back together.

Is it done?

no, and I won't.

Why?

you lied to me.

About?

you know exactly what. I won't.

Then I'll just have to find someone else.

you can't! you'll hurt someone.

And if you don't do this, then I'll make sure you take the blame. Do you think you're my only insider?

you can't. I didn't. I won't.

So you keep saying.

if you do this, i'll tell them the truth.

Will you?
[picture message attached]

you're a monster.

No, I'm simply following the rules.
What will it be, love?
It's entirely your decision

find someone else. it won't be me.

Very well, then. It's your funeral.

– Text message exchange between two prepaid mobiles, 17 January 2024

My mother doesn't leave my side all evening as I sob miserably into my pillow.

I don't tell her why I'm crying – I can't find the words, and even if I tried, I'd have to tell her about Aoife and the ABR, and I already feel like I'm at my breaking point. But once she realizes I don't want to talk about it, my mom doesn't push, and instead we curl up together underneath my blanket, and she tells me stories.

Most of them are fictional and only meant to distract me – the plots of books she's read, movies she half remembers, myths she's always liked – but inevitably they remind her of something that's happened in her life, and she veers into the truth. Stories about her childhood that I've never heard. About her friends growing up, and how they used to make jewellery to sell at craft fairs and how she designed the covers of all her high school yearbooks. She tells me about her time at Oxford, about the classes she took and the traditions I have to look forward to next year, and Alexander slides in and out of her anecdotes like his presence is as natural as breathing.

I don't remember falling asleep, but I must at some point, because I start to dream of her life like I'm her. Like my childhood was normal, or as normal as it could be when her own father died when she was three, and like the only thing eighteen-year-old me has to worry about is making it to my next class on time. But in the middle of this montage of memories that aren't mine, a shrill sound pierces the lecture hall I'm sitting in, spun entirely out of her words and my imagination, and my eyes fly open as my mom and I sit up in the darkness together.

"What is that?" she says, her voice low and sleepy, and I'm relieved she can hear it, too.

"I don't know," I say, already wriggling towards the edge of the bed. My limbs are heavy, and my head feels like it's full of sand, but the screech penetrates my brain like an ice pick. "It almost sounds like a—"

"Miss Bright!"

My bedroom door bursts open, and a protection officer holding a flashlight rushes inside, stopping only a few feet from the bed as he shines the light in our eyes. "Miss Bright – Ms Bright – we need to go. *Now.*"

I shrink back, but his free hand is already reaching for my elbow, and he seizes it with the kind of force that makes it clear he'll drag me if he has to.

"What's going on?" says my mom, already on her feet.

"There's a fire in the private apartments," he says, pulling me upright. "The castle's being evacuated."

I stumble across the carpet, my mind fuzzy. My rooms are technically in the visitors' apartments, but the private ones –

"Maisie," I gasp, her name caught in my throat, and suddenly everything she said to me flies out of my mind like it was never there at all. "Is she—"

"Her Royal Highness is being seen to," he says, and this is so infuriatingly vague that I can't even begin to interpret what he's really saying. "I'm afraid we must go."

For a split second, I think he's going to pull me out the window. Instead, he leads me and my mother through the sitting room and into the corridor, which is already hazy with smoke.

"Maisie!" I shout down the long gallery. "*Maisie!*"

"This way, Miss Bright," says the protection officer, and he all but jerks me in the other direction. The exit and the safety that comes with it aren't far, but I can hear other panicked voices call to one another in the distance, and adrenaline spikes through me.

"Let me go," I say, trying to free my arm, but his grip is impossibly tight. "I said let me *go*—"

Out of instinct, maybe, or pure fear, I twist my wrist in the way Ingrid taught me, pushing against his thumb, and I finally break loose. Instantly I take off deeper into the gallery, towards the thickening smoke.

"Evie!" cries my mom as a crackle of radio static fills the air. "Evie, get back here!"

It's irrational – I know it's irrational. But after nearly losing

Alexander, the thought of my sister, trapped and frightened and gasping for air, drives me forward as fast as my legs can carry me. The shouts grow louder as I dash towards my sister's apartment. But I don't know where I am, exactly, not with the smoke so thick now that I can hardly see, and I'm coughing as I stumble directly into someone's arms.

"Found her!" calls a man whose voice I don't recognize, and before I know what's happening, he picks me up around the waist and carries me around the bend in the corridor.

"Maisie!" I yell, but her name dissolves into another coughing fit. Suddenly ruddy orange flames flicker through the haze, and I see the outline of a doorway – the entrance to Alexander's apartment.

"This way," booms another voice nearby, and just as I spot a second door – Maisie's, which is wide open as smoke pours from her sitting room – my so-called rescuer veers to the left and out into the freezing courtyard.

Almost instantly, the air clears, and I suck in a deep breath between coughs. Dimly I hear my mother calling my name nearby, and within moments, her arms are around me.

"Don't you *ever* do that again," she gasps, clutching me so tightly that I really can't breathe. "What were you *thinking*?"

"Maisie's still in there," I wheeze. Sirens sound nearby, and blue lights reflect off the walls of the courtyard as several fire trucks appear, along with multiple ambulances.

"And you were going to rescue her yourself?" says my mom, but she holds me even closer. "Come on – let's get you checked out."

I don't want to go anywhere without knowing my sister's

all right, but another pair of protection officers usher us both towards the centre of the courtyard, where an ambulance has parked. I crane my neck as we go, anxiously watching the doorway closest to Maisie's room, but no one comes or goes for nearly a minute.

"She probably went out through her window, sweetheart," says my mom as a technician presses a stethoscope to my chest, half an inch from my healing wound. "She'll be in the garden, no doubt."

"But it's a drop," I manage. "And if she jumped out the window—"

Suddenly the doors burst open, and a protection officer with an ash-streaked face barrels out of the castle, cradling a bundle with strawberry-blond curls.

My sister.

"*Maisie!*" I cry, even though my throat is raw from the smoke. This time, I dodge both my mother and the protection officer hovering nearby as I race across the courtyard towards a second ambulance near the doors. My lungs are on fire, but I don't care. All I can focus on is the fact that she isn't moving.

I reach the ambulance just as Maisie's rescuer sets her on a stretcher, and I skid to a stop a couple yards away. "Maisie?" I say as terror spreads through me, rooting my bare feet to the ground. "*Maisie.*"

She's still – too still. The sleeve of her flannel pyjamas is scorched, and her arm is red and angry, but the paramedics pay it no attention as they place an oxygen mask over her face. They move over her, listening to her heart and her lungs with calm urgency, but just as tears sting my already-watering eyes, hers fly open.

"Get – *off* – me!" she gasps, and my legs damn near give out from relief. But as soon as these three words escape her, she dissolves into a coughing fit so violent that I half expect her to expel a lung. She sits up, hunching over as her entire body contracts with each rattle, but even as the crowd around her gathers, she looks at me.

"Maisie," I choke out, only partially because of the smoke now. "Are you—"

She pushes aside a paramedic who has to be twice her size, and despite the way she's shaking, she slides off the stretcher and crosses the narrow distance between us, her hand pressing the oxygen mask to her face. I meet her halfway, and without a word, she hugs me fiercely, once again clinging to me like I'm the only thing keeping her standing – which, after a second or two, might actually be true.

"I'm sorry," she wheezes as she pulls her mask away. We're surrounded by protection officers and paramedics alike, but she shrugs off their touches as she holds on to me instead. "What I said—"

"It doesn't matter," I say. "Let them take care of you, okay? I'll be right here."

At last she allows the officers and medics to lift her back onto the stretcher, but as they tend to her, her gaze doesn't leave mine. And while the words she said and the accusations she slung hours earlier still hang between us, with the smoke rising from the castle and the flames flickering towards the night sky, they seem to fade until they, too, drift away on the wind.

Chapter Thirty-three

> A fire has broken out in the private royal apartments of Windsor Castle, the main residence of His Majesty, Princess Mary and Evangeline Bright. The status of the royal family is currently unknown.
>
> – Breaking news alert from the BBC,
> 5:14 a.m., 18 January 2024

Rather than yet another trip to the hospital, which our protection officers deem unsafe, Maisie, my mother and I are escorted by half the city's police to Apartment 1A in Kensington Palace, a sprawling brick maze of a manor that borders a massive park in the heart of London.

"I'll come inside with you," says my mom, a hint of nervousness in her voice as we pass through the gate and into a dark courtyard. "But once you're both settled in, I think I'll head back to the hospital."

While the thought of her leaving sets my already-frayed nerves on edge, I don't argue. It's no secret why she doesn't want to be here – Apartment 1A is where Helene and Nicholas have been secretly living together since the summer, and after the interview Helene gave to the BBC, I can't blame my mom for not feeling welcome.

Both Helene and Nicholas are waiting for us beneath the inky predawn sky in front of their apartment, which is really a four-storey, twenty-room wing of the palace that no one could ever seriously compare to the apartments in Windsor Castle – or any other actual apartment in London. One of the protection officers helps Maisie out of the car, her bandaged arm held tight against her chest, and Helene hurries towards her in a flood of tears.

"Oh, my darling," she cries. "Look at you. The doctors have already arrived, and we've arranged for you to be treated in one of the reception rooms."

"I'm perfectly all right, Mummy," says Maisie, but her voice is hoarse, the burn on her forearm is swathed in gauze, and there are still smudges of ash on her cheeks. "This is all completely unnecessary."

"I'll believe that once the doctors have said so themselves," says Helene, and she gently guides Maisie inside, leaving my mom and me behind without a hint of acknowledgement.

Nicholas lingers, however, and he clears his throat in the awkward silence. "Laura," he says with a nod. "Evangeline. We're relieved you're both all right. Have you been seen to?"

"I'm fine," says my mother before I can jump in. "But the paramedics were concerned about the amount of smoke Evan breathed in. She went after Maisie," she explains, giving me a hard look. "Straight towards the flames, like the entire building wasn't already looking for her."

My face grows warm. "I know, Mom. I'm sorry."

"We'll make sure she's examined, too," says Nicholas, ushering us both through the double doors. "That was brave of you, Evan. Reckless, but brave."

"Maisie would've done the same for me," I say, but that almost definitely isn't true. And judging by the quirk of Nicholas's left eyebrow, he's thinking the same thing.

As we walk across the marble floor of the foyer, warm light spills out from one of the reception rooms, and the crown moulding over the arched doorways casts strange shadows on the walls, making this feel like some kind of fever dream. But my mom takes my hand, and I'm painfully aware that it's all very, very real.

She stays with me in the makeshift clinic until one of the doctors – a blond woman with a sleek bun – does a thorough exam, draws some blood and declares that the worst I'll have to deal with is a temporary cough. Relieved, my mom kisses my forehead.

"If anything happens, let Jenkins know, and I'll come back immediately," she promises. "You're sure you're all right if I go?"

I nod. "I need to get some sleep anyway," I say, even though I want her to stay. But now that she knows I'm okay, I can tell she's desperate to check on Alexander. "I'll visit the hospital later today."

"Only if you're feeling up to it." She gives me one more lingering hug. "I love you, Evie."

"Love you, too, Mom," I say. And as I watch her with a heavy lump of unexplained dread in the pit of my stomach, she slips back into the foyer and the darkness beyond.

While my exam was relatively quick, Maisie is subjected to a battery of tests on the other side of the room. My eyelids grow heavy as the adrenaline finally begins to wear off, and I can hear the low murmur of concerned voices while they examine her chest X-ray.

"...need plenty of oxygen and rest," says Gupta. "We'll re-evaluate her progress this afternoon, and should there be any concerning changes—"

"I'm *fine*," wheezes Maisie, who's once again holding an oxygen mask to her face. "Really. Please don't put me in hospital. Everyone already thinks I'm weak—"

"Darling, if you need further treatment, then we'll do whatever we must," says Helene. "But I'd rather she not be exposed to the public unless absolutely necessary."

"Agreed, ma'am," says the protection officer who brought us bandages the night before. "I'll have a team secure King Edward VII's Hospital just in case."

"Evan," says Nicholas quietly, and I jerk my head up so fast that I think I sprain something. My uncle stands beside the antique chaise I'm curled up on, his mouth pinched and his expression haggard. "Why don't I show you to one of the guest rooms?"

"Thanks," I say, "but I'd rather stay here."

Nicholas smiles faintly, like he was expecting this. "Then I'll have a pillow and blanket brought in for you. And some water," he adds, as on the other side of the room, Helene tries to coax a miserable Maisie to drink.

I don't know why he's being so nice to me, but I nod, too tired to really question it. Maybe it's guilt, or maybe with Alexander fighting for his life, Nicholas has decided it's his job to step up and make sure I don't suddenly keel over. Either way, I thank him again, and when the pillow and blanket and water arrive, I drain the glass and make myself comfortable, only intending to doze.

Instead, I wake up a disorienting amount of time later, to the sound of Helene's gasp. "You're certain? You're *absolutely* certain?"

"Yes, ma'am," says a deep voice I recognize, but can't place. "My team took pictures of the scene, if you'd like to see them."

I sit up groggily and rub my eyes. Grey winter light streams through the sheer curtains in the reception room, and as I glance around, I notice Maisie lying in a bed twenty feet away as a nurse checks her blood pressure. But even though Maisie should be asleep – we should both be asleep – her eyes are open, and she's watching me.

"Hey," I say softly. "How are you feel—"

Before I can finish, a series of curses echoes through the foyer, growing louder as the click of heels approach. "After all we did – after everything she's put us through—"

"Ma'am—" says the familiar voice, but suddenly Helene appears in the arched doorway, the fury on her face so consuming that for a split second, she looks like a completely different person.

"*You*," she growls, rounding on me. "*You* did this."

"What?" I say, sitting up so fast that I'm light-headed.

"*You* set the fire," accuses Helene as she advances on me. "*You're* the one who nearly killed my daughter."

My mouth drops open. "I had nothing to do with—"

"Palace security found accelerant hidden in your sitting room," she says. "The same accelerant used to start the fire."

I stare at her, gaping, as a man I recognize from the morning council meetings appears with a tablet clutched in his hand. Stephens – the royal family's head of security.

"Turpentine," he clarifies, angling his screen to show me a picture of several bottles of paint thinner stored in a cabinet in my sitting room. "The brand matches the supply used by Ms Bright in His Majesty's private apartment over the past few weeks."

"I—" For a moment, I forget how to breathe. "I don't know how those got in my room, I swear. I didn't put them there. I don't paint—"

"Then are you saying your mother is the one responsible for the fire?" says Helene viciously.

"Of course not," I protest. "Why would she do that? Why would *either* of us do that?"

"Why don't you tell me, Evangeline?" says Helene. "Every time something dreadful happens lately, it all seems to come back to you, doesn't it? Maisie's protection officer said you were in my daughter's room last night. You would've had ample opportunity to splash turpentine around her bedroom—"

"I wasn't anywhere near her bedroom," I argue. "I would never—"

"Actually, ma'am," says Stephens abruptly, "we believe the fire started in His Majesty's bedroom and spread into Her Royal Highness's."

Helene lets out a humourless gasp of a laugh. "Lovely. Was it Laura after all? Have we been hosting an entire family of arsonists? No one's forgotten why you were expelled from your last boarding school," she adds, blue eyes narrowed at me. "You certainly have experience with this sort of thing, don't you? Perhaps your mother asked you for help, and you were all too eager to offer it."

I stand then, toe to toe with Helene, and even though I'm barefoot and more than half a foot shorter than her, I refuse to cower. "My mom and I didn't have anything to do with this. We were both in my apartment all night, and we didn't leave. Aren't there cameras all over Windsor? Can't you check the footage and—"

"There are none in the private apartments, at the request of Their Majesties," says Stephens, and his uncomfortable glance at Helene tells me exactly why. Because during her years of sneaking around with Nicholas, neither of them wanted to leave any evidence behind. And Alexander undoubtedly went along with it – probably out of guilt, or a misguided attempt to keep the peace.

And now I have no way of proving I didn't try to barbecue my own sister.

I let out a choking laugh, though while I mean for it to be sardonic, it comes out as more hysterical than anything. "Great. Terrific," I say, glaring at my stepmother. "I can't say anything to change your mind, can I? I could find whoever did this and have them confess in front of you, and somehow you'd *still* be convinced that it was me. But it wasn't. I would never hurt Maisie. She's my sister—"

"*Half*-sister," corrects Helene sharply.

"She's my *family*," I say. "And that actually means something to me. I am not the source of all your problems, Helene. I'm sorry that my existence hurts you. I'm sorry my parents made some pretty awful choices, and you had to pay the price. But I didn't do this. My mother didn't do this. And the longer you insist that we did, the longer the real culprit is still out there, and the longer *you're* the one putting your entire family in danger by refusing to believe anything but the worst in me."

She stands there, cold as ice, for the better part of ten seconds. "Get out," she snarls.

"Mummy," says Maisie pleadingly. "Evan didn't do this. Someone must have planted the bottles, or maybe Laura stored them there ages ago, and—"

"Stay out of this, Maisie," orders Helene, her tone as hard as diamonds. To my dismay, Maisie falls silent, but I can see her staring a hole into the back of her mother's head. "*You*, Evangeline, will leave my home and stay away from my family. You've been nothing but a plague on us since the day you were born, and if you ever come near us again, I will go straight to the *Daily Sun* and tell them you were the one who started the fire."

I shouldn't be surprised – there's no low Helene won't stoop to, apparently, though I still stare at her in disbelief. "But I didn't," I insist. "*It wasn't me*."

"And yet all evidence points directly to you. What a terrible coincidence, if it truly wasn't." The honeyed venom in her voice is back, and a shiver runs through me like I've stepped outside into the winter chill. "You've already given the world plenty of reasons to hate you, Evangeline, but I am more than happy to offer them another. Now *go*, before I have you dragged out by your damn ear."

I swallow hard, and for a moment, I think I might cry, but I refuse to give Helene the satisfaction. Maisie looks furious, too, but she doesn't speak up again. And Stephens stares at his feet, still clutching his tablet and clearly uninterested in correcting his queen – or maybe he thinks I did it, too. Maybe they all do, and there's nothing I'll ever be able to say to get out of this one.

Fine. If Helene wants to burn it all down, then so be it.

"No matter how much the people hate me," I say through gritted teeth, "it'll never make them love you again. You will *always* be the heartless monster who left the King for his own brother – who lied to the people about your marriage for *decades*, and who hasn't visited her husband a single time since he was nearly blown to pieces. That's your legacy. That's what the world will remember about you. And there is nothing – *nothing* you can do to change it."

For a split second, Helene looks like I've slapped her, and part of me wishes I had. But as she opens her mouth – maybe to retort, maybe to tell Stephens to throw me into the courtyard by my hair – I slip past her and head towards the archway, refusing to look anyone in the eye. Even Maisie.

The entrance hall isn't empty, like I expect. Instead, Nicholas stands near the front door, along with another familiar man in an equally familiar suit. Suraj Singh.

Though I'm still in my pyjamas, which carry more than a faint whiff of smoke, I hold my head high as I stride towards the exit, intent on ignoring them completely. But as I approach, Nicholas moves between me and the double doors.

"Evangeline," he says, barely audible over Helene's furious screeches echoing from the reception room, her words mercifully indecipherable. "Please accept my apologies for Her Majesty's behaviour. We – she's had quite a scare this morning, and I'm afraid with everything else that's happened as of late, she isn't handling it well."

"I don't care," I say coldly. "She's your problem, not mine. I need to go."

"You're welcome to stay," he says, but we both know that's a lie. I give him a look, and he grimaces. "Well – at least let me escort you to Clarence House. Mother has plenty of room, and…"

He falters again at the expression on my face, and it takes all the effort I have left in me to be polite. "Thank you," I manage, "but I don't need your help. I'm going to the hospital to see my mom and Alexander."

"And after?" he says. "Perhaps I can ask the staff to ready Nottingham Cottage, or a room at Buckingham Palace, or any of the other properties nearby—"

"I'll figure something out," I say. "I just – I need to go."

Nicholas looks oddly crestfallen, but he nods. "There's a car waiting for you outside," he says. "It'll take you anywhere you want to go. And if there's anything you need…"

"Thanks," I say again, barely able to force myself to speak. But while he, at least, doesn't seem to believe I started the fire, there's no doubt in my mind that he'll follow Helene's lead, no matter where it might take him.

The cobblestones are icy against my bare feet as I step into the courtyard, and sure enough, there's a Range Rover idling several yards from the door. I'm halfway there when a sharp pebble digs into my heel, and I wince, pausing long enough to rub my foot against my other leg to dislodge the tiny rock.

In those few seconds, Singh appears in front of me, his hands in his pockets and his breath visible in the freezing morning air. I try to step around him, but he moves with me, blocking my way again.

"I don't want to hear it," I say sharply. "I didn't set the fire. I was in my room the entire night, and I had nothing to do with—"

"I never suspected you," says Singh in an infuriatingly neutral tone that doesn't give anything away, but it's enough to steal my indignation right out from under me.

"Do you know who did it, then?" I say warily.

"Haven't a clue," he admits, "but I am certain it wasn't you – or as certain as I can be, given the circumstances. Someone seems desperate to make everyone believe it was you, though, don't they? And that, to me, is exceptionally curious, especially considering everything else that's happened lately. Once again, this is all so very, very neat – and so very, very sloppy at the same time."

I frown. "You think the ABR might've been behind this, too?"

"They haven't taken credit, but the day is young," he says. "Though I sincerely hope they haven't breached the palace. If they have…"

I shiver again, and not because of the cold. "I just know it wasn't me or my mom."

"And as I said, Miss Bright, I believe you. In fact…" Singh reaches into the inner pocket of his suit jacket and produces a phone. "This belongs to you."

I take it gingerly, like this, too, might explode in my face. "You're giving me back my phone?"

"And your laptop, though I'm afraid I haven't got that in my pocket," he says with a hint of humour I'm too miserable to appreciate. "They were clean, as you undoubtedly know, other than a stray number under Aoife Marsh's name."

"It wasn't hers?" I say, confused.

"Not unless she's the owner of a Pizza Express in Derby," he says, and while this time I should be surprised, I'm not. Of course Kit didn't give me her real number, and I'm suddenly glad I never used it.

"What about Kit's phone?" I say as I press the power button. "Was it…?"

"Lord Clarence's personal items have also been returned to him," he says. "Other than the emails and messages he exchanged with members of Fox Rex, all of which he shared willingly, we found nothing to connect either of you with the bombing."

It isn't until that moment that I realize part of me – a minuscule part, but one that still exists – worried that Kit was lying, and that something on his devices would incriminate him. Maybe both of us. But as I watch my phone boot up, my eyes sting with tears, and I nod mutely.

Kit's innocent. We're both innocent. And someone is still coming after us with everything they've – he's – got.

"I took the liberty of adding my direct number to your contacts," says Singh after it becomes clear I can't speak. "Not strictly above board, but I thought it would be best if you had an easy way to keep in touch, should anything else pop up. I'm on your side, Evangeline," he adds. "I believe someone close to the royal family is framing you, with the assistance of the ABR. And whoever it is, I'm as keen to catch them as you are."

We both know exactly who it is, but all I can manage is another nod as I wipe my eyes with my sleeve. Even if I could form words right now, there's no use making my case again, not when I don't have proof. But Singh's support is an antidote to Helene's poison, and I almost – *almost* – believe him.

Singh opens the door to the Range Rover, and a blast of heat emanates from inside. "Keep in touch, Miss Bright," he says. "This is unlikely to be the end of it, I'm afraid, but if you and I are both lucky, perhaps we might find a way to help each other."

I have no idea what that means, but he doesn't elaborate as I climb into the SUV. Without another word, he closes the door behind me, and even though the windows are tinted, I can feel his gaze on me for a long moment before he heads back inside.

Closing my eyes, I try to take a deep breath to calm myself down. My irritated lungs aren't thrilled with the concept, however, and I end up in the middle of a coughing fit, painfully aware of the driver watching me through the rear-view mirror.

"Good morning, Miss Bright," he says as soon as the coughs subside. "Where would you like to go?"

"The hospital," I say. "I want to visit my dad."

He nods, and as he radios in our location, I tug on the seat belt. It locks up before I can pull it all the way across my body, and I mutter to myself, vaguely wondering how this day could possibly get any worse – and that's when I hear it.

"*Evangeline.*"

The sound of my name echoes off the brick and stone courtyard, and I clench my jaw. Not again. Not here – not now, not when everything else is falling apart.

"*Evangeline.*"

As the Range Rover starts to roll down the concrete drive, my name grows louder, and I resist the urge to cover my ears. It won't help, not when it's in my head. But without any warning, the driver hits the brakes, and I have to catch myself on the seat in front of me.

"Evangeline!"

This time, when I hear my name, it's through the door, and I do a double take when I realize that Maisie's on the other side. She's breathing heavily, and Helene and Nicholas rush out of Apartment 1A after her, but there's a determined look in her eye that I know better than to challenge.

"Will you open the bloody door?" she says, exasperated, and I fumble with the handle until it pops open.

"Maisie? What are you—"

"Move," she orders, and I hastily shift to the other seat. Helene and Nicholas shout Maisie's name as they hurry across the courtyard, but she ignores them and slams the door shut. "Palace Gardens Terrace, Matthew," she says to the driver. "You know the number."

"Yes, Your Royal Highness," he says, and seconds before Helene and Nicholas reach the Range Rover, we take off, and neither Maisie nor I look back.

It's only as we pass through the gate and onto the main road that I realize Maisie is clutching a tablet – the same one Stephens was holding minutes earlier. "You should be resting," I say. "Not – whatever this is."

"You sound uncannily like Mummy," she mutters, waking the screen. "And I'm going with you. I would've thought that was obvious."

"Yes, but – why?" I say. Maybe it's a question I shouldn't be asking, but I can't help myself, not after our argument the night before.

"Because," she says simply, and she hands me the tablet. "You're right about Ben. And I've found proof."

Chapter Thirty-four

We at the *Regal Record* have exclusively learned that while His Majesty fights for his life, Laura Bright, his reported mistress, is treating the King's private apartment as her own – and even sleeping in his bed.

While one might argue that this is nothing short of expected for a woman who's spent more than two decades chipping away at the marriage between the King and Queen, to do so while His Majesty remains hospitalized in a critical state is perhaps Laura's most audacious move yet. Palace insiders claim that even after the revelation that her daughter, Evangeline, is working with the Army of the British Republic, Laura has insisted on spending much of her time ordering around the household staff, in anticipation of His Majesty's recovery.

"She's delusional," says an anonymous royal insider. "Maybe it's her illness, but she really is acting like she'll be queen someday."

As our country is thrown into chaos in the wake of the terrorist attack that claimed the lives of eight people, one would hope that Ms Bright might spare us all the reminder that a home-wrecker remains at Windsor Castle – and that the British people are paying for her royal accommodations.

– *The Regal Record*, 18 January 2024

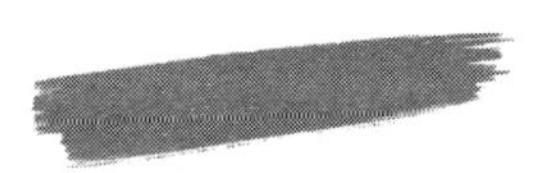

You're right about Ben.

As Maisie hands me the tablet, her voice ricochets in my head like a bullet, and I examine the picture on the screen. Her supposed proof doesn't look like much – just a piece of metal no bigger than a dime taped to the inside of a hollowed-out book. Hardly irrefutable evidence that Ben enlisted someone inside the palace to leak secrets. Or potentially try to kill us.

"What's this?" I say, zooming in, but I still can't identify it. Instead of answering, my sister swipes to another photograph, this time of the same kind of device concealed in the folds of a red velvet curtain. A third image shows one inside a lampshade, and then one more nestled in a wooden crevice that might be part of an armoire.

"I don't get it," I say as she swipes through several more. "What am I looking at?"

Maisie huffs. "I don't know how it's possible that your skull keeps getting thicker with age, but clearly you're a medical marvel."

She stops at a photograph of an entire room – my sitting room. It looks like a crime scene, with numbered markers seemingly everywhere, and from this angle, I can see the open cabinet where security found the paint thinner. The thought of anyone searching my apartment makes my skin crawl, but even amidst the feeling of utter violation, something else clicks.

"Are these…?" I swipe back to look at the last picture. "Are these *bugs*?"

"If by 'bugs', you mean covert transmitters and listening

devices, then yes," says Maisie curtly. "They found no fewer than twenty in your apartment."

"Twen…?" The word dies halfway off my tongue, and suddenly I feel like I'm falling through the air at a tremendous speed, as every single one of my internal organs finds a new place to settle. "Maisie—"

"Someone's been spying on you," she says. "And I'm positive that Ben had something to do with it."

"How?" I say in a choked voice, cycling through the pictures again. "How can you possibly connect this to Ben?"

"Because he used to do it to me," she says, and at my startled look, she waves off my concern. "Nothing untoward, of course. We were children. We saw these devices used in some film, I think, and we begged our parents for a set to play with. We used to hide them in the nursery – try to eavesdrop on our nannies, and even sometimes each other. It was fun," she added defensively. "We didn't have secrets then, of course."

My mouth is still dry, and it takes me a moment to speak. "And you think…you think he's behind this, too? You can prove it?"

"Well – I mean, no, I can't *prove* it," she says. "Not unless there are fingerprints on any of them. But he was here last week, wasn't he? He could've planted them then, or maybe he really does have someone in the palace working for him, and they did it ages ago. If he's been listening in, it would explain the leaks, wouldn't it?"

My mind is racing, and I shake my head, as if that'll somehow force things into neat little boxes so I can begin to make sense of it all. "I never talked to anyone about your injuries, though. Or about Thaddeus's roses, or any other secrets the *Regal Record* made public. I don't think Tibby ever brought them up, either. I don't even think she knows."

Maisie considers me for a long moment. "You're absolutely certain? There's no way you could've...I don't know, mentioned it to Kit, perhaps?"

"Maybe." I frown. "But I really don't think any of it came from..."

I pause as a horrifying thought swims to the forefront of my mind, as if it's been there all this time, waiting for me to notice. "Maisie," I say slowly. "Are these just listening devices? Or are they speakers, too?"

Maisie takes the tablet and swipes to another picture. "Most are listening devices, but Stephens said that the ones that look like these are tiny speakers."

Every inch of me freezes into place, and I stare at the image until it's nothing but a blur of colours.

Speakers. I've had speakers in my apartment. Maybe for days, but possibly for weeks. Or longer.

My throat is tight, and I gasp for air, barely managing enough to speak. "Maisie – I've been hearing things – voices—"

"You've what?" she says, startled.

"For weeks, ever since Sandringham. I thought they were real. Or – that they were in my head, I mean," I say. "But I think – I think it was Ben. You're *sure* this is something he'd do?"

She nods, her eyebrows knit as she zooms in on the device again. "Positive. It's exactly his style."

I reach for one of the miniature bottles of water stored in the centre console, my thoughts reeling. It was Ben. It was Ben this entire time, whispering my name, freaking me out, making me think I was having hallucinations –

"The day of the bombing, the voices told me I was going to die," I say, struggling to get the words out. "Kit was there – I don't think he heard them, but I told him, and – I was a mess."

"The day of the bombing?" she says, with a hint of scepticism. "You're sure?"

"That's not the kind of thing you forget," I mutter. "But I think...I think Ben was trying to scare me. To make me believe I was losing my mind, or – that maybe I was showing signs of schizophrenia."

Maisie scowls so deeply that she looks almost like a cartoon. "That's *ghastly*. Why on earth would he do that?"

"I don't know," I say, slumping against the seat as I twist off the plastic cap. "Why is he sending me flowers? Why did he give me that photo album? Why did he tell me it should've been me? Why is he trying to convince me I'm having auditory hallucinations? It doesn't make *sense*."

Maisie takes a water for herself, and she drinks half of it before slowly setting her bottle down. "Yes, it does. He's trying to discredit you. No one believes the mad girl, do they? That's why he felt he could say those things to you – because you've already been cracking, and don't deny it. I've known something was wrong for ages, but I thought it was – well, you know, getting shot. PTSD. That sort of thing."

"The voices started before then," I say, thinking back. "The morning you tried to get me and Kit to go hunting with you – the morning of the shooting. That's when they began."

Maisie sighs. "Well, it certainly fits the timeline, doesn't it?

Of Ben lurking about and being…*Ben*."

"But why?" I press. "What's the point? No one cares what I think or do. Why bother with all this in the first place?"

It's the same question I've been asking myself for months. But even now, with so many new pieces of the puzzle snapping into place, I still can't see the bigger picture – I still don't understand why Ben is torturing me. And I'm beginning to wonder if I ever will.

"I don't know," says Maisie. "And neither do you, so let's focus on what we do know, shall we? We *do* know that yesterday, someone poured turpentine all throughout Daddy's apartment, including his bedroom, and set it on fire. But who was it?"

"Not me," I say automatically, and Maisie rolls her eyes again.

"Yes, *obviously*. I'm not accusing you. Honestly, Evangeline, you're too bloody sensitive sometimes."

"I'm not—" I pause and sip my water. It isn't worth the fight. "You really believe me?"

"Of course I do," she says with a faint wheeze. "The fire started in Daddy's apartment, and your mother's the only one staying there at the moment. You have no reason to hurt her. If anything, you go a bit feral whenever anyone so much as insinuates that she's not the single greatest human being on the planet—"

"You think whoever did this wanted to hurt my mom?" I say, stunned. But now that she's said it, it makes perfect sense, and a wave of nausea hits me.

"Well, yes," says Maisie. "I suppose they could've been coming after me, considering how close my rooms are to his, but it seems a rather roundabout way of assassinating someone, doesn't it?"

My mind is racing again, and I take another sip of water in hopes of calming my roiling stomach. "If they were going after my mom, why yesterday? Because she finally came back from the hospital? Was it their only opportunity? But it can't be, not when she's been staying at the castle for weeks. The whole staff knew. The family, everyone—"

I freeze, and Maisie leans in, her blue eyes bright. "What?" she says. "I know that look, Evan. What is it? *Tell me.*"

"I—" I swallow painfully. "You're not going to like it."

"I don't bloody care," she says, breathless again. "Spit it out already."

The last thing I want to do is reignite the fight we had yesterday, but I don't have a choice. Not really. Besides, it all makes sense, and I hate myself a little for not seeing it sooner.

"When my mom and I got back from the hospital yesterday..." I hesitate again. "I ran into Rosie, right by Alexander's apartment. My mom went inside, and...Rosie asked me about her."

"What did she say?" says Maisie, and I can hear the familiar defensiveness in her voice already.

"Something about how she had no idea that my mom was staying in Alexander's suite. That she'd thought she'd gone back to Virginia, and..." I take another sip of my water, but it does nothing to alleviate the dryness in my throat. "I don't know. The whole thing was weird. She almost seemed guilty, and she kept saying she had no idea, but..."

I trail off. Maisie isn't looking at me any more, and there's a strange expression on her face as she types something into the tablet. A moment later, the *Regal Record* appears. The latest headline announces the fire, and as Maisie skims past the article that follows, I spot my name alongside *a history of arson*. And even though I should expect it – even though I know I've already been linked to the ABR, and no one in the country will give me the benefit of the doubt now – the reality of what's happening outside our isolated palace bubble hits me like a brick wall.

Everyone hates me. The *Daily Sun*, the *Regal Record*, every troll on social media – no doubt they're claiming that I'm the one who set the fire that could've killed my sister. Worse, I have no defence except my word. Because I *was* there that night. The turpentine *was* in my room. And even though I know it's all some twisted set-up, most of the world already believes I was involved in the bombing, and I'm coldly certain that they won't think twice before accepting this as the truth, too.

It doesn't matter that I didn't do it. No amount of innocence will ever wipe the slate clean, and for as long as I live, these whispers will follow me around, one more black mark on an already scandalous list. *Treasonous* list, now, with the bombing and two attempted murders to add to my count.

At last Maisie turns the tablet towards me again, and I see the headline she was searching for, time-stamped shortly after midnight.

WHILE ALEXANDER FIGHTS FOR HIS LIFE,
LAURA PLAYS WIFE

I blink once, twice, certain I'm reading it wrong, or at the very least making connections that aren't really there. But at the same time, I know I'm not – for exactly the same reason that, even though this article is made up of rumours and anonymous sources that add up to nothing but hot air, it happens to be right. That all the articles on the *Regal Record* happen to be right.

"Did you ever tell Rosie and Gia about my mom staying at Windsor?" I say, choosing my words carefully despite my racing pulse.

"No," says Maisie, though she's already pulled out her phone and is scrolling through what looks like a group text. "No, I – no, I never talked to them about Laura. Even at Klosters, we all avoided the subject. No one wanted to upset Mummy."

"Did your mother mention it during the interview?" I press. "She didn't, right? I would've remembered that."

"I don't think she did, either," says Maisie, her voice slightly panicked now as she continues to scroll through her texts. "Evan…it can't… Rosie *wouldn't*…"

"Maybe not," I say, because as much as I dislike her, I can't imagine her trying to burn my mother alive. "But if there's even a chance that she knows who did…"

Maisie's eyes flutter shut, and her throat works convulsively, like she's trying not to cry. "It's just a coincidence," she says. "She would never."

I stay silent, partially because I really am afraid of starting another fight, but also because I can tell she doesn't need my help coming to the inevitable conclusion. And sure enough, when she opens her eyes again, they're red and watery, but there's a look of determination on her face, too.

"We need to talk to her," says Maisie, her wheeze back now. "Even if she has nothing to do with any of it, even if it's…it's nothing, maybe…"

"She could've seen someone else lurking around," I say. "Or maybe she heard something while we were in your room. Anything's possible."

"Anything's possible," she echoes, but there's no real feeling behind it. She plucks a tissue from the console and dabs at her eyes. "She'll deny it all, though. Even if she has vital information, she won't admit it, not if she thinks our friendship is on the line."

I shrug. "Then we'll just have to find another way to get her to talk."

The Range Rover begins to slow, and when I glance out the window, my heart skips a beat. We're on a residential street now, with a row of neat white town houses on either side and expensive vehicles parked along the pavement. And just up ahead, standing by a wrought-iron gate, is a boy with a familiar head of wavy dark hair.

"How?" says Maisie miserably. "The more we push, the more scared she'll be."

Our driver stops in front of the gate, and even though it takes everything I have, I look back at Maisie and squeeze her hand.

"I think I have an idea," I say, and I flash her a reassuring smile before opening the door and leaping onto the sidewalk, where Kit is waiting for me with open arms.

Chapter Thirty-five

Kit:

Rosie, are you awake?

Rosie:

omg hi! yes, just taking snickers for a walk xx

Kit:

Did you hear about the fire?

Rosie:

fire?? what fire??? xx

Kit:

At Windsor this morning. Maisie's safe. She's at KP with Aunt Helene

Rosie:

evan and her mum were there?

Kit:

Yes. And I think . . .

Rosie:

?????
kit???
is everything okay????

Kit:

Are you free?

Rosie:

right now? do you want to ring me? xx

Kit:

In person, if you can. I'd rather not discuss this over the phone

Rosie:

i can pop by in an hour xx

Kit:

Perfect. Thank you, Rosie. I don't know who else to trust

Rosie:

you can always trust me xx
i'll be by right away xx

Kit:

Thank you. xxx

– Text message exchange between Lady Primrose Chesterfield-Bishop and the mobile of Christopher Abbott-Montgomery, Earl of Clarence, 18 January 2024

The doorbell of the Abbot-Montgomerys' town house rings at ten o'clock on the dot.

As Maisie and I watch through the nearest strategically placed security camera, Kit, wearing a grey sweater and black trousers that fit him a little too well, pads to the door and opens it, revealing a pink-faced and breathless Rosie.

"Kit!" she squeals, and even though Maisie and I are listening through headphones in the basement, we both wince at her high pitch. Without waiting for an invitation, Rosie leaps over the threshold and throws her arms around Kit, embracing him like they've been reunited after years apart.

"Rosie," he says, hugging her affectionately in return, though I don't miss the look he gives the camera. "It's lovely of you to pop by so quickly. I didn't interrupt anything, did I?"

"Of course not," she says as she finally releases him. "It sounded important. Is everything all right?"

"I..." Kit glances out towards the street in an impressive show of paranoia. "Let's go inside, shall we? I have a tea tray ready."

Rosie doesn't need persuading. She hugs his arm, and Kit leads her into a cosy sitting room as I switch the feed to a second camera. "What's this about?" she says as they sit side by side on the love seat, even though there are two armchairs and a separate sofa to choose from. "Are you sure Maisie's all right? Some people on social media are saying—"

"She's fine," he assures her. "The palace isn't releasing any information right now for security reasons, but no one was seriously injured."

Rosie nods, and while it might be the camera, she seems paler than usual. "Security reasons? Is something else going on?"

"I..." Kit hesitates. "I'm not supposed to say anything, but... Stephens and the protection officers think the fire was set on purpose."

Her mouth drops open a split second too late to be truly

convincing. "*Really?* Do they know who…I mean, do they have a suspect, or…?"

Kit stares at his knees, and his hair falls into his eyes, hiding his expression. "You have to swear you won't breathe a word of this to anyone," he says, so quietly now that the microphone barely registers his voice.

"Of course," she says immediately, and she takes his hand in hers. "Kit, you know I won't say anything. You can trust me."

Beside me, Maisie is slowly tearing a tissue to shreds. "Liar," she mutters, and even though I silently agree, I don't say a word as Kit launches into the story the three of us concocted. Which is, admittedly, less a work of fiction and more what everyone else will think by the time the sun sets.

"Palace security found accelerant in Evan's sitting room," he says in a hushed voice. "They think…they think she set the fire. And they think Maisie was the intended victim."

This time, the surprise on Rosie's face is real. Not, I suspect, because I've been framed, but because Rosie knows that Maisie was never supposed to be targeted.

"They…*what?*" she gasps, and there's an eagerness in the way she leans closer to Kit. "You really think it was Evan?"

Kit nods and rakes his hair out of his eyes, not quite looking at her. "I don't want to, but – what else am I supposed to believe? I just…I never thought she would ever…"

His voice breaks, and for a split second, I forget this isn't real. Rosie throws her arms around him, pressing her cheek to his. "Oh, Kit," she murmurs. "I'm so sorry. Of course you had no idea. None of us did. She seemed all right, didn't she? But she's had a troubled life, and all that nasty business with her mother…

well, sometimes the apple doesn't fall far from the tree."

Kit's entire body tenses, but Rosie doesn't let go. "I just wish I understood why," he mumbles into her shoulder. "I thought she loved Maisie. They've fought a few times, but that's normal for sisters, and Maisie's always been a bit prickly –"

"I'll show you prickly," mutters Maisie, and I elbow her in the side.

"– but I never thought Evan would try to kill her," continues Kit. "It doesn't make *sense*."

Rosie is quiet for several long seconds, her fingers now toying with the ends of Kit's hair. "Well...maybe it does," she says, and Maisie and I both go still.

"What do you mean?" says Kit, and he pulls away enough to look at her – but, I notice, he doesn't untangle himself completely.

"I..." Rosie pauses, and I can feel my heart pounding. For a few seconds, I don't breathe, terrified she might not finish. But then Kit takes her hand, and I can practically see Rosie melt.

"Go on," he says gently, lacing his fingers through hers. "I won't tell anyone. Not if you'd rather I didn't."

"It's important people know," she says, her voice wavering. "Motive is important. But...they can't know it came from me, all right?"

"They won't," he says, his eyes locked on hers now, and as she stares back, the tension seems to drain from her until she's curled against his chest.

"Do you know anything about the Legitimacy Act of 1959?" she says, and beside me, Maisie sucks in a breath.

"Er...I'm not acquainted with the particulars," says Kit, sounding as baffled as I am.

"Well," says Rosie, and there's a note of exhilaration in her voice now – either because she has a captive audience in Kit, or because she knows something the rest of us don't. "It's all a bit complicated, but it basically legitimizes children born of an adulterous affair – *if* their parents later marry."

The way she words this doesn't sound like her – it sounds like someone fed her this exact phrase, and she's relishing the chance to pass it on to Kit. But I'm so distracted by the way she says it that *what* she's saying doesn't start to sink in until I feel Maisie's nails digging into my forearm.

"*Ow*," I hiss. "What are you—"

"I know what's going on," she says, her eyes wide. "I know why Ben's doing this."

But before she can explain, Kit leaps to his feet, dislodging Rosie and forcing her to sit up. "Wait – *wait*," he says, like he's also having trouble fully grasping the concept. "You think Evan tried to kill Maisie because…?"

"Because if her parents marry, she'll be legitimate, and then she'll get to be queen," says Rosie, though she doesn't sound as sure of herself now. "That's what the law says, doesn't it?"

Kit shakes his head, and he begins to pace. "No – no, that's not true. Even if she's legitimized, she won't be placed in the line of succession. She can't be, not without an act of Parliament."

"But her heirs would be," says Rosie, yet again triumphant at knowing something he doesn't. "So if Maisie's dead, even if Evan can't be queen, her oldest child would still become the monarch."

Finally everything she's saying hits me, and something inside me – something I can't name – caves in on itself, suffocating me in the process. "Maisie, is that—"

She's already standing, though, and she flings her headphones aside as she hurries towards the stairs. Reeling, I race after her, and even though Maisie is wheezing so loudly that it's a miracle she can make it up the steps at all, she's still somehow faster than I am.

"Maisie—" I hiss, but it's too late. She marches straight through the kitchen and into the sitting room, stopping in the dead centre of the archway.

"I didn't realize you were such a scholar when it came to succession law," says Maisie, her tone deceptively mild despite her heavy breathing, and Rosie's jaw practically drops to the floor.

"Maisie! Are you—" She scrambles off the love seat, but Kit loops his arm around hers.

"I think it'd be best if you stayed here with me for now," he says, and confusion flickers across Rosie's face – until she glances at the archway again and finally sees me lingering behind my sister.

I've never seen anyone lose their colour so quickly, and for a split second, I'm positive she's about to faint. But somehow she manages to stay on her feet, and though she sways, Kit is there to steady her.

"Evan – you're here." She chokes out my name like it hurts, but I'm too stunned to feel any sense of satisfaction. "And – and Maisie – you're okay? Kit said—"

"How kind of you to be so concerned," says Maisie, her voice sweet venom now. "If Evan was the one to set the fire because she wanted the throne to herself, then explain to me why she started it in Daddy's bedroom, not mine."

"I—" Rosie gapes at her, but this time, she doesn't look the least bit surprised. "I don't know."

"And why would she be so careless as to keep evidence of her crime hidden in her own sitting room?" says Maisie. "She may be American, but even she has the brains to think that one through."

"Really, Maisie?" I say, but there's no bite behind it. I don't have it in me. I don't have anything in me right now except bewildered disbelief and a healthy dose of panic.

"I – I don't know," says Rosie again. "Maybe...maybe the other doors were locked."

"Maybe the *hundreds* of other doors in Windsor Castle were locked," repeats Maisie, as if this is a legitimate possibility. "I see."

"I don't know. I don't *know*," cries Rosie. "Maisie, please—"

"You can't explain why you think Evan's the main suspect in a fire that could've – *should've* – killed her mother, yet you can paraphrase obscure and nearly obsolete legislation from sixty-five years ago," says Maisie calmly. "How curious."

Instantly Rosie shuts her mouth, and she yanks her elbow from Kit's grip. He lets her go, and she stumbles backwards towards the mantel, her arms crossed tightly over her chest. "Maisie, I don't – whatever's going on—"

"That's precisely what I'm trying to discover," says Maisie. "Because you're one of my best friends, and because I know none of this could've possibly been your idea, I'll give you one chance to explain, Rosie. Tell me everything – and I do mean *everything* – and we won't involve the police."

Rosie stares at her, so pale now that her lips are bloodless. I expect her to object again, to insist this is all some kind of misunderstanding, but instead, her chin quivers, and she bursts into tears.

"It was him," she sobs. "All of it – it was all him. He wanted me to start the fire, and he told me how – he threatened me – but as soon as I saw Evan's mum there, I refused, and he threatened me again, but—"

She's crying so hard now that the rest of her words are lost on me, but neither Kit nor Maisie moves to comfort her. Instead, with her legs shaking like a newborn fawn's, Rosie teeters towards the nearest armchair and collapses.

"Who?" demands Maisie, but Rosie ignores the question as she weeps into her hands.

"I didn't hurt anyone. I didn't start the fire – I *didn't*, I swear. It was just supposed to be gossip. Tidbits. You know, things that – things that didn't matter. But then he kept asking for more, and more, and more, and—" She hiccups. "Then he wanted pictures and information and secrets, and I tried to refuse, but his threats got worse, and I couldn't tell him no, Maisie. I tried, but—"

"*Who?*" demands my sister.

"No one was supposed to get hurt," says Rosie. "He swore – he *swore*—"

"Rosie, if you don't say his name this instant, I will come over there and rip your curls out one by one," snarls Maisie, and Rosie gives her such a desperate look that for a moment, I almost feel sorry for her.

"You already know who," she whimpers.

Maisie advances across the threshold and into the sitting room. "Tell me."

"I can't."

"*Say his bloody name, or so help me*—"

"I *can't!*"

Rosie flies to her feet again, and Kit barely manages to dodge out of her way as she takes a few furious steps towards us. Then, almost as if she loses her nerve, she backtracks until her legs hit the edge of the armchair once more.

"I can't, Maisie," she whispers. "You don't understand. The things he has on me...the things he could do to me..."

"What about the things *I* could do to you?" growls my sister. "Because believe me, I am sorely tempted."

Rosie wipes her eyes. "He could do so, so, *so* much worse. He has pictures...and video...he could ruin my family...he could ruin *everything*."

With nauseating clarity, I flash back to the night that the *Regal Record* posted the video of Jasper assaulting me. I remember how it felt, watching it all unfold, knowing that millions – *billions* of people could watch it, too, if they wanted. With a single click of a button, the worst thing that had ever happened to me was viewable to anyone with an internet connection and a questionable moral compass. And there isn't a doubt in my mind that if Ben had given me a chance, I would've done damn near anything to prevent it from going public.

"Do you swear on your life – on Snickers's life – that you had nothing to do with the fire?" I say, as Maisie struggles to sputter out a coherent response. Clearly Rosie has never told her no before, and the idea isn't landing well.

Rosie nods miserably. "I can show you the texts. He gave me a prepaid mobile – it's how he keeps in touch. He told me to spread the paint thinner and sneak the cans into Evan's room, and he said someone else would light it so it couldn't be traced back to me. I didn't want to, but maybe – maybe I would've – but as soon as I saw you and your mum there, I knew I couldn't. I swear," she says, crying again. "Evan, I *swear*."

"Okay," I say quietly, my stomach churning with acidic fury that has nowhere to go. "Right now, until you give us a reason to change our minds, we're going to move forward like that's the truth."

"It *is*," wails Rosie, even as Maisie hisses my name, but I ignore them both.

"Now let's talk about the rest of this," I say, the steadiness of my voice an act of sheer willpower. "Is it true? That if my parents get married, I'll be legitimized?"

"Yes," says Maisie before Rosie can answer. "Though Kit's right – you wouldn't be in the line of succession, not without an act of Parliament that will never, ever happen."

"But my theoretical heirs would be," I say, and now it's Kit who nods.

"The line of succession would treat you as if…well, as if you weren't alive," he says. "But you're still the King's daughter, and if you were legitimized, your children would be placed after Maisie."

"And ahead of Ben," I say, and this time it isn't a question.

Silence settles between us as everything – *everything* finally falls into place. Why Ben's been after me since the moment I stepped foot in the UK. Why he's dragged my name through the mud again and again. Why he tried to make me question my own mental health. Why he convinced an actual terrorist group to claim me as one of their own and brand me a traitor who tried to kill my own father.

It's because he's afraid of me. And he's afraid of losing the crown that, since the moment he found out about Maisie and Gia, he thought was his for the taking.

I swear softly and lean against the archway, not sure I can hold my own weight any more. Kit steps towards me, but I shake my head. He has to stay where he is, as close as Rosie will let him, in case she bolts.

"He's been doing this from the start," I say, a little light-headed as it all clicks. "He and Jasper – they drugged me and assaulted me and filmed it to try to chase me out of the country. To make sure I was too humiliated and broken to stay. And when that didn't work, when we figured out Ben was behind it and Alexander banished him, he stopped playing nice and tried to have me killed at Sandringham. And the bombing...he knew about it beforehand. What he said to me and Kit – he's connected to the ABR somehow. I know it. I *know* it. And the fire..." I grit my teeth. "Maisie's right. It should've killed my mom. He must have someone else in the castle, too – someone who really did light it, without realizing my mom was in my room instead."

Kit is already on his phone, texting someone – palace security, I assume, or maybe Helene – but Rosie looks back and forth between Maisie and me, terror written on her face.

"So – the whole point *was* to...to hurt your mum?" she manages.

"The whole point was to *murder* her mother," says Maisie flatly, but her eyes are wide now as she puts the pieces together, too. "Daddy, Laura and Evan are the only ones standing in Ben's way now. If one of them dies, it's over – the line of succession stays as it is, and he's safe. That rotten bastard," she mutters.

"That knob-headed, spiteful *maggot*—"

She goes on for several rounds, and I let her, mostly because I'm still stunned by how simple it is. How utterly transparent, now that I have all the facts. I'm not paranoid. I'm not imagining things. I'm not connecting dots that aren't there.

Ben really is behind every horrible thing that's happened, and we can almost – *almost* prove it.

"Rosie," I say, interrupting Maisie as she delves into what I'm fairly certain are curses in several different languages. "Has he ever mentioned the ABR to you?"

"The what?" she says faintly as she wipes her eyes again, creating a black smudge of mascara on her cheeks.

"The Army of the British Republic," I say. "The group behind the bombing."

"No. No, of course not," she says, a note of panic in her voice now. "I was just – I was only supposed to give him gossip, that's all. For the *Regal Record*. He and Jasper started it, and he runs it now, and sometimes he has me write bits, but I swear, it's all him—"

"It's *him*?" says Maisie, still sputtering. "All that rubbish – it's him?"

Rosie nods wretchedly. "I'm sorry, Maisie. I wanted to tell you, but—"

"It's not important," I say, and the three of them look at me like I've proclaimed Marmite and ham to be the best sandwich combination on the planet. "Not right now, anyway. We need to prove that he's connected to the ABR. Rosie, you're *positive* he's never mentioned it? Even in passing?"

"Yes," she whispers, so faintly I can barely hear her. "I swear, I had no idea. I would've never…I would've *never*."

"Yet you did," says Maisie bitterly. "And now you have to find a way to live with that."

Rosie stares at her for a long moment before dissolving into tears yet again. I sigh inwardly, but her emotional well-being is the least of our problems right now.

"Ben is being extraordinarily careful to ensure that none of this can be traced back to him," says Kit as he tucks away his mobile. "The burner phones, being out of the country during the attacks…and if he's using blackmail to get what he wants…"

"Then anyone could be caught in his web," says Maisie, still glaring at Rosie. "Even the people we trust most. And unless we catch them in the act, then it's highly unlikely anyone working for him will come forward of their own accord. Especially with treason on the line."

"*Treason?*" says Rosie, anguished, and she's crying so hard now that I think she might drown in her own tears.

"But the ABR is different – they have their own agenda," says Kit, ignoring her. "It's possible he's using them, and they're happy to be used, so long as they get what they want in the end."

"Which, if you'll recall, is the fall of the entire monarchy," says Maisie. "How Ben thinks *that* will help his cause—"

"Wait," I say suddenly. "I have an idea. Maisie – how far does your power extend?"

She squares her shoulders and raises her chin, as if just the thought of *not* getting her way is a challenge. "Significantly."

"Good," I say. "Because we're going to need it."

Chapter Thirty-six

"Henrietta, with the news of a fire breaking out at Windsor Castle this morning, it's time to ask ourselves the obvious question – is our royal family under attack?"

"After the shooting at Sandringham, the bombing of the Modern Music Museum, and now reports of a fire intentionally set in the private apartments of Windsor, I'm afraid there's little room for doubt any more. Our royal family – our monarchy – our *country* is under attack from the so-called Army of the British Republic."

"For our viewers who may have missed our breaking news bulletin just minutes ago, the ABR has released another video taking credit for the fire and yet again thanking Evangeline Bright for the role she played. What do you make of this? With so much suspicion now being cast on His Majesty's illegitimate daughter, why has she been allowed to remain on royal grounds?"

"Well, the answer's clear, isn't it? The palace doesn't believe the accusations have any merit."

"And yet the ABR insists she was the one who started the fire. Who are we supposed to believe?"

"There are those who will jump to the very worst conclusions without a second thought, of course, but I believe it is vital we all keep an open mind. Remember, Evangeline has only been in the country for seven months, and much of her time has been spent sheltered in Windsor Castle. How would she have made these connections? How would she have been radicalized so quickly?"

"We already know, of course. Lord Clarence, the nephew of Her Majesty the Queen and Evangeline's rumoured boyfriend, also has proven ties to the group through his friendship with terrorist Aoife Marsh."

"Perhaps, and perhaps I'm naive in thinking there's more to the story. But something about this doesn't add up for me. Evangeline was, after all, the alleged victim of the Christmas Eve hunting accident at Sandringham, which is now speculated to be the first of the ABR's attacks on the royal family."

"A hunting accident for which the ABR has never taken credit."

"A point well made. But let's put this all into perspective, shall we? What would the ABR gain by revealing such a well-placed member of their operation? And what would Evangeline gain by continuing to do their bidding after they revealed her supposed involvement in the bombing?"

"Perhaps she is being blackmailed."

"The royal family employs some of the most highly trained and decorated security experts in the world. If anyone tried to blackmail a member of the royal family... well, let's just say it wouldn't end well for them."

"Nor does it seem like this will end well for Evangeline. With calls for her arrest being made not only on social media, but by celebrities, international figures, and even members of Parliament, it is only a matter of time before the public loses their faith in the palace's judgement."

"We have no way of really knowing what's going on behind closed doors, particularly now that the royal family's inner circle has closed ranks. But should there be even a kernel of truth in the rumours of Evangeline's involvement, then we can only hope that for the sake of the country, the palace allows those investigating these attacks on the royal family to seek justice."

"And if she is found guilty?"

"Well – let's not get ahead of ourselves. The royal family is going through enough right now without us all playing judge, jury and executioner for one of their own."

"But no one is above the law, are they?"

"No, of course not. Not even those of royal blood."

– ITV News's interview with royal expert
Henrietta Smythe, 18 January 2024

As I step into the interview room, which is little more than a featureless box only a few degrees above frosty, the heavy metal door clangs shut behind me, and the lock slides into place.

Suraj Singh is already inside, standing in a corner like a well-dressed sentry, and he acknowledges me with a single nod. His presence in the room is a condition of the deal Maisie and Jenkins managed to strike with the Home Office, but while I'm not thrilled about it, my attention immediately snaps to the girl sitting on the far side of the long metal table, her wrists and ankles bound in handcuffs and chained to the concrete floor.

Despite the red waves tumbling over her shoulders, Aoife Marsh seems colourless somehow, as grey as her oversized sweatshirt. Any hint of the bubbly girl I met in the gift shop near Sandringham is gone, replaced by hollow cheekbones, dark circles and a hopelessness in her dull green eyes that feels excruciatingly familiar.

For a split second, when she sees me, there's a spark of something on her face – excitement, or possibly relief. Maybe even hope. But when she offers me a tentative smile and I refuse to return it, that spark vanishes so fast that it might as well have never existed at all.

"I can't believe you're really here," she says, and even though *here* is a Category A prison, surrounded by so many layers of security that I feel claustrophobic, her voice is as sweet as ever. "I've been begging to speak to you, and my lawyer promised he'd pass the message on, but of course they say those things, and I never thought—"

"No one asked me to come," I say flatly. "I'm here because I need answers."

"Oh." She parts her lips to say something else, but it takes her a moment to speak. "Did they tell you I'm innocent? It was all a set-up, God's honest truth. I had no idea what they were planning—"

"Is Ben involved in the ABR?" I say. After listening to Rosie sob all morning, I have no interest in hearing more excuses. "Prince Benedict. Is he in any way connected to you?"

"Prince...?" Her voice trails off, and she shakes her head. "Dylan talks about him sometimes, but I've never met him. Evangeline, I swear it on my grave, they were using me. I didn't know what was happening. I didn't know what Dylan and the others were planning. The club – Fox Rex, it was just supposed to be a laugh – something to do together at uni, an excuse to drink and meet other people who weren't so keen on the royals. I had no idea they were recruiting for a – a terrorist group, and if I had, I would've told someone, cross my heart—"

"What does Dylan say when he talks about Benedict?" I say, cutting her off. Aoife blinks.

"I – I don't know. He comes up sometimes, when Dylan mentions Eton. I think they were mates, but I can't say for sure. I didn't know about the photo, Evangeline, I swear it. No one told me to hug you, and I didn't know they had a camera – I didn't know what they were planning—"

"So as far as you know, Benedict isn't involved in the ABR?" I say.

"I didn't even know there *was* an ABR," she insists, her voice cracking with desperation. "I was only at the museum because of your text."

"My text?" I say, startled. "What text?"

Aoife bites her lower lip. "You know, the one where you said you wanted me there. It's on my mobile. The police took it, but—"

"I didn't text you," I say, sharper than I should, given she looks like she's about to burst into tears.

"But – but it came from your number. It's the only reason I

went to the opening. It's why I've been asking to see you – because you could prove that you invited me. Because you did, right? It had to be you. I'm sure it was."

Even though I know I shouldn't, I glance nervously over my shoulder. But Singh's already been through my phone – he knows every single message I've sent, and that none of them were to Aoife. Or the number Kit pretended was hers. "I never texted you, Aoife," I say. "Whoever gave you my number…it wasn't really mine."

"I…" Aoife falls short again, and this time she looks so crestfallen that I almost feel sorry for her. "It wasn't?" she whispers. "But…but Dylan said…"

A lump of frustration forms in my throat, and I force it down as I push my chair back with a hair-raising screech of metal against concrete. "I'm sorry if they really did trick you," I say in a measured voice, even though my patience is frayed to the last thread. "But if you don't know anything, then there's no point in me staying."

"Wait." Her voice catches as I stand. "Evangeline, please – you have to believe me. I didn't do this. I had no idea."

"You must've known something, Aoife," I say. "You can't tell me you spent months hanging out with terrorists and didn't overhear anything about Ben, or their leaders, or what they planned to do—"

"The leader's name is Guy," she blurts. "Except – I don't think that's his real name. But it's what everyone calls him."

"Guy? As in Guy Fawkes?" I say, and out of the corner of my eye, I see Singh shift his weight. This must be new information. "Who is he?"

Aoife's lips part, and she averts her gaze, staring at her ragged nails instead. Even from a distance, I can tell they've been bitten to the quick. "He's older than us. A graduate student, I think. He was with me at the museum opening. I didn't know he was there until – until he found me in the crowd, but he was."

I take my seat again, my mind racing. "Was he wearing a teal scarf?"

Her eyes dart back up to meet mine. "How did you…?"

"I'm pretty sure he's been stalking me," I mutter. "Has he ever mentioned Ben?"

"Maybe. I don't know. He gives me the shivers, so I don't usually…I don't usually talk to him."

"Why does he give you the shivers?" I press, and Aoife lets out a single rueful laugh.

"Some people, you just know they're trouble, don't you? But everyone else loved him. Flocked to him when he bothered to show – which wasn't all that often, mind, but when he did, the rest of them thought it was grand. Like meeting a celebrity."

"Do you know the names of the other members of the club?" I say, but Aoife shakes her head.

"A few, maybe. But I was really only there for Dylan."

We're getting nowhere again, and my irritation must show, because she leans forward, her hands tugging at her chains.

"I know they have loads of contacts and donors – people who were part of the club when they were students, that sort. I couldn't say how many of them know about the ABR, or if they're in the dark, like me. But Guy likes to brag about it – how we're part of an illustrious group dating back decades, including members of Parliament, lawyers, doctors, journalists, barons, viscounts, and even people inside the palace—"

"People inside the palace?" I echo, alarmed. "Who? Did he ever give you names?"

"No, no one told me anything," insists Aoife. "I didn't know about the ABR, I didn't know about – about the bombing – but..."

She trails off, and I can see the wheels turning in her mind. "What?" I say, but it takes her another few seconds to respond.

"Outside of the museum opening," she says slowly – so slowly that I'm on tenterhooks now, "Guy seemed...happy. Like everything was going according to plan. I thought maybe he was pleased that Kit was there, since he was a new recruit to Fox Rex, and maybe Guy was chuffed to have a member so close to the royal family. But..." She gulps. "I didn't think anything of it at the time, because Guy can be a bit...off, yeah? He said something about...about being glad the appearance hadn't been cancelled. That it was the perfect location, exactly where he wanted it to be—"

Suddenly there's a buzz behind me, and I glance over at Singh again, only to see him punching a number into his phone. "If you'll excuse me," he says, and he hastily moves to the door and knocks. A beat later, it opens for him, and as he crosses the threshold, he starts to speak.

"Cooper. It's Singh. I need a list of staff at—"

The door shuts behind him, and for a moment, Aoife and I stare at each other, both of us confused into silence. I want to ask what this means – what clues Singh noticed that went over my head – but Aoife's eyes are overflowing again, and she tugs at her restraints like she wants to reach across the table for my hand.

"Evangeline, please," she begs, softer now. "You have to believe me. I'd never hurt anyone – I swear it. I'll admit, I'm not overly fond of the royals and all they stand for, but it's not personal. And I like you. I like Kit. I'm not a murderer. I'd never – I'd *never*—"

She's sobbing now, every bit as hard as Rosie was in Kit's sitting room. I should comfort her, maybe. Offer her words of assurance, promise to get to the bottom of it. But all I can see as I watch her are the bloody remains of Ingrid's body, and my father lying broken in a hospital bed, a single complication away from death.

"The ABR protested outside Sandringham the day we met," I say, and even to my ears, I sound hollow. "Were you part of that?"

"N-no," she hiccups, her watery eyes round, and even though I don't want to believe her, I think I do. "I arrived maybe an hour before Dylan suggested we go into town. And once we were there, he said there was an ice cream shop we had to try – that's why we went in. He suggested it. He suggested the whole thing."

She sniffs loudly, and her restraints rattle again as she tries to raise her hand. With a wince, she rubs her nose against her shoulder instead, leaving a streak of tears and mucus across her sweatshirt. I watch her, feeling strangely detached from her overt show of emotion, and at last I ask my final question.

"Do you know who shot me and Kit?"

Aoife's mouth opens again, and this time there's no mistaking her shock for anything but real. "I – it was both of you? I thought...the tabloids said it was only you."

"He threw himself in front of me," I say coldly. "And I want to know who almost killed him."

Aoife is silent for several seconds, but her hands are shaking now, and I know that finally, *finally* I've found a secret.

"I don't know," she whispers. "But...that morning, Dylan was texting someone, and he left early. Really early. Said he had a few more gifts to buy in town, but...but I peeked out the window to watch him go, and...he had...he had his rifle slung over his..."

Her face crumples as she chokes on the rest of her words, but she's already said enough. While this small bit of circumstantial evidence is just one more stone to add to the mountain that should – but doesn't – prove Ben's involvement, it's the piece of the puzzle that finally shows me the full picture.

Ben, who bugged my room at Sandringham, heard Kit telling Maisie where we'd be walking that morning. And there's no doubt in my mind that Ben sent Dylan to do his dirty work for him.

This time, when I stand, I'm careful not to drag the chair along the floor. I head towards the exit on silent feet, but once I reach it, I turn back to Aoife. "Dylan is a good shot, isn't he?" I say, and she manages a jerking nod.

"Y-yes," she gasps. "Please, Ev-Evangeline – *please*, you have to – to believe me – I didn't – I *didn't*—"

"Okay," I say, knocking on the door. "I believe you."

Her eyes widen, and she sits up straighter, her tear-streaked face full of astonishment. "You – you do?" she says, and the hope in her voice is a knife to my gut.

"I do," I say as the door opens. "But it won't make a difference, Aoife. You know that, right? Because the entire world thinks I'm guilty, too."

Her jaw goes slack, and she stares at me with dawning horror.

But before she can say another word, I turn and walk away, and I don't – can't – look back.

Kit and Jenkins are waiting for me in a room down the hall, where three more agents from the Home Office are watching a weeping Aoife on a monitor and speaking quietly among themselves. Jenkins reaches me first, and he places his hands on my shoulders, his gaze searching mine.

"That was a brave thing you did, darling," he says, and I shake my head.

"Didn't really have a choice. She only wanted to talk to me," I say quietly, and as Jenkins lets me go, Kit takes his place, silently gathering me in his arms. But while I bury my face in the crook of his neck, I'm numb. Even though I finally have the answers I've been looking for, I still don't have the one thing I need – the one thing that ties this all together: irrefutable evidence that Ben is responsible for everything.

"What if we can never prove it?" I mumble. We can't speak freely, not in front of the agents, but Kit knows exactly what I'm talking about.

"We will," he murmurs as he rubs my back. "He'll slip up eventually."

I close my eyes as the soft sound of Aoife's wails echo through the room. "Maybe," I say. "But how many more people are we going to lose first?"

Someone clears their throat, and I look up to see Singh standing on the threshold, phone in hand. "Mr Jenkins. I'm afraid that call is necessary," he says, and Jenkins stiffens.

"Very well," he says, and after offering me a small smile that isn't remotely convincing, he excuses himself to the other side of the room and pulls out his mobile.

"What's going on?" I say, but Singh gestures towards the hallway.

"If I could have a minute with both of you," he says, and it's the kind of request that isn't really a request at all.

Confused, I take Kit's hand and follow Singh into the wide corridor. It's empty, except for a few doors that remain firmly closed, and Singh glances over his shoulder before facing Kit and me head-on.

"Four of the doctors working at the hospital where His Majesty is staying studied at Oxford," he says in a low voice. "Three from colleges we know Fox Rex recruits from. We've pulled them from the floor, but that's only a temporary solution. As soon as it's safe to do so, I've recommended that His Majesty be moved to a more secure location, along with the rest of the royal family."

I frown. "But the hospital's crawling with security."

"I'm aware. Until we track down a full list of Fox Rex members, both past and present, however, we must assume that anyone who fits the profile could be working for the ABR," says Singh, and I stare at him, horrified.

"Wait – so anyone who went to Oxford—"

"Is to be treated as a danger to your family," he says. "Yes."

"But – that has to be thousands of people," I say. "Tens of thousands."

"Hundreds of thousands," he corrects. "Including several royal courtiers and senior advisers – such as Harry Jenkins."

I glance back through the open doorway and catch a glimpse of Jenkins pacing the length of the office, his spine ramrod straight as he speaks into his phone. "He's not a suspect," I say firmly. "He's family."

"So is Prince Benedict," says Singh, and I scowl.

"Don't you dare compare him to Jenkins—"

"It's not a comparison, Miss Bright," he says. "It's an example of how close the ABR could be. And as it stands, we have no way of knowing who might be an alumnus – or potentially still working for them."

"What if there is no list?" says Kit, taking my hand in what feels like a silent effort to calm me down.

"I guarantee you a record exists, if only to feed their leader's ego. We're already working on it, but it'll take time to get someone on the inside."

"What about Aoife?" I say. "If she's telling the truth about being used…"

Singh tilts his head. "Did you believe her story, then?"

I consider it. "Depends. Was she lying about the text I supposedly sent?"

"No," he says. "She wasn't lying. Someone was texting her as you under an unrelated number. And that someone asked her to come to the museum opening, exactly as she described."

My entire body goes cold. "So she really is innocent?"

"It's possible," he allows. "Or it could've all been set up in such a way to give her the benefit of the doubt, in hopes she might be released. Either way, she's not a viable asset to us. At best, the leaders of the operation will hold her at arm's length, *if* she's allowed back into the club at all. And if it turns out that she did in fact play a part in the bombing, then we'll be releasing a terrorist, and you and your family will have one more enemy out there gunning for your lives."

My fingers are now laced so tightly between Kit's that by all rights, he should pull away. But he doesn't. He strokes his thumb against the back of my hand instead, tracing invisible circles into my skin, and slowly I loosen my grip. I don't let go, though, and neither does he.

"Even if she's innocent, this will follow her for the rest of her life," I say.

"Yes," agrees Singh. "Some marks never rub off completely."

"And everyone thinks Kit and I…that we're part of it, too," I add, and he studies me for a long moment.

"Yes," he says again, slower this time. "They do."

I glance up at Kit, and he peers down at me, his warm brown eyes searching mine. We don't speak – there's no need, not really, not when we both know what the other is thinking. But there's a question there, too, that neither of us is ready to ask. Or answer.

"Why don't I walk you both out?" says Singh. "My colleagues will see to Jenkins once he's ready."

This time it's Kit's hand that tightens around mine. But he doesn't shake his head, and at last, with my heart in my throat, I tear my eyes away from his.

"Okay," I say. And as Kit and I follow Singh through the soulless corridor, the brick-and-concrete fortress weighs heavier over us with each step we take, threatening to bury the last dregs of everything familiar to us both.

Chapter Thirty-seven

Why has Evangeline Bright not been arrested? It's the question on everyone's mind, as the palace refuses to make a statement about her alleged ties to the terrorist organization known as the Army of the British Republic, which has claimed responsibility for the Modern Music Museum bombing that killed eight and grievously wounded His Majesty the King.

We certainly have the evidence. The pictures and video of Evangeline hugging friend Aoife Marsh, who was arrested at the scene of the attack and is a reported member of the ABR, have been confirmed as genuine. The leader of ABR himself has publicly thanked Evangeline for her help in the attempted assassination of her father, the King. And if that wasn't enough, with news breaking this morning of a fire at Windsor that reportedly targeted Princess Mary, palace insiders have revealed that accelerant was found in Evangeline's bedroom – and that the half-sisters had fought the night before.

What more does MI5 need? The members of the royal family have long enjoyed a certain amount of privilege when it comes to bending the laws that the rest of us must follow, but we're not talking about a traffic ticket or a bit of light fraud. This is murder. This is terrorism. This is *treason*.

How many more people have to die before MI5 finally admits that the King's own daughter is responsible? How many more times must our beloved royal family fight for their lives before the senior courtiers stop using the palace's substantial power to protect a killer?

Evangeline Bright is a traitor – not only to her family, but to this country and its people. And we shudder to think of how many more tragedies we as a nation must face before she is finally brought to justice.

– *The Regal Record*, 18 January 2024

As the Range Rover races down the expressway towards London, Jenkins stares at Kit and me, his silence louder than any rebuke.

He's in the passenger seat, his upper body twisted in what must be an uncomfortable position, but even when we hit a bump, he refuses to budge. The seconds tick by slowly, and though I expect him to speak, he doesn't have to – the look on his face says everything, and I toy with the cap on my water bottle as I hold his incredulous gaze.

"I know it's reckless," I say. "I know there are risks—"

"This is more than a risk, Evan," he says, his voice so rough that he doesn't sound like himself. "This is…it's unthinkable."

I shrug. "He gave me an opening, Jenkins. I have to take it."

"No, you don't," he says with gentle firmness. "As long as I've known you, Evan, your first instinct is to right wrongs with wrongs. You'll do whatever it takes to fight a *perceived injustice*, even when it means getting expelled, or setting your classroom on fire, or risking your future – or, it seems, your life."

"This isn't a perceived injustice," I insist. "He's trying to kill us. Not just me, but Kit, my mom, Alexander—"

"I know, sweetheart," says Jenkins. "And we have the best people in the world doing everything they can to protect you."

"But it isn't enough," I argue. "He knows the royal family's security protocols too well, and he also knows the loopholes and how to exploit them. He's grown up in this life – he knows exactly how to get to us, and I need to prove it's him before it's too late."

Jenkins sighs. "Even if you're right, darling, there's absolutely no reason it has to be you."

I look at Kit, who's tight-lipped and staring at his hands. "I think it does, though," I say. "I think I'm the only one who has a chance of making this work."

Before either Jenkins or Kit can respond, my phone buzzes in my lap, and I automatically check the screen.

"It's Maisie," I say as I accept the call and put the phone to my ear. "Hey, we just left the prison. Aoife Marsh didn't know anything about Ben, but—"

"Evan?" The connection crackles, and Maisie's voice sounds oddly distant as a swell of noise fills the background of the call. "What's going on? The prime minister's insisting we evacuate to Balmoral, which is positively *arctic* this time of year. And Daddy's coming by air ambulance even though he's still critical, but no one will tell me why—"

"It's the ABR," I say. "MI5 are worried they've infiltrated the hospital and the palace staff. Talk to Agent Singh – he'll give you the details. But they're right, Maisie. You need to get out of London, okay?"

Maisie mutters a few choice words under her breath, mostly about Scottish winters. "Yes, all right, fine. But I certainly won't enjoy it. How far away are you? The helicopter's already landed on the lawn at Kensington, and Mummy's insisting we leave as soon as possible."

"I—" I hesitate and look at Jenkins, whose stony expression offers me nothing in return. "My mom's going with them, right?"

"What? Who are you talking to?" says Maisie, confused, but I'm still watching Jenkins. At last the corners of his mouth tug downward, and he exhales in a heavy sigh.

"I'll make sure your mother remains with His Majesty," he promises, and I nod, grateful.

"My mom's going to join you at Balmoral, Maisie," I say. "Will you look after her for me? Make sure she takes care of herself?"

Maisie huffs. "I know you and Mummy had a bit of a spat, but Balmoral is my castle, not hers, and if I have to be there, then you most certainly do, too."

"I'll join you when I can," I promise. "But not yet, Mais. I'm sorry."

"What are you talking about?" she says, the indignation in her voice rising. But I hear a hint of fear, too. "You're coming with us, Evan. That's the whole bloody point, isn't it? He's after *you*."

"While I'm gone," I say as if she hasn't spoken, "let him take my spot on the council."

"*What?*" she sputters. "Evan—"

"You need to keep him close, all right? Close and busy. Let him think he's won. Let him think you believe I started the fire. Let him think you hate me, and that he's back in your good graces, or at least on his way. Pretend I'm not invited to Balmoral, that Kit and I are both being investigated—"

"Kit's part of this madness, too?" she says furiously. "Let me speak to him—"

"I need you to do this for me, Maisie, okay?" I say, talking over her once more. "It's important. *Keep him busy.*"

"I—" I can practically see Maisie opening and shutting her mouth. "Yes, all right, I'll keep him busy, but—"

"And don't let him anywhere near Dad," I say. "Not even for a moment, okay?"

"That we certainly agree on," she mutters. "Fine. I'll keep him busy, and I'll keep him away from Daddy – and your mother, naturally. But you *must* tell me what's going on."

My shoulders slump, and I lean forward, my seat belt cutting into my neck. "I'm going to fix this."

She scoffs. "That's alarmingly vague."

"I know. I'm sorry. Just – trust me, okay? Please. I love you."

"You – what?" says Maisie, and for a moment, her surprise overrides her fear. "Evan, what on earth—"

"I'll see you as soon as I can," I promise. "Stay safe. And don't trust anyone."

"Evan – *Evan!* Don't you *dare*—"

I hang up with her voice still ringing in my ears, and the silence in the vehicle is thick. Kit is watching me now, though his expression remains unreadable, and I desperately wish he'd say something. Even if it's not what I want to hear.

"I cannot condone this," says Jenkins, his words like steel as they cut through the quiet hum. "It's far too dangerous. If your father finds out—"

"Don't tell him," I say quickly. "Please. If – when he wakes up—"

"I cannot – I *will* not lie to my king," he says, and I hesitate, my mind a jumbled whirl.

"Then try to hold off on telling him for as long as possible," I say. "You don't have to lie, but just...buy me some time. Please."

Jenkins holds my pleading stare as the Range Rover veers towards an exit. He and I both know that this all might be a moot point – that Alexander might never wake up, and Jenkins will never have the chance to lie to him. Or tell him the truth.

But at last, his chin dips in the slightest of nods, and I reach forward, squeezing his fingers gratefully. "Thank you," I say, relieved. But Jenkins isn't looking at me any more, and after a beat, he lets my hand go. Most people would hardly notice, but to me, it's a stab in the heart.

My throat tightens, and I force myself to push past the brief ache as I turn towards Kit. "You don't need to do this," I say. "I can figure it out on my own."

"I know you can," he says, his voice so low that he sounds hoarse. "But you won't have to."

My heart is thumping, and I don't know if it's from fear or nerves or excitement, or a potent combination of all three. "Are you sure?" I say, searching his face for any hint of reluctance or doubt.

But Kit takes my hand – the same one Jenkins dropped – and raises it to his lips, brushing them against my knuckles. "We're in this together," he says, his breath warm against my skin. "Let's finish it."

The cold rushes in as he lets me go, setting his palm on my knee instead, and I hold his gaze for several long seconds before picking up my phone once more. I dismiss another call from

Maisie and open my contacts, where I have to scroll to find the right name. And as Jenkins speaks to the driver, grudgingly giving him our new destination, I type out my message.

We're in.

Acknowledgements

This series wouldn't exist without the support and guidance from my agents, Rosemary Stimola and Allison Remcheck, Alli Hellegers, and everyone at the Stimola Literary Studio. I have no idea where I'd be without you all, but it'd probably be nowhere good.

The team at Delacorte Press continues to knock it out of the park in every possible way, especially my editor, Kelsey Horton, whose unending patience and wealth of creative knowledge have been equally invaluable to the process of creating this book. A huge thank-you to the rest of the team, including Beverly Horowitz, Shameiza Ally, Kenneth Crossland, Colleen Fellingham, Joey Ho, Shannon Pender, Tamar Schwartz and Ray Shappell, and to Yordanka Poleganova for the incredible cover art.

Most of my friends are used to me sneaking chapters into their inboxes or snippets of new ideas into our texts, but it takes a special kind of dedication to commit to reading and offering feedback on sequels. My undying thanks to Sara Hodgkinson, Carli Segal, Caitlin Straw and Andrea Hannah for reading this one and letting me pick their brains far beyond the point most people would tolerate.

Thank you to Veronica O'Neil, Malcolm Freberg, Kristin Lord, Becca Mix, Ashley Zajac and Austin Webberly for the friendship and support, as always, and for listening to me spoil this entire trilogy. One day I'll learn to keep my mouth shut, but probably not anytime soon.

Several difficult situations cropped up in my life during the various writing and editing stages of this book, but especially towards the end, when we were up against a very strict deadline, and missing it would have meant moving the release date – something I am loath to do under any circumstances. But because of the understanding and grace of my publishing team and the support of the people in my life, this book was finished (mostly) on time. Thank you, thank you, thank you to Sadie Betro and Anthony Jacaruso, Ashley Oswald, Karla Olson-Bellfi, Ruth Rydstedt and Jessica W. for being there when we needed you most.

Shout-out to my pets for the company during the writing process, and especially to Fred, my cat, who nearly died while I was editing this book but somehow came out of it even sweeter and more lovable than ever. I'm sure there's a lesson in there somewhere. A huge thank you to the medical teams that kept her alive and made room in their schedules to see her literally dozens of times, which in turn helped me not be such an anxious mess – Dr C., Kelsey, Courtney, Hayley, Dr J., Sam, Lindsay, Terri, Rebekah and Andrea.

And thank you to my dad, as always, who is the best person I know and my favourite human being. His love of writing has always inspired my own, and his support from the very first time I expressed interest in writing is the only reason any of my books exist. I love you most.

aimeecarter.com

#RoyalBlood

X @usborne @aimee_carter

Instagram @usborneYA @aimeemoc